T0278910

# EMERALD ROAD

## ORLANDO ORTEGA-MEDINA

AMBLE
PRESS

2025

Amble Press

Copyright © 2025 Orlando Ortega-Medina

Print ISBN: 978-1-61294-302-2

Amble Press First Edition: January 2025

Printed in the United States of America on acid-free paper.

Cover designer:
TreeHouse Studio

Amble Press
PO Box 3671
Ann Arbor MI 48106-3671

*www.amblepressbooks.com*

Lyrics from "Bella Ciao," the 19th-century Italian folk song are in the public domain.

*For William with love and déjà vu*

"If we walk far enough, we shall sometime come to someplace."

—*The Wonderful Wizard of Oz (1900)*

# FOREWORD

Coming-of-age novels have long been popular with readers, and for good reason. We all struggle in one way or another when we pass from being children into young adulthood. Some of us are still on that journey. Most cultures mark the transition in rites of passage that often include a community celebration such as Quinceañeras, Bar and Bat Mitzvahs, Confirmations, and the like. At the heart of coming-of-age ceremonies across diverse cultures is the collective acknowledgment and celebration of a person's transition from childhood to adulthood, suggesting a person's willingness to abandon the toys of youth to take on new, more complex roles, responsibilities, and rights within the community.

This common experience can be more difficult for some young adults depending on the circumstances: poverty, violence, illness, and bigotry can add hardship to an already fraught period in a person's life. But in the end, we as readers—regardless of life experiences—recognize and can empathize with a protagonist's rocky road toward adulthood. And a coming-of-age novel succeeds when a writer creates a protagonist we can empathize with and root for.

Orlando Ortega-Medina's novel, *Emerald Road*, introduces

us to such a protagonist in the person of Isaac Perez, a teenager who teeters on the precipice of adulthood during El Salvador's Civil War of the 1980s. Added to this mix is Isaac's sexual awakening as a gay man who not only must navigate his country's violent conflict but also confront unwelcoming cultural bigotries. Also, our hero suffers from a health challenge that makes his journey into adulthood that much rockier. All the while, Isaac—as a fictional character—is fully realized, likable, and relatable. Plus, he has a canine friend named Ahbhu who is much more than a boy's loyal companion (I will not spoil your discovery of what makes this adorable creature so unusual). Simply put, we can't help but serve as Isaac's cheerleaders on his journey to adulthood and the kind of freedom that we all seek in our own way.

Ortega-Medina has created a compelling, thrilling, and extremely readable coming-of-age novel that will enthrall readers of all backgrounds. Welcome to Isaac's journey. Cheer him on as he travels his "Emerald Road" toward adulthood, self-fulfillment, and ultimately freedom.

Daniel A. Olivas
*August 9, 2024*
*Pasadena, CA*

# EMERALD ROAD

# AHBHU

*Tijuana, Mexico: February 7, 1986*

My best friend and love of my life Ahbhu vanished on me tonight. He'd gone missing just as our group's final dinner was winding down, a few hours before we were scheduled to gate-crash the border. His sudden, unexplained absence alarmed me as he'd rarely left my side in the eight years since I'd rescued him back home in San Salvador from an alley behind the National Theater.

My heart throbbed in my ears as I combed the area around the safehouse where we'd been holed up for the past week, my breath coming in short, anxious gasps as I searched the neighborhood. I found him minutes before midnight, weak and struggling to breathe, cowering in a pile of garbage behind a grimy dumpster.

"Ahbhu!" I'd cried, a wave of sorrow washing over me as I lifted him into my arms.

"Leave Ahbhu, mijo," he groaned as I stood, his dog voice laced with pain. "It's almost time . . ."

"Hush, Ahbhu!" I struggled down the deserted, litter-strewn side street toward Avenida Revolución. "I'm not crossing over

3

without you! Please, just hang in there!"

Each step back to the safehouse was a leaden anchor pressing down on my shoulders, increasing in weight as I moved, my chest tight with grief as I clutched Ahbhu close, navigating the bustling boulevard, jammed with vehicles, trinket sellers, and pedestrians, the air tainted with the pungent odor of exhaust and burning trash, fearful our time together was slipping away.

As I turned off the main boulevard, I held Ahbhu against my chest, cradling him like the precious friend he was. Tears slipped from my eyes and mingled with his fur as I buried my face in his bristly coat. After all we'd gone through together, it was unthinkable it was all going to end in this hellhole of a Mexican border city. "Hold on, Ahbhu," I'd pled. We're nearly there."

On reaching the safehouse, Ahbhu's breathing shallowed, and I choked back a sob that threatened to undo me. With every ounce of love in my soul, trying my best to stay strong, I lowered him onto my bunk and held him tight, hoping against hope I could save him again. We had come full circle, Ahbhu and me ...

# PART I

*San Salvador, El Salvador: 1978–1980*

# CHAPTER 1

## IN THE SHADOW OF THE VOLCANO

My journey began on the upper slopes of El Boquerón, a majestic and ever-grumbling volcano that looms over San Salvador, the capital of El Salvador. It was there, in the ring of fire, in the canton closest to the cone, that I was born.

From the moment I drew my first fevered breath in the shadow of that volcano until the day I fled my war-torn native country twenty-three years later, I lived with my parents and two older brothers, Neto and Arturo, in a bright yellow adobe house built around a spacious internal courtyard where we cultivated coffee plants.

For much of my young life, I was a lonely and nerdy twig of a boy, the personal punching bag of my brother Neto, the elder of the two. But everything changed for me on the day I turned sixteen, the day Ahbhu came into my life.

My mother had organized a Sunday lunch to celebrate my milestone birthday. It was November 12, 1978, and I was at the start of my three-month break before beginning secondary school, marking the beginning of a new chapter in my life. I remember "Shadow Dancing" by Andy Gibb was playing on the radio in the background.

Just as we were about to start in on the main course, Neto had turned to my parents and announced: "Let's not lose sight of what this is all about. Isaac's a man now!" I remember him gesturing across the table at me with his fork.

Though he was twenty-five, Neto had dominated the household since he was thirteen. Everyone in our family was intimidated by him, my parents included. Standing only five feet six inches and weighing barely one hundred thirty pounds on a good day, he was the viper in our nest. We never knew when he might strike.

"Now that he's a man, it's time he started acting like a man and carrying his weight in work around here. You hear that, brother? No more lolling about reading books and gazing at stars. Today, we close the chapter on that phase of your spoiled life." He looked around the table, his gaze settling on my mother, who was seated to my left. "You got that, mamá?"

A hollow sensation opened up in my stomach, migrating into my chest, as I lowered my fork to the plate and blinked back tears of suppressed anger at his having spoiled my celebration.

"Don't start, Neto," my father warned, his withered hand trembling as he reached for a glass of water. I could tell he was keen to get back to his garden, to escape what was coming. I didn't blame him.

My mother's fingers fidgeted on the edge of her plate. Arturo, my twenty-year-old brother and champion, placed his hand on Neto's extended arm in a silent plea for calm. Sleek and dark as a panther, Arturo outweighed Neto by a good fifteen pounds and could have taken him in a fight if it ever came to that. But he respected Neto's status as our older brother and rarely defied him.

Realizing he was outnumbered; Neto pulled his hand back and shot an infuriated glare at Arturo before redirecting his attention at me. "Fine! But tomorrow, you'll be helping me transport the coffee harvest into town. *That's* what it means to turn sixteen around here. Understand, little man?"

I clenched my teeth and locked eyes with Neto, feeling the heat rising in my cheeks. Everyone at the table stared at me as I pushed my chair back and stood up, gripping the table for support to keep myself from collapsing from the fury building inside me. Neto was right, I *was* sixteen, and I was done taking his abuse.

"Steady there, little brother," Arturo said.

My mother tugged on my sleeve, begging me to calm down. She signaled the chair with a nod of her head, hoping to defuse the confrontation.

Neto smirked, relishing the moment. "Seems the little squirt has something to say." He glanced around the table and chuckled, then turned his head towards me. "Speak up, *bicho!*" With a challenging lift of his chin, he dared me to continue. But just as I was about to let loose, El Boquerón let out a loud groan, silencing us all.

We exchanged nervous glances, each of us holding our breath and bracing for the possibility of an earthquake—often heralded in just this way. Time stretched as we waited, ready to dive for cover. After a few tense moments, the groaning ceased, and we released a collective sigh of relief, crossing ourselves in gratitude for yet another near miss.

Having lost my nerve, I settled back into my chair, wiping my eyes with the back of my hand. "Why *anyone* would build a city next to an active volcano is beyond me," I muttered.

My comment attracted a hard slap from Neto that knocked me to the floor.

"Neto!" my mother screamed, bringing her fist down hard on the table, startling all of us.

"Don't you *ever* disrespect El Bóque again!" Neto shouted. He rounded the table and towered over me. "You'll be the death of us all!"

Arturo leapt up and pulled him away from me. "What the hell's wrong with you, man?"

As the stars cleared from my vision, all the anger I'd been suppressing erupted. Jumping to my feet, I grabbed a dish of beans off the table and threw it in Neto's face. A chorus of shocked exclamations arose from everyone in the room.

"You little shit!" Neto roared, swiping the dripping food off his face. "I'll fucking kill you." Trembling with rage, he advanced on me with clenched fists.

Seeing his intention, my mother screamed for him to stop, interposing herself between us, and just missed getting slugged. Realizing how close he'd come to striking her, Neto stumbled backward, angry and embarrassed, spluttering an apology.

Just then, a sudden jolt caused us all to freeze. El Boquerón had come alive again. A second jolt sent them all diving under the dining table. Seizing the opportunity, I grabbed my book bag and ran out the front door with the ground rolling under my feet.

Reaching the edge of our property I took shelter in the shade of a banyan tree to catch my breath. I couldn't believe I'd stood up to Neto at last. I looked back at the house and at El Boquerón looming above it with its fat black cone spearing the bank of clouds that hovered there, shuddering with pent-up emotion, tears flowing down my cheeks, deciding my next move. In a split-second decision, I shot off down the steep hill in the direction of the Metropolitan Cathedral in the historic center of San Salvador nine miles away.

Winding around the deserted tree-lined roads, I sought out any shadow I could find for some relief from the merciless midday sun that beat down on me. The thick humid air intensified the heat, mirroring my fiery emotions.

With each stride down the hill, I tried to shake off my lingering anger, but it clung to me like the sweat streaming down my face. The road ahead felt endless, wending through the rugged terrain.

Though I could still feel El Boquerón rumbling under my feet, I focused instead on the whisper of the rustling leaves and the distant calls of birds. The serenity of the surroundings seeped into me, coaxing me to let go of my anger and find peace in the beauty of my journey out of our rural district and into the urbanized colonias below.

By the time I reached the chaotic streets of the city center three hours later, my anger had been replaced by exhaustion and a sense of resignation. I knew my mother would be worried, and I knew there would be hell to pay with Neto, but for now it was just me and the bustling squares and elegant buildings of my city of birth, ravaged by time and neglect, mirroring the tumultuous state of the nation as it teetered towards civil war.

Despite the desperation etched into every corner of the city center, a flicker of hope ignited within me as I approached the Metropolitan Cathedral—the very sanctuary where I'd been baptized. Years of turmoil and strife had left their mark on the building, its grandeur tarnished by the ravages of history. Yet, amid the peeling paint, weathered concrete, and jutting iron buttresses, there remained a sense of sanctity for anyone who sought refuge within its walls. Over the years, whenever I was tempted to give up on my life, I'd found comfort there.

Gazing up at the imposing, as-yet-unfinished structure, a sense of awe and reverence washed over me, and I whispered a prayer. Then I ascended the worn steps and moved inside.

# CHAPTER 2

## THE RESCUED PUP

On entering the cathedral, I was greeted by its comforting coolness, a welcome respite from the heat outside. Seeking out a quiet corner in the back, I settled onto a weathered pew and allowed the sacred stillness to rejuvenate my weary body. Enveloped by the quiet murmur of prayers and the gentle glow of candlelight from a nearby chapel, I closed my eyes, only to find that when I reopened them, several minutes had slipped away, and the Mass was drawing to a close.

Despite the restful interlude, my heart still weighed heavy with the memory of my argument with Neto. With a lump in my throat, I rose from the pew and drifted toward the grand altar, past the cathedral's hodgepodge of sacred art, unfinished concrete walls, and protruding reinforcement bars.

My footsteps echoed as I traversed the cracked stone floor, surrounded by the murmur of voices, the scent of frankincense, and the distant sound of jackhammers, all of which lent an otherworldly atmosphere. Then, slipping into the front pew with tears in my eyes, I prayed for help as the priest brought the Mass to its conclusion.

Just as he offered the final blessing, my gaze landed on an altar boy around my age who stood nearby, dressed in a simple white robe, cinched at the waist by a green cord. He was handsome, with a striking angular face, short black hair, and dark, intense eyes that lent him an air of mystery.

In those heart-pounding moments, I found I couldn't tear my eyes away from him. I watched transfixed as the Mass came to an end, the rich Latin hymns of the recessional filling the cavernous space. In the midst of the grandeur, the altar boy sensed my gaze. Our eyes met, and in that electric instant I felt a surge of exhilaration at the sense of connection between us. It was as though the cathedral itself had conspired to bring us together. I didn't understand it at the time; it had no name yet for me, but I was experiencing my first pang of desire in that sacred space and felt it reflected back at me.

Just as the intensity of our moment reached its peak, a priest's call summoned the altar boy back to the vestry. With a reluctant glance and a faint smile, he turned away, leaving me with the indelible memory of our brief encounter.

As the cathedral emptied out, I found myself sitting alone, flustered yet strangely expectant, waiting for . . . something. After a couple of minutes, a middle-aged priest with thinning red hair approached me and indicated that the Mass was over. Gathering my book bag, I exited the cathedral into the waning light, feeling anxious and hungry.

I wandered across the street into the Civic Square with the statue of General Barrios on horseback in the center. The altar boy's image lingered in my mind, amplifying the emptiness I'd been grappling with as of late. Clutching the edge of my shirt, my fingers trembled as I surveyed the nearly deserted square.

Spotting the full moon rising over the square, I was seized by a sudden urge to counteract my darkening mood with something reckless. Arching my back, I let out a howl that echoed off the grand buildings surrounding the square. Tears streamed down my face as I bayed like a deranged animal, releasing all the pent-up emotion that had been building inside me throughout this disastrous day.

After the last echo faded, I fell back against the statue of General Barrios, exhausted but feeling a little better, and whispered a prayer to whomever might be listening. Then, I readied myself to return home, conscious of the trouble that awaited me there.

I hurried past the cathedral down Second Avenue toward the National Theater, the most beautiful building in San Salvador, hands down. The bus stop for my journey home was located on Calle Delgado, just catty-corner to the theater. As I neared the building, rather than head directly for the bus stop, I decided to linger a bit longer to take in the sight of it at night.

Crossing Calle Delgado, I sat on the steps descending from Morazán Plaza opposite the theater. Its neoclassical façade with its tall columns and sculpted pediment was illuminated and looking lovelier than I'd ever seen it. Mesmerized by the sight, my mind soon drifted and I found myself thinking again about the handsome altar boy, wondering if I'd ever see him again.

After losing myself in pointless daydreams, I readied myself to return home. But just as I was headed for the bus stop, a faint whimpering caught my attention. Intrigued, I glanced around, trying to identify where the sound was coming from. After a moment, I determined it was somewhere off to my left.

Curiosity guided my steps to a dark alley a stone's throw from the theater, my heart pounding with anticipation. There, in the shadows, I found a wounded and forsaken scrap of a dog, barely more than a puppy. I suppressed a scream at the sight of it. It looked like someone had taken a mallet to the poor thing. Half of its left ear looked chewed off; the other one was flopped over, and what was left of its dark mottled coat was matted with dry blood, clinging to its fragile quivering frame. Soft moans escaped its mouth, a desperate plea for help that echoed through the trash-strewn alley.

Without a second thought, I knelt beside the injured pup. Its gleaming eyes, filled with pain and vulnerability, met mine. Gently, I scooped up the poor thing and cradled him in my arms. His frail body nestled against my chest, seeking warmth and protection. His heartbeat felt rapid and irregular, a testament to whatever trauma he had endured. As I held the pup close, a surge of determination flowed through me. In that moment, I vowed to protect him no matter what, to provide him with the love and care he so desperately needed.

I removed my shirt and wrapped him in it, then I hurried bare-chested toward the bus stop to catch what I knew would be the last bus home.

As I sped down the sidewalk, careful not to squeeze the pup too tightly, I was surprised to see his expressive, intelligent eyes looking up at me, fixing me in their gaze. It was as if he were acknowledging that ours was a destined bond. It was then I knew without a doubt that our paths had crossed for a reason.

Lowering my face to his fur, I kissed him and rubbed my cheek against his bristly head. Then I looked up and saw my bus whiz past, barreling in the direction of the bus stop, which was still a good two blocks away. Cradling the pup against my chest, I rushed toward the stop, yelling for the driver to wait. Out of breath and with still a half block to go, I watched in disbelief as the bus lurched from the stop and sped away, leaving us panting in a cloud of diesel.

# CHAPTER 3

## THE CHRISTENING

I trudged up the steep and snaking road, preparing to tackle the last turn on my interminable journey home that night. The imposing form of El Boquerón cast its brooding shadow over me like a threatening cyclops. It loomed above our house, a sentinel of darkness embodying my childhood fears. The full moon hung high above it, bathing everything in its ethereal glow. I couldn't help but notice the bright twinkle of Jupiter, steadfast in the night sky. Saturn, with its delicate rings, gleamed nearby. But tonight, even my beloved stars shimmered less brilliantly as my heart raced with trepidation, my mind torn between the wonders above and the worries that awaited me at home.

Feeling a sharp pain in my shoulders where my book bag was digging in, I shifted it around to my chest and checked on the pup, relieved to see his eyes blinking at me in the moonlight. I'd made room for him by dumping my precious sci-fi collection along the roadside when it became clear that carrying him in my arms would take forever. So, as delicately as I could, I'd placed him inside my bag and continued my journey beside the bustling highway, and up the deserted road toward Canton El Regreso.

I arrived home at a quarter past ten. Moving stealthily up the asphalt, I slipped in through a side door. As I crept down the hallway toward my bedroom, I was surprised to hear conversation coming from the front room that doubled as the general store my mother ran for the neighborhood. Poking my head inside, I found her and Arturo sitting next to each other on a pair of wooden chairs among crates of fruits and vegetables. They were trading random comments as my mother busied her hands with a pair of knitting needles and a spool of yarn and my brother cradled a thick university textbook in his lap.

I recall my mother wearing a flower-patterned house dress, her mane of salt and pepper hair held back with a matching hairband. Arturo sported a snug black tracksuit with a bold white stripe down the side. Their heads swung in my direction at the sound of a whimper from my book bag.

"Hijo!" my mother shouted, suppressing a scream with the back of her thin hand. She leaped up from the chair and hurried over to me.

Arturo set aside his book and stood, wagging his head, his face spoiled with disappointment, as my mother drew me into a hug. The pup let out a yelp at the sudden, unexpected movement and popped his raggedy head out of the bag to investigate. On seeing him, my mother drew back.

"What's this?" She stared at the pup for a moment, her eyes widening. Then, as if remembering something, she refocused on me. "Where have you been, hijo? You've been gone for hours! Your brother and I have been sick with worry." She stepped back, trembling with suppressed rage. "And just look at the state of you!"

If I hadn't been holding the pup, I swear she would have cracked me one across the face. But I had a greater worry. Shifting my gaze to Arturo, I asked: "Where's Neto?"

"Óye!" Arturo shot back, his voice rising. "I cruised around for two hours looking for you before I finally threw in the towel.

Answer mamá! Where were you? And what is that?" He pointed at the pup.

"I went downtown," I said, giving my backpack a protective squeeze. "But seriously, where's Neto?"

Arturo let out an exasperated sigh and plopped back onto his chair. "He's at his latest girlfriend's I think," he said, opening his textbook again. "You're safe for now."

Coming the rest of the way into the room, I sat on an upturned crate opposite them and gestured for my mother to sit down. "I'm sorry I worried you, mamá," I said. "Both of you. And papá, too. But if I didn't get out of here when I did . . . Well, you saw what happened. I had to calm down and clear my head." I paused for a moment and looked at each of them in turn. "Anyway, I went downtown and walked around for a while, and I found this puppy in an alley by the National Theater. He's hurt really bad."

I lifted the pup out of my book bag and held him up for them. My mother let out a gasp on seeing his injuries, and Arturo rose from the sofa. He came over and assessed the pup, examining its damaged ear. The pup blinked glassy brown eyes and turned his head to me, looking weaker than ever.

"Bring him some water, please," I begged Arturo. He nodded and sped to the kitchen down the long corridor. Turning to my mother, I asked: "Are there any scraps we can feed him? I'd like to get something into him, and then I need to tend to his wounds."

Despite his injuries, once the pup took his first halting sips he perked up enough to swallow a few strips of chicken before he lost interest and moved his head away from the bowl. Then I carried him to the bathroom where I checked his wounds. Fortunately, I didn't see any signs of infection and though he cried out in pain from time to time, he didn't seem to have

18

any broken bones.

Once I was satisfied I knew what I was dealing with, I used a pair of blunt-nosed scissors to trim away what was left of the pup's blood-matted fur. Then I gave him a warm bath, using a tiny bit of shampoo to make sure I didn't irritate his skin.

My mother and Arturo hovered in the background as I lathered and rinsed the pup, taking care to avoid getting water in his ears and eyes. Focusing on me as I bathed him, the pup held me in his gaze, which took me aback. It was as if he were trying to say something. I stopped a moment and stared back at him.

Those eyes . . . it seemed crazy at the time. After all, he was only a dog, a stray even. But as he held my gaze, the pup's eyes seemed full of understanding. Whatever it was, the expression in those eyes made me tear up.

After the moment of shock passed, I wiped my face, kissed his wet soapy head, and finished rinsing him. My mother handed me a soft towel, which I used to pat him dry. Then we wrapped him in a warm blanket and took him to the bedroom I shared with Arturo.

My mother watched from the doorway as I placed the pup on my cot. Once I was satisfied he was comfortable, I drew her into a hug. "Thank you for this, mamá," I said. "I'm sorry I worried you."

My mother kissed my head and looked past me to the pup. She stared at him for a moment, lost in thought, then withdrew from the room without saying a word, closing the door behind her, and Arturo locked it from the inside.

I snuggled in bed next to the pup. Arturo took in the sight of us from his cot, a wry smile animating his face.

"Are you planning on keeping it?"

"He's not an 'it'. . ." I kissed the pup, and he shifted closer.

"And, yes, of course I'm planning on keeping him."

The pup opened his wet eyes and blinked at me. He still looked so weak and trembly, which got me teary-eyed and choked up. I kissed him again, then looked over at Arturo and added, "That is, if he doesn't end up dying on me."

Arturo cocked his head and gazed at the pup, the corners of his mouth turning down. Then he looked at me and said in a low voice, "We'll see what Neto has to say."

"I don't care what he says. This dog is mine!"

Arturo shrugged. "That's what it looks like." He flashed a smile the way he always did when he wanted to make me feel better. "What's his name?" He lifted his head at the pup.

"He doesn't have a name yet." The pup had closed his eyes again. "I don't want to jinx anything. Once I know he's in the clear, then I'll name him." At that, the pup's eyes drifted open and landed on me.

"Did you see that?" Arturo said, his voice tinged with wonder. He shuffled across the room and stroked the pup's head. "The little guy wants a name!" He pressed his lips to the pup and kissed him. "Isn't that right, little runt?"

The pup kept his eyes locked on mine as if waiting for something. Then Arturo held out an open hand at him. "Go for it!"

In hindsight, it feels as if I'd always had his name in my back pocket, waiting for the right moment to unveil it, the perfect handle for my pup. I'd stumbled upon it in a favorite novella and had tucked it away in my heart, waiting for the right occasion. And that moment had arrived.

I glanced at Arturo with a grin, holding the pup in my arms, my stomach turning somersaults. Then, placing him on a simple wooden chair dubbed "the naming chair" by Arturo and me, I leaned over the pup, who gazed up with curiosity, extended my arm, and with all the drama I could muster, I announced, "Your name is: Ahbhu!"

A spark of recognition ignited in the pup's eyes, as if he'd always known his true name. Scooping him close, I welcomed his slobbery kisses on my face and turned to Arturo, whose mouth hung open in amazement.

"What do you think?" I asked.

"Ah-bhu!" Arturo repeated, savoring each syllable. Then he beamed at me. "I love it! Looks like he does, too." He raised his head at Ahbhu and pumped his eyebrows.

"I think so, too." Wrapping Ahbhu in his blanket, I watched as he closed his eyes and drifted back to sleep.

Arturo slipped across the room and hugged me. I remember it was a long, lingering, reassuring hug that made me feel like melting into him.

"Happy birthday, little brother," he said as he went back to his cot and turned off the light. "It was a good day after all."

The next morning, I carried Ahbhu outside to do his business in the shade of a big banyan tree that grew along the edge of our yard. I remember he looked over his shoulder at me as if seeking permission. I flashed a little smile and nodded at him. Taking my cue, he lowered his head and shuffled to the base of the trunk. Even though the sun was just coming up, it was already hot and muggy. My shirt and pants were sticking to my body, and the mosquitoes were dive-bombing me.

Once he was finished, Ahbhu glanced back at me with an embarrassed look. I picked him up, gave him a quick hug, then took him back into the shelter of the house, where I filled a bowl of water for him in the kitchen. Ahbhu lapped at it eagerly, while my mother hurried around us getting things ready for her shop. She squeezed past us on her way to the front room, carrying a big pot of something, and called out that she'd already set up breakfast in the back room.

Sensing we were in her way, I carried Ahbhu to the back of the house. There, I found my father sitting at the long dining table, alternating between eating fried plantains and reading the morning paper. His favorite tango piece, "La Cumparsita," filled the room from an old-fashioned Victrola he'd brought with him from his hometown of Jucuapa. He glanced up when I entered the room.

"Good morning, hijo. You had us worried yesterday."

I kissed his forehead with its receding hairline of thick graying hair. "I'm sorry, papá. I had to get away. And then I missed the bus home and had to walk all the way back with this one." I pointed at Ahbhu, who was still focused on the water bowl. "Meet Ahbhu!"

My father looked over his half glasses at the pup, then back at me. "Ahbhu?"

"Someone hurt him, papá. He was in a real bad way when I found him. He's a little better now."

My father looked back at Ahbhu, who had settled onto his haunches and lowered his head, raising his eyes at us as if he knew we were talking about him.

"You've done a good thing, hijo," my father said with a hint of pride. "Now sit and eat."

Arturo strolled into the room, carrying a basket of fresh tortillas and a pot of coffee, and refilled our cups. Then he joined us at the table where we chatted for a bit about random stuff. Before long, he and my father got into it about politics, being that Arturo was a bit of a left-winger and my father was decidedly on the right, the two of them on opposite sides of the fault line of our country's developing conflict. I focused on feeding Ahbhu some scraps, trying my best to ignore their raised voices.

Just then, Neto poked his head into the room, and everything went quiet. He was wearing a plain black T-shirt and pressed blue jeans, and his hair was slicked back, which accentuated the hard angles of his face. As he strode up to the table, his eyes fixed on Ahbhu, and he halted.

"What's that?" He pointed at Ahbhu, his voice as hard as granite.

I looked at Arturo and my father, both of whom had lowered their eyes to the table. Then I turned back to Neto, who was waiting for my response. Sensing trouble, Ahbhu raised his head at Neto. His little body had tensed up, and a deep growl rumbled from within him.

"I found this puppy downtown," I explained. "Someone hurt him and dumped him in an alley. His name is Ahbhu."

Neto barked a sarcastic laugh. "So, now you're what? Mother Theresa for *aguacateros?*" He sat at the table and pulled a plate of beans toward him. "Once it's recovered, that flea-bitten mutt goes."

I held Ahbhu close and opened my mouth to respond. Arturo held up his palm to silence me and pivoted his head toward Neto.

"The dog's staying, brother."

Neto lowered his fork and glared at Arturo. "What did you say?"

"You heard me," Arturo said, his voice low and steady, staring Neto down. "Isaac rescued him, and now the pup's his. He deserves to have a pet like any normal kid. Plus, he's not in anyone's way, least of all yours."

"It's a good thing your brother has done, hijo," my father added.

Despite Neto's authoritarian demeanor, he remained my father's favorite. You could see it in his eyes and in the deferential way he addressed him. It was the only thing that could calm Neto when he got into a mood.

"Let the boy enjoy the reward of his good deed." He placed his thin hand on Neto's arm.

"Just look at him, Neto, he's so cute," I said, holding up Ahbhu, who let out a whimper. "How can we refuse him a home?"

23

Neto stared deadpan at Ahbhu for a beat; then he shook his head and turned back to his food. "All right, you can keep the mutt."

His agreement defused the tension at the table, although I didn't believe for a second that the matter was closed as I lowered Ahbhu to the floor and stroked him.

"Just make sure he doesn't make any messes," he warned. "Otherwise, he's out of here."

# CHAPTER 4

## BECOMING A MAN

Neto found me later that morning perched on a wooden crate behind the house in the tranquil shade of our largest banyan tree, engrossed in a tattered copy of Ray Bradbury's *The Martian Chronicles*. Ahbhu lay resting at my feet, gazing up at me as I read. We heard Neto approaching, crunching over dead leaves, even before he appeared from around the corner. Ahbhu lifted his head and let out a little growl as Neto bore down on us, and I lowered the book to my lap, preparing for a confrontation. He halted a couple of steps from us and stared down at me.

"About yesterday," he said.

I rose to my feet, *The Martian Chronicles* dangling by my side.

"I was serious about you carrying your weight in work around here." He snatched the paperback out of my hand, provoking a bark from Ahbhu who rose on his unsteady feet. I reached for the book, and Neto held it behind his back.

"Give me that!" I demanded, my heart pounding in my chest as my frustration boiled over. At that moment, I felt smaller than I'd ever felt, overshadowed by Neto's imposing presence.

I wanted so much to hate him, but all I felt was a profound sense of helplessness and insignificance. I made another grab for the book, and he pushed me against the crate, causing me to stumble to the ground.

"In due time." He shoved my book into his back pocket and I heard the pages tear. "You'll read at night. During the daytime, whenever you're not at school, you'll work like the rest of us. Understand?"

I hauled myself back to my feet and brushed off the dry leaves that had adhered to my clothes. "Why do you hate me so much, Neto? What did I ever do to you?"

Neto blinked at me, surprised by the question. "I don't hate you. Why would you say that?"

"For starters, you're always mean to me. In fact, I can't remember a single time you've ever been nice to me, not one kind word, not a hug, nothing. If that's not hate, I don't know what is." I picked up Ahbhu and buried my face in his fur before looking back at Neto, who was staring at me, his mouth hanging slightly open.

"Listen, kid, life is hard, and it's only going to get harder. A lot of shit is about to come down on us; you have no idea." Neto's eyes had turned red and shone in the sunlight in a way that scared me. "Mamá and papá, they're living in the past, raising us as if we were going to live normal lives in a normal country: books, pets, stable homes, careers. But all that bougie shit's going to disappear soon, and I want all of you to be ready for what's coming, especially you."

I lowered my eyes, not knowing how to respond although I had an idea of what he was talking about from the arguments around our dinner table. After a moment, I looked back up at him. He looked afraid and a bit lost, and I suddenly felt sorry for him.

"Okay, Neto," I said, softening my voice, not sure what I was agreeing to but keen to bring an end to whatever this was.

"Whatever you say."

"Good." Neto nodded and his mouth pulled into a half-smile. "And I'm sorry. Maybe I have been a bit too hard on you."

"Kind of, yeah."

My comment drew a frown from Neto, but it soon passed and was replaced by an icy grin that sent a chill through me. "Well, then, let me make it up to you. We'll leave the work for tomorrow. Today, let's go out, just you and me, after lunch, a fresh start, older brother and younger brother. What do you say?"

"Really?" I hugged Ahbhu close to my chest like a security blanket, sensing a deep growl of suspicion gurgling around inside of him.

"Yes, really." Neto turned on his heels. "We'll head out after lunch," he said over his shoulder. "Wait for me in the shop."

"Wait! Where are we going?" I called out as he walked back to the house. I never knew whether he heard the question or if he chose to ignore me as he disappeared around the corner.

I lowered myself back onto the crate, puzzled and conflicted, a sense of unresolved tension still hanging in the air. A quiet whimper brought me back to myself, and I found Ahbhu blinking at me, his head cocked to one side, which brought a smile to my face.

"What do you think, Ahbhu?" I asked as if he could understand me.

Ahbhu pivoted his mottled head toward the house for a considered beat, then looked back at me and lowered his head to my lap with a little grumble.

Later that afternoon, I slipped into the shop and sat on an unopened crate of green mangoes while my mother transacted business over the counter with an endless stream of women from the neighborhood. She sold produce, freshly butchered meat, and some prepared food. Ever since I was a little boy, whenever I wasn't at school, I loved to sit in the shop to keep her company, help her grab this or that from the shelves, and maybe run an errand or two for her. Today, though, I was excitedly waiting for Neto to come get me for our big-brother-little-brother outing, and somewhat scared too, since I wasn't sure how much I could trust him.

After a few minutes of nervous waiting, I peered into the book bag resting on my lap to check on Ahbhu and was relieved to see he was sound asleep. The sound of someone clearing his throat made me look up, and I found Neto staring down at me. I scrambled to my feet so I could look at him eye to eye, threading my arms through my book bag and shifting it onto my stomach like a mother kangaroo. The maneuver woke Ahbhu, and he poked his head out of the bag to investigate.

"You're not bringing the dog," Neto said. He narrowed his eyes at Ahbhu, who stared back at him, sensing a challenge.

"But—"

"Huh-uh, no way. The dog stays here."

He reached for the book bag and drew an angry yap from Ahbhu, making him pull back his hand. "Damned aguacatero!" he snapped, glaring at Ahbhu.

"Oh, my God," I said. "He's only a puppy. Give me a break."

At that, Arturo strolled into the shop and halted at the scene. "What's happening here?"

Neto swung around and flashed a sarcastic grin. "Well, if it isn't Superman come to the rescue."

Arturo crossed his arms. "Say what?"

"Babysit the kid's dog, will you?" Neto said, looking askance at Ahbhu. "We'll be back in a couple of hours."

As much as it pained me to leave poor Ahbhu, I felt sure he'd be in good hands with Arturo. Plus, I wanted to go out with Neto since I'd never done that before. Something told me I might finally be starting a new chapter with my eldest brother, whom I both hated and loved—a better chapter I hoped.

I kissed Ahbhu and whispered that I'd be back soon. Then I turned him over to Arturo, making him swear he'd take good care of him, and sped out of the shop with Neto.

Neto thrust a helmet into my hands, and I climbed onto the back of his motorcycle with a sense of unease. I gripped him tight around the waist as we shot out of the driveway onto the bumpy road. He tore downhill, maneuvering around the winding paths like a daredevil, scaring the bejeebies out of pedestrians who leapt out of our way. Gripping him for dear life, we zoomed through the posh neighborhoods on the lower slopes.

After a heart-pounding five minutes, Neto slowed as we merged onto the main highway, blending with the sluggish traffic, which allowed some time to catch my breath. When we finally exited the highway, we cruised down an unfamiliar boulevard, swerving to avoid burning tires left by left-wing, anti-government protesters until we reached a rundown neighborhood.

The streets were lined with parked cars, and every other building seemed to be a shop, eatery, or bar. Most structures sported faded pastel colors—pinks, blues, or aqua greens—with cracked concrete and peeling paint adding to the sketchy vibe. Despite the apparent activity, there was an eerie lack of pedestrians in sight.

Neto pulled up in front of an abandoned movie house and wedged between a VW van and a Chevy El Dorado. Hopping off the bike, he locked up our helmets. Then he swaggered across the road like a badass, dressed all in black—black T-shirt, black jeans, black boots, and a pair of black sunglasses that presto appeared on his face like magic.

"Follow me," he called without bothering to look back.

"Hey, wait up!" I hurried to catch up with him, dodging cars as we crossed the road. "Where are we going?"

He jumped up onto the sidewalk on the other side, quickstepping past a couple of snack shops, and screeched to a stop in front of a dark blue single-story building. It had a flat roof, no windows, and a neon sign advertising Regia beer. Slapping his hand on the black wooden door, he flashed a grin and said, "We're about to make history, brother." Then he yanked me inside by the arm, and the door slammed shut behind us.

I found myself within the dim confines of a smoky, windowless tavern, painted a depressing shade of red with black trim. Along the back wall stretched a bar manned by a bald bartender in a white tank top. Opposite the bar was an empty stage extending into the middle of the room with a mirror ball dangling over it. A smattering of patrons crisscrossed the floor, most of them guys, some young, some old, looking like they were waiting for something to happen. A Juan Gabriel song was leaking out of a pair of cracked speakers.

Neto glanced around as if he were expecting someone; then he shepherded me onto a bar stool and left me alone while he went to the toilet. The creepy bartender flashed a mouthful of gold teeth at me. Feeling nervous, I looked away, disappointed and mad that Neto had brought me to this freaky place. Looking around, I noticed people sitting in dark corners, women and men it seemed, doing stuff I couldn't see very well.

Just then the music changed and "Eres Tu" by Mocedades came on, which was a song I liked. I turned back around and found the bartender still staring me down. Having had enough of the place, I was about to hop off the stool when Neto appeared at my side.

"Sorry, sorry." He held up two fingers at the bartender. "I got distracted on my way back from the restroom. Anyway . . ." He squeezed my shoulder not finishing his sentence.

"What is this place, Neto?" I moved away from his hand and

shook my head at the bartender as he deposited a shot glass in front of me and another in front of Neto.

Neto raised his glass, pumping his eyebrows at me. "This is wonderland, Alice, and today is your initiation." He indicated my glass with a nod of his head. "It's saying *Drink Me*."

Neto downed his drink, slammed the shot glass back on the bar, and ordered another. "Now it's your turn."

I sniffed at the contents, wrinkling my nose at the sharp-smelling liquid. "What is it?"

"Don't ask so many questions," he snapped. "Drink it!"

"Mamá wouldn't like it if I did, Neto." I crossed my arms and scooted away from him. "Neither would Papá. I'm only sixteen."

Neto downed a second shot and ordered another, and I felt a spike of panic blossom in my chest. As the tension in the bar mounted, a strange metallic taste filled my mouth, and my vision seemed to blur, which scared me.

"Like I said yesterday when you so rudely baptized me with mamá's finest cooking," Neto said, leaning toward me, "you're a man now. A sixteen-year-old is a man as far as I'm concerned. Right, Chango?" he said to the bartender, who nodded and pushed the shot glass toward me. "In fact, I had my first drink at twelve. Chango here is my witness. He served it to me."

Both of them burst out laughing, loud cackling guffaws that made my stomach drop and brought out a cold sweat all over my body.

I stole a glance at the door across the room, calculating how long it would take me to reach it if I launched myself off the stool and made a break for it. But what then? Panic surged within me, my heart pounding faster, palms growing clammy, as a feeling of dread crept over me. I had no clue where I even was. Perhaps I'd spot a policeman outside and flag them down. Regardless, I was determined to do a runner, because there was no way I was going to drink that stuff.

"I'm counting to three, brother," Neto said. "Just three, got it? If that glass is still full when I finish my count, I'm going to pour it down your gullet myself."

"You're doing this because of yesterday, aren't you?"

Neto chuckled. "What do *you* think?"

"I'm sorry about that, Neto, really," I tried. "I shouldn't have reacted that way. I don't know what happened. I think something's wrong with me."

Neto narrowed his eyes for a moment, as if he was trying to figure something out; then he squeezed my arm and said in a low voice, "Apology accepted, brother." He tapped the shot glass closer. "But you'll still need to partake. Consider it a peace offering."

"If I drink it, can we go?" I glanced around the place once more. "I mean it, Neto. I hate it here. Promise me we'll go, and I'll drink it. But you can't tell mamá or papá or Arturo."

Neto glanced at the bartender and raised his shoulders then swung his head back at me. "Sure, kid, one drink. Our secret. Then I'll introduce you to a friend, a nice lady you'll like a lot, and *then* we can go."

I glared at Neto, struggling to hide my fear and resentment. I didn't want to be in this place, and I didn't want to drink, but I was desperate to get it over with and go home. So, lifting the shot glass to my nose, I sniffed at it for half a second, then tilted it into my mouth and felt the cool liquid burn its way down my throat. Dropping the glass back on the counter, I swatted it away and lifted my chin at Neto. "Happy now?"

"Good boy," Neto said in a low serious voice. "Now then, it's time for the main event." He waved at someone over my shoulder.

Out of the shadows emerged a woman, like no other woman I'd ever seen. Striking and statuesque, her thick black hair cascaded down her back in a sleek ponytail that swayed with her every move. The vibrant colors of her flower-patterned skirt mirrored her vivacious personality, drawing every eye in the room. Her low-cut blouse showcased ample cleavage, daring yet elegant. But what really set her apart was a tiny heart-shaped beauty mark on her lip that added a naughty touch to her broad smile.

The woman swept up to Neto and planted a lingering kiss on his mouth; then she turned to me and took me in from head to foot. "So, *this* is the one?" she asked Neto, never taking her sparkling eyes off me.

Without waiting for an answer, she patted me on the head and flashed her teeth. "Hello, young man!" she purred, slipping onto the stool next to me and planting a little kiss on my right cheek that made my heart jump. She smelled like jasmine.

"His name's Isaac," Neto said. He slammed back another shot and wiped his mouth on the back of his arm.

The woman arched a wire-thin eyebrow at him and tapped his glass. "Maybe you should slow down with those."

"Never mind that, pumpkin," Neto said. "Isaac, this here is my good friend Celestina. Around here, we call her *La Chispa*. She's going to show you a good time. Consider it my birthday present."

I swung my head at Neto. "What do you mean?"

Neto grinned at me for a beat then looked over at the woman. "He wants to know what I mean. Isn't that just the cutest thing?"

I turned back to Celestina. "Seriously, what's he talking about?"

Celestina slinked up from her stool and held her hand out at me. Confused, I looked at it then back up at her. Taking my hand, she eased me off my stool. "Come with me, darling."

"Where are we going?" I asked, digging in my heels, fearing I was about to be kidnapped.

"Relax, darling," she said in a soothing voice. "We're just going to relax in the back for a little while."

"I don't want to relax in the back!" I pulled my hand away and turned to Neto. "I want to go home!" I shouted, making all the people in the bar look in our direction.

Neto put his hand on my shoulder, and I shrugged it off. "You said I could go home if I had the one drink and after you introduced me to a friend, and we've done all that! I drank the stupid drink, and now I've met your friend." I swung on Celestina. "Did he tell you I'm only sixteen? Did he?"

Celestina dropped back and cast a bewildered look at Neto; then she held up her hands at him. "I'm sorry, mijo, I didn't sign up for this." Then she turned to leave.

"Hold on a second!" Neto shouted, stopping her in her tracks. He grabbed my arm and pushed me toward her. "Don't make this more difficult than it needs to be. Believe me, kid, you'll thank me for this one day."

In that instant, something happened to me that had never happened before: I was overcome by a sudden, overwhelming surge of dizziness, as if the world had tilted on its axis. My muscles tensed, and an eerie tingling sensation rippled through my limbs. A wave of panic spread over me, accompanied by a sense of profound disorientation. And then, as if a shadow had descended over my consciousness, everything faded into black.

# CHAPTER 5

## MY NEW ABNORMAL

A gentle warmth enveloped me as I regained awareness of my surroundings. There was no pain, just a lingering sense of dislocation. I struggled to grasp where I was and what had happened. As I slowly emerged from the haze, the sounds of the world seeped into my consciousness.

Amid a mixed-up whirl of beeps and ringtones, soft and concerned voices reached my ears—whispers carried on a gentle breeze. I recognized these as the familiar, worried voices of my parents. And then . . . a sound reached me that brought a smile to my face, even in my groggy state: the excited whimpering of a puppy, *my* puppy Ahbhu. His joyful yips filled the liminal space around me with an infectious energy.

As my eyelids fluttered open, I realized I was lying in a hospital bed. The sterile scent of antiseptic lingered in the air, mingled with the warmth of human presence. Arturo stood beside me, holding Ahbhu in his arms, the little pup wagging his tail furiously. The sight filled me with a surge of joy and comfort.

"He's awake," Arturo exclaimed to my parents, who were behind him.

They rushed to my bedside, their tear-filled eyes meeting mine. My mother gently stroked my hair and planted a tender kiss on my forehead. My father held my arm, waiting his turn, his expression reflecting a mix of relief and concern.

"I'm back," I managed, offering them a weak smile.

"I'll go get the nurse!" Arturo said, turning to leave.

"Wait!" I called out, my gaze shifting to Ahbhu. "Bring him here, please."

My parents made way for Arturo as he brought Ahbhu to me. The pup smothered me with affectionate licks, his tail fluttering with unbridled enthusiasm.

"This one went crazy when you left," Arturo said, as I nuzzled Ahbhu. "He didn't stop crying the entire time."

"Really? Is that true, Ahbhu?" Ahbhu responded by cuddling against my chest.

"I'll be back," Arturo said and disappeared into the corridor.

My parents returned to my bedside and held onto each other.

"What happened to me?" I asked.

"We don't know yet," my mother said in a trembling voice. "They ran some tests. We should have the results soon."

"Neto brought you," my father added. "You collapsed. It seems you may have had a seizure."

My mother's head snapped around at my father's words. "He definitely had a seizure," she corrected. "I know about these things. My brother Paco suffered from them."

"Uncle Paco did?" I asked. "I never knew that!"

"We kept it quiet, of course," my mother said. "Nobody outside the family needed to know." She looked at me with moist eyes. "Please don't say anything to him yet."

"Neto explained what happened," my father said, changing the subject. "He feels terrible. Your mother and I have asked him to stay away for now until we can figure everything out."

Just then, Arturo and a pretty nurse with large eyes and short brown hair entered the room. She drew up short at the sight of Ahbhu, her expression turning serious. Lifting him out of my hands to his wriggling protests, she handed him to Arturo with a curt shake of her head, as if she'd already scolded him about it.

"Welcome back to the world, young man," she said, turning back to me with a sweet smile. "How are we feeling?"

"Okay, I guess. Sort of confused."

She checked my vitals, seeming satisfied with what she saw, then examined my eyes with a little flashlight and nodded. "Do you have an appetite?"

"My stomach feels upset, but I feel hungry, too," I said with a shrug, feeling a mix of conflicting sensations. "Does that make sense?"

The nurse patted my head. "Perfect sense. I'll have some lunch brought to you. It's beef soup today."

"When can we take him home, miss?" my mother asked.

"We're just waiting for Doctor Rodriguez," the nurse replied. "He should be here soon."

A few minutes later, they served me lunch. The warm aroma of the hearty soup filled the air. I did my best to eat but, hungry as I was, I could only get down a couple of spoonfuls. Just as I was about to try the dessert, a tall man in a white coat with thick red hair and freckles entered the room, carrying a clipboard.

He took us all in and then focused on me. "Good afternoon, young man. I'm Hernan Rodriguez, the head of Pediatric Neurology. I've already met your parents."

"Hello, doctor," my parents said.

"I'm Arturo," Arturo chimed in. "Isaac's brother."

Arturo's comment drew a concerned glance from the doctor.

"The good one," Arturo clarified. "And this is Ahbhu." He lifted up Ahbhu, whose sparkling eyes were fixed on the doctor.

Doctor Rodriguez's gaze landed on Ahbhu, and his face clouded over as he took a closer look at him. He raised questioning eyes at Arturo.

"He's Isaac's," Arturo said. "He rescued him a couple of days ago. Poor thing was in terrible shape. Still is, in a way. Isaac was nursing him back to health. Then this happened." He raised his head at me.

Doctor Rodriguez nodded without saying a word, then came to my bedside, looking like someone about to deliver bad news. I moved my food tray aside, having lost what little appetite I had left, and readied myself for what he was about to say.

"Isaac," Doctor Rodriguez began, his voice calm and soothing, "after reviewing your medical history and conducting some very preliminary tests, I can confirm that you had a seizure, most likely an epileptic seizure. It was fairly severe in terms of these events." His words hung in the air, heavy with the weight of uncertainty. "From what I understand, you were in a stressful situation just before the seizure. We know that stress can be a trigger."

My mother's eyes welled up, and my father gripped my hand. Their faces were etched deep with worry. I wanted to be strong for them, but my own chest felt tight with fear at what it all meant. Ahbhu also sensed something dire was being discussed as he struggled in Arturo's arms, stretching his head in my direction.

Doctor Rodriguez glanced at Ahbhu for a moment, then continued. "Epilepsy is a neurological condition characterized by recurrent seizures. With the right treatment plan, we can aim to control these and improve your quality of life. That said, I'd like to run a full battery of tests in the next couple of weeks to make sure we get to the bottom of exactly what's going on."

I felt a flicker of hope at his mention of a treatment plan, as if maybe this wasn't the end of the world or the start of a bleak future for me. Maybe I could still have a normal life.

My father, his voice trembling, asked about the prognosis. Would I outgrow this?

Doctor Rodriguez explained that while it was difficult to

predict, many young people with epilepsy did outgrow their seizures as they transitioned from their teens into their twenties, although he couldn't guarantee anything. Still, I clung to that ray of hope.

Doctor Rodriguez asked my parents to schedule a follow-up in the next few days for additional testing and to discuss a specific treatment plan. As a preview, though, he explained that a combination of medication and a service dog might be beneficial.

"A service dog?" I asked, my eyes meeting Arturo's, then Ahbhu's.

Doctor Rodriguez nodded. "Some dogs can be specially trained to detect and respond to seizures." He glanced again at Ahbhu, then set aside his clipboard and took him into his arms, which surprised all of us, including Ahbhu. "Your dog, for example," Doctor Rodriguez said. "His ancestors were bred for herding. He's a mix, of course, but he's probably about eighty percent Australian Cattle Dog. A dog like this can be trained to be the perfect service dog. He could be trained to provide you comfort, which reduces stress; alert you and your parents before a seizure occurs; and even assist during an episode. The costs of the training would be borne by a charity I'm on the board of. That is, if you're interested." He handed Ahbhu to me and stepped back.

"Yes! We're interested! Right?" I asked my parents, who nodded their agreement.

"Good," the doctor said, stroking Ahbhu. "He's still quite young and in the early stages of his development, so we'll have to wait until he's at least a year old to start his service training. In the meantime, Isaac, your primary focus should be on socialization, basic obedience training, and building a strong bond between Ahbhu and yourself. We'll give you some booklets on this. How does that sound?"

My heart swelled with joy as Doctor Rodriguez explained

everything. Ahbhu had already brought a sense of purpose into my life, and now he could play a critical role in helping to manage my condition. I buried my face in Ahbhu's neck and wept tears of gratitude while my parents booked my follow-up.

Later that afternoon, after learning more about my condition from the nurse, I was discharged with some medication and a couple of pamphlets. Doctor Rodriguez swung by to say goodbye and gave us a referral to a trainer for Ahbhu, who lived a couple of miles down the hill from us, an American lady named Sue Martin. According to the doctor, Sue had already agreed to help me with the obedience training as a first step once Ahbhu was recovered enough to walk around.

I spent the next couple of weeks recovering at home with Ahbhu. The seizure had taken a lot out of me and had left me feeling weak and unsteady and pretty depressed. It also took me a few days to get used to the anti-seizure medication, which I was supposed to take twice a day on an empty stomach. But it still made me dizzy and nauseous. Considering all of that, it was a good thing I had one month left of vacation to get my head around my "new normal" as Arturo called it, but which I preferred to call my "new abnormal" since there wasn't anything especially normal about me to begin with.

I couldn't believe what had happened. I found myself wondering whether things would be different if I had reacted differently at my party, if I had just played along with Neto like the obedient younger brother instead of doing what I did. Perhaps then, I'd still be my ordinary self.

Arturo said I was being silly, that my condition wasn't my fault and that I probably would have had a seizure at some other point anyway. He said the epilepsy was probably inside of me, waiting for something to trigger it, and that I was damned lucky it happened when it did, with someone from the family to intervene—that it would have been far worse if it had happened in some random public place. My parents agreed with Arturo. They told me to focus on getting stronger by eating the tasty food my mother brought to me whenever she had a break from the store. When I felt well enough, they advised taking walks around the house with Ahbhu, getting outside, and breathing fresh air.

On the plus side, taking advantage of the down time, I was able to rip through Frank Herbert's *Dune*, *Dune Messiah*, and *Children of Dune* back-to-back. That was fifteen hundred pages, which was something I'd always wanted to do. The constant, unsettling rumble of El Boquerón as ambient noise added to the weirdness of it all.

On his part, Ahbhu recovered more of his strength with each passing day. He was soon hopping on and off my bed on his own, lolling in the sunlight that pooled on the floor in the early morning, and trotting from one side of the room to the other, staring at me as if to say, "Look at me! If I can do it, you can too!" Whenever he needed to do his business, he'd slip out of the room on his own for a few minutes. But he'd always come straight back to cuddle and watch me read, or listen to the radio with me, or follow me to the bathroom, or to the kitchen whenever I got hungry, and back to the bedroom again, always keeping close as I moved from room to room.

Ahbhu also adored watching me from afar. Whenever Arturo stepped out, he would bound onto his cot, remaining there for hours, his eyes bright and attentive, fixed on my face. He seemed to analyze every expression and gesture, mirroring them with surprising accuracy. Strangely, his intense gaze would often catch mine, prompting me to meet it without uttering a word. It felt as though our hearts communicated through our eyes, cementing the unspoken bond between us.

After about a week of trotting around and staring at me,

Ahbhu started playing hide-and-seek with me. He'd crouch under the cots, or in different corners of the room, and then call out in his own special way, a mix of barks, yips, and a cute howling sound I'd never heard from any other dog. If I got too close, he'd slip away, keeping the game exciting. Then, when he was ready to be caught, he'd pop his head out and wag his tail like crazy. That was my signal to jump on him, wrap him up in my arms, and give him a big hug while repeating his name over and over again. He'd always reward me with a sloppy lick on the face and one of those funny Ahbhu sounds, the yipping and howling. It was as if he was telling me, "Hey, you did good!" I soon got the feeling he was training *me*, pushing me to get up and be more active.

With each passing day, Ahbhu's coat filled in, starting with a dense, bristly undercoat followed by a softer topcoat. His appearance was becoming ever more striking, a mesmerizing blend of blue hues adorned by small patches of black, tan, and white that speckled his fur. His caramel brown eyes were captivating, the left one accentuated by a black pirate patch. I soon took to grabbing his triangle-shaped head between my hands and staring into those eyes, touching his chubby wet nose with mine. Then I'd shake his head back and forth, all the while calling him mean names he understood were actually love names: menso, loquito, tonto, mi chulis! Once I let go of his head, Ahbhu would respond by biting down on my hand so hard it left teeth marks that would make my mother scream and threaten to toss him out. But I knew it was just his weird doggie way of showing love, and I defended him each and every time.

One morning, a couple of weeks after the seizure, Ahbhu nudged me awake. As I opened my eyes, I noticed a subtle shift in the room's atmosphere. Everything seemed brighter, more vibrant, infused with a renewed sense of life. Sitting up, I surveyed my surroundings, and it dawned on me that I felt different—like my old self again, before the seizure. It was the strangest thing, almost as though I'd been inhabiting a parallel version of myself for a time, and now I had awoken as Isaac Perez once more. Ahbhu sensed it too. He peeled back my sheet and urged me off the cot.

"Good morning, Ahbhu," I said with a delighted laugh, giving him a quick peck on the head. Then I stood and stretched in the morning light and pulled on a pair of shorts.

Feeling both hungry and thirsty, I headed into the kitchen with Ahbhu trotting close behind.

I found my mother getting things ready for her shop. She stopped what she was doing and gasped, her hand flying to her mouth as she noticed the change in me too.

"Hijo!" she cried, drawing me into her arms.

"I'm better, mamá," I announced, tears pooling in my eyes.

She stepped back and took me in, hardly believing it, as if she was seeing someone who had come back from the grave. It made me believe I really had been inhabiting a parallel version of myself.

Conscious she was in a hurry to open the store, I told her I'd take care of my own breakfast, then poured myself some coffee and some water for Ahbhu and took them to our back room. There, I munched on *pan dulce*, while looking out the back window.

Arturo and Neto were outside in the courtyard, tending to the coffee plants. Neto still wasn't allowed into the house on account of what had happened to me, and I had no idea when he would be. But I agreed it wasn't a good idea for us to be too close to each other for a while even though I did miss him in some strange way I didn't understand.

Ahbhu jumped onto a chair to see what I was looking at. Spotting Neto, he growled and bared his teeth, and I stroked his head to calm him down. "It's okay, Ahbhu. It's only Neto."

Ahbhu looked at me and squinted as if trying to understand.

"Neto," I repeated. "He's my brother, like Arturo, only older

43

and more serious."

Ahbhu stared back out the window, his gaze lingering on Neto as he wielded a pair of pruning shears, and let out a sharp bark. Both Neto and Arturo stopped work, turning their attention to us. Arturo beamed a smile and raised his hand in a greeting, while Neto nodded a sheepish hello. After a moment, they refocused on one of the plants.

I felt guilty to see the two of them laboring in the hot sun while I watched them from inside, as if I were some kind of pampered pet, especially after what Neto had said about my needing to step up. But I honestly couldn't see myself working out there. I had other ambitions for my life. I wanted to study science and astronomy. If I was lucky and worked hard, I might get into a good university and go on to become an astrophysicist or maybe even an astronaut. Working on coffee plants, I told myself, was not going to get me any closer to that. So, on that note, I grabbed my empty plates, deposited them in the kitchen, and headed back to my bedroom with Ahbhu.

"Today," I told Ahbhu, who was perched on the naming chair and panting, "I'm going to give you the grand tour of the house and the yard. What do you think?" Even though he had already explored most of the rooms on his own, I wanted to properly introduce each one to him by name before moving on to the next.

Ahbhu hopped off the naming chair and joined me on the cot, flashing a happy doggy grin, which I took as a yes. "Awesome!" I said, pulling a NASA tank top over my head and heading for the door. "Let's go!"

To give him the full experience, we went out the side door and down the driveway to the street. Our house stood proud and pink in the late morning sun. Through the front window,

I could see my mother conducting business over the counter in her shop.

"*That's* where we live, Ahbhu!" I pointed at the house. "We call it '*La Casa*.'"

Ahbhu looked at me when I said his name, then followed my gaze to where I was pointing. "La Casa," I repeated a few more times. Then I picked him up and whispered it in his ear, which made him howl with excitement.

Just then, El Boquerón decided to shake things up, causing Ahbhu to squirm out of my arms and look around as if to say, *What's going on?*

I'd planned to introduce him to the volcano later on. But since it had decided to make an entrance just then, I scooped him up and stepped out onto the road, pointing at the massive cone looming over our house.

"That's El Boquerón, Ahbhu." I shook him gently and said the name again, trying to get it into his head that El Boquerón was the reason for the shaking. I repeated the routine a few times, even adding a rumbling sound effect. Then I mixed it up by saying the name, shaking Ahbhu, and letting out a little howl. Soon we were howling together.

"El Boquerón!" Little shake! Big howl!

Ahbhu bolted out of my arms and ran in circles, stopping to howl at El Boquerón each time I said the name. From that moment on, whenever someone mentioned the volcano, Ahbhu would howl. Whenever the volcano shook us, he'd howl again. And whenever El Boquerón rumbled, no matter how slight, Ahbhu would pace around growling until the rumbling stopped.

I sat on the curb, and Ahbhu crouched by my side, pressing up against me. "I've been scared of El Boquerón my whole life, Ahbhu," I confessed, pointing once more at the big cone. This time, he just stared at me, listening to what I had to say. "See that jacaranda over there?" I indicated the gorgeous blossom-filled tree in front of our house. "When I was a baby, my mother would set up an empty mango crate with a blanket and put me inside it. Then she'd place me under that tree, like I was Moses in the bulrushes, where she could keep an eye on me from the store. To this day she likes to say I was happy in that box, cooing and laughing, as if all I needed was a pretty tree." I stroked Ahbhu's head, focusing on the sweet spot behind his ear. "But that's not how I remember it."

I shut my eyes, recalling my earliest memories, then opened them again, gazing at the jacaranda. "What I remember from that time isn't the flowers, Ahbhu. What I remember was the scary sight of El Boquerón towering over me."

Ahbhu howled.

"Yep, that's right, Ahbhu." I pointed at the volcano again, unable to look at it directly at that moment, because it stirred up a nervous feeling, as if another seizure might be around the corner. "I remember that black cone poking through a dark cloud ring, blocking the sun as it moved west; I remember the constant rumbling, bubbling up from deep in the ground into my makeshift crib." I shuddered at the thought and hugged Ahbhu close.

"When I learned that it could blow its stack anytime or that it could set off a huge earthquake that could flatten everything, I couldn't get it out of my head. To deal with the anxiety, I buried it deep inside. I tried my best to ignore it like everyone else in this crazy place does. That's why I'm such a jittery scaredy-cat, Ahbhu, in case you were wondering."

I laughed at my little dog-cat joke, then got up from the curb.

"Anyway, Ahbhu," I said as we crossed the road back to the house, "let's continue with our tour!"

# CHAPTER 6

## CONQUERING AND EMBRACING

The next morning, Ahbhu surprised me by dragging the sheet off me, urging me out of bed with loud yips and barks. It was still early, and the sun hadn't come up yet. Arturo groaned at the noise and pulled a pillow over his head, instructing me in a muffled voice to take Ahbhu outside.

Thinking Ahbhu needed to do his doggie business, I got up from my cot, groggy as a zombie, and made my way to the side door. But when I opened it, Ahbhu didn't run out as I expected. Instead, he head-butted my legs, nudging *me* out of the house.

"What's up, Ahbhu?" I crouched beside him, stroking his bristly fur to calm him down, but he kept pushing me.

Right then, my mother crept past us on her way to her shop. She halted and narrowed her eyes at us. "Why are you up so early?"

"Ahbhu woke me up. I think he wants me to go outside with him. Is that right, Ahbhu? You want me to go outside?"

Ahbhu wagged his tail and let out a cute little howl that made my mother frown. "Shush, you!" she scolded in a hushed voice before disappearing down the hallway.

47

"Okay, okay, Ahbhu. Wait here."

I went to the bathroom and doused my face with water with Ahbhu following close at heel. Then I went back to my bedroom and changed into jeans and a T-shirt. When I went for my trainers, Ahbhu grabbed them with his teeth and tossed them away, surprising me and catching Arturo's attention. He disappeared into the closet and came back with my muddy-weather boots, dropping them at my feet.

"Look at that!" Arturo said. "He wants to take you on a hike!"

"Seems like it," I said, still half-asleep and puzzled by the whole thing.

Ahbhu danced around my boots and scooted them closer. Then he sat down and waited, panting with excitement. Realizing I didn't have much of a choice, I slipped into them and laced them up.

Since it looked like we really were going on a hike, I grabbed some water and snacks for us and stuffed them into my backpack along with a library copy of Samuel R. Delaney's *Dhalgren*, in case Ahbhu allowed me some downtime, and headed out the door, nearly tripping over him on the way.

Ahbhu galloped ahead down the driveway, past the jacarandas, and stopped, waiting for me, ready to lead the way. Pausing a moment, I stretched in the early morning sunlight, feeling the increasing warmth, and breathed in the sweet scent of the flowering trees my mother so adored but rarely had the opportunity to enjoy. Ahbhu barked impatiently, and I jogged over to him.

Expecting we'd be turning out of the driveway to the right, heading down the hill toward the city center, I was taken aback when Ahbhu turned the *other* way, toward where the road ended and the trailhead leading to El Boquerón began. When I realized his intention, I skidded to a stop. Sensing I wasn't following anymore, Ahbhu looked back at me.

"No, Ahbhu," I protested. "Not there."

Ahbhu trotted over and sat down in the road right in front of me, panting with anticipation. He glanced back at the trailhead and then at me before standing up again.

"I told you I'm scared of it, remember? Scared of El Boquerón!"

Ahbhu let loose a howl and tugged on my pants with his teeth, trying to pull me in the direction of the trailhead.

"I said no, Ahbhu! I'm not going up there."

With shaking legs and a racing heart, I sank onto the curb. I reached into my backpack for my medication, which I hadn't taken yet, worried I might have a seizure. Popping open the bottle, I remembered I had an appointment at the hospital in a couple of days for more tests, which only added to my anxiety.

Seeing me take the pill, Ahbhu raced over and pressed himself into my arms, the way he did when he wanted a hug, or maybe to give me one. Either way, I held him close until my anxiety faded. When I finally let go, he pulled me toward El Boquerón again, more gently this time but just as determined, as if to say, *Trust me; Ahbhu knows you can do this!* I swear, I could almost hear his voice.

And so, trusting Ahbhu, I did something no one had ever managed to persuade me to do: I stepped onto the trailhead and started my ascent to the summit of the volcano that had so terrified me ever since I could remember, with Ahbhu leading the way, both of us feeling the rumbling beneath our feet.


The climb proved arduous, each step testing my resolve. My heart pounded with childhood fears as I grappled with the uncertainty of the hike ahead. With every upward stride, the weight of my apprehension pressed on me. But now that Ahbhu had gotten me this far, I did my best to suppress the scary image of myself collapsing and tumbling backward down the hill.

Ahbhu's barking brought me back to myself, and I continued forward, letting him lead the way.

The trail was treacherous, winding through rugged terrain and steep inclines, demanding every ounce of strength and determination I possessed. Ahbhu, with his sharp senses, guided me through the rocky sections, his paws confidently navigating the terrain as if he'd been hiking the hill all his life. His presence cooled my burning doubts, reminding me I wasn't alone in this scary endeavor.

As we ascended higher, the air grew thin, adding an additional layer of difficulty to the climb. I had to stop to guzzle some water and offered some to Ahbhu. But he seemed unaffected by the altitude and danced around me as I rested. When I was ready, he continued leading the way up the winding path, his tail wagging in encouragement.

Midway up, we encountered a couple of American hikers on their way down from the summit, two middle-aged hippie guys in ripped jeans. They'd hiked up early in the morning when it was still dark, they told me, to watch the sunrise. They went on and on about how amazing the view was from up there. Ahbhu didn't seem to like them much, crouching down, watching them, suspicious, and emitting a low growl, which put me on my guard, too. When one of them tried to pet him, Ahbhu snapped at him, which quickly ended the conversation. We waited as they disappeared around a corner before pressing on.

After what felt like forever, we broke past the tree line and reached the summit. Tears welled up in my eyes and spilled onto my cheeks when I realized what I'd just accomplished. Ahbhu raced back and forth along the trail urging me on a little farther to the lookout point.

Mopping away the sweat that was now streaming down my face, I jogged the last few meters up the hill to the observation platform. The sight that greeted us was nothing short of amazing. The crater itself stretched out before us. Its steep walls, adorned with a tapestry of green, seemed to defy gravity itself. At its heart lay the smaller secondary crater known as *El Boqueroncito*, the active vent, a testament to the raw power that lay dormant beneath the surface. Ahbhu, his eyes shining with triumph, let out a joyous bark, as if to proclaim our victory to the world.

In that moment, all my fears were vanquished, replaced by a sense of triumph that surged through me. It was as if someone had flipped a switch. Old Isaac had vanished and was replaced with New Isaac, an Isaac resolved never to be cowed by anyone or anything ever again. We had conquered the mountain— Ahbhu and I—both within and without.

Turning away from the crater, I was startled by the amazing sight of San Salvador sprawled out below, shimmering in the bright sunlight. It was a sight I'd seen countless times from the safety of my home, but from this vantage, it felt like an entirely different world. The bustling city, the distant ocean, and the surrounding landscapes stretched out before us like a magnificent tapestry. My breath caught and the rhythm of my heart accelerated as I gazed out at the place that had birthed me. Ahbhu sensed it, too. He stood like a sentry, facing the city, his tail standing straight back.

With tears streaming down my cheeks, I raised my arms to the sky as if to embrace the entire metropolis, open to all the possibilities of the future, and I let out a howl. Ahbhu dropped onto his haunches and joined me, our voices echoing through the thin mountain air. Both of us spent the rest of the afternoon baying at the sky.


We made our descent in the waning sunlight. The journey down was no less challenging in the advancing shadows than the ascent. But with Ahbhu's guidance, a blossoming sense of self-assurance had taken hold of me. Going forward, I felt sure I'd be able to overcome obstacles, both external and internal, with the same courage I had shown that day on El Boquerón.

By the time we reached the trailhead, it had gone dark, and the stars stood out in the sky, like a carpet of diamonds above our heads. The moon was just peeking over the top of the black cone. With that awesome backdrop looming overhead, I couldn't help but feel a profound sense of gratitude toward Ahbhu. He had not only helped me conquer the volcano, but he'd awakened a spirit of exploration as well, and I was excited by the prospect of future adventures with him.

Arturo and my parents were relieved to see us when we finally arrived home. They'd expected our hike to be a short one. The sight of us returning after so many hours left them astounded, especially after I told them where Ahbhu and I had spent the day. I regaled them with the story of our trek, emphasizing how Ahbhu had played a pivotal role in helping me tackle my fear of the volcano.

Arturo, who'd been skeptical of Ahbhu's insistence on the hike, now looked at my pup with newfound respect. "Seems the little guy knew exactly what he was doing," he teased, delighting Ahbhu by planting a big, sloppy kiss on his belly.

# CHAPTER 7

## MEETING GERÓNIMO

After a few days of being scanned, poked and prodded, I was sitting in Doctor Fernandez's office on a Friday morning, flanked by my parents, trying to appear calm despite my growing unease. We'd gotten permission for Ahbhu to accompany me throughout even though I could tell some of the nurses weren't so thrilled about it. But Ahbhu had behaved like a perfect gentleman, sensing the seriousness of the situation. He'd kept close to me, watching everything that was going on and only rarely making a comment under his breath. Today he lay on the floor next to me, resting his head on crossed paws.

A sharp rap on the door startled us as Doctor Fernandez announced his arrival. Stepping into the room, he regarded us with a tight expression before sitting at his desk. He looked tired and stressed as he read through my file. We hadn't seen him since that first night in the hospital as all the extra testing had been performed by the hospital staff. But he was here now to go over the results with us.

"Mr. and Mrs. Perez, Isaac. . ." He glanced at Ahbhu for a moment then looked back at us. "I appreciate your patience with the additional testing. But we needed to make sure what we were dealing with." He passed his fingers through his hair and drew a deep breath.

At that, my parents and I exchanged a glance, and Ahbhu lifted his head.

"First, Isaac, how have you been feeling since we last saw each other?"

"The first few days were rough," I said. "But after some rest, I was fine."

"But no more seizures," he stated, as if he already knew the answer.

"No, although at the beginning I was afraid I'd have another one. But so far so good." I fished the bottle of medication out of my backpack and rattled the pills. "I've been taking these like you said. They upset my stomach—a lot."

My mother fidgeted with the hem of her skirt while my father held his breath, his hands clasped tightly together. Ahbhu looked concerned as well, nuzzling my dangling leg in a gesture of reassurance. But I was determined not to be afraid. I lifted my chin at Doctor Fernandez, prompting him to continue.

"The results of the EEG and brain imaging tests we conducted have all come back negative. That means we haven't found any structural or electrical abnormalities in your brain that would typically explain the seizures."

My father exhaled in relief, and I couldn't help but look down at Ahbhu, who tilted his head curiously. My mother's eyes remained locked on Doctor Fernandez, hanging onto his every word, sensing there was more to the story.

"However," he continued, "this doesn't necessarily mean we're out of the woods yet. Sometimes, epilepsy can be challenging to diagnose, especially when the standard tests yield normal results. That said, it's *also* possible the seizure you suffered could have a psychological cause."

My eyes widened at this, and I glanced at my parents, who

seemed as surprised as I was. Sensing the shift in the room, Ahbhu sat up.

Doctor Fernandez offered a reassuring smile. "I appreciate this is a lot to take in, Isaac, but please understand that a psychological cause doesn't mean the seizure you suffered wasn't real or significant. No doubt, it was a very real experience for you. To help us determine the exact cause, though, I'd like to perform a couple of more advanced tests."

"More tests?" I interrupted.

"I'm afraid so," he said, looking kinder than ever, which settled me down. "The tests I have in mind are designed to capture any subtle changes in brain activity and monitor you more closely. We can set these up in the next few days."

"If it's something psychological, would the anti-seizure medication even work?" I asked.

"Probably not. But we wouldn't want to dispense with it altogether until we're sure. Instead, I'll be prescribing some additional forms of treatment at this point, such as psychotherapy and stress management, which are good ideas anyway. We'll confer again once we've completed our investigations."

"Doctor," my mother inserted, "Isaac starts school on Monday."

"It's my first day of secondary," I said. "Everyone will think I'm even more of a weirdo if I have to be pulled out of classes for medical stuff."

"We can arrange for testing on Saturdays," Doctor Fernandez said, standing up, ready to wrap up the consultation. "Isaac, I'd like you to continue taking your anti-seizure medication. But let's decrease your dosage from two pills a day to just one in the morning. This will help us understand if the medication is still necessary."

I nodded slowly. Reaching the end of his patience, Ahbhu had started to pace the room like a caged lion. I waved him over and held him steady.

Doctor Fernandez handed a form to my parents. "I've written referrals for the advanced tests we'll need. Also, let's schedule a follow-up appointment in a couple of weeks to discuss the results and our next steps."

Doctor Fernandez patted me on the shoulder and smiled at Ahbhu, who looked up at him with his soulful eyes. "We'll do everything we can to find answers. Remember, we're here to support you every step of the way."


After the intense morning at Doctor Fernandez's office and the uncertainty still hanging over us, my parents and I decompressed on a bench in the hospital's rose garden. The fragrant blooms and babbling fountains offered a moment of quiet respite. I took a deep breath, releasing some of the tension that had gripped me during the appointment.

Ahbhu, though, continued his restless pacing. I unclipped his leash, and he wasted no time dashing around the garden with complete abandon. His joyful antics drew smiles from the other people enjoying the serene surroundings. As I watched Ahbhu dancihg and leaping, his boundless energy and vitality filled me with warmth and hope. He had come so far from the scared, battered pup I'd rescued a few weeks earlier.

Turning to my parents, I proposed an idea. "Is it okay if Ahbhu and I stay behind for a while? I want to show him around Morazán Plaza where I found him. We'll catch the bus home later. I swear, I won't miss it this time."

My father initially hesitated, but my mother touched his arm, conveying her agreement. After some begging on my part, he eventually acceded to my promise to be back in time for dinner. With that settled, my parents headed out of the garden, leaving me brimming with anticipation as I was eager to explore the city with Ahbhu. Once he had exhausted himself chasing butterflies, we set off for the heart of the city.

As we approached the National Theater from a distance, its facade glowed in the warm afternoon light. As we drew nearer, though, Ahbhu grew skittish. By the time we reached Morazán Plaza, he dug in his heels, growling and refusing to budge.

I knelt beside him, understanding that he might still associate this area with whatever had happened to him before he was abandoned. "Don't worry, Ahbhu," I reassured him. "Nobody's going to hurt you."

Resisting my attempts to pick him up, he retreated in the opposite direction, shooting me an annoyed look, his leash trailing behind him.

I jogged over to him and crouched down, attempting to soothe his fears. "It's okay, Ahbhu. We don't have to go there." I stroked his head softly. "We can go somewhere else!" Gathering his leash, I redirected our path to the Civic Square a couple of blocks away.

On reaching the square, I released Ahbhu to let him roam freely. As he frolicked around, I sat at the base of the equestrian statue, ready to call him back if he strayed too far. Ahbhu was cautious about his limits, and once he reached the other side, he circled back to me, jumping into my arms and showering me with affectionate licks.

"I love this square, Ahbhu," I said once he'd calmed down. "It's my favorite place in all of San Salvador." Ahbhu grinned at me, his eyes filled with excitement. "See that building over there?" I pointed at a magnificent neo-Gothic structure with a distinctive portico and Romanesque columns. "That's our National Palace."

Ahbhu let out a short bark, drawing disapproving glances from passers-by. Ignoring them, I continued, "It's beautiful, isn't it, Ahbhu? And that unfinished building over there is the Metropolitan Cathedral, where I was baptized."

Growing bored with the impromptu tour, Ahbhu slipped

out of my arms and wandered away. I continued to gaze at the cathedral, memories of the last time I'd sought refuge there flooding back. I recalled the handsome altar boy who'd so captivated me that day. I'd since pushed aside that memory amid the turmoil in my life. But now that I was back, with the cathedral looming before me, his image returned, burning as bright as it did on that Sunday weeks ago. I soon found myself moving toward the building. Spotting me from across the square, Ahbhu galloped toward me and fell in at my side.

Ahbhu and I stepped into the cathedral, greeted by its cool and tranquil atmosphere. We'd arrived during a quiet interlude between Masses, with only a few people scattered about, engaged in personal devotion. Some knelt in prayer, while others sat in contemplation.

I scanned the surroundings, hoping to spot the altar boy even though I knew it was a long shot since it was a Friday. I had last seen him on a bustling Sunday when multiple altar boys served. After a few minutes of fruitless searching, I decided to give it until the next Mass.

Suppressing a yawn, I found a quiet corner where Ahbhu and I could rest while we awaited the start of the Mass. Feeling super hungry, I discreetly gobbled down a banana and fed Ahbhu some doggie treats from my book bag. Then, surrendering to the serenity of the space, I closed my eyes.

"Are you okay?" I heard a voice say, distant at first but growing closer, followed by a shake. "Excuse me! Are you all right?"

I pried open my eyes and found myself reclined on the pew, using my bookbag as a lumpy pillow. Sitting up, I blinked at my surroundings. The cathedral had filled up, and I could see a couple of priests talking to each other up front near the altar.

Glancing around, I saw a young guy in a white robe gazing down at me. It was the altar boy from the last time I was there. I couldn't believe my luck!

"Welcome back to the world," he said, offering a concerned smile. Up close he looked even more handsome than I remembered.

"Sorry. . ." I held my book bag against my chest. "I must have fallen asleep. I didn't mean to." I looked around for Ahbhu, who had disappeared from my side.

"Did you lose something?"

"My dog. He was just here."

The altar boy's mouth pulled into a half smile. He turned around and pointed at a side chapel. "Is that him?"

I sat up and saw Ahbhu sound asleep at the foot of the Virgin, her arms spread wide, her eyes gazing heavenward. I suppressed a chuckle and nodded. "Yeah, that's him. His name's Ahbhu."

"Ahbhu . . .?" His voice trailed off as he took in the sight of Ahbhu. Then, with a vague nod, he settled beside me on the bench and held out his hand, his white robe rustling slightly. "I'm Gerónimo, one of the altar boys here." He indicated his robe. "I guess that's obvious."

I shook his hand, feeling its warmth against my skin and spreading into me. I couldn't help but notice the softness of his palm in contrast to the rough calluses on my own.

"And you are?" Gerónimo prompted.

"I'm Isaac Perez. I live in Canton El Regreso—up there by the volcano." I gestured hesitatingly in the direction of El Boquerón.

"Canton El Regreso, really?" He let out a soft whistle. "You're a long way from home."

"Tell me about it."

"Why do I feel like I know you from somewhere?"

"I was here a few weeks ago, on a Sunday. You must have seen me then."

Gerónimo squinted, reaching back into his memory, then he glanced back at me. "Up by the altar, right? You strolled in just as the Mass was ending."

I nodded.

"Right. . ." Gerónimo reddened as he recalled our moment.

Just then, the priest stepped out to call the Mass to order, accompanied by another altar boy, and greeted the congregation. Awakened by the priest's voice, Ahbhu lifted his head. Seeing someone unfamiliar so close to me, he shot toward us and leapt into my lap, eyeing Gerónimo with curiosity. Gerónimo extended his hand to pet Ahbhu, who surprisingly welcomed the touch without resistance.

"He seems to like you," I remarked, determined not to let our connection slip away this time.

Gerónimo met my gaze with an intrigued expression. "Does he really?"

I hesitated a moment, then, taking a chance, I added: "We *both* do. A lot."

His eyes fixed on mine, and I saw he had grasped my meaning. "I like you, too," he replied, his warm smile lighting up the space around us. "Both of you." After a moment of awkward silence, he rose from the bench and pointed at the altar. "I have to go help."

"Wait a sec," I said, rising from the bench and shouldering my bag, feeling a pang of disappointment that our interaction had been cut short. "Maybe we could meet again sometime."

"You're not sticking around for the Mass?" he asked.

"I wasn't planning on it," I admitted. "Should I?"

"I'll be done in a half hour." He indicated the exit. "Wait for me in the square."

A thrill of excitement coursed through me at the prospect of spending more time with Gerónimo that afternoon, competing with my growling stomach. It had been hours since breakfast and I was out of snacks. "I'm not sure I can wait that long," I whispered as I followed him into the aisle, holding Ahbhu in my arms. "I'm starving."

"Me, too!" he whispered back. "We'll grab something together. I won't be more than thirty minutes, I promise!"

# CHAPTER 8

## THE EMERALD ROAD

Gerónimo emerged from the cathedral in his street clothes, a crisp white dress shirt that enhanced his broad shoulders, tight blue jeans that hugged his powerful legs, and black trainers. The sky had turned dark and was threatening rain heralded by a cool breeze that cut through the humidity. I stood as he jogged to the bench where Ahbhu and I were waiting, slaloming through the late afternoon crowds and hordes of street vendors. I was still pinching myself in disbelief that I had actually met him and that he'd turned out to be so nice.

A shiver of anticipation danced along my skin as he drew me into a hug. I remember his hair smelled like some kind of herbal shampoo. We were interrupted by the first few drops of rain and set off across the square in search of shelter and food.

We ended up at a nearby *pupuseria* just as the skies opened. There, we gorged on a variety of *pupusas*, which we washed down with a couple of glasses of *horchata*. At first, the owner wouldn't let Ahbhu inside and said I needed to tie him up by the door, which upset Ahbhu. When I clarified that Ahbhu was my service dog and that he was supposed to accompany me everywhere I went, he relented and even offered Ahbhu some *chicharones* to munch on.

"Service dog, eh?" Gerónimo said once the owner had retreated into the kitchen, his dark eyes reflecting the overhead lights.

Ahbhu glanced between us, aware we were talking about him.

"That's a long story for another time if that's okay," I said, not ready to share my problem with him.

Gerónimo lifted his shoulders and stroked Ahbhu. "Sure, not a problem. It's just that service dogs are for blind people, aren't they?"

"I'm obviously not blind." I reached across the table and playfully touched his arm, surprised by how delicious his skin felt to my fingertips.

Gerónimo drew back, surprised by the gesture. His gaze flickered around the restaurant, then settled back on me, having recovered himself. "Pretty daring, aren't you?" he said with a discreet little grin.

"More so lately," I said as the owner dropped a plate of pupusas in front of us and we dug in. "Thanks to Ahbhu."

"How so?"

"He's been helping me get over a few things. Thanks to him, I'm feeling a little more confident these days. I'll tell you more about that later." I held his gaze for a moment. "Sorry about the arm thing."

Gerónimo glanced at the owner, who was busy behind the counter, then leaned forward and said in a low voice. "It's not a problem, really."

"That's good to know," I said, feeling relieved I hadn't scared him off as he tucked back into his food.

"Where did he come from anyway?" He gestured at Ahbhu with his pupusa. "Can you at least tell me that?"

"I found him near here," I said between bites, "all banged up.

The day I first saw you. Why?"

He studied Ahbhu, contemplating him as he had in the cathedral. "Not many dogs look like this one." He said this more to himself than to me, it seemed. "I have a cousin with a similar-looking dog. She was pregnant a few months back." My heart froze as he looked up at me and said: "Nobody knows what happened to the litter. It was like one week she was blown up like a balloon, the next week she wasn't. But no puppies." He frowned and looked back down at Ahbhu. "He was banged up, you said?"

I fought back tears at what Gerónimo was telling me. "I literally dug him out of a pile of trash where he'd been left for dead," I said through gritted teeth. "If I hadn't come along when I did. . ." Sensing the change in my emotions, Ahbhu stopped eating and rose to his feet, his one good ear perked up and alert. "What's your cousin's name?" I demanded.

Gerónimo sat up and blinked, unprepared for the question.

"Don't worry," I said, "I'm not going to say anything. I just want to know who's responsible for what happened to Ahbhu."

"I didn't say he was," Gerónimo corrected.

"Maybe he was and maybe he wasn't. But I still want to know his name."

Gerónimo shifted his gaze to Ahbhu and the two of them stared at each other for a beat with Ahbhu standing stock still. "His name's Sisler."

At the mention of the name, Ahbhu lowered himself to the ground and growled, looking ready to spring. A few patrons looked in our direction, and the owner glanced our way from over the counter. I stroked Ahbhu to calm him, but he kept growling. Gerónimo scooted back, a mix of surprise and caution crossing his features.

"What's your cousin's last name?" I grabbed hold of Ahbhu's collar just in case.

"Izquierdo," Gerónimo said, "just like mine. Sisler Izquierdo."

Straining against his collar, Ahbhu looked back at me with a pleading look in his eye, and he let out a bark.

"It's okay, Ahbhu," I reassured, bending down to kiss his head. "You're safe." I jerked my head up at Gerónimo. "*Right?*"

Gerónimo nodded and released a long breath.

"This'll be *our* secret," I emphasized. "You won't say anything to anyone about this. I don't want any trouble. Ahbhu's *my* dog now!"

Gerónimo held up his hands and swore he'd keep what I'd told him a secret. We shook on it and carried on with our lunch.

Ordering another round of pupusas, we shifted onto calmer subjects as the tension in the air gradually dissipated. Ahbhu soon settled against my feet and listened to us with half open eyes.

The warmth of the pupusas contrasted with the chill of the afternoon. As we hungrily dug into our selections, we exchanged stories and shared laughs. My heart raced as I realized how easy it was to talk to Gerónimo, how quickly the walls I'd built up over the years were crumbling in the presence of this stranger who felt like an old friend. I found myself hoping that this was the start of something meaningful and lasting and not just a one-off.

It turned out Gerónimo was seventeen, one year older than me. He'd been set to start his second year of secondary school, but his plans had changed over the break thanks to his involvement at the church. Instead of continuing at his old school, he'd been accepted into a special religious school where he could finish his studies, he said, as a *seminarian*, which sounded strange to me.

"You know what a seminarian is, right?" he asked, his dark eyes holding me fast.

"Of course, I do. It's someone who's studying to be a priest. I've just never talked to one before. I mean, I've met two or three seminarians at church functions over the years, but I've never talked to any of them one-on-one like we're doing."

"There's a first time for everything," Gerónimo quipped with a crooked smile, the hint of a dimple forming on his cheek. My lips curved in response, a faint echo of a smile that mirrored Gerónimo's. His deep eyes held my gaze.

"Guess so," I said, glancing around the snack shop, which had pretty much emptied out. "You really want to be a priest?"

"I do," he said, his voice turning serious.

"Why?"

Gerónimo lifted his eyes and took in the sight of a few new diners coming through the door, shaking the rain off before finding a table. "I want to help people," he said. "The poor and the marginalized. The way Jesus did. Like Archbishop Romero is doing now."

I winced at the mention of Archbishop Romero, recalling my father's strong disapproval of him as a symbol of opposition to the government. I lowered my eyes and focused on the space between us, which was now clear of plates. "That's left-wing stuff," I said after a moment.

Gerónimo jerked upright. "Left-wing stuff?"

"That's okay," I said. "My brother Arturo's a left-winger, too. My father hates all that. They have arguments about politics all the time. I'm more of an in-betweener myself."

Gerónimo's mouth pulled into a lopsided smile that made my stomach flutter. "So, there's hope for you yet."

"What about sex?" I asked, moving our conversation away from politics.

"What about it?"

"Priests can't have sex."

Gerónimo stared at me for a long moment, then shrugged.

"Good luck with that," I said, rolling my eyes. Even though I was only sixteen and probably still a few years away from having my first real sexual experience, I couldn't imagine a life without someone to call my own, whether male or female it hadn't even crossed my mind at that time.

"Yeah, we'll see. Anyway, changing gears," Gerónimo leaned in and asked: "What about you? What does the future hold for Isaac Perez?"

I stared into what was left of my *horchata* and raised my eyes to him. "I want to be an astronaut one day."

Gerónimo's eyes flashed, and he suppressed a chuckle.

"What's funny?"

"I'm sorry, but fat chance with *that*. No one here's going to give you that opportunity, even if you were the best of the best. I mean, have you ever even been on a plane?"

"No. But I hope to."

"You'll need more than hope if you want to be an astronaut, my friend. Maybe if you lived in the United States or Russia."

I looked down and muttered, "Yeah, well, you never know."

Gerónimo snorted and flashed sad eyes. "That's Wizard of Oz stuff, amigo."

"What do you mean?" I shot back, my frustration mingling with a growing regret at having allowed myself to be so vulnerable with him.

"You know, the magic castle, a wizard at the end of the Emerald Road ready to grant all your wishes. Pure fantasy."

"What would you know?" I turned away from him and retrieved my book bag from the floor. "And, by the way," I said, trying not to sound too annoyed, "it's the Yellow Brick Road."

"I beg your pardon?"

"You said 'a wizard at the end of the Emerald Road, but it's the Yellow Brick Road. The Emerald *City* and the *Yellow Brick Road*." He sat up at that, looking bemused. "If you're going to lecture me," I added, "at least get your facts right."

"My *facts*?"

"You know what I mean."

"Okay, Dorothy," he bowed with an exaggerated show of deference and winked at me. "No need to get your panties in a twist."

We burst out laughing, attracting the attention of the last few customers, as even he seemed surprised by his campy response. Once we'd recovered ourselves, he held out his hand. "Friends again?"

Dying for another hug, I leaned into him and pulled him against my chest. He held me close, and I could feel the thump of his heart. After a few seconds, he let out a long breath and released me, then stood and signaled for me to follow him.

The rain had stopped, and the wind had blown away the clouds, leaving the evening air fresh and cool as the afternoon wound down and people hurried home for the weekend. We made our way across the square, dodging puddles left behind by the showers.

I let Ahbhu run free again as a reward for behaving himself at the restaurant, and Gerónimo and I sat at the base of the statue of General Barrios to watch the sun go down, neither of us speaking much. We simply enjoyed each other's company.

"Do you mind if I ask you something?" Gerónimo said, breaking the silence. "Sorry if it's personal."

I shrugged. "Go for it."

"What brought you down from Canton El Regreso today on this nothing Friday?"

His question caught me by surprise. I hadn't thought of the hospital or my condition for the past couple of hours. Formulating a response brought the whole ugly thing crashing back in on me.

"Sorry," he said, noticing my change of mood. "I didn't mean to—"

I held up my hand to stop him from apologizing. "No, it's okay. I just need a moment."

Gerónimo leaned back against the statue and closed his eyes, looking serene in the dim light of the advancing evening.

"No pressure. Take all the time you need."

I looked across the square at the cathedral and focused for a beat on the stragglers from the last Mass exiting the building. One of the priests was waiting to one side to lock up for the night. He glanced in our direction and held us in his view for a long spell before disappearing inside. I turned back to Gerónimo who was staring at me, his face illuminated by one of the spots lighting up the statue.

"I had a seizure a couple of months ago," I said after a brief hesitation. "The doctors initially suspected epilepsy. Now they're not so sure. I underwent a few more tests at the hospital this morning to try to find some answers. Afterward, my parents gave me permission to hang around here with Ahbhu."

"Ahbhu . . . your service dog," he confirmed, staring out across the square. After a moment, he looked back at me. "Sorry for asking. I didn't mean to pry, really."

"It's okay." I scooted closer to him. "I've been keeping it bottled inside for a while. It feels good to have finally told someone outside of my family. Thanks for not getting weirded out about it."

"No problem. I'm all ears anytime you want to talk, okay?" He squeezed my shoulder.

"Thanks." I stood and whistled for Ahbhu, who came running at lightning speed. I fastened his leash and turned to Gerónimo, who was looking on amused. "Anyway, we need to get going."

"You can stay at my place tonight if it's too late for you to go back. I'm sure my parents won't mind. We can call your parents."

I shook my head. "Thanks, but I promised my father I'd be home for dinner. Plus, we don't have a telephone. I'll just catch a bus up the hill."

We hugged each other and made plans to meet again on Sunday afternoon once he was done with the Mass. Then he was gone.

As I watched Gerónimo's silhouette grow smaller in the distance, a profound ache settled in my chest. The warmth of his presence that had enveloped me for the past couple of hours was slipping away, leaving me standing there, shoulders slumped, my heart strangely hollow. Gathering Ahbhu, who had grown quiet, I held him close and trudged to the bus stop, wondering how I would endure the time until Sunday without losing my mind.

# CHAPTER 9

## ARTURO'S APPROVAL

Everyone lifted their heads from their dinner plates as Ahbhu and I appeared at the doorway still breathless from running up the hill from where the bus had dropped us off. The delicious aroma of stuffed peppers and Spanish rice filled the room.

"I made it!" I announced, dropping my book bag and slipping into my chair next to Arturo, who shot me a discreet look that said he had something to tell me.

I held up my hands for my father to inspect them, having washed them on the sly on my way in. Once he was satisfied they were clean, my mother pulled a strained smile and served me dinner. Ahbhu slurped some water from his bowl and curled up at my feet.

I spent the next few minutes filling them in about my day, including meeting Gerónimo and how we'd planned to meet on Sunday, with their permission, of course.

"To do what exactly?" Arturo asked.

"I don't know," I said. "We'll probably just hang out like we did today."

"What's this boy's name?" my father asked. His face had

grown serious when I mentioned going back to meet Gerónimo, trading a look with my mother, who'd shrugged like she didn't care one way or the other.

"I already told you, Papá," I said. "His name's Gerónimo."

"Gerónimo what?" Arturo asked.

All of them were staring at me, waiting for my answer. Even Ahbhu lifted his head and stared at me. My father switched off the Victrola and the room fell silent.

"Izquierdo," I said after a beat.

My father scoffed at that, as I expected, since the word *Izquierdo* literally means left, as in the direction. And since my father was a right-winger, to the point of being fanatical, he hated anything that even smelled of the left.

"It's just a name, Papá," Arturo said, coming to my rescue. "You can't hold someone's name against them."

After a few tense moments where Arturo and I did our best to talk sense into my father, he reluctantly admitted he was probably being overly sensitive. It was a big climb-down for him as he almost never admitted he was wrong about anything, especially when it came to politics. And there was a lot of politics in the air in those days: left, right, rich, poor, fascists, Marxists, and nothing much in between, with increasingly desperate attempts at collective action that the government swiftly and brutally snuffed out. It was making everyone a bit nuts.

In the end, he agreed I could get together with Gerónimo on Sunday on the condition that Arturo took me to meet him and was satisfied it was safe for me to hang around with him. I was so excited I was going to get to see Gerónimo again that I couldn't finish my dinner, as hungry as I was.

Later that night, as we were getting ready for bed, Arturo mentioned my parents were worried the doctor had said my seizure might have had a psychological cause, as if it meant I had a mental illness. They'd spent all afternoon talking about it, which explained why they were acting so weird and protective.

Arturo had convinced them to wait until all the tests were in before jumping to conclusions. As we turned off the lights, Arturo gave me a reassuring hug, promising everything was going to be fine, even though I could see he was worried, too.

I spent the next day reading and playing around the yard with Ahbhu. We even tried another hike up the side of the volcano, this time on another trail that branched off from the main one. But I couldn't concentrate on anything for very long, as I was preoccupied with thoughts of Gerónimo. The day dragged on as if it would never end. I even went to bed early to cut the day short and ended up tossing and turning all night, bothered by Arturo's and Ahbhu's snoring and every creak of the house.

At the first hint of light, I threw off the covers and got dressed. After breakfast, as soon as my parents headed off to Mass, I hopped on the back of Arturo's motorcycle with Ahbhu nestling between my legs, and we roared off to the city center. The day was already hot and sticky, and the noonday sun bore down on us as we traveled a half hour through light traffic.

We arrived at the cathedral twenty minutes before the end of the Mass. Arturo wasn't much for religion, so we waited on a bench in the Civic Square. In contrast to Friday, the square was bustling with families out for the afternoon. Once the Mass was over, the congregants would stream out and join the throng, which would make it difficult to spot Gerónimo. So, to make sure we didn't miss each other, I left Arturo on the bench and crossed the road, with Ahbhu trotting at my side.

Creeping inside, we found a place at the back of the packed sanctuary near where Gerónimo had found me. My stomach fluttered as I spotted him assisting the priest with the last bits of the service along with another older boy. I lifted my hand at him when I thought he might be looking in our direction, but he didn't seem to have seen me. Before I knew it, the service was over.

With the recessional swelling in the background, the priest processed down the aisle, carrying a large cross, followed by Gerónimo. The other altar boy stayed behind to extinguish the candles and organize things for the next service. Sliding to the end of the pew, I caught Gerónimo's eye as he moved past, and his face lit up. Just as he reached the door, haloed by the bright sunlight outside, he looked back and motioned for me to follow. I shot out the door after him.

I came up alongside him in the crowd and tapped his shoulder.

"You made it!" he said, looking as handsome as ever in his robe in the bright sunlight.

"Of course I made it!" I moved closer to him, buffeted by the horde pouring out of the cathedral. "Wild horses couldn't have kept me away."

He glanced down at Ahbhu, who was straining at his leash, uncomfortable in the crowd and trying to move me toward the square. "Hi, Ahbhu? Remember me?"

Ahbhu looked sharply at Gerónimo at the mention of his name. I picked him up, and Gerónimo scratched his head, bringing his eyes level with him and smiling.

"You remember Gerónimo, Ahbhu, don't you?" I said. Perking up, Ahbhu licked Gerónimo's nose. Gerónimo pulled back with a cute mock scream and dabbed at his nose.

"That was obviously a yes," I said.

We were joined by Arturo, whom I introduced to Gerónimo before he was called back inside by the other altar boy to help him with something or other. A few minutes later, he emerged in his street clothes, sporting white linen trousers and a black shirt that accentuated his eyes and perfect teeth. A newfound air of confidence radiated from him as he joined us at a bench in the square. Arturo had refrained from commenting on him while we'd been waiting, leading me to think he didn't care much for him. However, as Gerónimo approached, Arturo sat up, barely containing his curiosity.

"So, is this the brother you were telling me about?" Gerónimo stood over us and gestured at Arturo with a playful smile animating his face.

Arturo turned his head toward me with a questioning look.

"The one that drives your father crazy with his political views," Gerónimo clarified.

I felt myself redden, afraid I might have revealed something Arturo would be upset about. Ahbhu looked back and forth between us and whined a bit trying to understand what was happening.

"Oh, sorry," Gerónimo said, lowering himself to the bench. "I didn't mean to ..."

"It's fine," Arturo said, "It's just a bit of a sore subject these days, you know."

"Is it okay if I explain?" Gerónimo asked me, and I said yes, worried about where the conversation was heading and wanting more than anything to be alone with Gerónimo.

"The other day I told Isaac that I admired Monsignor Romero's work with the poor and disenfranchised. He mentioned he had a brother, who was on the same page with that, or something to that effect. I was just curious if you were that brother. That's all. Sorry."

Arturo tossed me a glance that said we had to talk, then offered Gerónimo a tight smile, indicating he didn't wish to be drawn into any further conversation on the subject. Taking the hint, Gerónimo seamlessly changed gears.

After a few minutes of idle chitchat, Arturo left us, declining Gerónimo's invitation to join us for lunch. His parting words, which he whispered in my ear, were: "I like him. But be careful with what you disclose. You've only just met him."

Gerónimo took me to his house for lunch, where I met his parents and two older sisters, all of whom were nice, but a touch distant and reserved. They lived in a roomy townhouse a short walk from the cathedral, and they had a maid, which told me they were a lot better off than we were.

After lunch, Gerónimo and I retired to his bedroom, where we kicked back and talked for hours, while Ahbhu grumbled in the background. It got so annoying at one point that I had to pick up Ahbhu to calm him down. He reared his head and stared triumphantly at Gerónimo as if to say, *He's mine, not yours!* That drew a laugh from Gerónimo. He tried to appease Ahbhu by scratching his muzzle, but Ahbhu was having none of that, moving his head every which way to avoid the touch of Gerónimo's fingers.

"Wow," Gerónimo said, pulling back his hand and glancing at me. "Is this going to be a problem?"

"I hope not." I kissed Ahbhu and set him down again. He sat at my feet for the rest of my visit and continued to stare down Gerónimo.

Aside from Ahbhu's antics, it was all so laid back and comfortable as if Gerónimo and I had known each other all our lives. We spent the time sharing all about our families and our childhoods, our hopes and dreams for the future, the things we liked to do for fun and the things we avoided as well. Every so often, the maid would check in on us to see if we were all right, which I found nosy and annoying. Gerónimo would just roll his eyes once she'd gone and carry on.

Later, Gerónimo took me onto his roof terrace, which was decked out like a country club, complete with fake grass, a wet bar, and bolted-down lawn chairs. There, we watched the sunset, leaning against each other like some old couple. It was weird and nice at the same time, Gerónimo and I in those early days, with our developing, still-innocent boy crush.

Gerónimo insisted on driving us back home that night. I declined the offer at first, feeling embarrassed for him to see how I lived compared to him. But Gerónimo reassured me, insisting I was just being silly, and that he wasn't the snob I was making him out to be.

"I wasn't suggesting that, sorry," I said, feeling bad he'd assumed I meant such a thing.

Gerónimo's father tossed him the keys to the family car, a shiny black Mercedez Benz, and we piled into it—Gerónimo, Ahbhu, and me—and drove up the hill. There was no moon that night, and the stars were shining brightly.

Gerónimo had never been to Canton El Regreso before and was taken aback at the sight of the volcano towering above our house as we pulled up in front.

"Once my nemesis, now a respected friend," I said, pointing at the black cone. "Thanks to Ahbhu." Ahbhu let loose a little howl, which drew a puzzled smile from Gerónimo. "Anyway, come inside to meet my parents. We can talk later about the volcano."

"I should be getting back. Maybe some other time." He made to hug me goodbye, but I backed away.

"I met your parents; you should meet mine as well," I said.

Looking chastised, Gerónimo raised his hands in a mock surrender. "Okay, boss, lead the way."

We found my parents nestled in the back room sipping coffee and listening to the news. They looked surprised by Gerónimo's sudden presence but covered up by offering him coffee once I'd made the introductions. Gerónimo glanced at me sidelong as he accepted a cup from my mother, discreetly signaling his discomfort, then offered her a gracious smile. It was then I realized I'd miscalculated by springing him on them without any advance notice.

My mother tried her best to initiate a bit of casual talk while my father studied Gerónimo, interjecting only a word or two here and there, and I looked on nervously. Just as things seemed to be winding down smoothly, my father jumped in with some questions of his own.

"Isaac tells us you serve at the cathedral as an altar boy," he said.

Gerónimo set down his empty coffee cup and smiled at my father. "Yes, sir, that's right."

"And how are you finding that?" my father probed.

Sensing trouble, my mother crossed the room to fill Gerónimo's cup as a momentary distraction. Gerónimo declined the second serving, smiling at her and holding his hand over his cup. Then he returned his attention to my father. "I've enjoyed the experience, sir. So much so that I've decided to go to seminary."

At that moment, Arturo popped into the room and halted as his eyes landed on Gerónimo. Exchanging a concerned glance with me, he jumped in just as my father was about to respond to Gerónimo's revelation.

"Well, look who's here!" he said, coming around to Gerónimo and shaking his hand. "I see you've met the folks."

"Hey, Arturo," Gerónimo said, standing and looking like he was ready to go.

"I'll just see Gerónimo out," Arturo said to my parents. "I'm sure he needs to get back home. It's pretty late."

"In due time," my father said. "Isaac's friend was just telling us about seminary."

"I haven't started yet," Geronimo clarified. "Tomorrow's

actually my first day of classes. So I don't know a lot about it yet."

"Well, I know a thing or two about it," my father interjected. "The place is crawling with leftist Jesuits intent on cultivating a crop of leftist priests."

"Papá, please," I said.

"I don't know about that, sir," Gerónimo said.

"Well, I *do* know," my father shot back, his voice rising. "If you ask me, priests should stick to religion and keep out of politics."

"And with that," Arturo said, tugging at Gerónimo's shirt sleeve, "let's bring this lovefest to a close, shall we?"

But Gerónimo held his ground now that my father had thrown down the gauntlet. "If by politics you mean caring for the poor and the weak and standing up against repression, sir, may I remind you that this was our Lord's mission as well. I'm sure you don't consider Him to have been preaching politics."

"Our Lord would be *ashamed* of what the priests in this country are saying and doing in his name, starting with that so-called Monsignor Oscar Romero. Wolves in sheep's clothing, communists in cassocks! That's what they are."

"I'm sorry you feel that way, sir, with all due respect," Gerónimo said, the light draining out of his face. "Perhaps if you were better informed you might have a different opinion."

My father blinked at Gerónimo, stricken speechless by the challenge, looking as though he were on the verge of having an apoplectic fit.

"Good night, Mrs. Perez," Gerónimo said. "Thank you for the coffee."

And with that, Arturo hustled us out of the door and down the driveway to Gerónimo's car.

"Well, that went swimmingly," Geronimo said, digging the keys out of his pocket. "Wouldn't you say?"

"I'm so sorry about that," I said. "I should have expected something like that."

"Guys, this doesn't bode well for your friendship," Arturo said, looking back and forth between the two of us.

"I pick my own friends," I said, looking at the house, a note of defiance in my voice.

"Me, too," Gerónimo said, matching my tone to my relief.

Arturo thoughtfully sucked in his bottom lip. "In that case, someone's going to have to run interference for you if you want to avoid an all-out war between yourselves and Papá."

"Are you volunteering for the job?" I said a bit too sharply and immediately regretted disrespecting my brother, who was only trying to help. Gerónimo touched my shoulder to steady me. "Sorry. . ." I muttered to Arturo, who looked as frustrated as I felt.

"Anyway, I'd best be going," Gerónimo said, drawing me into a hug. "Next Saturday, ten o'clock, in the square by the statue. Be there." He drew back and forced a smile, putting on a brave face. "Wild horses . . .!"

Inside the house, my father was fuming. "You're not to get mixed up with that boy!" He pointed a finger at me, trying his best to control himself.

Misunderstanding the gesture as a threat, Ahbhu snarled and bared his teeth at my father, startling him into silence. Arturo quickly scooped him up and whispered a few calming words, while Ahbhu whined and tossed me a worried look.

"That's not fair, Papá!" I protested. "Why should I be punished just because you don't agree with him? Everyone's entitled to their opinion, aren't they?"

"These are dangerous times, hijo," he shot back. "People are disappearing. We can't afford to be associated with the wrong people."

"This isn't about you!" I shouted.

Just then my mouth went dry, and I noticed a familiar metallic taste rising in my gorge. "Oh, crap," I said, moving aside the chair I was standing next to and lowering myself to the floor, terrified of what was coming. The last thing I remember before everything went black was Ahbhu's desperate barking and my mother's piercing scream.

Feeling like Bizarro Dorothy, I regained consciousness in my bedroom a couple of hours later, exhausted and surrounded by my family. Ahbhu, who was curled up on the cot next to me, licked my face when my eyes fluttered open and whined with concern. Arturo and my mother rushed to my side, and my father hung back, looking guilty.

I glanced down and noticed I was in my pajamas. "I'm sorry," I said, feeling embarrassed as Arturo slipped me a glass of water to soothe my parched throat.

"Not at all, hijo," my father said. "I'm the one who should apologize."

"We need to avoid scenes like that, Papá." Arturo said in a firm voice, casting a brief glance in my direction, implying the advice applied to me as well.

Somehow, I could tell the seizure hadn't been as intense as the one I'd had at the bar, and I told them that. Still, my parents insisted, they thought it best if I skipped school the next day to recover.

"I don't want to miss my first day of secondary," I moaned, rising on one elbow. Feeling I was getting upset again, I drew a few deep, calming breaths and lay back down on my pillow.

In the end they agreed I could try going to school if I felt better in the morning, which was one heck of a way to start my freshman year.

# Chapter 10

## AWAKENING

Over the weeks and months that followed, the bond between Ahbhu and me grew ever stronger. He was my constant companion, accompanying me everywhere I went, including to classes with the wholehearted support of my teachers and the school administration. Most of my classmates accepted him as the loyal and devoted friend he was, drawn to his affable nature. Ahbhu, in turn, welcomed almost everyone, as long as he didn't perceive a threat to me or, worse, a rival for my affections.

Our bond was further cemented by his training as a service dog, which started a couple of weeks after the start of my school year. Twice a week, after classes, Ahbhu and I would ride on the back of Arturo's motorcycle the short distance to Sue the trainer's house, where she would spend each session teaching Ahbhu different tasks like alerting me when I was about to have a seizure, helping to move me into a safe position, clearing away dangerous objects, and fetching assistance.

During the course of our sessions, Sue soon discovered Ahbhu was gifted with a unique talent for picking up on people's vibes, whether good or bad. He'd cozy up to those he liked, huddling by their feet and sharing his warmth with them. But he could equally sniff out people he perceived as having bad intentions, steering clear of those who, in fact, later proved untrustworthy. Impressed, Sue commented that she'd never before seen such a highly developed protective instinct in a dog as young as Ahbhu, emphasizing how fortunate I was to have him in my life.

Given Ahbhu's uncanny ability to read people's character, I learned to depend on his judgment, using it as a compass for my own life. If Ahbhu signaled he didn't like someone, I became wary of them. Sometimes, though, Ahbhu surprised me with the people he accepted.

The most notable example happened one evening in April when, out of the blue, Neto showed up in the middle of dinner, wearing dress pants and a button-down shirt. Even though I'd often seen him through the back window working on the coffee trees, it had been months since we'd inhabited the same room. I'd expected Ahbhu to go mad at the sight of him in such close quarters to me. But he didn't. Instead, he trotted up to Neto and offered his head for a scratch. Then he returned to me and stood at attention, looking back and forth between us, as if he'd just negotiated a truce. It was then I realized Ahbhu and Neto must have been interacting when I wasn't aware, perhaps in the early mornings when Neto arrived for work. I'd been taken by surprise when Neto entered the room. But seeing that Ahbhu was okay with him, I resolved to trust his judgment.

After securing my parents' permission to enter, Neto approached me and apologized for his past behavior. There was a genuine warmth in his voice, and his sincerity was evident in the way he made direct eye contact with me and in the conviction with which he spoke. He added that he was sorry if he'd contributed to my illness and that he was glad that Ahbhu had come into our lives. It was the last thing I expected from him, and I broke into tears, feeling all the more grateful to Ahbhu for having brokered this reconciliation.

Neto drew me into an awkward hug that lasted a few seconds. Then he shocked us all by calling in Celestina, of all people, whom he introduced as his fiancée. Compared with the way she had looked at the bar, Celestina presented as demurely as a nun in a modest gray dress that reached her calves and a matching head scarf. I rubbed my eyes in disbelief, and Celestina responded with a friendly wink that didn't escape Ahbhu, who pressed close to me and stared at her questioningly. After recovering their composure, my parents offered congratulations and invited Neto and Celestina to join us at the table. And so began a new, uneasy era of Perez family détente.

Although I hadn't suffered another seizure since the night of my argument with my father about Gerónimo, Doctor Fernandez insisted we follow through with the additional testing. The results revealed what he'd suspected: there was no identifiable physiological explanation for my seizures. As a result, he suspended the anti-seizure medication, as it wasn't an appropriate treatment, and referred me to a psychologist named Doctor Elsa, who specialized in adolescents.

I met with Doctor Elsa once a week every Saturday morning at the children's ward of the hospital, accompanied by Ahbhu. She was a grandmotherly woman with kind eyes, who reminded me of a big velvety pillow, soft and comfy. We'd spend the first half hour or so talking about my life and various topics. Then she'd spend the rest of the session leading me through a series of calming exercises like deep breathing, and meditation, and even talking to Ahbhu, whose voice I'd started hearing in my head, though I didn't want to tell Doctor Elsa about this in case she thought I was going crazy. These calming exercises were supposed to keep my stress levels down. The idea was that if

I ever felt a seizure coming on, I was meant to call on these exercises to help defuse the episode.

After our first couple of sessions, I felt comfortable enough to open up to her about my feelings for Gerónimo, something I'd never shared with anyone before. It took everything I had to get it out the first time I broached the subject.

"That's what I'm here for, Isaac," Doctor Elsa reassured, her tone gentle yet firm. "It's better to talk about these things than to keep them bottled inside. Inside, they can only hurt you."

"It's just that I haven't even talked about it with *him*. Although he's probably already figured it out," I admitted.

"Figured what out?" she prompted.

"That I might like him . . . in a wrong way."

"What do you mean by a wrong way?"

"I mean that I want to be with him all the time. When I'm with him, I don't want to leave him—and when I'm not with him, he's all I can think about. That can't be right."

"Isaac, dear, you're still quite young. At sixteen, it's perfectly normal for you to feel close to another boy. It's very common, believe me. You'll eventually grow out of it, of course. But for now, you shouldn't worry about it. It's likely Geronimo feels very much the same."

"Are you sure?" I asked.

"Quite sure, dear," she said reassuringly.

I hesitated, my words stumbling out in a jumble of uncertainty. "But . . . I've never felt this way before. And I'm scared. What if . . . what if I'm gay?" I said, finally putting my worst fear into words.

Doctor Elsa paused a moment and regarded me with a compassionate, understanding expression. "Are your feelings for Geronimo sexual?" she asked gently.

"I don't think so. I mean, I've never really given it much thought. I just like being close to him."

Doctor Elsa's hand found its way to my arm, offering

85

comfort and reassurance in a single touch. "Then, no, Isaac. I doubt very much that you're gay. Your feelings for Gerónimo may be intense, but they don't necessarily define your sexuality. In fact, I can almost guarantee in ten years' time you'll be married with children."

As our session came to an end, Doctor Elsa offered one last reassurance. "You need to learn to trust yourself, Isaac. You have the strength and resilience to navigate these feelings in your own time."

With a grateful smile, I nodded, feeling relieved and lighter than I had in weeks.

Gerónimo and I could only see each other on weekends since we went to different schools. Sundays were out of the question because, as a seminarian, he had his church duties. Curious about that aspect of his life, I'd sometimes drop by the cathedral to snatch a glimpse of him. He now wore a black robe, which I thought suited him better than the white one he'd worn as an altar boy. Mostly, though, I left him alone on Sundays as he seemed uncomfortable with my presence.

My main day, then, for getting together with him was Saturdays, right after my sessions with Doctor Elsa. It was the highlight of my week. And I felt a lot better about it now that I'd talked to Doctor Elsa. We would meet on the hospital steps and spend the rest of the day doing homework or just walking around town, talking about anything and everything and making plans to do things further afield. If his parents happened to be away, we'd hang out at his house, with Ahbhu keeping a wary eye on us.

"Doesn't he ever lighten up?" Gerónimo asked me once, inclining his head at Ahbhu as we kicked back on his bed.

Ahbhu's ears immediately perked up, and he focused an intense gaze on Gerónimo.

"Sure, he does," I said. "But it's in his nature to be protective. It's how he's wired."

Gerónimo arched an eyebrow. "You don't trust me, Ahbhu? Is that it?"

Ahbhu stood and tilted his head.

"Don't tease him, please," I said. "If he weren't okay with you, you'd know it, believe me. Sit, Ahbhu!"

After a beat, Ahbhu lowered himself to the floor and rested his head on crossed paws, looking chastened.

A few weeks into my therapy, Gerónimo showed up at the hospital in a new Toyota Corolla and announced we were going to spend the afternoon at Lago Ilopango, a huge crater lake outside San Salvador. He'd even packed a picnic lunch for both of us. I was so excited to be going on an outing with him my legs went momentarily weak, and I grabbed hold of the door to steady myself. Gerónimo rounded the car and gave my shoulder a friendly squeeze, oblivious to how I was feeling. Then he opened the front passenger door for me and let Ahbhu scramble into the back.

A half hour later, we arrived at a secluded lakeside spot Gerónimo said not too many people knew about. He spread out a blanket in the shade of a big ceiba tree and we kicked off our shoes, picnicking on different kinds of savory snacks. He'd even brought some doggie treats for Ahbhu, who turned up his nose at them to Gerónimo's chagrin before launching into a run around our campsite.

Once we were sated, Gerónimo leapt to his feet and announced we were going for a swim, stripping off his shirt and exposing a nicely muscled chest with a light dusting of hair. The sight of his bare torso made me catch my breath. "Come on!" he said.

"But . . . I don't have a swimming suit," I spluttered, trying not to stare.

Gerónimo flashed a mischievous grin. "Neither do I!" Then he stripped off his jeans and stood before me in his underpants before racing headlong for the water.

A couple of nervous minutes later, I joined him, and we spent a long while splashing about in the sun-warmed water and swimming laps. At one point, Ahbhu paddled out to check up on me. Satisfied I was all right, he made his way back to shore and waited there.

After we'd exhausted ourselves, Gerónimo and I swam back to shore, where he handed me a towel. Then I watched in disbelief as he peeled off his underpants and shamelessly dried off in front of me.

Having been raised in a home that prized modesty as one of the highest virtues, nakedness was considered taboo in my family. Up until that moment, I had *never* seen a naked person, not even my own brothers with whom I had shared a bedroom. So the sight of Gerónimo, my closest friend for whom I felt a strong affection, behaving so uninhibited, both horrified and confused me.

Spinning away, I dried myself under cover of my towel and slipped back into my clothes. Gerónimo didn't comment about my shyness and steered the conversation to more mundane subjects as we drove back to the city. Still, I couldn't extinguish the image of his body from my mind for the rest of the afternoon.

Sometime in the middle of the night, I was abruptly awakened from a dream about Gerónimo at the lake. Checking myself, I groaned in frustration to find that my sheets were sticky and I needed a wash. Slipping out of bed, I was relieved to see Arturo sleeping soundly. I made my way to the bathroom, followed by a concerned Ahbhu, who pattered alongside me, screwing up his eyes at me. "Never mind, Ahbhu," I muttered, shutting the bathroom door on him.

This sort of thing had happened to me before, but never after dreaming about another boy, and definitely never about Gerónimo. As I washed up, still trying to puzzle it all out, I was jolted to my core by a sudden epiphany, as if I'd been pierced through by lightning. In that moment, the scales fell from my eyes, and I saw Gerónimo in a completely different way—a way that both scared and excited me. And I realized then that Doctor Elsa had gotten it wrong.

The next time Gerónimo and I met, a couple of Saturdays later, his eyes told me he felt the same as he greeted me outside the hospital. His gaze was intense, with a focused, penetrating look that conveyed a sense of longing that aroused me. Perhaps it had been there all along and I just hadn't noticed it, like the innocent klutz that I was back then. But on that day in early May, our attraction for each other was as clear as the cloudless expanse above us. We retreated to his house, which was devoid of parents and sisters for the weekend, stripped off our clothes, and spent the rest of the day exploring each other, while Ahbhu whined and scratched at the bedroom door.

"Are you all right?" Gerónimo asked once we were done as I'd gone quiet on him, feeling suddenly guilty.

"I guess so," I said, propping myself up against a pillow. "This isn't something I was expecting, that's all. I mean, it's my first time. I've never even been with a girl before. I feel kind of bad about that."

"Neither have I," Gerónimo confessed. "But just to be clear, this wasn't my first time."

"It wasn't?" I asked.

Gerónimo laughed. "No. My first time was a couple of years ago. You might say I've been around the block a few times already."

"Oh," I said, feeling a mix of jealousy and anger. "So, I'm just another conquest, is that it?" I reached for my undershirt, ready to leave, and Gerónimo put it behind his back.

"No, that's not it. And calm down, please. I actually like you. In fact, I've liked you from the beginning, and not just in a physical way," he said. "I've been waiting for you to come around of your own accord the way I thought you would."

"That's thanks to you and that strip show you put on the other day at the lake."

"Yeah . . . I thought you needed a little help." Gerónimo smirked as he reflected on our camping trip. "Seems it worked."

Scooting closer, he eased me against his chest and told me not to feel bad about what we'd done because we both wanted it. I stayed quiet, enjoying being held by him, feeling his warm breath on my neck, his wet kisses on my cheek, afraid to ask a question that was burning inside me.

"What is it now?" Gerónimo asked, noticing my changing mood.

"Isn't it a sin . . . what we just did?" I asked, afraid of my own voice. "That's what everyone says!"

We sat up on his bed, and he held me close.

"Can I tell you a secret?" he asked in a low voice. "It's something that needs to stay between you and me."

I nodded, pivoting around to face him, my curiosity piqued.

He pulled aside a lock of hair that had fallen into my face and tucked it behind one of my ears, stalling for a beat. Then he became serious and held my gaze. "I don't believe in sin."

"You don't?"

Gerónimo shook his head slowly and meaningfully.

"But..." My mind reeled at what he was telling me. I scooted away a bit and cocked my head. "You're studying to be a priest! How can you not believe in sin?"

Gerónimo held up his hand and cut in: "Hang on a sec. First, I'm not a priest yet. Second, I'm not the only one of us who doesn't believe in sin, even if that's the official doctrine of the Church."

I crossed my arms skeptically. "Will they even let someone become a priest if they don't believe something the Church teaches?"

"Darling," Gerónimo chuckled, "I've met seasoned priests who don't even believe *in God.*"

"What?" I blurted, completely thrown. "Then why are they even priests? That doesn't make any sense."

"They're priests because they want to make a difference in the world in a way regular people can't, like what I was trying to explain to your father about helping the poor and disenfranchised, defending their rights against institutional injustice—making El Salvador a better place than it is at the moment."

I scoffed at that and shook my head. "If that's what you want, then become a lawyer and leave the priest stuff to people who actually believe in what they're supposed to believe."

Gerónimo sat back, a troubled expression spreading over his face. After a few minutes, we slipped back into our clothes in silence. Afraid I'd offended him, and hoping our discussion hadn't ruined our friendship, I grabbed his hand and apologized.

"I really like you," Gerónimo responded after a moment of reflection. "I want us to keep seeing each other as friends—and like this too." He indicated his bed. "Discreetly, of course."

"I want that, too."

"Good. So, Isaac, for the time being, to keep the peace between us, let's avoid talking about religion and politics and just enjoy the time we have together for as long as we can. Honestly, I don't know where my head will be about the priesthood as I go along. I've only just started. Maybe I *will* decide to become a lawyer instead. But it's still early days for me, and I'd rather keep that part of my life separate from our thing until I know for sure. Will that work for you?"

Of course, I agreed to the arrangement, overjoyed our

relationship would continue. We sealed the deal by promising to remain exclusively committed to each other, come what may.

As we parted ways that afternoon down the hill from my house, my mind fast-forwarded to our next meeting. I was keen to share something special with Gerónimo to initiate this new phase of our relationship.

"I've got an idea for next weekend, a little escape from all the heavy stuff," I said as we sat in his idling car.

"Go on," he said, his interest aroused.

I pointed at the black cone looming ahead. "Let's go on a night hike to the top of El Boquerón. I'll bring my telescope, and we can do some stargazing. What do you say?"

Gerónimo squinted up at the volcano then looked at me doubtfully. "A night hike up there?"

"Yes, up there. It's totally safe. I do it all the time. Ahbhu can help lead the way. Plus, it's the best place to see the stars!" I could feel the excitement building as I spoke.

"Sure, okay, I'm game." Gerónimo looked anything but convinced, then surprised me with: "But we don't have to wait until the weekend, do we?"

"I guess not."

"Tomorrow night then, after everyone's gone to bed. How's that?"

# Chapter 11

## INTO THE CRATER

The following evening, after my parents had gone to bed and the lights were off, I heard Gerónimo's light tapping on my window. I'd told Arturo about our planned outing, and he seemed fine with it. Flinging back the curtains, we found Gerónimo crouching below the sill dressed in dark joggers and shouldering a pack. Ahbhu was already outside sniffing at him, giving him the once-over.

"Be careful up there," Arturo whispered as I gathered my things and prepared to slide out the side door. "It's super dark tonight."

"That's the idea!" I said, patting my telescope.

He nodded and glanced in the direction of my parents' bedroom. "Make sure you're back before dawn."

I rounded the house and hugged Gerónimo, then handed him a high-powered flashlight and held up my own. "Don't turn it on until I tell you," I whispered. "Follow me."

"What's that?" He gestured at the black leather case dangling at my side as we moved down the driveway.

"It's my refractor." I slapped the case. "We'll be able to see a lot more up there with it." I pointed at the moonless sky, which was awash in stars.

Switching on my flashlight as we reached the trailhead, I asked Ahbhu to lead the way. El Boquerón loomed above us, its black cone a shadow obscuring the sky behind it.

"Watch your step," I warned. "There are lots of loose rocks. Point your flashlight at the path like this and keep your eyes on me. I'll be following Ahbhu."

Gerónimo huffed behind me after a few minutes of intense hiking. The night air was fragrant with the smell of cinnamon as we crushed it underfoot, the darkness occasionally split by the cry of something weird and nocturnal.

"We're lucky the mountain's quiet tonight," I commented. "It's usually grumbling like a crotchety old man."

A half hour later, we stood at the summit, our bodies streaming with sweat as we refreshed ourselves from our canteens. Before us, the sparkling city lay spread out like a carpet of diamonds. Mesmerized by the beauty of it, I turned to Gerónimo, who had fallen silent. To my surprise, tears streaked his cheeks. Ahbhu pawed at his leg, issuing plaintive whines, which told me they weren't tears of joy.

"What's wrong?"

"I've never seen it like this before," he said, his eyes fixed on the view. "But it's a deception."

I dropped my pack to the ground. "What's a deception?"

He held out his hand. "That is! The beauty of San Salvador seen from this height. It camouflages what's really going on there."

I felt my heart sink. "I thought we weren't going to talk politics."

"I'm not talking politics; I'm talking reality. There's so much inequity out there, so much suffering. Do you know that ninety percent of the wealth of our nation is owned by only fourteen families?"

Pushing down my anger, I looked away from him. "Yes, Gerónimo, I know that."

"And now with the CDP and that fascist Duarte in power, none of that is *ever* going to change." He nodded at the view. "That's why *that* is a deception. If you allow it, it can lull you into believing everything is fine when it's light-years from fine."

"I know you're passionate about all that, Gerónimo, and I don't want to be dismissive. But I invited you here to show you something *I'm* passionate about. Can we just do that?"

Gerónimo blinked at me, looking suddenly chastened. "Sorry."

"Next time, we can have an outing to wherever *you* want, and I promise to be all ears about anything you want to talk about, politics included. I'll even hold my tongue and listen. But tonight is about us and those guys." I pointed at the sky, which was throbbing with stars, the band of the Milky Way streaked across it. "Deal?"

An embarrassed smile animated Gerónimo's face. He pulled me into a hug and kissed my cheek. "You do know I'll take you up on that offer, right?"

"Yep, I know." I picked up my pack and led him to the edge of the darkened tree-filled crater, facing away from the city. It was softly illuminated by the starlight.

"This is the main crater we're looking at. In the center lies a smaller, secondary crater, El Boqueróncito. If the volcano were ever to erupt, the lava would flow from there."

Gerónimo peered into the darkness, his eyes a pair of slits. "You're not scared to live so close to it?"

"I used to be. Big time. But Ahbhu helped me get over that. Right Ahbhu?" I bent down and scratched Ahbhu's head. He panted with anticipation, sensing what was coming next. "Good boy! Good Ahbhu!" I straightened up and smiled at Gerónimo. "The truth is nobody in San Salvador is safe if El Boquerón erupts or even if it decides to shake the hell out of us. We'd be the first to go, of course. In an instant, in fact. But the casualties down below could be in the tens of thousands, and the city would never be the same."

Shouldering my pack, I switched on my flashlight and took a step toward the crater, which drew a gasp from Gerónimo. "Follow me," I said.

Ahbhu blazed over, ready to lead the way.

"Wait!" Gerónimo called. I looked back at him, and he shielded his eyes against the powerful beam. "Where are we going?"

"Into the crater, obviously." I pointed the beam at the well-worn trail. "I know a flat spot that isn't affected by the city lights where we can set up the telescope. Trust me!"

We picked our way down the rocky trail, moving single file behind Ahbhu. The air was cooler and fresher inside the crater. At one point, I paused and switched off my flashlight and instructed Gerónimo to do the same. We were immediately enveloped by the near-total darkness. Overhead, the stars stood out ever more intensely. They were practically vibrating. Gerónimo's eyes widened and he let out a breath, astonished by the sight.

A few minutes later, we arrived at the spot I'd selected. We'd been there a few times before, Ahbhu and me, as it was the perfect place to pick out the planets, constellations, and the occasional meteor shower. Gerónimo helped me clear the ground of a few dry twigs and stray stones, and we spread out a tarp while Ahbhu watched on and growled.

"What's up with him?" Gerónimo asked as we secured the corners of the tarp. "He seems extra tetchy tonight."

"He's just jealous, that's all. I've never brought anyone up here before so it's understandable."

I gazed at Ahbhu, feeling a little guilty. Then I made to stroke his fur to reassure him, but he backed away and whined. "I'm sorry, Ahbhu," I said.

Gerónimo watched us with an amused expression.

I tried again, but Ahbhu moved farther from my hand and wagged his head.

"I'll make it up to you, Ahbhu, I promise. I just want to show Gerónimo the Pleiades." I pointed at the sky then crouched down close to him. "I won't bring him up here again, cross my heart." I mimed an X across my chest. Ahbhu relaxed at that and scuttled forward. He pushed into me, letting me know I was forgiven. Grabbing his head with both hands, I shook it from side to side, eliciting a satisfied little groan from him.

"Why did you promise him that?" Gerónimo asked as I extended the legs of the telescope. He spoke in a lowered voice, tossing a glance at Ahbhu, who was cavorting around a bush, playing hide-and-seek with himself and keeping an eye on me at the same time. "I wouldn't be surprised if he actually holds you to it."

"He will." I pressed my eye against the eyepiece and focused the telescope on the area of the sky I wanted to show him. "But let's not talk about that now," I said, straightening up. "Come over here."

Gerónimo crunched over to me, and I extended my hand to the sky. "Are you familiar with the Pleiades?"

Gerónimo shrugged. "It's a constellation."

"Obviously," I snorted. "I'd be worried if you didn't know that at least. Do you know *which* constellation it is?"

Gerónimo shook his head. He glanced again at Ahbhu, who had stopped his playing and was watching us from a distance.

"It's up there," I said, pointing a finger at the sky, a note of impatience creeping into my voice.

Gerónimo blinked at me for a beat, then raised his eyes to where I was pointing. "No, I don't know which one it is. The only constellations I know are the Big Dipper, which is right there, and the Little Dipper—" He drew an imaginary line from the Big Dipper across to Polaris, the luminous North Star in the handle of the Little Dipper "—which is right there."

"That's it? You don't know Orion, the hunter?"

"Oh, right." He screwed up his eyes at the sky and scoured it for a bit. "It's that one there, the hourglass-shaped one with the three stars across the middle."

"Bravo," I said, relieved I wasn't dealing with a complete tabula rasa. "You're sure you don't know the Pleiades? Some people call it the Seven Sisters. It's my favorite constellation."

"I honestly don't. Which one is it?"

I stepped close to Gerónimo and pointed out the shimmering cluster of stars that made up the constellation, feeling suddenly breathless with emotion. I told him the story I'd first heard from my father when I was around five, about how the Greeks believed the Seven Sisters, who were being pursued by Orion, transformed themselves into stars to escape him. "I loved that when I was a kid," I said, smiling at the memory, "the idea that you could turn yourself into a star to escape your troubles."

"Maybe that explains why you want to be an astronaut," Gerónimo suggested, staring up at the constellation, the hint of a smile brightening his face. "Maybe it's your grown-up way of escaping your troubles." He held my eyes. "Ever thought of that?"

"Maybe." Feeling suddenly defensive, I covered up by lowering myself to the telescope and looking into the eyepiece, making sure it was positioned correctly. "Anyway," I said, making a final adjustment, "the Pleiades consists of hundreds of stars, but only a handful are visible to the naked eye. With a telescope, you can see more of the individual stars within the cluster." I moved to one side to make room for him and inclined my head towards the telescope. "Take a look."

Gerónimo regarded me for a beat, as if he was still trying to figure something out; then he shrugged and lowered himself to the refractor and peered into the eyepiece.

"Wow," he murmured after a moment. "It's incredible."

"You should be able to make out some subtle color variations among the individual stars in the cluster. Colors you can't see with the naked eye."

Gerónimo nodded slightly. "Yeah, I see that."

"And if you look closely, concentrating on the middle region, you might even notice a faint nebulosity that adds to the cluster's beauty. That's known as reflection nebulosity. It's caused by scattered light interacting with dust and gas in the region."

"It's incredible," he repeated, his voice filled with wonder. "I've never seen anything like it before. It's literally as if someone scattered a handful of jewels across the night sky."

"I know, I love it. I could gaze at it all night. And that's just one constellation!" My heart raced as I spoke. "And check out the edges surrounding it. You should be able to make out a few other celestial objects you can't see without a telescope." I massaged Gerónimo's neck and he moved his head side to side, still glued to the eyepiece. "Even a telescope as simple as this one offers an amazingly wide field of vision. I can't even imagine what I could see with an observatory telescope!"

Gerónimo sat back on the dirt and grinned at me. "Or from outer space itself!"

"Exactly."

I lowered myself next to him, feeling our connection had deepened by the shared experience.

"That's what I love about you," he said, "your passion for things, that sweet feistiness. Also, your undying optimism, maddening as it is sometimes." He sat up and took my hand. "Those are the things that attracted me to you, aside from the fact you're as cute as hell." He smirked and touched my nose, which drew a low growl from Ahbhu.

We sat in silence for a few minutes, our hair rustled by a faint current of warm air from El Boqueróncito. Then I took him by the hand and led him to the tarp where, in full view of the celestial pantheon pulsating overhead, I made love to Gerónimo while Ahbhu bayed at the night sky.

Afterward, I pulled a light blanket over us and held Gerónimo to my chest, kissing his broad shoulders. He lay so quietly I was sure he'd fallen asleep so I closed my eyes and surrendered to my exhaustion. Just as I was drifting off, he let out a sigh and turned to face me, looking like he had something on his mind.

"Ready for another round?" I joked, drawing a chuckle from him. Then he went serious again. "What is it?"

"There's this thing I'm going to next Saturday. It's supposed to be really special. I want you to come with me."

"What kind of a thing? And where?" I pushed down a sudden apprehension and kept my voice neutral.

"In Panchimalco, at the church. But I don't want to spoil the surprise by saying too much. Let's just say it's something close to my heart, like *this* is for you," he said as he pulled on his clothes.

Still naked and wrapped in the blanket, I stared at him as he laced up his shoes. "Is it something political?"

"Some might see it that way." Now fully dressed, he sat cross-legged on the tarp and handed me my underpants, silently urging me to get dressed. "I'm mainly going to help with the Mass. There will be a lunch and other activities afterward. But I don't want to say more. It'll spoil things if you know too much beforehand."

"People are getting killed now, Gerónimo," I said as I slid into my jeans. "Just last week, some people broke into my friend Vero's house and took her brother, and nobody knows where he is now. We hear gunshots in the night. This isn't just about protests anymore."

Gerónimo shook his head and stared hard at me. "Do you even hear what you're saying? Don't you think it's insane we have to live in fear of being murdered, just because some people believe things can be done better than they're being done now? Look, all I'm asking is for you to come with me to a special Mass and to have some lunch afterwards, nothing more. It would mean a lot to me. Do you think you could do that?"

Gerónimo and I finished folding the tarpaulin in silence and packing up for our journey back down the hill. Every so often, he'd glance in my direction, waiting for a response. But I kept tight-lipped, not wanting to commit to anything under pressure. That said, I reasoned, Gerónimo had come stargazing with me and listened to me blab on about telescopes and constellations when that obviously wasn't his thing. And, after all, weren't relationships about compromise and doing things you're not thrilled about out of love for your partner? But stargazing isn't dangerous, I thought. That other stuff, the things Gerónimo was passionate about, definitely were, not to mention my parents were absolutely against my getting involved in anything that could put me or my family in danger. But hadn't I already crossed that line by continuing to secretly see Gerónimo? When I considered *that*, then how much worse could it be to go with him to a Mass and a communal lunch?

In the end, with my heart in my throat, as we reached the bottom of the hill and paused to say goodbye, I agreed to go with Gerónimo to Panchimalco the following Saturday.

# Chapter 12

## PANCHIMALCO

It was already a scorcher when Gerónimo swung by the hospital to pick me up a couple of hours earlier than usual. The weather couldn't make up its mind, switching between sudden rain showers and relentless sun. I had told my parents that Doctor Elsa had moved my therapy session to ten in the morning instead of the usual eleven, but truth be told, I'd canceled it to get an early start and had passed the message to Gerónimo through a mutual friend. I didn't want to feel rushed during my therapy session, especially knowing we'd have to speed off straight afterward to make it in time for the Mass.

As Ahbhu and I climbed into Gerónimo's Tercel, I saw he'd gotten a buzz cut that complemented the handsome angles of his face. He looked extra nice in a pair of black dress trousers and a white polo that showed off his biceps. I tried to coax Ahbhu into the back seat, where Gerónimo preferred him to ride, but he insisted on sitting up front with me. He grinned triumphantly at Gerónimo, who smoldered for the first few blocks until his annoyance passed. Then he reached down and held my hand the rest of the way.

We arrived in Panchimalco an hour later. Despite the erratic weather, the town was alive and buzzing. Although it was my first time there, I'd heard plenty about its vibrant colonial houses and quaint cobblestone streets, so my excitement had been building during the drive.

As I stepped out of the car, a gust of wind tousled my hair and sent a shiver down my spine, even though it was sweltering. The town's energy was contagious. The streets bustled with vendors lining the sidewalks, their stalls overflowing with handcrafted trinkets, from colorful textiles to intricate wood carvings. The air was thick with the tantalizing aroma of sizzling pupusas and fresh corn tortillas.

Gerónimo led me a short distance to the town's renowned church with its distinctive white colonial facade that glowed in the bright sunlight. Ahbhu trailed behind on his leash, captivated by the new sights and sounds as we crossed the square and climbed the steps to the church's arched portico.

Inside, the pews were packed with congregants engaged in hushed conversation. Gerónimo, now in his black robe, guided me up a side aisle to a space at the front where Ahbhu and I could sit and left us there to marvel at the amazing Baroque altarpiece and coffered wooden ceiling. I'd never seen anything so lovely in my life.

As the Mass kicked off, I was shocked to see Monsignor Romero himself ascend the altar, accompanied by two other priests and Gerónimo, who beamed a proud smile. I'd seen the Monsignor on TV and in the newspapers but seeing him in person was something else. He exuded a commanding presence, his piercing eyes holding a sense of purpose as he led the Mass. Even Ahbhu, who usually dozed during the service, sat up, alert and interested in what was going on.

Listening to Monsignor Romero intone the Mass, I couldn't help but feel a mix of fascination and inner conflict. My father had long complained about the Monsignor's involvement in politics and had cautioned against our being drawn into his orbit. His words echoed in my head, adding an extra layer of guilt to the experience.

By the time the Monsignor began the homily, my head was spinning. He addressed what he called urgent matters, the repression of the marginalized, challenging the notion that only a select few were fit to rule. I caught Gerónimo's eye, trying to convey my discomfort, but he just shrugged and indicated the rest of the congregation. Looking around, I saw lots of folks exchanging approving glances as the Monsignor spoke. He wrapped up his homily with a message about unity and collective responsibility for constructing a better society.

Overwhelmed and disoriented, I hugged Ahbhu and held him close until the Mass was over, burying my face in his fur. Afterwards, Gerónimo came over, excited to introduce me to the Monsignor.

"Why didn't you tell me he was going to be here?" I asked.

"If I'd told you, you wouldn't have come."

"So, you tricked me."

Gerónimo's face fell. "It was meant as a surprise, not a trick." He glanced at the vestry and then back at me, his eyes moist. "You know I love the Monsignor and the work he's doing to make things better for all of us. This was a special event, maybe even a once-in-a-lifetime one. I just wanted to share it with you. I didn't mean to upset you."

He looked so hurt, which made me feel horrible. I apologized with a hug and followed him to the church hall, my emotions all over the place.

As we stepped into the bustling room, the Monsignor's humble yet charismatic presence filled the air, just as during the Mass. He warmly welcomed guests, graciously showing them to their seats at the lunch table. When Gerónimo introduced me to him, I couldn't help but feel a sense of awe and admiration as I shook the Monsignor's hand. Ahbhu danced around my feet, which drew a laugh from the Monsignor, who bent down to pet him, much to the dismay of a couple of priests looking on.

"All God's creatures, brothers," he said, standing up straight and surveying the room. "All are welcome at the Lord's table."

Once we were seated, Gerónimo said grace at the Monsignor's invitation, his voice strong and humble, and we dug into our meal. As we ate, Monsignor Romero shared his stories and his unwavering commitment to social justice. His message was clear: the fight against repression and the pursuit of justice were top priorities, rising to the level of a religious duty. Listening to him, I felt the weight of his words and the strength of his convictions. They seemed to resonate with most at the table. But with my father's warnings ringing in my ears, I couldn't help but experience a disturbing blend of inspiration and turmoil. Having lost my appetite, I pushed back my plate and glanced at Gerónimo, who was utterly focused on the Monsignor.

As lunch drew to a close, the distant sound of barking caught my attention. My heart caught in my chest as I looked around for Ahbhu. The last I'd seen him, he'd been resting at my feet. But with all the activity and discussions around the table, I'd lost track of him. Noticing my growing anxiety, Gerónimo placed his hand on my arm as the barking intensified.

I excused myself from the Monsignor and rushed out of the hall with Gerónimo close behind. We followed the noise around the corner. It grew louder as we approached a clothing store with a small crowd gathered at an open door. Gerónimo tugged on my arm and mentioned he had something he wanted to explain, but I was desperate to find Ahbhu. Pulling away from him, I rushed into the packed shop.

"Where's the dog?" I asked the first person I ran into. He pointed to the back of the shop. Pushing through the crowd, I burst into a large storeroom.

Inside, I found my brother Arturo in jeans and a T-shirt,

struggling to restrain Ahbhu, who was angrily straining on his leash, barking, growling, and baring his teeth at a tall, lean man with a pockmarked face. Quickly assessing the situation, I realized the room was filled with men and woman of all ages, assembling placards, obviously organizing for a protest. They had stopped what they were doing and were fixed on the chaos Ahbhu was causing.

"Ahbhu, stand down," I shouted, my voice cutting through the commotion. Everyone turned to look at me, including Arturo. But Ahbhu kept trying to attack the tall man.

"Ahbhu," I shouted again, snatching the leash from Arturo and tugging on it the way Sue had taught me. At that, Ahbhu turned his head, still growling. The moment our eyes met he whined loudly, then looked back at the tall man, who had retreated into the crowd, his face red with anger. Gerónimo swept past us and spoke to the man, defusing the situation.

I led Ahbhu out of the shop and away from the crowd, where I spoke soothingly to him, doing my best to quiet him. I made sure to hold my own emotions in check to avoid triggering a seizure. Arturo followed us and stood by silently.

"What are you doing here?" he asked once Ahbhu had calmed down.

"What are *you* doing here?" I shot back. "And who was that man Ahbhu was barking at?"

"His name's Sisler," Arturo explained. Ahbhu's ears immediately perked up and he took to growling, verifying my suspicions. Arturo looked down at him and frowned with concern. "He's the organizer."

Gerónimo appeared at the shop door and approached us. As he neared, I stood and pointed at the shop. "That guy in there is your cousin, isn't he? Your cousin with the vanishing litter!"

"Wait!" Arturo said, now thoroughly confused, "What's going on here?"

"Gerónimo told me he had a cousin with a pregnant dog

that looked a lot like Ahbhu. But once she gave birth, nobody ever saw her litter again. It was as if the puppies disappeared from one day to the next. Ahbhu must have been one of them."

Ahbhu let out a loud whine, confirming what I was saying.

"You remember the condition he was in when I found him!" I said, holding back hot tears.

The crowd had cleared enough for me to see Sisler standing at the door, staring our way. Determined to avoid another confrontation, I pulled Ahbhu in the opposite direction, not exactly sure where we were going. Gerónimo and Arturo both fell in at my side.

"Why did you bring him here?" Arturo hissed at Gerónimo. "I don't want him mixed up with any of this."

"Isn't that a bit hypocritical?" Gerónimo retorted. "It's okay for you, but not for him?"

"*I'm* politically active!" Arturo argued. "*He's* not."

"Well, maybe he should be!"

Arturo halted and stared down Gerónimo. "That's not up to you, Gerónimo. It's up to him! It's wrong of you to lure him into something he's never showed any interest in, especially when the stakes are so high. Isaac is made for other things."

"What other things? You mean like being an astronaut?" Gerónimo edged in, his voice dripping with sarcasm.

"Just shut up, both of you!" I shouted, cut to the heart. "Stop talking about me as if I weren't standing right here." I swung on Gerónimo. "Arturo's right. I'm not interested in any of this, I'm sorry. I know it's important for you, and I know you want to share it with me. And thank you for introducing me to the Monsignor. He's a great man, for sure. But if you and I are going to stay friends, this has to be the last time you bring me to anything political. Understand?"

Gerónimo stared at me, on the verge of tears. He glanced at Arturo, who was waiting for a response to what I'd just said, then looked back at me and simply nodded. "I'll grab my things from the vestry, and we can go."

"*I'll* take him home," Arturo said.

Gerónimo shot me a questioning look, and I shrugged. As much as I adored Gerónimo, I'd had enough of him for the day. I sidled up to Arturo, and he slung an arm over my shoulder, and we watched Gerónimo head back to the village center, his head hanging low as he went.

Ahbhu and I sat behind Arturo on his motorcycle through a beating rain shower that let up as we started our ascent toward Canton El Regreso. As we neared our home in the waning light, Arturo pulled to the side of the road. He suggested we come up with a story to tell our parents about where we'd spent the afternoon.

"I don't want to lie!" I countered, tired of feeling manipulated by everyone. "I prefer to just keep quiet . . . if that's okay with you."

Arturo fell silent, surprised at the intensity in my voice.

I hopped off the bike and let him roar on ahead, and Ahbhu and I walked the rest of the way up the hill in the advancing darkness.

# Chapter 13

## THE END AND THE BEGINNING

In the months following the incident in Panchimalco, Gerónimo and I continued to explore our relationship. Things had become markedly colder between us, though, as his political interests were effectively closed off to me, and he showed little interest in anything I cared about. Worse yet, his promise of exclusivity had gone out the window. All that was left for us then was physical and superficial, which worked well for us under the circumstances. As the world around us grew more turbulent, our secret rendezvous in the hidden corners of San Salvador served as a kind of lifeline, an island of normalcy in the midst of the increasing insanity.

Ahbhu was an ever watchful, if reluctant, presence during these clandestine meetings. His loyalty to me never wavered. Yet, ever since Panchimalco, a hint of distrust had crept into his heart whenever Gerónimo was around, creating a palpable tension. I did my best to ignore it and carry on as normal. But every so often, I would catch Gerónimo staring darkly at Ahbhu, and a shiver of fear would course through me, prompting me to cut short our meetings. It didn't take many such incidents before things between Gerónimo and me began to deteriorate even further.

The gradual breakdown in our relationship coincided with El Salvador's slide into utter chaos as the political situation spun out of control. With the government on one side and the labor unions and church leaders on the other, the rest of us, the majority, were caught in the middle, under pressure to pick a side.

Fear and paranoia lodged in the hearts of my countrymen as the streets daily heaved with protests that were met with violent repression. The heart of our city, once our sanctuary, became engulfed in rising tensions. Suspected agitators were regularly detained for questioning, or they disappeared entirely, never to be seen again in this life. Even Arturo, as cautious as he was, was rounded up near his university and held without charge for over a week before he was finally released to the custody of my traumatized parents with a firm warning from the police to cease his association with a certain teachers' union. The experience nearly killed me, I'd been so worked up with worry for my brother, afraid I'd never see him again. Arturo, though, had played it off as an unfortunate misunderstanding and never mentioned the incident again.

Such was the panic engendered by the political situation that one either surrendered to fear and holed up at home, as my parents chose to do, or one carried on, willfully oblivious to the conflagration threatening to engulf us. Almost everyone I knew preferred to dodge the bullets, hop over corpses, take the long way around a random massacre, and pretend they didn't notice whenever a neighbor went missing, while keeping their heads down and praying they weren't next. It was that same mentality, that same willful ignorance, that had kept us going despite the active volcano that threatened to rain destruction on us at any moment. Given the constant disruptions to our lives, my meetups with Gerónimo diminished to a trickle as they became virtually impossible to arrange amid the turmoil.

When it seemed things couldn't get any worse, our own homespun version of Armageddon arrived with a vengeance. On the morning of March 24, 1980, the news exploded that gunmen had shot and killed Monsignor Romero while he celebrated morning Mass in the chapel of the Hospital of Divine Providence in San Salvador.

I was at home when the news struck and was mortified by my father's reaction. It was no secret he hated the Monsignor for his leftist views and for what he considered his political agitation. "The man should stick to religion!" he'd often roared at the TV whenever the Monsignor's activities were reported, prompting Arturo and me to leave the room to avoid another lecture. It was something we'd gotten used to. But that morning, I watched in disbelief as my father cracked open a bottle of his favorite wine to toast the archbishop's assassination, my disbelief boiling over into rage. To keep from disrespecting him, I bit down hard on my tongue, collected Ahbhu, and together we hiked to the top of El Boquerón. Tears flowed freely as I wound my way up the stony path.

When we reached the top, I gazed out over our city, our very country, terrified of the storm that was coming—that had, in fact, arrived—and I screamed out my lungs, with Ahbhu howling at my side, until I felt my legs buckle and everything around me went black.

# PART II

*San Salvador, El Salvador: 1984–1985*

# Chapter 14

## LA CASONA

Ahbhu and I followed Gerónimo through the imposing wrought-iron gates toward the once-grand hacienda we affectionately called La Casona. Now a dilapidated relic on the outskirts of San Salvador, the house loomed large in the moonlight, adorned with a few simple but heartfelt Christmas decorations. A string of rainbow-colored lights had been hung on the trees lining the overgrown gravel path, casting a warm festive glow. The broken cobblestones and tangle of weeds we navigated were a metaphor for the crumbling world around us.

La Casona was Doña Pepe's secret refuge for gay and bisexual men seeking anonymity, a haven in the midst of the madness. The aged owner, a seventy-year-old "bachelor," provided us with a discreet gathering place where we could momentarily escape the full-blown civil war that had torn our nation apart for nearly five relentless years now.

Widespread violence had erupted after the brutal assassination of Monsignor Romero, who was denied even a proper funeral. During his funeral Mass, a deadly explosion in the Civic Square opposite the cathedral claimed the lives of forty innocents trampled in the ensuing panic. This was the inciting event in a conflict that, by 1984, had left thousands dead. Among them were a South African ambassador snatched off the street and murdered, three American nuns who'd been raped and killed, and numerous priests and their household staff mercilessly machine-gunned to death by shadowy paramilitary groups operating with impunity.

Disheartened by it all, Gerónimo had abandoned his aspirations for the priesthood and instead pursued a career in law. I, on the other hand, found myself stuck in academic limbo, struggling to complete my university studies due to the government-enforced school closures that disrupted my classes. Our rendezvous at La Casona, whenever Doña Pepe graciously opened his doors, became our sanctuary. Though we were estranged in all other aspects of our lives by this point, at La Casona we found refuge and a fleeting reconnection in the laughter, the music, and the moments we stole together.

As Gerónimo and I climbed the steps to the house, we exchanged a nod with Lupa, a deceptively sweet fortyish lesbian friend of Doña Pepe who stood watch. She was our sentry, meant to raise the alarm at the first sign of soldiers approaching. The truth was, we'd never been bothered by anyone there. Both the government and the rebels had more pressing concerns than a gathering of queers, dancing and celebrating life under the shroud of darkness. Still, we took every precaution to ensure our safety, having preplanned our routes of escape should it ever come to that.

To suit the occasion, Lupa wore a Santa hat and a jingle bell necklace, infusing a touch of whimsy into her watchful presence. She greeted us with a warm smile and a festive "Merry Christmas, boys! Hello, Ahbhu!" She crouched down to pet Ahbhu, who greeted her with a friendly lick. Gerónimo rolled his eyes and pushed into the house without waiting for us.

Noticing the tension, Lupa offered to watch Ahbhu for me.

Ahbhu flashed me a look that said: *No way!* As fond as he was of Lupa, his place was at my side at all times. That was the deal.

Politely declining Lupa's offer, I hurried to catch up with Gerónimo, pulling Ahbhu along by his leash, sensing his reluctance to go inside. That evening, as I was getting ready, he'd told me he didn't think I should go to La Casona anymore. He felt something bad was going to happen, maybe not that night, but soon. Since Ahbhu usually was proved right about things, I promised him that that night would be my last and determined to make the best of my final outing at La Casona.

I found Gerónimo standing at the bar in the cheerily decorated living room. There were already quite a few men there mixing about, around twenty or so of all ages, from young guys in their late teens to those in their fifties or sixties. Jose Feliciano's "Feliz Navidad" was playing in the background, and some of the men sang along and moved to the music. Though I knew most of them by sight, we never exchanged names. That was a strict house rule. If we bumped into each other out in the real world, we were not to let on we'd ever even seen each other before.

"What'll you have?" Gerónimo rolled a beer bottle across his forehead to cool himself and glanced about the room.

"Something sweet."

"He'll have a cosmo," Gerónimo said to the ancient guy minding the bar. We speculated he was Doña Pepe's lover but never had any confirmation of that. Men in those days didn't openly partner up with other men. If you were wired "that way," you either married and carried on with other men on the side, the same way straight guys had affairs with women, or you stayed single forever like Doña Pepe.

"Let's head to the back," Gerónimo said as soon as the drink was in my hand, leading the way through the crowd to the dance floor at the back of the house.

"Are you okay?" I asked as we moved down the long hall

117

with the infectious pounding of Aretha Franklin's "Freeway of Love" spilling toward us. "You're acting standoffish, more so than usual."

He took a long swig of beer and wiped his mouth on the back of his arm. "Sorry, it's been a fucked week." He gifted me a wet kiss and grinned. "Nothing to do with you. I just need to get onto the dance floor, and I'll be good as gold."

We burst into the jammed salon, equipped with colored lights and a mirror ball. Gerónimo peeled off his shirt, waded into the middle of the crowd, and went for it. Eyes closed, he gyrated with those around him, his arms held high, a blissful smile breaking out on his face. Ahbhu and I stood to one side and watched.

*Gerónimo's off tonight*, Ahbhu warned. *Ahbhu doesn't believe his bad week story. Isaac should leave.*

"No, Ahbhu," I said. "We're staying. He's just being his moody self. Plus, I need to talk to him."

"Well, if it isn't the dog and his boy," Doña Pepe shouted over the music as he approached from the shadows. "Happy holidays to you both!"

*Oh, no . . .* Ahbhu groaned, taking shelter behind me.

I greeted Doña Pepe with a peck on both cheeks, Euro style, and he draped his arm around my shoulder and pulled me close.

"He's magnificent tonight, darling." He indicated Gerónimo on the dance floor. "Your boyfriend, I mean."

He was right. Gerónimo looked especially beautiful that night, with his slicked-back hair, his glistening muscled torso reflecting the rainbow of lights, the tight jeans that left nothing to the imagination. He was the center of attention, and he knew it.

"He's not my boyfriend," I grumbled. "We're just old friends. With benefits."

Doña Pepe pulled away and raised an eyebrow. "You *do* know that boy has been with half the men on that dance floor, don't you? If I were you, I wouldn't get my hopes up."

*Tell the old coot to mind his own business*, Ahbhu muttered, showing Doña Pepe his teeth.

"I'll keep that in mind, Pepe, thanks." Pushing down my annoyance, I shifted away from him.

He hadn't told me anything I didn't already know. Gerónimo had always been promiscuous and had become even more so with each passing year of the war. I doubted he used protection during his countless encounters, which made me fear for him. Even though AIDS had not yet reached El Salvador, the disease had already arrived in Mexico, just one country away, making its eventual landfall in El Salvador inevitable. But despite Gerónimo's recklessness, my feelings for him remained unwavering, and I stayed completely loyal to him. Up until that point, Gerónimo was the only man I'd ever slept with, and I didn't expect that to change. I was hopelessly in love with him and secretly prayed he'd eventually come around and feel the same. Silly me.

Sensing I was watching him, Gerónimo waved me over to where he was dancing in the middle of the fray. "Freeway" had segued to REM's "Losing My Religion," one of his favorites, and he danced for all he was worth, twirling his T-shirt over his head. I didn't usually dance, to avoid Ahbhu getting trampled. But that night, my last night at La Casona, I felt a pain in my chest seeing Gerónimo surrounded by a bunch of guys pawing at him. He was mine; that was *my* place there. Lowering myself to Ahbhu, I grabbed his head on either side. "I need to be out there, Ahbhu, okay? Stay right here, please."

Ahbhu stared at me for a moment, his dark brown eyes gleaming in the low light, sensing my anxiety; then he nodded and sat on his haunches to wait for me.

I pushed through the crowd, making a beeline for Gerónimo, and wrapped my arms around him. Delighted I'd joined him, he planted a deep kiss on my mouth, drawing catcalls from a few of the guys; then we spent the next hour dancing nonstop. I'd never felt closer to him than I did that last night at La Casona. Doña Pepe had warned me not to get my hopes up. But that night, I believed we might actually have a chance to make it together after all, Gerónimo and me.

At midnight, just as the DJ spun Madonna's "Material Girl," I took Gerónimo's hand and led him off the dance floor. We bought a couple more beers at the bar; then we paid Doña Pepe to use one of the rooms upstairs. Ahbhu kept close as Gerónimo and I slowly walked up the steps, holding each other close. His heartbeat thudded against my side as we moved, his breath warm on my neck with every kiss.

When we reached the second-story landing, I made to turn right, but Gerónimo pulled me left. "It's this way," he said pointedly.

Ahbhu's ears perked up at that, and he moved away with the clear intention of going to the right.

"Ahbhu, no," Gerónimo ordered. "Follow us."

Ahbhu halted at Gerónimo's words, still staring down the hall to the right. After a beat, he turned and trotted behind us to our assigned bedroom.

Our established custom, after so many years, was for Ahbhu to wait outside the door whenever Gerónimo and I had sex. Gerónimo preferred it that way, and so did I. But that night, I was surprised when Gerónimo opened the door to the room and let Ahbhu go in ahead of us. "I don't want him bothering anyone," he explained.

Without a second thought, Ahbhu slipped into the room. He sniffed around a bit before climbing onto an old stuffed chair with a clear view of the double bed and settled there.

Locking the door, Gerónimo dimmed the lights, and we stripped. Then we fell onto the bed and made love with an intensity I'd never experienced before. Gerónimo had learned a few things since the last time we'd been together, and I went for it on the condition we use protection, determined to make the most of what was left of the night.

When it was finally over, we held each other as we caught our breath, drenched in sweat. Gerónimo cracked open the window for some air. I ached at the sight of his body glowing in the silvering light of the advancing dawn, not ready to let him go, and I held out my hand to him. Flashing a lascivious smile, he crawled back into bed and eagerly explored my mouth with his tongue, ready for another round.

"Man, that was good," Gerónimo sighed when we were finally done. "Best sex we've ever had, you and me. Maybe the best I've had with anyone."

I grinned at that, my body reacting to the memory of it all. He was right. That night had surpassed anything he and I had ever experienced together. I was ready for more. Seeing my intention, Gerónimo pulled on his boxers and handed me mine. Then he leaned back against the headboard, his expression turning suddenly somber.

"We could have this all the time, you know," I ventured after a moment. "Not just in these stolen moments, living as if we're on the run."

Gerónimo pivoted his head to me. "What do you mean?"

"I mean, why don't we move in with each other? We could get an apartment or a house together."

Gerónimo scoffed. "My parents are lining up a match for me with the daughter of a friend. They say it's time I settled down and got married . . . this summer."

My stomach dropped at the unexpected news, and I struggled to keep from crying. Gerónimo squeezed my shoulder reassuringly. "You and I can keep seeing each other on the side if you want."

I shifted away from his hand. "Is that what *you* want?" I asked, my voice barely audible.

*Isaac is wasting his life chasing Gerónimo,* Ahbhu grumbled in the background.

I whipped around and glared at him. "Shut up, Ahbhu. Just shut up!"

Gerónimo narrowed his eyes and cocked his head. "What the hell was that?"

"Never mind," I said. "Just tell me, is that what you really want for yourself? To marry a woman? You like men, for God's sake, not women. How will a woman ever be able to please you the way you like? Are you going to spend the rest of your days cheating on your wife, living a double life, maybe even risking your reputation and the reputation of your family?"

"It's the way things are, Isaac. The way things have always been. Men settle down and have their dalliances on the side; women do it, too."

"Then let's go someplace where they do things differently! We can go north. Men like us can make a life together. Openly."

"There you go again with the fairy tales."

"It's not a fairy tale, and you know it!"

"I'm sorry, Isaac. I'm not going to abandon El Salvador and leave behind my family, my career, everything I know and love, just to live a pipe dream with you up there. I'm not willing to start from zero, working in some damned restaurant, earning less than the minimum wage to scrape by, just to be able to have it off with you every night." He hauled himself off the bed and pulled on his clothes. "It's not worth it."

"You mean, *I'm* not worth it," I said, shocked by the reversal.

"Nobody's worth it," Gerónimo corrected. He tossed my trousers at me. "I'm happy for us to keep seeing each other like we've been doing over the past few years. But no more than that."

"Exclusively?"

"I can't promise that," Gerónimo said. "You'll always be my main guy. And I *do* love you if that means anything to you. But this will never be exclusive like before. You know what I'm like."

I finished getting dressed, then faced off with Gerónimo. "I won't see you again once you're married, Gerónimo. As much as I adore you, I refuse to be your thing on the side."

"Then maybe we should call it quits now."

"Maybe we should."

We stared at each other from across the room, neither of us apparently willing to make the final call.

The grind of tires on the gravel outside brought us back to ourselves, and we moved wordlessly to the door. Ahbhu shot out the moment we opened it and sped down the hallway. Seeing Ahbhu's direction of travel, Gerónimo sprinted after him, and I ran behind, confused at what was happening.

Gerónimo caught up with Ahbhu just as he reached the door at the end of the hall and nudged it open. Inside, a group of around six men and a couple of women were gathered around a table. They all looked up at the interruption and two of the men brandished handguns. I recognized one of them as Gerónimo's cousin Sisler. Ahbhu took to barking at the sight of him. Swooping in, Gerónimo scooped up Ahbhu and apologized to the group, then shut the door firmly and shoved Ahbhu at me.

"What was that back there?" I asked once we were outside and hoofing it down the long driveway to Gerónimo's car.

"You didn't see anything, all right?" Gerónimo said, opening the passenger side door for me. "Do you understand?"

"I thought you weren't involved in that anymore," I protested.

"I'm not!" Gerónimo rounded the car and started up the engine. "I just made the introductions."

*Ahbhu told you so!* Ahbhu said.

I whipped around and glared at Ahbhu, shutting him up with a raised hand. Then I looked back at Gerónimo. "You know, you're right. Maybe it *is* best if we call it quits. At least until all of this is over and we can reevaluate where everything stands."

Just then we were shaken by a sharp jolt, and the ground rolled beneath us. Gerónimo pulled the car to one side and engaged the brake, narrowly avoiding a minor rock slide that tumbled to the road from the slopes above us.

We waited in silence, our eyes locked on each other, preparing for the next jolt. But it never came. After a few minutes, we let out a sigh of relief. The flicker of terror in Gerónimo's eyes subsided and, a moment later, he switched the car back on. "I hope to God that there's something left standing *once all of this is over*," he said.

# Chapter 15

## CHECKPOINT

Our bus rumbled along the dark road from Sonsonate, filled with a mix of tired university students and teachers. Now an assistant professor, Arturo had organized a charitable mission there to rebuild a war-damaged schoolhouse during a temporary ceasefire. We had all put in an exhausting ten-hour day of labor, and my body ached.

As the bus made its way through the winding roads, a haunting chant filled the air, passed from one voice to the next like a burning torch.

*Bella ciao, Bella ciao, Bella ciao, ciao, ciao!*

The refrain from an Italian folk song synonymous with international revolutionary movements echoed through the bus. Some passengers took to thumping their seats in rhythm with the chant, creating a relentless cadence:

*If I die as a partisan, make sure you bury me up there in the mountains in the shade of a beautiful flower;*

*Bella ciao, Bella ciao, Bella ciao, ciao, ciao!*

As the chant continued, a sense of unease ate away at me. Ahbhu felt it too and growled softly. Arturo had promised me this mission would remain apolitical. Yet here we were, caught in the cadence of a potentially dangerous anthem.

Surveying us through his rearview mirror, the driver's angry eyes terrified me. Lunging forward, I whisper-screamed to Arturo, who was seated in front of me and had joined in with the chanting. "What the hell are you doing? You promised this wasn't going to turn political!"

Arturo turned in his seat, his expression grave. "Everything's political these days, hermano."

"But . . . if someone finds out. Arturo, you *know* what could happen! Tell them to stop!" Panic welled up, and I felt a seizure threatening to come on.

I was still reeling from the news I'd received earlier that week. Gerónimo had told me that the army had raided La Casona and arrested a bunch of guys there—just as Ahbhu had predicted. Machine gun fire had been heard echoing off the surrounding hills. It was rumored Doña Pepe had been dragged into the trees behind the house, never to return. La Casona was now sealed off from the main road, and the grand old mansion was to be bulldozed.

In an attempt to calm my distress, Ahbhu pressed his warm body against mine and calmly instructed: *Isaac, breff, Isaac needs to breff. Big breffs like Doctor Elsa taught. Ten in, ten out, okay?*

I closed my eyes, clung to Ahbhu, and followed his instructions: *Ten times in, ten times out.*

*Good*, he said. *Again!*

When I opened my eyes a couple of minutes later, I found Arturo staring at me, his eyes shining with concern. He squeezed my arm. "Are you all right, buddy?" His gesture elicited a low growl from Ahbhu, prompting Arturo to pull back his hand. "I'll get them to stop in a moment," he said, scanning the bus.

"*Now*, Arturo!" I urged, trying my best to channel calm. I had narrowly escaped a blackout and was determined to avoid another episode.

Arturo nodded and moved to the front of the bus. He activated the PA system and addressed the passengers. "Compañeros, pipe down for a second, please." He smiled and raised his hand. The group fell silent, all eyes fixed on him. "I just wanted to thank you all for your efforts today," he began. "In these difficult times, it takes great courage. Thanks to you, children will be able to resume their education as they were meant to, in a proper classroom. We should all be proud of ourselves." His words drew cheers and applause.

Arturo continued, "We'll soon be joining the main highway. As such, I feel it would be appropriate to finish the balance of our journey in a spirit of quiet contemplation, out of respect for those who've been lost or are suffering—on both sides of the conflict. May this war soon come to an end."

The passengers murmured their approval and fell silent.

As Arturo returned to his seat, he winked at me. I exhaled, relieved, my heart rate settling as the driver dimmed the interior lights. After a moment, I curled up against the window and dozed off as the bus continued its journey toward the highway.

A few minutes later, an abrupt gear change jarred me awake. Through half-open eyes, I caught a faint glow of flames in the distance. Arturo sat up, peering through the windshield. "Stay put," he told me, then darted to the front of the bus.

Crouching next to the driver as the bus slowed to a crawl, he snatched up the microphone and announced in a low voice, "Compañeros, it looks like we're approaching a checkpoint. It's important that you all remain calm. Let the driver and me do the talking."

"What kind of checkpoint is it?" one of the female students asked anxiously.

I looked around and saw fear etched on the faces of everyone around me.

"I can't tell yet," Arturo responded, his eyes focused on the distant flames. "But it looks like a sizable group of people, most probably soldiers. But again, keep calm and we'll be all right."

Rather than calming the group, Arturo's words provoked a quiet panic. Some passengers lowered their windows and strained to catch a better look at the impassable barrier of burning tires and flaming oil barrels in the middle of the road. The smell of burning rubber permeated the night air and echoes of shouting reflected off the surrounding hills. A cold sweat of fear broke out over my body, and I reached for Ahbhu.

*Isaac, stick to Ahbhu,* he instructed, *no matter what happens, stick close to Ahbhu.*

Suddenly, an explosion of light strafed the inside of the bus from some kind of high-powered searchlight, and an amplified voice ordered: "Bring the bus to a stop now."

The driver slammed on the brakes, tossing us forward and then back against our seats. Arturo was thrown against the windshield and collapsed. I made to go to him, but Ahbhu ordered me to stay put. In spite of myself, I obeyed, suppressing the sobs that threatened to overwhelm me.

As we recovered from the initial shock, a retinue of masked uniformed men cantered forward from the shadows and surrounded the bus, four on each side, two at the back, each of them bearing a machine gun held diagonally across their chests. Fear gripped my fellow passengers, mirroring my own terror, their faces ashen and voices trembling, clutching onto the person next to them.

I desperately kept my eye on Arturo, who had come to and was lifting himself into a vacant seat just as a loud pounding shook the bus, and the driver opened the bus door.

An instant later, a soldier in a gray officer's uniform and a black beret climbed inside. He locked his cruel eyes on the driver. Another soldier, twenty at the most, with a set of gold teeth, followed close behind. The soldier in charge demanded the driver's papers and read through them; then he shoved them at his second and glared at us before turning his attention back to the driver.

"Where are you coming from?" he barked.

"Sonsonate," the driver answered, keeping his eyes down.

"What were you doing in Sonsonate?"

Catching sight of Arturo in his rearview mirror, the driver jerked his thumb at him. "Ask that guy. I'm just the driver."

"You're *just* the driver?" The soldier turned to his junior. "Did you hear that, Cano? The man says he's *just* the driver."

"Sí, mi Capitan, I heard him," Cano answered, addressing the officer as his captain.

"Show him how we deal with drivers that talk back."

Cano tossed aside the driver's papers and drew a pistol. "Off the bus, Señor Driver."

"Wait!" Arturo said, rising to his feet. "It's true he's just a driver. The university hired him to take us to Sonsonate."

The captain's head snapped in Arturo's direction, and he focused his black eyes on him. "Is that so. . ." he said drily. "And who are you?"

"I'm the organizer."

"The organizer of what?"

Arturo drew himself up and spoke confidently. "We're a charitable mission sponsored by the university. We spent the day in Sonsonate repairing a schoolhouse. Our aims are purely educational. Nothing else."

The captain stared deadpan at Arturo, then turned and instructed his second: "Cano, the driver."

Before we even had a chance to react, Cano dragged the driver off the bus, shoved him onto the ground, and put a bullet in his head, the sound of the single gunshot ricocheting off the hills.

Arturo collapsed to his seat as if he'd been punched in the chest, his face radiating terror; panic and shouting broke out among the other passengers. Some of them leapt into the aisles seeking to flee but finding no outlet; others, like me, cowered on the floor, dreading the worst.

Four of the black-masked soldiers stormed the bus and started dragging us off one by one. A few passengers managed to jump out the bus windows but were immediately apprehended and hauled to an area of level gravel to one side of the bus within view of the driver's body, which was face down in the dirt.

"Lose the dog!" one of the soldiers ordered as he hauled Ahbhu and me off the bus toward the group of passengers gathered on the gravel.

*Stay calm and wait for Ahbhu's sign*, Ahbhu whispered. *Remember your breffs, ten in, ten out.*

The soldier with the gold teeth took over and ordered us to assemble in two parallel single-file lines in the glare of the spotlights. We tearfully complied, trying our best to keep our heads despite the fact he'd just murdered our driver.

We moved into position, fearing what was coming next. Ahbhu shepherded me to the end of the second line. *Don't move, whatever happens*, he said. *Ahbhu will be back.* My heart rose into my throat as I watched him race into the trees behind us, feeling suddenly vulnerable without him.

Refocusing on what was happening around me, I saw that Arturo had taken pole position in the first line. He was trying his best to reassure those around him, but his ashen face belied the fear that gripped him. I felt like a coward hiding in the back, but Ahbhu's words echoed in my mind. *Don't move, whatever happens.*

The captain ordered us to surrender our identity cards, and his soldiers snatched them out of our wallets and bags. Then he stepped up to Rubén Menendez, a young freshman, and said, "That school you rebuilt today was being used by *guerrilleros.* We officially decommissioned it. Did you know that?"

Rubén looked down and shook his head. "I don't know anything," he said, his voice trembling.

"Which of you knew this?" the captain called out. "Which of you *charity workers* knew the school you rebuilt today was being used to cache arms?"

A hard nudge at my leg told me Ahbhu had returned. *When Ahbhu gives the sign,* he said, *Isaac will run to those trees.* He indicated where with a lifted paw.

Desperate to save the group, Arturo spoke up. "As I said, sir, our interest was purely educational and charitable. The children of the town had no place to go for—"

"I wasn't speaking to you!" the captain said. He waved at the soldier with the gold teeth and pointed at Rubén. The soldier swept forward and yanked Rubén onto his knees and pointed an automatic rifle at his head.

"Anyone here who knew the school you rebuilt today was being used by guerrilleros, raise your hand, or your *comrade* here gets the next bullet," the captain declared.

Arturo leapt forward, tears of desperation streaming down his face. "Brothers, no! Please, don't do this. We can talk this over like civilized people."

The soldier with the gold teeth swung on Arturo, savagely cracking him on the head with the butt of his rifle. Arturo hit the ground, and his attacker laid into him with his boot. I watched in horror and total impotence as he kicked Arturo again and again, with Arturo groaning loudly with each kick. Some of the other soldiers joined in, kicking Arturo with increasing frenzy, calling him names as they did so:

"Comunista! Izquierdista! Guerrillero! Gusano de mierda!"

The captain watched on with mild amusement. The soldier nearest me ran over to join the others and aimed a kick at Arturo's head. Seeing that, one of the others took a step back and applied an even harder kick, reminiscent of a goal kick in football. The gesture drew laughter from the others, each of whom took turns kicking Arturo's head.

*Don't watch,* Ahbhu ordered, and I squeezed my eyes shut, hearing the frenzied laughter of the soldiers as they kicked Arturo again and again.

I wanted to scream: "Stop! That's my brother! You're killing him!" But I obeyed Ahbhu, biting my fist to keep quiet, feeling guilty and ashamed.

"Okay, men," the captain called out. "That's enough. Get back to work."

But the soldiers continued taking turns kicking my poor brother, who had long since passed from this world.

The captain fired his pistol into the air. "Enough with the playing!" he shouted. "Get back to work!"

We were startled by another gunshot that rang out in the darkness followed by the unmistakable sounds of a brawl. A couple of the soldiers next to my brother disengaged from his side and sped toward what seemed like a full-blown fistfight that had broken out among the soldiers manning the roadblock. The captain fired his pistol in the air again and screamed for the men to come back. Realizing he was being ignored, he tore after them.

*Now!* Ahbhu said. *Follow Ahbhu. Keep low to the ground.*

I followed him, crouching as I ran, escaping into the darkness, the sound of machine-gun fire ringing out behind me. Ahbhu led the way, guiding me through the trees. The night air was thick and suffocating. The forest was so dark that it was almost impossible to see.

We reached a massive boulder sitting smack in the middle of the path, and I halted before it, gasping for breath, my heart pounding. The chirping of crickets surrounded us, and the darkness was disorienting.

"What now?" I asked Ahbhu, looking around for any sign of the soldiers.

He trotted to the left of the boulder and disappeared behind it. Tossing up my hands, I followed him, scraping the hell out of my arms between the boulder and the bushes that butted up against it. A few seconds later, I emerged on the other side, where Ahbhu was waiting for me. He pointed at a fresh indentation in the dirt at the base of the boulder.

*Isaac can hide there.*

"You dug that?" I asked, bewildered, feeling ready to collapse from exhaustion and fear. "When?"

*When Ahbhu was scouting the escaping way. Come, fast! Isaac to lay down there. Ahbhu will cover Isaac with dead plants.*

"What about *you?*"

*Ahbhu will keep watch. Maybe the soldiers will be gone soon. Isaac to stop talking now and lay down there.*

I lowered myself into the hiding spot Ahbhu had dug for me, the scent of damp earth and decaying leaves filling my senses. Then, curling into a fetal position, I closed my eyes and lost consciousness.

# Chapter 16

## ON THE RUN

Ahbhu's gentle push brought me out of my stupor. Reluctant to move, I kept my eyes closed, not yet ready to face reality, savoring the warmth of the damp ground beneath me.

*Isaac*, Ahbhu murmured, tapping me again with his paw, *Isaac, wake up.*

I groaned and slowly leveraged my body upright, blinking to adjust to the feeble light filtering through the trees. The effort to rise seemed like an arduous ascent, every muscle protesting the motion. The acrid smell of burnt wreckage filled the air, and Ahbhu paced nervously, his eyes filled with concern.

"Ahbhu, what happened?" I rasped, slowly recalling the events of the previous night. My throat was parched from lack of water.

*Soldiers set the bus on fire, Isaac. Dead people are everywhere. Trucks with red lights are coming now with new soldiers.*

"Arturo . . ." I choked, the memory of the attack on him flooding back.

Ahbhu shook his head slowly. His eyes were the saddest I'd ever seen them. Then he pushed into my arms, and I held him close. A moment later, the sound of distant shouting reached us, and Ahbhu pulled away, his intact ear perking up.

"What should we do?" I asked, my voice trembling.

Ahbhu's gaze remained resolute. *Ahbhu and Isaac to go back home, but the roads are not safe. Ahbhu will find another escaping way through the trees, Isaac to follow. But hurry. Soldiers are coming now!*

I rose to my feet as swiftly as I could, feeling unsteady after my time in the hiding place. The uncomfortable position had left my body stiff, and I worked out the kinks with some quick stretches. Then we set off.

Ahbhu took the lead, and we embarked on our escape through dense forest, following a path that eluded me but was clear to him.

The forty-five-mile trek proved grueling. We moved silently and cautiously, avoiding any signs of soldiers or danger. Ahbhu scouted ahead, ensuring our path remained clear, and guided me through the wilderness and along lesser traveled, poorly maintained lanes.

Two days passed like an endless nightmare, filled with exhaustion, hunger, and fear. We survived on the meager rations Ahbhu procured during occasional nighttime forays into the surrounding villages we passed, while I nervously waited for him in the trees.

When we finally arrived in Canton El Regreso along the backside of El Boquerón, it was deep into a moonless night, and the bright arch of the Milky Way was pulsating overhead. We crept into the village near the trailhead, keeping to the shadows cast by the surrounding foliage. My heart pounded at the sight of my family home shrouded in darkness. Looking in all directions to make sure nobody was watching, Ahbhu and I darted across the road and up the drive and slipped into the house through the side door.

The front of the house was dark and silent as death. I moved down the hallway, past my bedroom, and into the kitchen. A sliver of light shone under the door leading to the back room. I put my ear to it and heard soft murmuring with the radio in the background tuned to the government station. Then, taking a breath to steel myself, I gave the door a gentle push and stepped into the room.

Inside, I found my parents and Neto gathered around the radio, so focused on the broadcast they hadn't noticed me come in. To my surprise, the newscaster was reporting on an update to a guerrilla attack on a university bus on the road from Sonsonate two days before. The government had just announced that all passengers were now presumed either dead or kidnapped by the rebels. All families would be separately notified in the coming days. On hearing the news, my father broke down, and my mother reached to Neto for support.

"They're lying," I interrupted, tears streaming down my face.

They all spun in my direction, their faces a mix of terror and disbelief at the sight of the son they were sure was dead but who was now standing in their presence, like an apparition of Christ himself. Keen to break the spell, Ahbhu dashed forward and circled around Neto, who blinked at him then looked back up at me.

"We were attacked by soldiers," I said. "Not by guerrillas."

My mother leapt up from her chair and rushed to my side, taking me into her arms. "Hijo mio," she cried, squeezing me tightly. An instant later, she was joined by my father, whose kisses mingled with his tears. Neto watched from across the room, his eyes shining with emotion, concern carved deep on his face.

"Are you sure it was soldiers?" he asked.

"What does it matter if it was soldiers or guerrillas?" my mother snapped over her shoulder.

"I'm positive, Neto," I said.

As if suddenly remembering something, my mother straightened up and glanced around the room. "And Arturo?"

she said, asking the question I was dreading to answer. My father wiped his face with his sleeve and searched my face.

Gritting my teeth to keep from breaking down, I looked at each of them and shook my head. "Arturo's gone," I drew out painfully. "He's gone."

Both my parents fell back a step as if they'd been slugged in the chest.

"What do you mean he's gone?" Neto asked, stepping toward me. "What happened to him?"

I closed my eyes and clamped my hands over my mouth to suppress a sob, trying desperately to unsee the image of those soldiers savagely kicking Arturo as he lay helpless on the ground. But as much as I wanted to erase the memory of his murder, my family had the right to know what had happened to their son. So, lowering my hands, I took a steadying breath and started talking.

I barely got out the words, choking back tears, as I explained everything that had occurred, sparing no detail. When I got to the part about Arturo, I stopped for a beat and looked into the eyes of each of them, silently seeking their consent to share the harrowing event. My mother grabbed my father's hand on one side and Neto's on the other then nodded for me to continue. Taking another breath, I described the soldiers' assault on Arturo.

"Is there any chance he might have escaped?" my father asked, "I mean afterward, once the soldiers left."

I shook my head, the terror obvious on my face. "Arturo's with God now, Papá."

At that, my parents broke down, and Neto pulled me to one side. Ahbhu followed and stood nearby, his body tense and alert.

"You're sure they took your cedula?" he asked, casting a cautious glance at Ahbhu.

"They took everyone's."

Neto pursed his lips, the wheels turning behind his dark eyes. "If it was soldiers," he said, half to himself, "they'll be matching cedulas with bodies if they haven't done that already. Anyone they can't match they're likely to hunt down to keep them quiet."

He turned to my parents, who looked haggard and spent with grief. "Papá, Mamá," he started gently, "you'll probably get a visit from someone delivering the news about Arturo. You can't let on you know it was soldiers that killed him; otherwise, you'll become targets yourselves. Understand?"

My parents looked at each other and nodded. "What about Isaac?" my mother asked.

"Isaac can't be here when they come, Mamá. He's already in danger. They'll be looking for him."

"Where am I supposed to go?" I asked, feeling a fresh wave of fear. Ahbhu trotted to my side and urged me to keep steady.

Neto crossed his arms the way he did whenever he was about to deliver bad news. "The way I see it, we have only two choices: Isaac can either go into hiding until this all blows over or he can turn himself in. He can explain that he had no idea what the trip to Sonsonate was about and that he'd been roped into it."

"This is all your fault, Neto!" my father exploded. "You *knew* about the trip Arturo had planned, yet you never did *anything* to warn us or to discourage it. That was your responsibility as an older brother. We're in the middle of a civil war, damn it all; don't you get that?"

"I warned Arturo not to go, Papá," Neto argued. "But he insisted there was a ceasefire and that it was all right. I couldn't exactly lie down in front of the bus to stop him, could I?"

"I'm not turning myself in," I said. "That would be absolutely stupid."

Suddenly, Ahbhu's ear perked up and he released a low growl. An instant later we heard a soft rapping outside the kitchen. Neto held up his hand, signaling for silence, and then slipped out of the room to investigate. My mother gestured urgently at a leather sofa pushed up against one of the walls, and I hid behind it. We all waited in tense silence for Neto's return.

Shortly after, Neto reappeared, accompanied by Gerónimo, who was dressed in a black T-shirt and jeans with a black watch cap covering his hair. My father sprung up at the sight of him, his face registering alarm, and my heart leapt in my chest. The last time I'd seen Gerónimo was at the Christmas party, which now seemed like an eternity ago.

Gerónimo removed his cap and lowered his head. "I'm sorry to show up unannounced, Mr. Perez, Mrs. Perez. I came as soon as I was able. Have you had any news of Isaac or Arturo?"

My father growled, "How dare you come here?"

"You're putting all of us in danger, Gerónimo!" my mother added, tightly holding my father's hand. "Please go."

"Don't worry, Señora, I made sure I wasn't followed. I'm truly sorry to trouble you all, but I've been sick with worry and didn't know what else to do."

I crept out from behind the sofa, and Gerónimo's knees nearly buckled from the shock of seeing me. Neto rushed forward to keep him from collapsing and helped him into a chair.

Staring at me from across the room, tears pooled in Gerónimo's eyes. "Thank God," he whispered, wiping his face with the back of his trembling hand. "Thank God, Isaac."

My mother spat out, "Your kind don't believe in God!"

"Mamá, stop!" I said. She turned away angrily, crossing her arms and simmering with frustration. I took a seat across from Gerónimo, holding his gaze. "It wasn't God who saved me, Gerónimo."

Gerónimo glanced at Ahbhu and nodded. "And Arturo?"

I shook my head, and my parents broke down again, moving away for some privacy. Alarmed by the news and my parents' reaction, Gerónimo lowered his face into his hands and wept.

"Now you've seen him; now you can go," Neto said, towering over Gerónimo, his tone as hard as granite.

"Neto, wait," I said. "He's my friend. If he says he wasn't followed, I believe him."

"Ten minutes," Neto said, moving away from us and joining my parents.

Gerónimo raised wet eyes at me, brimming with unasked questions.

"It was soldiers, Gerónimo," I said in a low voice. "They dragged us off the bus and confiscated our cedulas. I got away thanks to Ahbhu. Maybe a couple of the others did as well, I don't know." I blinked away tears. "Most didn't."

His face had gone pale. "You can't stay here, not if they have your cedula," he said, the terror palpable in his voice. "They'll come looking for you." He looked at my parents and repeated. "He can't stay here."

"Yes, we *know* that," Neto said.

"Mr. and Mrs. Perez," Gerónimo said, ignoring Neto. "I know a safehouse where Isaac can stay. Nobody will look for him there."

"No!" my mother said, holding on to my father. "There's *no* such thing as a safehouse. People talk. Sooner or later, he'll be discovered."

"There's a secure cellar at the factory I supervise downtown," Neto cut in. "It's been abandoned for years. Nobody will look there."

"You're his brother, for God's sake," Gerónimo countered. "They're bound to come calling at your factory."

"Stop it, all of you!" I said, feeling the blood rush into my head. I called Ahbhu to me and held on to him. "I am *not* going to a safehouse, and I'm *not* going to hide underground in a cellar like I'm some kind of a rat. No way!"

"Then what?" they all said at the same time.

Feeling suddenly decided, I locked eyes with each of them in turn. "Ahbhu and I will go someplace where nobody will be able to find us, and we'll lie low there until I decide what to do next." I paused and kissed Ahbhu's head and rose to my feet. "I'll take a few supplies with me for now. But whenever I run low,

Ahbhu will come by here to pick up food and water. Mamá, just make sure to have stuff packed and ready for him to carry."

"But where are you going?" My mother said. The others looked on, speechless.

"It's best if I don't tell you," I said. "That way, if anyone asks, you can honestly tell them you have no idea where I am. But I promise, we'll be safe. Right, Ahbhu?"

Ahbhu barked his agreement and nudged me toward the door. "Hang on a sec," I told him; then I hugged my mother and held her as she wept. My father joined us and kissed my head, making me promise again to be careful.

Neto stood to one side, staring at the ground and shaking his head, holding his peace. Disengaging from my parents, I held out my hand to him. He stared at it for a moment, then pulled me into a hug before turning away and staring out the back window.

After excusing myself, I sped through the house to my bedroom with both Ahbhu and Gerónimo following close behind. Gerónimo watched from the doorway with a pained expression as I slapped together a backpack, pup tent, and my telescope, and positioned them on my back. Then I pushed past him and went to the kitchen where I packed some food and water.

"Isaac," he said as I made some final adjustments to my pack. "You're not going where I think you're going, are you?"

"Don't ask," I snapped. "And don't try following me either."

"But—"

"I'm serious, Gerónimo. Just back off. I'll contact you once I'm ready. Until then, give me some space. It's best for me, and it's best for you."

"But it's dangerous up there," he protested.

"What do you mean it's dangerous up there? It's dangerous down *here!* It's fricking dangerous *everywhere* in this crazy country. I'll take my chances with 'up there.' Now do me a favor and leave, please. Don't make this more difficult than it already is."

Gerónimo stared at me while I secured the backpack, looking the saddest I'd ever seen him. "Can I at least give you a hug?"

Without waiting for an answer, he hung on my shoulder and wept bitter tears, drawing a growl from Ahbhu. I felt completely numb and embarrassed at the scene he was making. After a few awkward seconds, I extricated myself and opened the side door for him.

"Goodbye, Gerónimo."

Gerónimo stared at me for a moment, wiping his eyes with the back of his hand. I pointedly held out my hand at the door. Shaking his head, he stepped out into the dark, and I slammed the door at his back, feeling against reason that he was somehow responsible for everything that had happened.

# Chapter 17

## THE HIDING PLACE

Ahbhu and I stood on the summit of El Boquerón, teetering above the crater in the soft starlight. Behind us, a distant, cool breeze carried echoes of explosions and machine gun fire from the city below. Now that I was there, my chest constricted at the prospect of taking refuge inside the crater. To steady myself, I crouched, sinking my fingers into Ahbhu's fur as I scratched his head, releasing a long sigh.

*Come with Ahbhu*, he said, pulling away and padding over to the trail leading into the tree-filled crater. *In here is best.*

"Yeah, I get that," I said jogging over to him. The dirt beneath my boots felt solid and cool, and the scent of pine and damp earth wafted through the air. "But for how long? That's the question!"

*Follow Ahbhu*, he said again, vanishing into the underbrush.

I caught up with him a few minutes later where the trees were densest, a stone's throw from El Boqueróncito.

*This spot is good*, Ahbhu declared, circling a dark stand of trees. The earthy scent was intense in there, and I brought my hand to my nose and pulled a face. *Inside the trees, nobody can see*

*Isaac.* He raised his head at the volcano's lip, now obscured by the trees.

"Just what I always wanted," I grumbled as I cleared the muddy ground and set up the tent. "To hide out inside a bloody volcano." The dank scent of the damp soil mingled unpleasantly with the muggy air.

*Think that Isaac and Ahbhu are camping,* Ahbhu quipped as he sniffed around the site for any hidden hazards.

Surveying our surroundings, memories of outings with Gerónimo filled me with sadness. "I'll do my best," I said in a low voice.

Wiping my face, I crawled into the tent with a flashlight and halfheartedly emptied my pack, spreading out my sleeping bag and arranging our provisions. "At least I'll be able to catch up on some reading." A feeling of dread crept up my spine as I spoke, and I sank onto my sleeping bag and swallowed hard.

Ahbhu poked his head into the tent and glanced around at the makeshift home I'd prepared for us. *Isaac did good,* he said.

A nocturnal screech echoed in the distance, startling us. Whether animal or human was up for debate. We held each other's gaze until silence descended once again inside the crater. It surprised me that it had unnerved Ahbhu as well; he was usually so level-headed. In any case, it didn't seem to bode well.

"Speaking of food," I said, changing the subject. "I'm starving." I grabbed a piece of bread and stuffed some cheese into it, then pointed at Ahbhu's food bowl. "Go for it."

Once we finished eating, Ahbhu licked my hand reassuringly before heading outside to explore a bit. I grabbed a book and crawled into my sleeping bag, intending to read. Within seconds, though, I transitioned to a deep, nightmarish sleep, the sounds and scents of our mysterious surroundings blending into my dreams.

The next few days crawled by, their monotony broken only by the haunting echoes of distant gunfire on those evenings when the fighting was the most intense. I grappled with a relentless boredom that only amplified the conflict beyond. Sleep became a fleeting refuge, my thoughts spiraling into a nightmarish labyrinth of uncertainty. During the day, I paced the thicket, which had become both my sanctuary and my prison.

Each afternoon, Ahbhu would slip away, his silhouette vanishing into the shadows. He would return under cover of darkness, carrying a bag of food and a couple of juice boxes from my mother, usually accompanied by a note from her updating me on the home front. Water was a problem that required Ahbhu to take another couple of short trips each day to wherever he could find a random puddle to slake his thirst since he could only carry so much between his teeth.

As expected, soldiers showed up at our home to deliver the news about Arturo and to discuss the release of his body to the family for interment. They stuck to the story that rebels had attacked the bus and expressed their deepest condolences on behalf of the government. Ever astute, Neto jumped in and asked about me, telling the soldiers he understood I had accompanied Arturo on the trip against the family's wishes and assumed I'd been a victim as well. Echoing Neto's concerns, my parents pressed the soldiers for more information. The soldiers appeared confused and conferred between themselves after which they answered that they didn't have any information about me. They could only confirm that I hadn't been found among the dead. Neto speculated that perhaps I'd been kidnapped by the rebels, forcibly recruited into their ranks. The soldiers then cut short the discussion. Three days had passed since that visit, and the soldiers hadn't returned.

Arturo's funeral was held the following weekend at the local parish church. I'd desperately wanted to attend, but Ahbhu staunchly opposed the idea, sensing a trap. He insisted on going in my place. My parents echoed Ahbhu's sentiments in the notes accompanying my provisions, cautioning me against attending due to potential government surveillance.

As anticipated, scores of people, including masked soldiers armed with machine guns, attended Arturo's funeral Mass. Positioned at the back, the soldiers claimed to be there to maintain order, but it was evident they were scrutinizing the crowd, searching for something. Ahbhu was convinced that "something" was me.

*Isaac to stay here one more week*, he announced once he was back at the tent later that evening.

"One more week? Ahbhu, I'm going out of my mind here!"

*One more week*, he insisted, *until the soldiers stop looking for Isaac. Then Ahbhu and Isaac can leave.*

"Leave for where?"

*Away from here. Someplace safe. North. Like Isaac always wanted.*

A sense of excitement infused Ahbhu's panting. He was right, I *had* always dreamt of heading north. But not under these circumstances. Not as a fugitive and not without Gerónimo. Despite everything that had happened between us, I still held on to the mad hope we might somehow make a life together up there, even more so now that he had come looking for me.

Sensing my ambivalence, Ahbhu nestled into my arms and rubbed his head against my chest. I held him close, promising I'd be sensible, and I prayed for a good outcome.

After a silent dinner, Ahbhu brushed my face with his rough tongue and sauntered outside to keep watch. Emotionally spent, I stripped to my boxers, slipped into the sleeping bag, and clicked off the flashlight, feeling a steady rumble beneath the tent for the first time since we'd sheltered in the crater.

The moment I switched off the light, Ahbhu's low growls pierced the night, signaling danger. Hastily abandoning my sleeping bag, I snatched up the hefty flashlight, ready to wield it as a defensive weapon. I moved to the tent's mesh side and peered into the murky darkness. Outside, I caught the unmistakable silhouette of Gerónimo, cloaked in black, facing off with Ahbhu, his hand held out defensively.

"What are you doing here?" I hissed, annoyed he'd followed me, but happy to see him nonetheless.

Gerónimo beckoned me outside, casting uneasy glances at Ahbhu, who remained on edge. "Hurry!"

I crawled out of the tent in my boxers, my hair sticking up like a crazy cockscomb. "I told you to stay away!"

Gunshots in the distance shattered the night. Both of us froze, waited, our eyes fixed on each other. Seconds of silence passed. Finally, Gerónimo let out a breath. "Yeah, sorry. I'll explain later. But you've got to come now!"

He edged toward me and Ahbhu bared his teeth in response. Gerónimo backed off, his eyes widening with fear.

"Easy, Ahbhu," I soothed, stroking his wiry fur. But Ahbhu continued to growl. "It's just Gerónimo."

I waved Gerónimo closer. "Give me your hand."

Hesitant, Gerónimo extended his hand, and I kissed it. "See, Ahbhu? It's okay. It's only Gerónimo."

I kissed Gerónimo's hand again, and Ahbhu looked back and forth between us. After a few tense moments, he sat back and fell silent.

Gerónimo exhaled with relief and met my eyes in the dim light. I guided him to the edge of the thicket where the trees were densest. Ahbhu remained vigilant, poised to defend.

"What's the big emergency?" I asked once we were cocooned within the dank canopy of branches. It was so humid I could practically chew the air. Ahbhu crouched at my feet never taking his eyes off Gerónimo.

"They found him." Gerónimo whispered, looking sidelong at Ahbhu.

"Found who? And who are 'they'?"

"Sisler and Yuri and them. They nabbed one of the soldiers that stopped your bus, headed home from the El Zapote Barracks. They think he might be the guy that killed Arturo."

A wave of nausea washed over me at the mention of Arturo's name, and I steadied myself against a branch. Ahbhu rose and leaned his warm body against my legs.

"They want you to try and identify him. To make sure they got the right guy."

My head snapped up at that. "What? No way." I started back for the tent and Gerónimo swiped at my arm, provoking an angry growl from Ahbhu.

Gerónimo drew back his arm. "You're the *only* one that made it out of there alive. So, *you're* the one who has to do it. Sisler said not to go back without you, even if I have to drag you."

Halting, I swung around. Gerónimo was barely visible, having backed up into the canopy of branches. "It happened too fast," I argued. "There were a lot of soldiers. I didn't get a good look at any of them."

"Please, Isaac. At least have a look. If you don't recognize him, fine. But I don't want any trouble from Sisler. He's crazy. He might kill me if I show up empty-handed."

In all the years I'd known him, Gerónimo had always played it cool. Here, though, was a new, more vulnerable Gerónimo, laying bare his emotions, his voice heavy with anguish as he pleaded with me, tugging at something deep within me. Feeling torn, I looked to Ahbhu for guidance. Sadness lingered in his eyes, reflecting the anxiety building inside me. Bending down, I kissed his fur and hugged him close, sensing his disapproval. After a moment, I peered into the darkness.

"I need to think about this, Gerónimo," I whispered. "Wait here while I get dressed."

Gerónimo nodded, his face suddenly hardening into an inscrutable mask. "Hurry."

Ahbhu followed me into the tent and stared at me skeptically as I slipped into my NASA T-shirt and blue jeans.

"What?" I said, straightening up and reaching for my trainers.

*Isaac is* not *going with Gerónimo.*

"You heard him! He'll get in trouble if I don't."

*If Isaac helps Gerónimo,* Isaac *will get in trouble, too!*

At that, Gerónimo stepped into the tent, eyeing us suspiciously. "Are you all right?" he asked after an awkward beat.

I shoved my feet into my trainers and bent down to lace them up. "I'm just getting dressed," I muttered.

"You weren't just talking to Ahbhu, were you?" he asked.

"I was talking to myself," I snapped, exchanging a look with Ahbhu. "Working out whether to go with you or not."

*Tell Gerónimo to go away!* Ahbhu growled.

"What if they got the wrong guy?" I asked Gerónimo, ignoring Ahbhu.

He shrugged. "I suppose they'd let him go."

"Are you *sure* about that?"

He looked away for a moment then back at me. "Sure, why wouldn't they? Our faces are covered, so he wouldn't be able to identify anyone."

Ahbhu let out an angry growl that suggested a more sinister outcome.

I glanced down at him and back at Gerónimo. "What if they caught the *right* guy, Gerónimo? What then?"

Gerónimo shook his head. "I don't know. They'll probably kill him."

*There it is!* Ahbhu said, furiously pacing the tent.

"Leave it with me! *Please, Ahbhu!*"

"Stop that!" Gerónimo shouted. "Stop talking to your dog! Are you insane, or what?"

149

"You know what's insane, Gerónimo?" I said, swinging on him. "Kidnapping a soldier! *That's* insane! You know what else is insane? Your getting involved in all that damned guerrilla shit. That's *completely* insane! But you know what, Gerónimo? I *am* going to go with you." Tears filled my eyes as I shouldered my backpack and pushed past him out of the tent. "And you know why? Because I love you, *that's* why. And that's *fucking* insane. Compared with all of that, talking to Ahbhu is as normal as it gets!"

Gerónimo stepped out and stared at me, at a complete loss of words. Ahbhu trotted over and stood at attention at my side, fuming. "I'm sorry, Ahbhu, but I'm going." I reached down to stroke him, but he yanked away.

Feeling on the verge of blacking out, I steadied myself with a few deep breaths and raised my chin at Gerónimo. "Come on then. What are we waiting for? Let's go, Ahbhu."

Gerónimo held up his hand at us: "Sorry, but you *can't* bring Ahbhu."

A flash of anger surged into my face. "Where I go, Ahbhu goes! That's not negotiable."

"Not this time, 'mano. If he acts up, Sisler will shoot him." Gerónimo squatted next to Ahbhu, who had started growling again, and cautiously offered his hand. "Sorry, guy, it's not safe for you."

"I'm not leaving Ahbhu, Gerónimo! No way!"

Gerónimo sprang up and snapped, "Fine, bring him! Just make sure he hangs back in the shadows." He locked eyes with Ahbhu, "You got that, buddy? Keep a low profile!" With that, he brushed past us. "But if something happens to him, remember I warned you."

# Chapter 18

## RECKONING ON THE LAKESHORE

To avoid detection, Gerónimo parked his car at the trailhead on the far side of El Boquerón, away from the city. We trekked there in the moonlight for over an hour, with Gerónimo leading and Ahbhu grumbling behind me the whole way.

When we arrived at his car, Gerónimo handed me a black bandana, his expression serious as he instructed me to tie it around my eyes. I examined the fabric, stalling, my mind racing with uncertainty.

"Sorry," he said, lifting a finger to my eyes. "It's only until we get there. Sisler doesn't want you to know where I'm taking you."

"Let's just pretend I put it on." I tossed the bandana back at him.

Gerónimo stuffed it into his pocket. "Will you at least keep your head down until we get there? You can lie on my lap."

*Sure, sure*, Ahbhu growled, his tone dripping with sarcasm. *Because that's what's best for Isaac.*

"What's he saying now?" Gerónimo asked, lifting his head at Ahbhu.

"Nothing! Let's just get this over with, please." Nervousness clawed at me as I feared things were about to spiral even more out of control than they already had.

Gerónimo gave my shoulder a squeeze, promising everything would be fine. He kissed me on the cheek before opening the car door.

Ahbhu raced ahead and jumped into the back, and I followed him in. Curling up on the front seat, I rested my head on Gerónimo's warm lap.

As we drove, Gerónimo's fingers glided through my hair, and he caressed my face. The contact of his hand sparked a pang of desire within me; it mingled with the sadness of our estrangement. Feeling the poignancy of the moment, I pivoted my head and tenderly kissed his thigh. Misinterpreting the gesture, Gerónimo lowered his hand to loosen his belt. I tapped his wrist, declining the invitation. He glanced down at me for a beat, then drew back his hand with a shrug and focused on his driving.

*Bad Gerónimo*, Ahbhu said from the back seat. His disgruntled barb was the last thing I remembered before succumbing to exhaustion.

The next sensation I became aware of was a sudden shaking as the car bumped over an unpaved road, snapping me awake. I tried to lift my head, but Gerónimo held me down, the steady pressure of his hand quieting my curiosity. He muttered an apology as the car continued its uneven journey. The vehicle soon came to an abrupt stop. Gerónimo retrieved the bandana from his pocket and placed it in my hand.

"Put it on now, please. We'll walk from here."

My heart raced as I affixed the blindfold over my eyes. Gerónimo helped me sit up then exited his side of the car. Shifting around in my seat, I whispered, "Ahbhu, where are we?"

*Lago Ilopango, Ahbhu thinks. Ahbhu sees water in front. Gerónimo's car is stopped in the trees close to the camping place.*

"Got it. Stay in the shadows, Ahbhu, just like he said. No matter what. Please!"

*No. If Ahbhu sees Isaac in danger, Ahbhu will give a sign. Isaac will run into the trees like before.*

Gerónimo pulled open the passenger side door and led me out by the crook of my arm, and we started down a stony path. Ahbhu's description of where we were helped me make sense of my surroundings, the mix of humidity and coolness, the smell of wet earth and vegetation, the sound of lapping water ahead, the cry of night birds in the trees above.

After a few meters of walking, with Gerónimo keeping tight-lipped, I caught the smell of burning lacing the breeze, the murmur of men, a distant moaning. I dug in my heels, suddenly disoriented, my breath shallowing as the blood rose in my face.

"Don't worry, I've got you," Gerónimo said in my ear, his breath warm against my cheek. "We're nearly there." But something unrecognizable in his voice told me something was wrong. Very wrong.

Desperate to abort, I pulled away from Gerónimo, but he held me fast. Twisting around, I tried to call out for Ahbhu. I was instantly silenced by a rough hand that clamped over my mouth. I felt myself dragged for several feet and deposited on the dirt. A moment later, the bandana was ripped off my face.

Blinking at my surroundings, I found myself on a fog-shrouded lakeshore illuminated by the flickering light from a torch held aloft by Gerónimo's cousin Sisler, his oily hair slicked back, dressed in white like an avenging angel. Next to him stood his sidekick Yuri and another guy I'd never seen before—a haunted-looking youth barely out of his teens holding a machete. Gerónimo stood to one side, avoiding my gaze, the bandana I'd been wearing dangling from his fingertips.

Glancing around, I felt my heart shatter as I recognized the location. It was one of Gerónimo's favorite places, the same secluded beach he'd brought me to many years before when we were just kids. I dropped to my knees and looked to him for an explanation. But he shifted his eyes away.

"Isn't this the part where you kiss my cheek?" I said angrily.

"Shut it!" Gerónimo snapped.

"Sounds like your friend has a Jesus complex," Sisler said, revealing a mouthful of crooked teeth.

"You asked me to bring him. Here he is," Gerónimo responded abruptly. "Just get to it!"

Sisler gestured to Yuri, who pulled me to my feet. I glanced around, searching for Ahbhu in the background, trying my best to look nonchalant.

"I understand you were on the bus when it was attacked," Sisler said. "When Arturo was murdered."

I looked over at Gerónimo, who was staring at the ground.

"*Yes*, I was on the bus," I answered in a low voice.

"My condolences," Sisler said. "Arturo's death was a great loss—for your family, of course, but more importantly for the movement. He was one of our key operatives."

"I doubt that," I said, feeling thrown by the revelation. "He sympathized with the left, for sure. But he was never actively involved."

Sisler chuckled and exchanged an amused glance with the others then focused back on me. "You can tell yourself whatever you want. What I want to know is how you were able to survive the attack when everyone else on that bus was slaughtered."

"What do you mean?"

"I mean what I asked. How many soldiers were there?"

I shrugged. "Maybe twenty-five or thirty, I'm not sure."

"How did you get away from that many soldiers? Do you expect us to believe they just let you go?"

A red alert flashed in my head as I realized what was going through their minds, perhaps the real reason why I'd been summoned. "What do you want, Sisler?" I asked. "You're not suggesting I cut a deal with them to get away, are you?"

"Did you?"

"Of course not! They got into some kind of argument and

started fighting with each other. They were distracted; I got away. With Ahbhu's help."

Sisler's head snapped up at the mention of Ahbhu, his eyes narrowing. "That mutt of yours was *there* with you?"

My confidence abandoned me as he uttered the question, afraid I'd confessed something I shouldn't have. Feeling suddenly lightheaded, I pushed down my apprehension. The edges of my vision were darkening, and that familiar metallic taste was seeping into my mouth. "Wherever I go, Ahbhu goes," I rasped, squinting into the darkness, wondering when Ahbhu was planning on making his appearance.

Sisler turned to Gerónimo. "Did you know this? About the dog?"

"Nope." Gerónimo's forehead was shining in the firelight, and a trickle of sweat hung off the tip of his nose. "I had no idea he was on the bus with them."

Sisler swung back on me. "Where is he now?"

"Who?" I asked, stalling.

"The dog, dumbshit! Where's the fucking dog?"

"Why?" I asked. "What does he have to do with anything?"

"If he goes everywhere you go, then why isn't he here?"

"Gerónimo said not to bring him, so I left him behind. Look, can we just get on with whatever it is you want me to do?"

Sisler stared hard at me, then he conferred with the others in a low voice. As they parleyed, Gerónimo came over to me and asked in a low voice, "How are you doing?"

I flinched at the touch of his hand. "How do you *think* I'm doing, Gerónimo? Since when was this supposed to be an interrogation?"

"They had legitimate questions. You did fine. Just relax and everything will be over soon. I promise."

"Thanks, but your promises haven't held much stock for me for a long time."

"Ouch."

"Do something, please. I'm losing my mind here."

Gerónimo stared at me for a beat; then he nodded. "Hey guys," he called out to the others, who had fallen silent. "Can we get this show on the road? It's nearly dawn."

Yuri disengaged from the group and jogged over to one of the vehicles gleaming in the trees—a late-model Chevy. The young guy with the machete took up what looked like a defensive stance, the weapon held across his chest.

Sisler scraped across the gravel to me. "One more question," he said once we were eye to eye. "Did you see who killed Arturo?"

Relieved to be back on track, I nodded. "I saw, but not clearly. It was dark, and I was scared. It was more than one, though. One soldier smacked him hard with a rifle butt, and a bunch of others kicked him when he went down, over and over until he was gone."

"How many?"

"I don't know. Five or six maybe. Like I said, I was scared. It's hard to remember."

Yuri jogged back from the car carrying what looked like a bundle of black sacks. He handed one of them to the guy with the machete, who slipped it onto his head. It fitted snugly, like a mask, with eye holes. Then Yuri put his on and handed the rest to Sisler.

"Gerónimo must have told you," Sisler said, "we managed to grab a soldier from the El Zapote Barracks. He's confessed to being there during the attack. We want you to take a look at him, since you were there. We want to know if he was one of the soldiers that attacked Arturo." He shoved a mask at Gerónimo.

"Bring him here!" Sisler ordered, sliding on the mask.

Yuri sprinted back to the car. The young guy handed the machete to Sisler and ran to help Yuri.

"Wait, cousin!" Gerónimo said to Sisler. "Doesn't Isaac get a mask?"

Ignoring the question, Sisler turned to watch Yuri and the

young guy returning, dragging a man between the two of them, his bare feet leaving shallow ruts in the damp earth. He was blindfolded and wearing a tattered, bloodied pair of cotton briefs and was barely struggling.

Gerónimo exchanged a worried glance with me then slid the mask over his head. He adjusted the eye holes as Yuri and the other guy deposited the half-naked man on the ground in front of me. From the wounds he bore, I could see he'd been mercilessly worked over. My knees nearly gave way at the sight of him, groaning in the dark. Feeling on the verge of vomiting, I turned away and gulped down draught after draught of the thick morning air, fighting against collapse.

"Take a good look at this guy when we remove his blindfold," Sisler said, shoving the machete at me. Surprised by the gesture, I held up my hands and backed away, tripping over some stones.

"Take it!" he ordered.

"Why?" I asked, feeling the sheer terror rising in me to a fever pitch.

"If he's one of the soldiers that killed Arturo, we expect you to return the favor. For Arturo, for the movement."

"I'm not killing anyone," I stammered.

Gerónimo jumped forward and grabbed the machete from Sisler. He held it out to me. "Just take it, Isaac!" he yelled.

In that moment, a roar echoed from behind us, and Ahbhu came bounding out of the trees. He flew at Gerónimo, knocking him backward, and the machete clattered away. Gerónimo held his arms in front of his face as Ahbhu savaged him, digging his fangs into him, ripping flesh, drawing blood.

"Ahbhu, no!" I screamed, launching toward them, trying to pull him off Gerónimo.

*Run, Isaac*, Ahbhu roared as he continued to attack Gerónimo.

Recovering from the initial shock, Sisler and his crew descended on Ahbhu. Between them, after a major struggle, they were able to yank him off Gerónimo and restrain him, smacking him repeatedly with the butt of the machete. Then they dragged him to a nearby tree and tied him by the neck to the trunk with a thick rope.

I screamed out for Ahbhu, and ran to where they'd tied him, but Sisler collared me and dragged me back to the soldier. He shoved the machete into my hand and ripped the blindfold off the soldier.

The moment our eyes met, the man grimaced, his gold teeth glinting in the moonlight, and I recognized him as the soldier that had struck the first blow. I felt my hand tighten on the butt of the machete. Coming back to himself, Ahbhu leapt to his feet and barked, struggling in vain to break free of the rope, crying out for me to drop the machete and run.

Hot tears filled my eyes as I cast about me in the waning torchlight, the sky silvering at the edge of the horizon above the steaming lake: Gerónimo was sobbing in the dirt, bleeding profusely, his arms ripped to shreds; Sisler and the others were screaming at me, urging me to kill the soldier, who had squeezed his eyes shut and lowered his head, ready for the blow.

The last thing I remember was the machete slipping from my grasp as an abrupt, dizzying rush overtook me. My muscles tensed, and a familiar tingling sensation spread through my limbs. Then, as if a veil had been drawn over my consciousness, everything went black.


My awareness gradually returned, a dim light piercing through the shadows that had enveloped my senses. The cold, hard ground beneath me became increasingly tangible, and the air carried a strange coppery scent that clung to my clothes. I pried open my eyes, disoriented about my location, then clamped them shut against the harsh morning sunlight streaming in and waited for my senses to adjust. As the memories of the night seeped back into my consciousness, I opened my eyes again, allowing my bleary vision to adapt to the light reflecting off the lake.

With the greatest of effort, I pushed myself up from the ground, feeling a dull ache in every joint of my body. Suddenly aware of a sticky wetness on my hands, I recoiled against the sensation, scrambling backward in panic as I looked down at myself. Every inch of me—my arms, clothes, even my shoes—was coated in blood. I glanced around and saw I was alone on the lakeshore. The blood-soaked machete lay in a tuft of grass off to my left, and a trail of gore led from where I'd been sprawled into the trees.

The implication of what I was seeing struck like a thunderbolt, and I fought against a sickening vertigo that threatened another seizure. Forcing myself to close my eyes, I drew in a series of calming breaths to regain control. After a few minutes, I opened my eyes again, and, channeling a stoic detachment worthy of a Vulcan, peered into the woods before moving forward to investigate.

Following the erratic trail into the trees, my breath caught as I stumbled upon the grisly aftermath. The nude body of the soldier lay sprawled on the forest floor, lifeless, hacked to death, his head severed from his body and deliberately parked face-up against a nearby tree trunk, revealing a grimacing mouth, propped open like a treasure chest, displaying its horde of gold teeth. The sharp scent of blood hung thick in the air. I fell backward against a tree and suppressed a scream, tearing my eyes away from the gruesome sight.

My thoughts immediately went to Ahbhu, and a dry crackling filled my head. Why had he left me alone? How could he have allowed this to happen? He'd promised to intervene at any sign of danger! To create a distraction, he'd said. Then I recalled Ahbhu's attack on Gerónimo, how he'd been set on by Sisler and the others moments before I lost consciousness.

I spun around, shouting for Ahbhu, fearing the worst. My screams echoed through the dense trees, unanswered except for the rustling leaves and the distant lapping of water on the shoreline. Sinking to the ground, I sobbed into my hands, vague memories playing at the edge of my mind—Sisler and Yuri dragging Ahbhu into the woods, tying him to a tree. The recollection jolted me out of my grief. I ran back to the lakeshore to regain my bearings, then moved purposefully back into the woods.

A few feet into the trees, I found Ahbhu's inert body at the foot of a tall pine, still tied to the trunk, his fur matted with blood. "Ahbhu!" I screamed, throwing myself down next to him. I scooped him into my arms, certain he was gone. But he was still breathing, only just. My heart leapt into my throat as I kissed him repeatedly, whispering his name and begging him not to leave me. A low groan escaped his mouth, and his eyes fluttered open. "Yes, Ahbhu, it's me, Isaac. Stay with me. You can do it!"

His neck strained against the thick rope. Desperate to untie him, I burned my fingers on the fibers, but the knot was vice-tight, and the rope too thick to dislodge. As I worked at freeing him, Ahbhu's mouth dropped open and his tongue lolled out. *The machete, Isaac. . .* he panted weakly, *bring the machete.*

Relief flooded through me at the sound of his voice, and tears spilled onto my burning cheeks, cutting black streaks through the caked blood on my face. I ran back to the lakeshore, located the machete, and returned to Ahbhu's side. I hacked off the rope from the tree and dislodged it from Ahbhu's neck in a matter of minutes.

Once free of the rope, he heaved a few dry coughs and begged for water. Cradling him in my arms, I staggered to the lake, lowered him onto the sand, and scooped water into his mouth from cupped hands until he signaled he'd had enough. I passed my hand over his fur, and he blinked moist eyes full of pain.

*Isaac, wash now*, he said after a moment.

Looking down at myself, horror replaced my relief that Ahbhu was alive, seeing my clothes still covered in gore. "Ahbhu, what happened?" I asked. "Did I—"

*Isaac, wash now!* Ahbhu repeated, lifting his snout at the lake. *Then Isaac and Ahbhu go away fast.*

"Wait, Ahbhu! Did I kill that soldier? Yes, or no?"

*No,* Ahbhu said, his voice growing weak. *Wash now . . . hurry.*

# Chapter 19

## CASHTŌKA

We threaded around the perimeter of the lake in the direction of the main road to San Salvador, keeping close to the trees for cover. A man in his boxer shorts carrying a dog slung over his shoulders along the lakeshore was too conspicuous to chance a sighting. It was no easy task winding our way in and around the trees, mindful not to leave footprints, all the while contending with insects incessantly dive-bombing us, lured by the scent of blood.

For a sedentary Poindexter in his early twenties, I was relatively fit thanks to my hikes with Ahbhu, who put me through my paces. But with each step I took along that shoreline, Ahbhu became heavier and heavier. Around a half hour after we started our walk, my legs gave out. Lowering him to the ground, I dropped next to him and examined his wounds. His eyes were closed, but he was still breathing, albeit shallowly. At least he was alive. That was something.

I kissed Ahbhu and gently stroked his fur, careful to avoid touching areas of obvious injury. I'd done my best to clean his wounds with lake water once I'd finished scrubbing the blood off myself. But I was going to have to tend to them properly as soon as we reached someplace safe, plus I feared he might have a broken rib or two.

The only thing keeping me from surrendering to despair was the fact that Ahbhu was still alive. Nothing else mattered: not Gerónimo's betrayal, not my stupidity in trusting him, not the reality of being on the run again. Only Ahbhu mattered. I kissed him, and his eyes fluttered open, unfocused.

"How are you holding up, buddy?" I asked him. These were the first words I'd spoken to him since we started our journey.

He slowly shifted his head and nuzzled my hand, letting out a low groan. I scooted closer and he rested his head on my leg and closed his eyes again. In the distance I caught the wail of sirens, probably headed in the direction we'd left. Ahbhu's ear pricked up and he raised his head.

"We've got a good start," I said. "But we need to get someplace safe soon, or they're going to find us."

Ahbhu rose to his feet and tested his legs. He limped when he walked, one of his back legs appearing slightly out of joint. He glanced around at the leg and licked it.

"Is it broken?" I asked.

*Don't know. Hurts, but Ahbhu can walk. Easier for Isaac.*

I stood and peered in the direction we'd come from and ran my hands through my damp hair. I estimated we'd traveled a couple of miles and had a lot more to go to reach safety. But the humidity was killing me, and the skies were clouding over, threatening rain.

"We'd better go," I said, feeling a second wind. "If it hurts too much, tell me, and I'll carry you again."

Ahbhu nodded and sniffed the air. He cocked his head and limped forward and sniffed again.

"What is it?" I asked.

*Ahbhu smells food*, he said, his mouth watering a bit. He lifted his head in the direction we'd been heading. *Coming from over there.*

I sniffed the air, trying to catch the scent. "I don't smell anything. Can you tell how far?"

*Ahbhu thinks far. Many steps.*

"Let's head for that, then," I said. "Lead the way."

As we pressed on, the sirens grew closer, probably traveling the same road we'd traveled with Gerónimo, on their way to the clearing. Someone had obviously alerted them, and I had a good idea who that someone may have been. A few minutes later, the sirens ceased. I imagined military vehicles arriving at the clearing, soldiers spreading out to search for their brother in arms, stumbling on his lifeless body. That's when they'd come looking for me.

Ahbhu picked up his pace, despite his limp, with me keeping up as best as I could, the sky above us growing increasingly dark. A few minutes later, we encountered a narrow dirt path leading into the trees.

*This way,* Ahbhu panted, pointing his nose up the path. He staggered forward, and I followed.

Just then a deafening crack of thunder echoed around us, and the heavens opened up, unleashing a torrential downpour. The rain descended in sheets, transforming the forest floor into a mire of mud. Undeterred by the weather, we pressed onward up the path.

A short time later, the trail widened to reveal a small settlement—two or three adobe buildings, painted in muted pastels. One stood out as the main house with a thin trail of smoke rising from its low-slung chimney, carrying the tantalizing aroma of cooking meat.

Exhausted and nearing collapse, I splashed past Ahbhu and pounded on the vividly painted wooden front door. It swung open abruptly, and I found myself facing the conversation end of a shotgun wielded by a slight, sharp-eyed woman in her late fifties or sixties with crepe-like skin the color of a dry carob pod. Standing barely five feet tall and dressed in a floral-patterned skirt and pink blouse, she had a thick braid of gray hair slung forward over her shoulder.

"What is it?" she barked, squinting at me with eyes narrowed to slits. Stunned into silence, I dropped back a step and held up my hands. She advanced on her bare feet, gesturing with the barrel of the gun. "Well then? Speak!"

Ahbhu, ever calculating, staggered forward and rested against my leg. He cast puppy dog eyes at the woman. Her face softened momentarily, but she quickly raised the shotgun again.

Over her shoulder, I spotted a photo of Monsignor Romero hanging on a cord on her living room wall and immediately knew where her loyalties lay.

"I'm so sorry to disturb you, Señora. We need help. My dog and I." I tenderly lifted Ahbhu to show her. "Please! His name's Ahbhu. He's injured. We're both hungry!"

"You're running!" she accused, dismissing my plea. "What are you running from?"

"Soldiers, Señora," I stammered, fear catching in my throat. "We're running from soldiers!"

She cocked her gun and brought it to her eye. "What are you doing bringing trouble to my doorstep? And what makes you think I'd help someone who's running from soldiers, eh?"

"Please, Señora! I only followed Ahbhu, who was drawn by the smell of food. If you can't help us, we'll go away. But we don't have much time. They'll be here soon."

The woman scrutinized me, sizing up the situation; then she glanced at Ahbhu. After an agonizing pause, she lowered the shotgun and grumbled to herself, "Soldiers, a half-naked man, and a wounded dog. I must be out of my mind."

Stepping aside, she nodded at her front room. "Wait in there." She grabbed a rake from behind the door, pulled on a plastic mac, slipped into leather sandals, and stepped outside to rake the path leading to her door.

I surveyed the room, absorbing every detail I could in her

absence. The furniture exuded a rustic charm, featuring a well-maintained stuffed sofa and family photos on a side table. A black-and-white photograph captured the woman in her youth, standing beside a man I presumed to be her husband. Another resembled a family portrait, showcasing the woman, her husband, and a young girl. There were a few more photographs of the same young girl, now a woman in her twenties, sporting a neck-length bob that imparted a boyish look. My gaze shifted back to the door, and I couldn't resist picking up the photo. The young woman had inherited her mother's intense eyes, only hers were green, possessing a penetrating, almost mesmerizing gaze.

"Put that down!" the woman's stern voice cut as she entered the room.

I sheepishly complied, placing the photo back on the side table, and muttered an apology. The woman's eyes bore into me, her gaze filled with a mix of anger and fear. She swiftly stowed away the rake and her mac; then, without a word she marched past us toward the photograph of Monsignor Romero. In one swift motion, she flipped the photo around, revealing a graphic of the Salvadoran coat of arms—a symbol suggesting loyalty to the current government.

Taken aback by the unexpected gesture, I felt a knot tighten in my stomach, fearing I'd read her wrong.

*The small woman is smart*, Ahbhu reassured, indicating her shrewdness.

The woman whirled around, her gaze piercing through me like a dagger. "What did he say?" she asked sharply.

The realization she'd perceived that Ahbhu had spoken was like a slug to the chest. "What do you mean?" I stuttered.

"Don't play games with me," she said, her eyes flashing fiercely. "I'm risking everything by sheltering you here. Tell me what your dog said, or I swear I'll throw you out this instant."

Coming to my aid, Ahbhu nudged my leg and growled softly, urging me to comply. "He said you were a shrewd lady—

just now when you turned around the picture of the Monsignor. That's all. It was a compliment. But . . . how did you know he'd said something?"

"It's a lost practice," she said. "Communication between humans and animals. It's right there in the first pages of the Bible."

"Okay," I said, nervously recalling the story of the talking serpent as a metaphor for the devil, "but if it's a *lost* practice—"

"It's not lost for everyone. My mother was a *shamana*, a practitioner of ancient rituals, like her mothers before her. She spoke with animals all the time. She passed down some of her knowledge to me."

I remembered hearing about shamanas from my mother, something having to do with Mayan religious practices. Some isolated tribes had survived into modern times in the hills near the border with Honduras and Guatemala.

"I don't understand," I said, my mind reeling with the implications of what she was telling me. "How am *I* able to communicate with Ahbhu? Nobody else in my family can."

"I don't have all the answers!" she snapped, irritated by my questions. "But perhaps it has more to do with Ahbhu choosing you than anything else. That said, who knows what secrets lie hidden in your own lineage."

Before I could respond, Ahbhu growled, his ear pricking up. He quickly hobbled to the door, his senses on high alert. *Soldiers coming*, he confirmed. *On feet. Moving slow on mud.*

I relayed the information to the woman, who instructed us to follow her into the kitchen. She shoved aside a wooden crate full of dry corn, next to a clay oven. Beneath the crate lay an ancient-looking handwoven rug. The woman threw back the rug, revealing a wooden trap door. Grabbing an iron rod, she pried it open.

"Hide in there!" she ordered, pointing at the opening with the rod. "Hurry!"

Ahbhu and I moved forward, discovering narrow concrete steps leading into a dark hole. Hesitating, I asked, "Is there a light in there at least?"

"No light!" she said. "Get yourselves settled and, when you're ready, I'll shut you in until it's safe."

*Follow Ahbhu,* Ahbhu said as he navigated the steps and disappeared below the ground.

Shrugging at the lady, I thanked her, then, drawing a breath, I descended into a dank cellar, more of a crawl space than a proper cellar. Locating a wooden bench against one wall, I huddled there with Ahbhu. Right before she slammed the trap door shut, the woman handed down a basket of tortillas and a leg of chicken, along with a couple of blankets. Then everything went dark. So dark I couldn't make out my own hand in front of my face. A moment later, I heard the woman drag the crate back over the trap door.

Fearing I'd been tricked into allowing myself to be buried alive, like some character in an Edgar Allan Poe story, I drew Ahbhu close and kissed him, more to comfort myself than anything. His silence spoke volumes. Unflappable even in the direst of circumstances, the fact he was scared, too, caused a sheet of cold perspiration to break out over my entire body.

Wrapped in the blanket, I listened intently in the tomb-like chamber. But it was as silent as it was dark, save for my own labored breathing and Ahbhu's panting. Closing my eyes, I was reluctant to fall asleep, fearing I might never wake up again. Yet keeping my eyes open in total darkness proved to be a challenging task. I found myself jerking awake a few times until, despite my efforts, I dozed off.

I stirred from my uneasy slumber as the muffled echoes of shouts and animated conversation filtered down into the oppressive darkness of the cellar. I immediately reached for Ahbhu to combat the disorienting panic. His comforting presence and the reassuring touch of his tongue helped me to center myself. Pressing a kiss to his fur, I silently thanked him for his friendship, my only remaining tether to sanity. At his urging, I focused on my breath, inhaling and exhaling, counting each deliberate cycle—ten times in, ten times out.

Above, the commotion persisted with shuffling and stamping feet, creating a discordant symphony. The woman's voice, sharp and shrill, cut through the clamor. "You've had your look," she screamed, "now leave an old woman be!" Her words, a defiant plea, pierced the tumult, only to be swallowed by an abrupt silence.

"What do you think is happening?" I whispered to Ahbhu, resisting the desperate urge to pound on the trap door for the woman to release us.

*The small woman is thinking*, Ahbhu said after a considered pause. *What to do with Isaac, what to do with Ahbhu.*

"She wouldn't just leave us in here, right?"

Before he could respond, the earth beneath us convulsed and trembled, prompting the disconcerting realization that Lago Ilopango occupies the crater of an active volcano.

*Bad shake*, Ahbhu muttered in fear, cowering against me.

Instinctively, I lowered my head against him in a futile defense against a potential cave-in, a reflex ingrained in me from my earliest days. Then, just as suddenly as it had hit, the rumbling ceased, and the two of us let out an audible sigh of relief.

"Freaking hell!" I said. "That's it! I need to get out of here!"

I stood and clenched my fist, ready to hammer on the trap door, when it flew open, and the woman's voice floated down to us: "Come out of there, boy!"

Bolting out of the cellar, I gulped down deep draughts of air in the woman's kitchen, nearly collapsing from the tension. My eyes landed on a couple of iron pots bubbling on her stove. Ahbhu sped past me into the front room where we found the woman standing over a table she'd laid out with a meat stew, beans, and tortillas, which made my mouth water. A few candles dotted the room, their flickering light the only source of illumination in the house now that the sun had set.

"Come on then!" she said, shoving a pair of jeans and a white cotton shirt at me. "Get yourself decent, then sit and eat. There's something there for your dog." She gestured at a bowl by the front door.

Grateful to this strange woman, I accepted the clothes, which looked a couple of sizes too big for me. Slipping into them, I stuttered my thanks.

"Never mind that," she said, sitting at the table and ladling some beans onto her plate. "Eat before it gets cold."

I glanced at Ahbhu, who was already wolfing down his dinner, then took my place next to the woman and dug in.

Whether it was down to the woman's culinary prowess or my intense hunger, I'd never tasted anything as delicious as that meal in my entire life. I helped myself to a second serving after securing a curt nod of permission from the woman.

As I washed down the last of the meal with some water, the woman pushed back her chair and fixed me with an intense look. "Your name is Isaac, is it?" she said, lacing her thin arms across her bony chest.

Taken aback by the suddenness of her question, I set down my glass and nodded. Ever alert, Ahbhu trotted over and sat next to me, his hind legs tense, ready to spring. I stroked his head to steady him. "How do you know that?" I asked.

"Those soldiers," the woman said. "They were looking for someone named Isaac. They described you exactly. They claim you killed a soldier. Is that true?"

Ahbhu bared his teeth and growled at the woman. "Down, boy," I said. "She's just asking a question." I looked up at the woman, who was waiting for my response, undaunted by Ahbhu's behavior. "Sorry about that; he's just being protective. You *are* only asking a question, right?"

"I have no love for soldiers," she said. "Soldiers once attacked my daughter Suchipila." She gestured absently at the photo of the young woman on the side table. "But make no mistake, I have no love for murderers either."

"I'm sorry," I said, staring at the photograph, which shimmered in the candlelight. "About your daughter—Suchipila. Is she all right?"

"We're talking about *you* right now, young man," she said cuttingly.

*Tell the small woman Isaac didn't kill the soldier!* Ahbhu urged. *Ahbhu saw everything. Tell her.*

The woman's head jerked at Ahbhu, clearly aware he was speaking. "Tell me what he's saying," she ordered.

I hesitated, grappling with the decision whether to disclose my condition and the events that led to my current predicament. Glancing at Ahbhu, who was urging me on, I made up my mind to tell her everything.

"I . . . I suffer from seizures and blackouts," I began, my voice wavering. "Some people I know, FMLN, I think . . . they captured a soldier who killed my brother. They ordered *me* to kill him in revenge, but I didn't want to. I told them so! Then . . . then I blacked out. Ahbhu was there. He saw everything."

My gaze shifted to the woman, who watched me intently, waiting for me to continue.

"Ahbhu says I didn't do it," I continued, my words gaining momentum. "The *other* guys did. Then they left me there to take the blame. I found the soldier when I came to and escaped with Ahbhu. That's what he wanted me to tell you."

The woman fell silent, absorbing what I'd just related. After a moment, she focused on Ahbhu. "How did you get injured?"

I opened my mouth to answer. The woman's palm immediately shot up to silence me. "Let him speak for himself."

Compelled by a force beyond his control, Ahbhu rose and limped over to the woman, and I marveled as he accepted a

171

scrap of chicken from her outstretched hand and an affectionate scratch on his muzzle. Then he blinked moist eyes at her and spoke: *Ahbhu tried to help Isaac. But bad men stopped Ahbhu; they tied Ahbhu to a tree, hit Ahbhu with fists and feet. Gerónimo stopped them.* Clearly disturbed by the harrowing memories, Ahbhu crouched to the floor and let out a whimper.

The woman tenderly kissed his head and looked at me. Something in her expression had changed. "Who is this Gerónimo?" she asked.

"You understood Ahbhu?" I felt suddenly disoriented, as if I'd crossed into an alternate reality.

"I'll explain later," she said. "But first, who is this Gerónimo person that saved your dog?"

Conscious that I had no choice but to trust this woman who'd taken us in and fed us at great risk to herself, I opened up as I'd never opened up to anyone before: "Gerónimo was my friend." My voice caught as I uttered the painful words. Was my friend. Past tense. "My best friend ever since we were kids. My only friend. We loved each other. Deeply. But he tricked me. He lured me to where those men were holding the soldier."

"But he saved your dog," she countered. "That says something, doesn't it? Are you sure he intended for you to take the blame? Maybe it was the others."

*Gerónimo stopped them,* Ahbhu repeated.

I shrugged, considering what they were suggesting. Maybe Gerónimo wasn't the villain I was making him out to be. I wanted to believe it. More than anything.

"In any case," the woman said, "now that we have that out of the way, I'm Cashtōka Ramirez. Let's tend to your dog's injuries before they get infected. Then we can chat some more."

# Chapter 20

## SUCHIPILA

Ahbhu and I spent the next few days recuperating at Cashtōka's home. Her hospitality, a seamless blend of warmth and tenacity, made the healing process more bearable. She even offered us the use of her daughter Suchipila's room—she was away in San Salvador working as a caregiver.

We learned that Cashtōka's roots traced back to Nahuizalco, a colonial market town nestled in the west highlands of the country, where a remnant of the pre-Hispanic Nahuatl-speaking Mayan people made their diminishing home. At the tender age of thirteen, she found herself entangled in the allure of Gino Ramirez, a charming merchant from Ilopango, eight years her senior. Gino, a charismatic figure who frequented the town, selling building materials to the municipality, was captivated by her early physical maturity and natural flirtatiousness.

Their clandestine courtship unfolded in the town's only hair salon, where Cashtōka styled both men's and women's hair under the watchful gaze of her domineering mother. Yearning to escape the constraints of her upbringing, she devised a plan with Gino through an intermediary to elope. A week later, under the cover of darkness, Gino returned and whisked her away. They eventually invested their pooled savings in this secluded plot of land, cultivating a modest farm where corn swayed in the breeze, and chickens clucked contentedly.

Suchipila entered the world seven years into their union, and tragedy struck five years after that. In a devastating turn of events, Gino lost his life in a gas explosion in town, leaving Cashtōka widowed at twenty-five. Bereft of her partner, she faced the daunting task of raising a daughter and managing the farm they had established. These days, Suchipila visited the homestead on weekends to check in on her mother and gather fresh eggs laid by the hens, destined for sale in the community where she worked.

Eagerly anticipating her daughter's arrival, Cashtōka commenced preparations early on my first Saturday at the homestead, enlisting my assistance as her sous chef. By the afternoon, with Cashtōka engrossed in adding the final touches to Suchipila's cherished turkey stew, the tantalizing aroma permeated the air. It was then that a new presence quietly materialized in the kitchen.

Ahbhu, who had been resting in the corner next to the oven, perked up at the sudden appearance of an intriguing woman in blue jeans and a man's work shirt standing in the doorway—presumably Suchipila, her salt and pepper hair cropped close to her head.

Setting down the ladle, I greeted her with a tentative smile, taken aback by the disparity between the woman before me and the mental image I had conjured. I recognized the same intense gaze from the living room photographs, but the passage of two decades was evident in her weathered appearance.

"Who is this, Mamá?"

"There you are, hija!" Cashtōka embraced her daughter, who continued to eye me with suspicion. Ahbhu approached Suchipila and sniffed at her, momentarily diverting her attention.

"This is Ahbhu, hija." Cashtōka squatted next to Ahbhu and scratched his muzzle, drawing a gentle groan of pleasure and setting his tail to wagging. "Ahbhu, this is my dear daughter Suchi."

Unimpressed, Suchipila pointed at me. "I meant *him*, Mamá."

"Oh, him . . ." Cashtōka, seemingly unfazed, removed her apron and gestured at me. "This is Isaac Perez, Ahbhu's human. Isaac, this is my daughter Suchipila."

Wiping my hands on my apron, I stepped forward and invited a handshake. "Hi?"

"What's he doing here, Mamá?" Suchipila asked, ignoring my outstretched hand.

"Let's go into the front room for coffee and a chat, shall we?" Cashtōka guided us to the dining table, then she retreated to the kitchen to brew some coffee while Suchipila continued to stare at me. Ahbhu positioned himself next to Suchipila, who absently stroked his head while keeping me in her sights.

"Your mother rescued me and Ahbhu from some soldiers a few days ago," I explained, hoping for some empathy from this woman who had her own reasons to distrust soldiers. "We were on the run, and she took us in. Ahbhu was injured, and your mother helped patch him up. They've grown close, your mother and Ahbhu. I've been helping around the house and with the chickens—"

"What did you do?" Suchipila's question held a weight of accusation.

"What do you mean?"

"Why were you being pursued by soldiers? You must have done something."

"I didn't do anything. I was framed. It's a long story."

"I have all the time in the world," she said, crossing her arms. "And it had better be good, or I'll turn you in myself. My mother can't be running any risks. Not at her age."

"Leave the boy alone, Suchi," Cashtōka intervened, carrying

175

in a tray with hot coffee and a few pieces of *semita*. "He's been nothing but an angel, and his dog is a delight. I've been happy for the company."

"Mamá! Company is one thing. But you're probably harboring a fugitive as far as the government is concerned, regardless of what he's done or hasn't done! I need to understand exactly what's going on here."

We spent the next couple of hours over dinner recounting to Suchipila everything that had happened in the lead-up to my rescue by Cashtōka. As I laid it all out, Suchipila's face transformed from suspicion to a mosaic of emotions. Her furrowed brow softened as the layers of my narrative unfolded. When I detailed the framed accusations and my perilous escape, her eyes widened, mirroring the incredulity etched across her features.

After a lengthy silence, Suchipila responded. "I also had an incident with some soldiers." Her voice was calm, but there was a hint of tension in her demeanor. "In the Barrio de San Jacinto, near the El Zapote Barracks, many years ago. I was walking alone on my way to visit my friend Amparo, the woman I work for. Back then, I didn't dress the way I do now." She looked down at herself pensively. "I was pretty in those days."

"Too pretty for her own good," Cahstōka muttered in the background.

Suchi cast a dark expression at her mother then continued, "A van pulled up next to me as I started down the hill from the presidential palace toward my friend's *colonia*. Some soldiers, three of them, all masked, hustled me inside and held me at gunpoint while they drove to a remote *barranco* not far from the city."

A chill ran through me as she spoke, shot through with a hot flash of anger. "Did they . . .?"

Suchi shook her head. "I fought those *hijueputas* with everything I had. I kicked and screamed and thrashed despite their threats to kill me. But I refused to give in, not even at the cost of my life. In the end, all they managed was to tear my dress and grope me a bit before deciding I wasn't worth the fight. They took turns delivering a few kicks while I lay defenseless and spat on me; then they abandoned me there in the dark." She raised shining eyes at me that made my heart ache. "I can't fathom why they didn't kill me."

Cahstōka gently stroked her daughter's back and kissed her. "Mi pobre hija," she sighed. "God protected you that day."

Suchi scoffed and drew away from her mother's hand. "God had nothing to do with it, Mamá. I was lucky, that's all. I don't know why, but I was. Anyway, ever since that day, I've dressed like this." Her hand went up to her hair. "Aside from a rude comment or two, nobody pays attention to me anymore, not in that way. I've made myself invisible." Suchi wiped her eyes and sat up straight, centering herself.

"That's horrible." I said, "I'm so sorry."

"It's a long time ago," she said, her voice steadying. She poured herself a glass of water and took a sip. "But just now as you were speaking, it all came flooding back. Anyway, this is supposed to be about you, not me. I want to know more about Isaac Perez. Who are you, where do you come from?"

With some hesitation, I cautiously unpacked my family history, the basics really, where I was from, who my parents were. I was careful not to reveal too much as I still wasn't sure what she wanted with the information. I guardedly confided about the differences of opinion in my household between my father and brothers, especially with Arturo. I nearly broke down at the mention of his name and had to take a breather. Once I'd steadied myself, I elaborated on my medical condition and how Ahbhu had come into my life just when I needed him most. I called Ahbhu over and hugged him. "He's the best thing that ever happened to me."

The room echoed with silence as the weight of my words

settled. Suchipila, perched on the edge of her seat, seemed suspended in thought. Ahbhu nudged closer to her, offering comfort in the midst of the heavy atmosphere.

As I prepared to broach the subject of Gerónimo, I felt unsure as to how much I could share about our relationship. I exchanged a glance with Ahbhu to seek his guidance. Licking my hand, he assured me I could be transparent with these women. So, steeling myself, I related to them my whole history with Gerónimo from our early days up through the present.

As I spoke, I noticed a subtle shift in Suchipila's demeanor. Her eyes, once guarded, now glistened with empathy. The lines etched on her face softened, revealing a depth of understanding that transcended the spoken words. Encouraged by her receptiveness, I confessed that despite everything that had happened, despite Gerónimo's unavailability, I still loved him and despaired I'd never be able to move on as long as he kept popping in and out of my life.

When my tale reached its conclusion, and the candles flickered in the waning light, Suchipila extended a calloused hand across the table. Her touch, though firm, carried a warmth that spoke volumes. It was a moment of connection, an unspoken acknowledgment that transcended the complexities of our individual stories.

"Thank you, Isaac," she said, her voice carrying a mixture of compassion and understanding. "For baring your soul. I didn't expect to find *common ground* in such a tumultuous story."

"There's no need to go there, hija; it's not relevant," Cashtōka interrupted, casting a sharp look at her daughter. "When we love, we make ourselves vulnerable. It's a law of nature. None of us is immune, period. Isaac has told us *his* story; let's leave it at that."

Suchi shifted her gaze at her mother and fixed her with her eyes. "But I think it *is* relevant, Mamá."

Cashtōka threw up her thin hands in exasperation. "Suit yourself, hija." She rose from the table, picked up a few dishes, and exited the room. "You always do."

Confused by Cashtōka's heated departure, I looked questioningly at Suchi. "I didn't say anything wrong, did I?"

"Not at all." Suchi frowned at the kitchen. "It's my mother. There are things she and I don't see eye to eye on." She turned back to me, her gaze softening in the fading candlelight. "You might say our relationship is still a work in progress."

I looked toward the kitchen and nodded slowly, still not fully grasping the situation. "Okay, but . . . what does that have to do with me exactly?"

Suchipila leaned back, her hands clasped, her eyes shining with pent-up emotion. "I've been living a delicate dance myself, Isaac. I was about to share that with you, to let you know you're not alone in this. My mother didn't think I should." Her voice, steady until now, carried a weight of vulnerability as she unraveled her own story.

"I'm also in love with someone who isn't fully available to me. Amparo, my friend in San Salvador. We met when we were at university. It was beautiful what we had back then." A wistful look clouded Suchi's expression. Her eyes, now glossed over with bittersweet memories, revealed a fragility that stirred a pang within me.

After a long pause, she refocused. "She's married now, my Amparo. Her parents arranged it. Her husband, Luis, drives trucks. He's usually on the road, transporting goods to and from Nicaragua during the week. Amparo arranged for me to work in their home, caring for their special-needs daughter Dinfita. When Luis is away, Amparo and I share our lives like any couple, more or less, careful not to be seen by anyone. But whenever Luis comes home, usually on the weekends, I clear out. I come here, visit my mother, waiting to go back to Amparo. And to Dinfita, of course." Suchipila flashed a sad smile and squeezed my hand. "We're lucky that way, I suppose. It could be worse."

I nodded, absorbing her words. The room had become a

crucible of shared experiences, where our individual narratives melded and transformed in the heat of the telling, as if the very air crackled with the energy of our revelations, forging a bond that transcended the boundaries of our stories. But while I felt happy for this woman who had been able to sort out a situation that allowed her to share her life with her lover, precarious and dangerous as it was, I didn't find much comfort for myself.

As if reading my thoughts, Suchi lowered her voice and said, "The truth is, Isaac, El Salvador isn't a place for people like us. It never has been and probably never will be. I have friends who've left for America, Canada, even Europe, where it's possible to live openly, fully ourselves, where love is love regardless."

"I've been thinking about that, believe me. My mother has a cousin in Los Angeles. But I haven't wanted to leave without Gerónimo." Feeling a sudden drop in my spirits, I lowered my gaze to the table and bit my lower lip. Suchi grabbed my hand and held it firm.

"You should consider fleeing, Isaac. You and your dog. The sooner the better. You're wanted by both sides for something you didn't do. If they catch you, I don't even want to think what they'll do to you. If Gerónimo is meant to be in your life, he'll follow."

"But how? And what about my parents, my family? I can't run away without consulting them, without at least saying goodbye."

She glanced over her shoulder toward the kitchen then leaned in and whispered, "Some people I know, they've been working at organizing a network of safehouses between here and the United States—for people who can't get visas. People like us."

I leaned forward, my curiosity piqued. "Really? How does that work exactly? I mean, I've heard about safehouses, but organizing a network seems . . . intricate."

Suchipila nodded. "It's a delicate system," she explained, her hands drawing invisible lines in the air. "A few of us who share similar experiences, who've faced persecution or danger, came together a while back to create it. It's not perfect, but it does the job thanks to the cooperation of a lot of good people."

Leaning back, I processed what she was saying. "But how does it operate day-to-day? I mean, how do people get from one safehouse to another?"

Suchipila considered her words, her eyes scanning the room as if gauging the safety of our conversation. "We've developed discreet communication channels, codes." She mimicked typing on an invisible keyboard, her gestures precise. "And, like I said, trusted contacts." She formed a circle with her hands. "When someone needs to move, they reach out to the network. We arrange transportation, usually inconspicuous vehicles, to take them from one safehouse to the next. It's all about minimizing risks and keeping under the radar."

I couldn't help but visualize the intricate web they had woven to protect people like me. My mind wandered to Gerónimo, recalling his old joke, and I found myself saying, "So, it's the Emerald Road after all."

Suchipila looked at me, puzzled. "I beg your pardon?"

"It's what Gerónimo used to call it, some imaginary road from here to America. Never mind." I chuckled at the memory. "In any event, I imagine my case would be more difficult with my being a wanted person. I wouldn't want to be a burden on the network or put anyone in danger."

"You wouldn't be a burden, Isaac. Just keep focused on staying safe, keep your head down, and I'll take care of the rest. We just need to get you from here to Guatemala undetected, since the authorities are likely to be keeping an eye out for you. After that, it would be a matter of following the trail through Guatemala and Mexico and into the States."

I caught myself wringing my hands. I didn't exactly relish the idea of embarking on a potentially dangerous two-thousand-mile land journey, being handed off from stranger to stranger. Staring absently into the darkness that had descended over the room, I felt suddenly like a passenger on a rudderless boat, unmoored on choppy waters, realizing there's no captain at the helm. Hoping for an alternative solution, I turned to Suchi and asked: "Couldn't I just catch a ride to Guatemala City and then fly up to the US border from there?"

"Airports have strict immigration controls, and enforcement measures are more robust than at land borders, not to mention you'd need a visa to get beyond Mexico City. Given the circumstances, it's unlikely you'd be able to bypass those controls at an airport, especially if the authorities are on the lookout for you. There are more opportunities to cross land borders undetected—as long as you have the right guide."

"You mean a people smuggler," I said, liking the idea less and less. "A coyote."

"I'm talking about someone trusted," she corrected. "Someone we've worked with over the past few years."

"What do you think, Señora?" I asked Cashtōka, whom I noticed had joined us and was sitting in the shadows.

Suchi shifted in her chair, surprised to see her mother in the room. "Mamá, how long have you been there?"

"I'd just as soon you stayed here until things die down," Cashtōka said quietly, ignoring Suchi's question. "Once they do, you can decide what to do calmly. Besides, hija," she said, turning to her daughter in a voice that was almost pleading, "I've gotten used to his company and his dog's as well."

"He can't stay here, Mamá!" Suchi protested. "It's too risky; they could come back. You know what they'd do if they find you're harboring a wanted man. They'd arrest you and take away the farm, everything we've worked for."

*The Suchipila woman is right*, Ahbhu said. *Isaac and Ahbhu have to go.*

"Whose side are you on?" Cahstōka rose and cast a

182

disappointed look at Ahbhu.

*Ahbhu is on Cashtōka's side,* he soothed. *But if Isaac stays, bad things will happen to Cashtōka, Isaac, Ahbhu and the Suchipila woman.*

"Wait!" Suchi leapt to her feet and glanced back and forth between her mother and Ahbhu. "What's going on here?"

"They talk to each other," I said, arching an eyebrow. "Something to do with your mother being a *shamana* or something."

Suchi tossed up her hands in a gesture reminiscent of her mother. "Oh, for God's sake, Mamá. Well, I hope he's 'telling' you that I'm right."

"He is," I said, dryly.

Suchi's head swung around, and she stared open-mouthed at me.

I held up my hand. "Don't ask."

Looking thoroughly confused, she lowered herself back into her chair and rubbed her tired eyes. "Whatever . . ."

"In any case, you've convinced me. Where do I sign up?" I turned to Cashtōka. "I'm sorry, Señora, but they're right."

"Of course they're right," she replied bitterly.

Suchi sat up. "Thank you, Mamá. I'll start making enquiries tomorrow."

"Also," I said, "how can we get word to my parents? I'll need money, too."

"You mentioned your mother runs a neighborhood market, yes?" Cashtōka said, resignedly joining us at the table.

"Yes, that's right. Monday to Saturday from eight in the morning until three in the afternoon. Why?"

"Suchi can drop in on her on the pretence of supplying her with fresh eggs. Nobody will suspect her. She can deliver the news that you're safe and let her know you're planning on fleeing the country."

"That's a brilliant idea, Mamá," Suchi said.

"My mother's a suspicious woman," I countered, "Both my parents are. They don't trust people easily, especially when money is involved. They'll want proof."

"He has a point," Cashtōka said. "I'd want proof, too, if it was me. Perhaps a note?"

"A note's too risky," Suchi said. "If I were stopped it could be taken as evidence." She turned to me, "Do you have anything else we could use, an article of clothing, a piece of jewelry?"

"I was barely wearing a stitch when I showed up here. I've got nothing."

*Ahbhu will be Isaac's proof!* Ahbhu announced. Cashtōka and I exchanged a glance as he rose to his feet and held his head high and proud, having settled the debate.

"What's he saying?" Suchi asked.

"He said he'll go with you." I kissed Ahbhu's muzzle and received a lick on the cheek in return. "If he's with you, my mother will know you're telling the truth."

"But he never leaves your side," Cahstōka chimed in. "If he shows up with another person, won't that look suspicious?"

"That's not entirely true," I said. "When I was hiding the first time, he used to pick up our supplies from her every couple of days. She's used to seeing him without me, especially lately."

"What if *other* people see him?" Suchi asked, calling Ahbhu to herself and stroking his head. "Won't they know he's your dog, a dog with half an ear and with this particular coloring? That might be a giveaway."

"People aren't that observant," Cashtōka said. "But just to play it safe, I can fix both those issues temporarily, if that's okay with the both of you."

"But how, Mamá?"

"Just leave it with me. Now, it's very late, and this old woman needs her beauty sleep. We can set all of this in motion tomorrow morning after breakfast."

# Chapter 21

## MAKEOVER

When I awoke the next morning, it was still dark outside. I had claimed the living room sofa as my sleeping spot, defying Suchipila's insistence that I continue using her room as her guest. Ignoring her protests, I stuck to my guns and climbed into the sofa, turning my back on her until she went away.

I might have slept into late morning but for a strange smell, cloyingly sweet and herby, that pulled me out of my deep slumber. Sitting up, I surveyed the dim living room, looking for Ahbhu. Noting a soft light emanating from the kitchen, I realized the smell was coming from there.

Peering through the doorway, I discovered Cashtōka in a nightgown, tending to a large cast iron pot emitting a strange odor. Ahbhu was lolling at her feet, his head resting heavily on his paws. On sensing my presence, he greeted me with sleepy eyes, then refocused on Cashtōka, who was muttering something rhythmic and sing-songy under her breath.

"Good morning, Señora," I whispered, careful not to wake Suchipila in the adjacent room. Cashtōka, engrossed in her task, continued stirring without acknowledging my presence. Moving closer, I crouched beside Ahbhu, who rose as my hand touched his head. Stretching, he returned to his spot by the bread oven. I looked at him questioningly.

*The Cashtōka woman is making a disguise for Ahbhu,* he explained.

"Mamá?" came Suchipila's voice from behind me. We exchanged a glance as she entered the kitchen, dressed in a flannel nightshirt. She touched her mother's shoulder. "What are you doing? What's that awful smell?"

"There's coffee there," Cashtōka said in a low, intense voice, signaling a pot with a nod of her head, "and there's semita in the cupboard. We'll join you later, the dog and I."

Suchipila shrugged and we gathered our breakfast and headed to the dining table.

"Ahbhu said she's making him a disguise," I explained as we tucked into the stale sweet bread, leftovers from the day before.

Suchipila's eyes widened as if recalling something important. When I asked for an explanation, she assured me her mother knew what she was doing. Then she turned to her plans for the day: she would start with a visit to my mother with Ahbhu if I was willing to part with him for a day or two. Assuming things went well there, she'd take him home with her to start reaching out to her contacts.

It would take a few days to prepare my itinerary, maybe even until the following weekend. Once everything was arranged, she'd come back to review the details with me. Then, we'd embark on a three-hour journey to Guatemala in Suchi's pickup, our first major challenge, since the roads would be closely monitored, especially near the border.

To avoid detection, Ahbhu and I would have to hide in a false compartment behind Suchipila. She'd successfully used it a couple of times before and was confident it was safe. Rubbing sweaty palms against my jeans, my breathing shallowed at the thought of being stuffed into a metal compartment for hours with Ahbhu. I was on the verge of saying I wanted to rethink the whole thing when Cashtōka strode triumphantly into the room followed by a black dog, his ears pricked up and alert. Confused by the presence of the strange animal, I jumped to my feet and looked around for Ahbhu. In response, the black dog limped over to me and nudged its head under my hand.

*I'm Ahbhu!* He licked my palm in a familiar gesture.

"That's amazing, Mamá!" Suchipila brought her hands to her mouth in surprise.

I squatted and grabbed the sides of his head and gently shook it side to side, hardly believing it was my Ahbhu.

Cashtōka proudly explained: "I cooked up a dye from some crushed berries, herbs, and flowers and applied it to the dog's coat, flattening out his distinctive coloring in favor of something dark and more discreet. Don't worry, it'll grow out eventually."

"What about his ear?" I asked, amazed at how much his now intact ear so dramatically changed his appearance.

"It's a simple prosthetic made from an old chamois dyed the same color as his coat. I attached it to his half-ear using a homemade adhesive made from gelatine and glycerin. It should be easily removable after a few days."

"It looks amazing! But how will my mother recognize him if even I didn't?"

*Ahbhu will make sure Isaac's mother knows Ahbhu,* Ahbhu reassured, lopsidedly parading proudly around the room, showcasing his new look. I was happy to see his spirits were up and he was walking better.

Once they were ready, I kissed Ahbhu goodbye and entrusted him to Suchi. From Cashtōka's kitchen window, I watched them trudge away from the house in a steady drizzle toward where Suchi had parked out by the road. As they disappeared into the trees, I raised my hand in a wave, then slowly lowered it and braced myself against the sill, feeling that something had shifted inside me forever.

I spent the next couple of days moping around the homestead, waiting for Suchi's return, silently assisting Cashtōka with her chores. The air in the house was heavy with the earthy scent of herbs and the aroma of Cashtōka's endless cooking, creating a cozy but somber atmosphere. It was difficult not to let my imagination run away with me, fearing the worst outcome. The creaks and groans of the old homestead echoed my anxieties, making the waiting even more unbearable. Cashtōka respected my silence, only offering her firm reassurance about Suchipila's shrewd judgment while we went about our chores.

On the second morning, following an agonizing night, Cashtōka called me into the kitchen. The pale light filtering through the window revealed additional clutter in the already cramped space: a high-backed wooden chair from the front room and a couple of tattered cardboard boxes on the floor. Answering my unspoken question, Cashtōka announced that, like Ahbhu, I should also have my appearance altered.

Slipping on a plastic apron, she pointed me to the chair and proceeded to apply a pair of scissors to my hair, the snipping sounds mingling with the rhythmic mutterings under her breath. The scent of fresh-cut hair filled the air as Cashtōka transformed my unruly black locks into a textured mullet. I felt the coolness of the morning around my ears as she skillfully created a spiky top, cropped sides, and a longer, layered back. Stepping away, she screwed up her face and surveyed her handiwork; then she applied a few additional snips before putting her scissors aside.

As I checked myself out in a hand-held mirror, admiring my new look, Cashtōka recommended that we bleach my hair to alter my appearance more dramatically. Digging around in the musty-smelling boxes, she produced a long-expired hair bleach kit, assuring me she knew how to salvage enough product to produce a good result. Then she mixed up the pungent-smelling stuff and applied it to my hair in batches.

By the time she rinsed it out, my scalp was burning as if it had been dunked in a vat of hot chiles. Cashtōka massaged in some aloe vera gel, which provided some relief, and then handed me the mirror again.

I nearly jumped with surprise at my reflection. Staring out of the mirror was an alternate reality version of me with straw-yellow hair that contrasted weirdly with my cinnamon-toned skin and thick black unibrow. Gobsmacked, I lowered the mirror and noticed Cashtōka frowning at me.

"What's wrong?" I asked, feeling slightly nauseated by the lingering smell of bleach and alarmed that my scalp was still tingling.

Cashtōka shook her head and dipped into her box again. "Something's still not right," she said as she rummaged around in it. A moment later she extracted a pair of tweezers and waved them at me. "That caterpillar of yours! It has to go."

"But—"

"It's a dead giveaway. Once I take care of that, not even your own mother will recognize you."

"But I *like* my eyebrows!"

Ignoring my protests, she wiped the tweezers with alcohol, then she tilted back my head and laid into my poor eyebrows. Each pluck of the tweezers brought a scream or a whimper to my lips. Undaunted, Cashtōka carried on until I feared I'd have no eyebrows left.

When she finished, Cashtōka carefully examined my brow. Then she stepped back and took in the sight of me, an approving smile spreading on her face.

"That's it!" she declared, handing me the mirror. "Your transformation is complete. We just need to find you some appropriate clothes."

I took another look at myself and felt my stomach turn

cartwheels over the edge of a cliff. Gone was Isaac Perez. I was staring out of the eyes of another person. For a moment, I felt ashamed of what I'd become—a total fraud—and lowered my face into my hands.

"There's nothing to be ashamed of," Cashtōka reassured me as she put away her styling kit. "Consider it a costume, a bit of fancy dress, nothing more. Once you're safe, it will all grow back, and you'll be you again."

"So, you approve of all this after all," I stated, as I dragged the chair back to the front room and helped her set the table.

"It doesn't matter what I think. It never has, not with my daughter. I love her deeply, and she's always been good to me. But we've never seen eye to eye on *anything*. This time, though, I must admit she's probably right. As much as I've enjoyed having you and Ahbhu around, you can't stay here." She swiped at her eyes with the back of her hand and withdrew to compose herself.

Later that afternoon, as Cashtōka and I were finishing lunch, Suchi and Ahbhu slipped in through the front door. I was so happy to see Ahbhu that I rushed past Suchi and caught him as he leapt into my arms. We rolled around on the ground for a bit while Suchi and Cashtōka watched on in astonishment. Once we were done with our horseplay, I jumped up, out of breath, and looked questioningly at Suchi, eager to hear her report.

"I honestly don't think I would have recognized you like that had I seen you on the street," Suchi said, dropping onto the sofa. "Bravo, Mamá. Good job."

Cashtōka crossed her thin arms and frowned at Ahbhu. "Apparently not good enough. This one recognized him right away."

*Cashtōka only changed Isaac on the outside,* Ahbhu explained. *Ahbhu sees inside.*

Relaxing her arms, Cashtōka appeared satisfied with Ahbhu's response. She turned to Suchi. "Well, out with it, hija. We're waiting to hear what happened."

Suchi rolled her eyes at her mother and focused on me. "Everything went just as you expected. Your mother was suspicious until she saw Ahbhu. I'm afraid to say she saw straight through his disguise, but that was all the credibility I needed. She closed the shop and introduced me to your father. They cried when they heard you were alive and were completely onboard with our exit plan for you. They agreed for me to act as their go-between until it's safe for you to call them yourself. Also, they asked me to tell you that they love you very much and that they believe wholeheartedly in your innocence."

Tears flowed freely down my cheeks as she spoke, and I swallowed hard against a lump that had risen in my throat. Cashtōka handed me a glass of water, which I drank in small sips.

"There was only one thing that didn't go to plan," she added after a pause. "Your friend Gerónimo showed up at the house to ask if they'd heard anything. He was adamant he needed to speak with you."

"Gerónimo?" I asked, feeling immediately conflicted at the mention of his name.

"Ahbhu knew to hide as soon as he heard his voice," Suchi continued, "just in case Geronimo recognized him. In any case, your father turned him out and threatened to call the police if he came around again. I almost felt sorry for him, he looked so miserable, like he hadn't slept for a while."

"He's no friend, that one!" Cashtōka weighed in. "He could clear Isaac's name if he wanted to, tell the authorities who *really* killed that soldier."

"It might be worth hearing him out, though," Suchi said. "Safely, of course."

"I don't know what to think," I said. "But regardless, I can't trust Gerónimo anymore, even if he *did* save Ahbhu. I *won't* trust him."

Suchi shrugged and continued, "After visiting with your parents, I spent the rest of yesterday and part of today reaching out to my contacts, making the arrangements. I'd like to go over them with you to make sure you're okay with all the details."

Suchi's plan hit me like a five-ton wrecking ball. First, the three-hour journey to the border crossing with Guatemala. Once safely over the border, Ahbhu and I would ride up front with her to the first safehouse in Ciudad Pedro de Alvarado, where she'd hand us off to her first contact. At dawn, someone would drive us to the next safehouse in Ciudad Tecún Umán, five hours away, on the Guatemala side of the border with Mexico. I'd spend a few hours there, waiting for the right time to be driven into southern Mexico, possibly in the trunk of someone else's car, depending on whether there was police activity or not.

The more Suchi got into the details, rattling off the strange names of places I'd never heard of, the reality of the journey began to sink in, and I felt my stomach churn with anxiety. Asking to take a break, I shut myself in the bathroom and splashed water on my face. Then I sat on the edge of the tub and focused on how I'd once conquered my fear of the volcano by climbing it, step by step, with Ahbhu by my side. Reminding myself he'd be with me on this journey as well, my heart rate soon returned to normal. I stood and held the gaze of the stranger in the mirror. "You've got this," I told him. He nodded and flashed me a thumbs-up. Ready to hear the rest of the crazy itinerary, I returned to the front room for more.

"Once you're safely in Mexico," Suchi continued, eyeing me with concern, "it's a five-hour drive through the state of Chiapas, from Tapachula to Tuxtla Gutierrez, where you'll be dropped off at the next safehouse. You'll bed down there, gearing up for the next leg."

"That's three days already," I said. "How long is the trip

anyway? And who are all these people? What's in it for them?"

Echoing my sentiments, Cashtōka let out a skeptical *harumph* and held her arms tightly across her chest. Annoyed, Suchi gave her mother her back and squeezed my hand.

"It's around sixty hours by car if one were to drive straight up without stopping, which is obviously impossible. We try to break it up into small chunks, five or six hours at a time, no more than seven, for everyone's sake.

"Once you get to Mexico City, you'll need to wait for your onward visa to travel the rest of the way. From there, it's an overnight bus ride to Mexicali, then a special cab to Tijuana where you'll be met by the coyote. So, ten days in total, give or take."

"Or a five-hour flight," I said, with a hint of sarcasm.

Suchi let go of my hand. "That's not an option here," she said. "As for who the people involved are, they're good, trusted folks we've vetted and a few others *they* trust, mainly the drivers, who are putting their lives on the line for a good cause."

"And for the money," Cashtōka dropped in, dryly. She absently stroked Ahbhu's head, who had taken up residence on the sofa next to her.

"Of course, for the money, Mamá! Nobody's going to put themselves out for free." Exasperated, she waved a dismissive hand and continued. "I'll write everything down for you before we take off, so you'll know exactly who'll be taking care of you as you make your way up. Plus, we can chat more once we're on our way. We should leave first thing tomorrow morning after a good rest."

"Speaking of money. . ." I said, miming empty pockets.

Suchi reached into her bag and handed me an envelope. "Your parents gave me this for the first part of your journey. They'll be wiring more when you reach Mexico City and some more when you reach Tijuana. I'll be providing them with instructions as to when. I'll also serve as your main point of contact. If you have something to communicate to them, you'll call me and I'll relay your message, and vice versa."

"Sounds expensive. My parents aren't rich people."

Suchi shrugged. "I don't know. I overheard them say something about your brother contributing something. Maybe they have savings you don't know about."

I peeked inside the envelope and counted out five thousand colones, the equivalent of around two thousand dollars—a small fortune for my parents. My heart sank as I felt suddenly guilty at having put them in this position, risking their very livelihood to help their fugitive son.

"You'll be able to pay them back in no time once you make it to the States," Suchi assured me. "It's easy to find a good-paying job there."

"That's if I even make it to the States," I muttered. "If I don't, they'll be ruined."

Silence descended over the room. Outside, the wind had picked up and was flailing through the trees, hurling dry vegetation against the windows. Ahbhu, who'd been listening silently from the sofa, pattered over and climbed into my lap, seeming more than ever like a normal dog, missing the attention of his master. I buried my nose in his fur and kissed him and received a reciprocal lick on my cheek, which helped buoy my mood.

"I honestly appreciate everything you're doing for me, Suchi. But I've never been good with strangers. No disrespect to anyone, but I *hate* the idea of being at the mercy of people I don't know, even if they've been vetted. On top of that, I still occasionally suffer blackouts. I'd be in real trouble if I experienced one at some random point along the way. And Ahbhu can only help so much if we're someplace strange or with someone unfamiliar with my condition. I'd just as soon go it alone once I'm in Guatemala."

"The young man's right, hija," Cashtōka offered. "He might not be the right candidate for this type of journey."

"Then what? We already agreed he can't remain here."

"Couldn't you accompany me to Mexico City, Suchi? If you want, we could stay in the safehouses you arranged. That wouldn't be a problem as long as you're there. I could pay *you* instead of a bunch of random drivers."

Ahbhu's head shot up, and he panted his approval. He hopped out of my lap and offered his head to Suchi. Surprised, she glanced down at him, and a hint of a smile animated her face for the first time since we'd started going over the plan.

"See!" I exclaimed. "Even Ahbhu agrees it's a great idea."

Cashtōka joined us at the table. "This is a good solution, hija," she urged. "I'd feel better knowing you're looking after the boy and his dog."

Suchi glanced at her mother and tentatively nodded.

"Some time away might do you good as well," Cashtōka added.

"Time away from what exactly, Mamá?" Suchi answered angrily.

"So, is it a yes?" I intervened, temporarily breaking the eternal stalemate that existed between these two.

Suchi squinted at me, considering my proposition. "I'd need a couple of days to put things in order back home and to make sure my pickup is properly serviced for such a long ride. But I think I could make it work." Her face brightened as she thought it through. "It might even be fun. We could approach the trip a bit as tourists, maybe even adding in a couple of interesting stopovers along the way, places I've always wanted to see."

With everyone on board with the new plan, the atmosphere in the room lightened. After coffee, Cashtōka fired up an old Victrola and put on some cumbia. For the rest of the afternoon and on into the evening, we distracted ourselves from what lay ahead with a few beers and some dancing that lasted long after darkness had descended over the forest.

# Chapter 22

## THE CYCLONE

Fifteen minutes into our storm-battered journey, folded like a German pretzel with Ahbhu in the compartment behind Suchi, I knew I wasn't going to be able to stand the three-hour drive. I'd been awakened that morning by an intense windstorm that had started in the early hours and had intensified into the dawn. By the time I became aware of it, the wind was screeching through the trees, threatening to tear the shuddering house off its foundations.

Over Cashtōka's vigorous objections, Suchi argued that the weather was ideal for our crossing as it would make inspections all that more challenging for the customs agents. I was more worried about our being blasted off the road into a side ditch. But Suchi was undaunted, dismissing what she dubbed my hysterics. And so, after a quick bite, we gathered a few provisions and battled our way through the wind to Suchi's pickup, where Ahbhu and I contorted ourselves to fit into the tight space behind the front bench.

As we drove, Ahbhu tried his best to soothe me with doggy kisses and the deep breathing mantra that usually got my anxiety under control. But nothing was working, and I feared I'd have a seizure in the cramped space. Desperate for release, I pounded on the back of Suchi's seat, screaming for her to let me out. Just when I thought I'd go mad with panic, the pickup jerked to a stop and Suchi pried open the compartment.

"What the hell is all that racket?" She ducked to avoid a small branch flying past her head, which made her pound the side of the truck in frustration.

Tumbling out of the cramped space, I bent over and drew in deep draughts of air among the dense trees she'd pulled into off the side of the highway, which was already busy with vehicles heading north. Ahbhu galloped past me into the forest to relieve himself. After a few beats, I straightened up and rotated my neck. Suchi watched on with a dark expression that threatened trouble, squinting her eyes against the flying dust.

"I'm sorry, Suchi, I can't do it! I don't mean to be a prima donna, but I'm seriously freaking out inside there. I'm terrified I'll have a seizure, or worse. Let me ride up front with you, *please*. No one will recognize me, not looking like this!"

I drew her attention to the ridiculous dashiki and drawstring pants she'd brought me from San Salvador. "I don't look anything like the Isaac they're looking for. Plus, I've got the fake passport you finagled." I pulled out the booklet, which bore the picture she'd snapped with a Polaroid and my new name: *Tlaloc Rodriguez*. If anyone asked, I was supposed to be Suchi's son. That was Cashtōka's grand idea. She'd always wanted a grandson, she said, her voice loaded with irony, and now she had one. "What's the point of *this* if I'm not going to use it."

Suchi looked away in the direction of the road, battling to control her anger. The sound of cars and trucks whizzing by reached us; we were that close. Mercifully, the wind had started to diminish. After a few moments of tense silence, she relaxed her balled-up fists. Ahbhu had returned and was circling her legs. Squatting next to him Suchi stroked his dark coat, her face drained of emotion. Then she glanced up at me.

"Supposing you *were* to ride up front—and I'm not saying I'll agree to that yet—even if they *don't* recognize you, the authorities will likely be on the lookout for a young man and his dog. We may attract unwanted suspicion if you're *both* riding up front with me. The stakes are much too high. It's one thing if you're willing to take the chance of being caught, Isaac. But I'm not."

Ahbhu trotted over to me, his eyes shining in the morning light. *Ahbhu will hide in the box so Isaac can ride with Suchi*, he offered.

"No, Ahbhu. It's too confined!"

"What's he saying?" Suchi asked.

"That he'll ride in the compartment alone. But—"

Suchi's hand shot up to silence me. "*That* I'll agree to."

"I'd rather he rode up front with us. He could lie down at my feet, maybe under a blanket. Nobody will see him."

"Absolutely not," Suchi declared. She marched back to the truck and pulled forward the seat, exposing the compartment again. "I'm not debating this one minute longer. It's getting late, and our side of the border will be crawling with soldiers by noon. We must go *now!*"

Before I could get another word out, Ahbhu dove into the compartment and Suchi slammed it shut. Then she climbed into the cab of her pickup and revved up the engine. "Are you coming or not?" she called, her patience wearing thin again.

Seeing I was outvoted, I held up my hands in surrender and jumped into the passenger seat. Suchi executed a crazy 180-degree turn and roared out of the woods and onto the highway, heading north.

Three hours later, after refueling and grabbing a bite to eat at a service station a few hundred meters from the border crossing, we joined a single-file queue of vehicles waiting for inspection. Three or four Salvadoran soldiers patrolled on either side of the queue, peering into the vehicles as we inched forward toward the border crossing. Suchi had loaded the bed of her pickup with a few crates of fresh eggs, lashed down against the wind. If asked the purpose of her trip, she would say she was transporting eggs to a relative in Ciudad Pedro de Alvarado, the town just over the border.

When we were just two vehicles away from the customs booth a young soldier, nineteen at the most, approached my side of the truck, an assault rifle slung over his shoulder. White knuckling the door handle, I swallowed hard against a sudden swell of nausea and deliberately rolled down the window, feigning fearlessness. I forced a smile at the soldier and nodded a friendly greeting. He acknowledged the greeting and returned the smile, then moved on to the next car.

"That was fucking ballsy of you," Suchi said under her breath, running her fingers over her damp scalp. "Well done!" She rolled down her window, preparing for her interaction with the Guatemalan customs officer and drew a deep breath.

Grabbing a bottle of water on the seat between us, I guzzled half of it in one go. Then I set it aside and faced forward, gritting my teeth, readying myself for whatever awaited us. When our turn arrived, there was a short delay due to a shift change. Suchi squeezed my hand reassuringly. Her hand felt cold and clammy, and I squeezed back, signaling I was ready.

After a couple of minutes, a bleary-eyed man in his late forties in an ill-fitting uniform took his seat in the booth and smothered a yawn. He asked to see our papers and took a quick glance at the bed of Suchi's pickup, then waved us through.

"Is that it?" I asked as Suchi's pickup rumbled forward.

She shook her head and indicated the low-rise pastel-colored building looming just ahead to our left. "That back there was Guatemalan customs. We lucked out with them, thank God. Next is Guatemalan immigration." She pulled into a parking space next to the building and shut off her engine. "Follow me." She exited the truck and trudged toward the building.

"Wait, what?" I sputtered, catching up with her. "What do we have to do in there?"

Whirling on me, she said, eyes blazing: "If you'd listened to me and waited where I told you to wait, it would just be me who has to face questions. Now it's the two of us. Get your passport ready." And with that she marched into the building.

I found her inside the hot, musty office, waiting to be called forward to the counter. A few ceiling fans placed around the room circulated monotonously above our heads to little effect. Dropping in beside her, I swiped the perspiration from my forehead and whispered an apology, feeling bad for having put her in this situation in the first place. Suchi waved me off and stared straight ahead, fidgeting nervously with her passport.

Behind the counter, several uniformed immigration officers were busy with paperwork. A lone officer, a statuesque young woman with dark flowing hair, attended to the public. She called us forward when it was our turn and inspected our passports.

"What's the relationship between the two of you?" she asked, looking first at Suchi then at me.

"This is my son," Suchi responded after a moment's hesitation. She draped her arm over my shoulder as if to prove the point.

The officer looked at our passports again, then narrowed her eyes at us. I imagined she was trying to find the family resemblance.

"What's your father's name?" she asked me, surprising me with the unexpected question.

Suchi jumped to my rescue: "I'm sorry, but what does that have to do with anything?"

"I'm asking the questions here," the officer said firmly, her eyes dark and intense.

Suchi raised her hands in a silent apology and stepped back slightly.

"I don't know my father's name," I answered, thinking fast. "She's never told me." I indicated Suchi with a nod of my head. "Some random someone, back when she was into men."

Suchi spun angrily on me: "How dare you speak about your mother that way!" She slapped me hard across my face, practically knocking me to the ground with the force of the blow. Stumbling away from her, I held my hands up defensively.

Everyone stopped what they were doing and stared in shock at the scene unfolding before them. The immigration officer, red-faced and embarrassed, ordered us to calm down and summoned a couple of her colleagues to coax us to opposite ends of the room. Someone in a uniform brought me a glass of water and stood by my side, awaiting instructions from the attending officer. Across the room, I saw her chatting with Suchi, who was beaming daggers at me as she answered additional questions. After she'd finished with Suchi, the officer called me back to the counter, directing me to a far corner, out of earshot of everyone else in the room.

"You should show more respect for your mother," she lectured, her voice no louder than a whisper. "Life is difficult enough for her as it is. Only God knows the sacrifices she's made for you. The last thing she needed was to have you publicly expose her in such a vicious manner. Shame on you!"

I stole a quick glance at Suchi. She was staring at me melodramatically with a hurt look. Turning back to the officer I asked: "What exactly did she tell you? My mother."

"Never mind that! My question was a simple one. Your response, though, was rude and uncalled for and deeply upsetting not only for your mother, but for everyone in this office. I should place you under arrest if only to teach you a lesson. But I'm prepared to give you a pass this time on your solemn promise to apologize to your poor mother and to show her the love and respect *all* mothers deserve."

Shortly after, Suchi and I surrendered our passports to the officer for stamping. She welcomed us to Guatemala, her eyes glistening with heartfelt satisfaction at having brokered a peace agreement between a mother and her son. Personally escorting us to the door, she wished us the best of luck as she saw us off.

Suchi and I stepped out into the bright Guatemalan sunlight, my cheek still stinging from her unexpected slap. I couldn't help but marvel at the theatricality of our exchange and the effect it had had on the officer.

"Well played back there, sonny boy," she said, a wry smile playing on her lips. "You certainly know how to keep things interesting."

"I was surprised you went all in like that."

Suchi chuckled, playfully ruffling my hair. "Sometimes a bit of drama can be a useful distraction. Keeps them guessing."

As we pulled back onto the road, a silent understanding passed between us. There was no question we were in it together now, mother and son, partners in an inadvertent dance of deception. I couldn't help but wonder what secrets and strategies awaited us on the rest of our journey north.

# PART III

*Guatemala & Mexico (1985–1986)*

# Chapter 23

## THE HIGHWAY

Ahbhu bolted out of the compartment the instant Suchi unlatched it, vanishing into the brush behind the filling station we'd pulled into just out of sight of the border. After three hours without food or water, thanks to Suchi's steadfast refusal to stop, I imagined he had some serious business to attend to.

The filling station boasted a convenience store and a toilet at the rear, with a few trinket sellers and currency peddlers loitering around the parked cars. The air hung heavy with the scent of gasoline, and the distant hum of the station's generators added an industrial undertone. Suchi and I agreed to rendezvous at the pickup after a few minutes while she went inside to buy some more water, and I set off in search of Ahbhu.

The sun was high in the cloudless sky and beat down on me like a searing mallet as I called out Ahbhu's name. I pulled my damp hair back, securing it with a rubber band, and surveyed the landscape. The distant rumble of engines and the lone call of a bird were the only sounds in the air. Despite our proximity to El Salvador, the view seemed remarkably different, though I couldn't pinpoint exactly what had changed. Turning toward El Salvador, I peered into the distance, struggling to discern the border. Then, looking in the opposite direction, I found Ahbhu sitting at my feet, his tongue hanging out.

*Ahbhu is back*, he said with a wide doggie grin.

I squatted next to him, overjoyed to see him. Grasping his head, I shook it side to side, the way he liked. He responded with a gentle head-butt, sending me tumbling onto the dirt. The soil, damp from earlier rains, clung to my pants. Ahbhu pounced on me, and his playful energy stirred the scent of nearby wildflowers. He licked my face, his mouth dripping wet. Pointing into the brush, he excitedly indicated he'd found a river, referring to it as *moving water*.

"Yes, I know, Ahbhu. We drove over it a couple of minutes ago. That's the dividing line between El Salvador and Guatemala," I replied, looking around. "It looks different on this side, though. But I can't tell what's changed."

*No volcanos*, Ahbhu quipped, galloping toward Suchi, who appeared in the distance.

Ahbhu was right. Scanning the surroundings, I saw hills teeming with vegetation, but no volcanos. Breathing a sigh of relief for the first time since the bus attack, I felt everything was going to be okay.

I ran to rejoin Suchi and Ahbhu. After securing his promise to keep his head low, I persuaded Suchi to let him ride up front with us.

We carried on down the road, rumbling through a bustling border settlement with restaurants, food stands, a motel, and a lively outdoor market. The aroma of street food wafting from vibrantly painted market stalls laced the air. Streets branched off into neat neighborhoods of rickety houses.

"We're not staying here, are we?" I wrinkled my nose at the crowded sidewalks.

"*Near* here," Suchi replied, turning onto a two-lane highway on reaching the end of the commercial strip. "We're almost there. Our contact Esperanza will be waiting for us."

A couple of minutes later, she took a left onto a small road leading to a quiet town made up of a municipal complex, a church, a grade school, and a handful of pastel-colored houses.

We turned onto a dirt road near the town's edge and followed it around a bend to our first safehouse—an isolated sky-blue shack with a tin roof, surrounded by a chicken wire fence. Two well-fed Doberman pinschers were lounging on the front porch. Their heads shot up the moment we pulled up to the fence, and they padded toward us. On catching sight of Ahbhu, the Dobermans erupted into loud barks and menacing snarls.

"I told you to keep him the hell down!" Suchi scolded, her face tense. Popping open the door, she ordered me to wait inside the truck and marched toward the fence.

Ahbhu retreated to the floorboard, in response to Suchi's angry tone, and curled around my feet. Just then, a woman I assumed was Esperanza appeared at the door to the shack and called the dogs inside. She looked to be a few years younger than Suchi, dressed in jeans, cowboy boots, and a T-shirt, and she wore her hair in a long braid down the middle of her back. She trod across the front yard and spoke with Suchi through the fence. The distant murmur of their conversation floated toward us, carried on the wind that had kicked up, causing their clothes to flutter and flap.

*What's happening?* Ahbhu asked.

"Hush, Ahbhu," I said, gently stroking his head.

Esperanza periodically glanced at me as she conversed with Suchi, who was shaking her head and gesturing at the truck.

"Keep down; I'll be back," I said to Ahbhu. Hopping out of the pickup, I joined the two women at the fence. They fell silent and stared at me as if I were an extraterrestrial.

"What's going on?" I asked, looking first at Suchi then at Esperanza.

"I told you to stay in the truck," Suchi hissed.

"I'm sorry, but you can't stay here," Esperanza said to me, her voice sympathetic but firm.

"Why not?" I asked, struggling to keep my voice steady. "Suchi?"

"When Suchipila first contacted us about you, she didn't mention you were on the run."

"You didn't?" I questioned Suchi.

Suchi turned away and shook her head in frustration.

"She only mentioned that you were one of us, heading north for a better life. That's what we're here for—to help our kind."

"But he *is* our kind, Esperanza!" Suchi protested. "Exactly like us."

"I'm sorry, Suchi." Esperanza glanced around as if checking for eavesdroppers. "There have been increased patrols and inquiries about strangers in the area. The authorities are on high alert. It's not safe to harbor someone like him right now. We can't take the risk," she added, her eyes apologetic.

"Does it matter that I'm wanted in El Salvador and not here—or, more importantly, that I'm innocent?" I pleaded. "You know what a mess it is over there!"

"I'm truly sorry," Esperanza said, meeting my gaze. Then she looked back at Suchi, her expression heavy with disappointment. "I haven't alerted the others, Suchi. Out of respect for you. But I hope you won't put them in a similar position."

"Thank you," Suchi retorted, sounding a defiant note. "What about El Garrobo?"

Esperanza spat on the ground, pressing her spittle into the dirt with her boot. "El Garrobo couldn't care less. He'd sell out his blessed mother for a piece of silver if given the chance." With that, she returned to the house, disappearing inside.

"Who's El Garrobo?" I asked.

"He's your contact in Tijuana, the coyote," Suchi explained, her eyes locked on Esperanza's front door, still fuming but losing steam. "He's meant to be the only wildcard in all of this."

"The *only* wildcard?" The name alone, *El Garrobo,* conjured images of a leather-skinned ogre. From where I was standing, none of what I was hearing bode well for the rest of the journey. That said, I had no choice but to press forward. The very thought of a retreat sent a current of dread through my entrails.

Suchi and I exchanged a glance, both of us battling against the urge to lash out at the universe. Seeing her on the verge of tears, I drew her close and hugged her, and we rocked for a few seconds. Then we crunched back across the gravel to the pickup and climbed inside.

We rode in silence for the next few minutes, each of us processing what had just happened, pondering how best to play our next move now that the rules of the game had changed. Raising his eyes at me, Ahbhu beamed a solution my way, encouraging me to propose it to Suchi. After a brief hesitation, I broached the subject.

"I'm really sorry to have put you in this position, Suchi," I began.

Suchi glanced at me out of the corner of her eye, a snort escaping her lips before returning her focus to the road.

"There's really no need for you to accompany me any further, not if the safehouses aren't safe for me anymore. Ahbhu and I should be able to manage from here on out."

Suchi's hand shot up dismissively. "Just shut it, okay? This is completely on me for not being transparent with my contacts from the beginning."

"Regardless," I said, "I think you should head home and let us handle it from here." I scooted up in my seat and leaned toward her. "All I ask is that you give Ahbhu and me a ride to someplace where we can hop a bus north. Maybe Guatemala City."

The pickup jolted to a stop as Suchi pulled onto the shoulder.

"Guatemala City's three hours from here in a different direction from where we're going," she growled. "We're heading up the CA2."

"But I—"

"I promised to take you to Mexico City, and that's what I'm going to do, safehouse or no safehouse. Once I'm satisfied you're good to go for the rest of the journey, with your Mexican visa and more funds from your parents, you can take it from there. Are we agreed?"

Ahbhu signaled his approval, and I nodded at Suchi. She squeezed my hand tightly in response, pleased she'd persuaded me. Then, maneuvering her juddering pickup back onto the highway, she gunned the accelerator, making a beeline to a cheap motel off the highway next to a muddy truck stop.

We bedded down in a windowless room decorated in a patchwork of mismatched wallpaper that was barely large enough to fit the lumpy queen-sized mattress. Over the door was a transom that let in some daylight and an air vent so guests wouldn't suffocate. The closet-sized bathroom consisted of a squat hole, a handheld shower, a threadbare towel, and a foul-smelling drain. When I suggested we were better off sleeping in her pickup, Suchi ordered me to stop complaining and dropped onto the bed to yank off her boots, grumbling about being thoroughly shattered by the long drive. Propping herself against the headboard she handed me a couple of stiff tortillas, a slice of hard-ripened cheese, and a carton of juice from her backpack.

"Eat," she instructed, tearing off a piece of tortilla and folding it over a piece of the pungent cheese.

On seeing the food, Ahbhu paced the floor, his mouth watering.

"Did you bring anything for Ahbhu?"

"I didn't pack any dog food if that's what you mean." She handed me another piece of cheese. "Toss him this. There's water in the bathroom."

Ahbhu sniffed at the cheese and retreated a couple of steps. *Let Ahbhu out.* He scratched at the door and glanced back at us, pleading with his eyes. *Ahbhu will find something to eat outside.*

I climbed out of bed and made to open the door for him.

"No!" Suchi said. "I don't want him running around loose outside. We can buy dog food for him tomorrow."

"He's going to have to go outside some time, Suchi! He *is* a dog, you know."

"Only if he's accompanied. That's a rule of the road from now on. Also, we should get him a leash."

Ahbhu cast an injured look at Suchi then backed away from the door and settled at the foot of the bed, covering his head with his paws. *Ahbhu will wait,* he muttered.

Swallowing my annoyance, I stripped down to my boxers and went into the bathroom to wash up.

Upon reentering the room, I was surprised to find Ahbhu on the bed curled up against Suchi, who was absently stroking his head while engrossed in a paperback edition of *Love Story.* Relieved to see they'd made peace, I joined them in bed and sulked under the covers, kicking myself for not having brought something to read.

"It's five hours from here to Ciudad Tecún Umán, depending on traffic and the state of the road," Suchi said abruptly, marking her place in the book. "It's a bit hit and miss. We'll stay in a nicer place and have some proper food tomorrow night, I promise."

"If you say so."

"And I'm sorry for being so ill-tempered. I was thrown by the whole debacle with Esperanza. She's been a valued friend and comrade over the years, a gem of a woman. I'm devastated at the thought that I spoiled the relationship."

Not sure how to respond, and afraid to set her off again by

saying the wrong thing, I rubbed her shoulder reassuringly. She responded with a sad smile then turned back to her book.

"I was thinking," I said after a few minutes of boring silence, "we should probably let my parents know I made it safely across the border."

Suchi set down her book and squinted at me, making me feel like duckling.

"There's a pay phone by the office," I said.

"You mean *now*?"

"Please. They don't even know that I'm riding with you most of the way. They should know that. Tell them we'll contact them again once we're in Mexico City. Only don't tell them where we are in case their phone is tapped."

Suchi nodded and wordlessly pushed her feet into her boots, controlling herself as best as she could. I'd never met anyone with such a short fuse, but I was determined to ride out her volatility come what may. I refused to play the victim with her, or with anyone.

"Take Ahbhu with you," I said.

Suchi stared daggers at me then slipped out the door followed by Ahbhu.

When they returned twenty minutes or so later, Suchi was a lot more relaxed, almost cheery and beaming a dreamy smile. It was as if someone had replaced Mean Suchi with Nice Suchi from some alternate universe; either that or she'd popped a chill pill, which freaked me out a bit. Sitting on the bed and holding my hands, she reported how she'd spoken with my parents. My mother had answered the phone on the first ring as if she'd been waiting next to it. After identifying herself using an alias they'd agreed on, Suchi filled her in on everything that had happened so far, careful not to say anything that could lead the authorities to us. Tears spilled down my cheeks as she dramatized the call for me. She paused to wipe my face dry with a tissue from her backpack.

"Toward the end, your mother passed the phone to your father," she continued. "She'd gotten super emotional; it was tough for her to speak."

Suchi paused again. Her face had turned serious, and she held my gaze for a moment. Anticipating something dire, my heart floated into my throat.

"Your father has had to chase Gerónimo off the property a couple of times. He's been showing up at odd hours, insisting on speaking with you, but refusing to say what about. Lately, he's taken to watching your home from his car, sometimes in the morning, sometimes at night."

"Why doesn't he just leave them alone?" I groaned, grasping the side of the bed, furious he was bothering my parents.

"Maybe you should speak with him," Suchi said. "At least that way he'd leave them alone. Otherwise, he's bound to keep showing up."

"I already told you I don't trust him! It might all be a ruse to find out where I am and turn me over to the authorities."

"But what if it's not a ruse? What if he wants to help you? It's worth a call, don't you think?" She dug a few coins out of her pocket and placed them in my hand. "Have faith in a mother's advice."

Ahbhu had crawled onto the bed and had been listening to our conversation. I stroked his side and asked him what he thought I should do. He pivoted his head and raised his eyes at me. *Call Gerónimo when Isaac is safe*, he said. *Isaac isn't safe yet.*

Surprised by his assessment, I asked: "When will Isaac be safe, Ahbhu?"

*When Ahbhu says.* Ahbhu closed his eyes, effectively ending our conversation, and cuddled against Suchi, ready to nod off.

"I'm guessing that's a no," Suchi said, arching an eyebrow.

"That's the verdict, for now."

Suchi shrugged. "It's your call. Anyway, I'm beat." She reached over to the nightstand and switched off the lamp, plunging the room into darkness. We were soon asleep, with Suchi on one side of the bed, lying on top of the bedspread still in her jeans, me tucked under it on the other side, and Ahbhu snoring between us.

We awoke at the first sign of dawn above the transom. Suchi had gotten up in a sluggish mood, turned inward, not keen on exchanging more than a couple of words as we gathered our things and trudged out to the pickup. It had poured overnight, and the ground outside was muddy and waterlogged. Before jumping on the highway, we made a quick stop at a convenience store to buy a bag of kibbles for Ahbhu. Inside the store, I was delighted to find a rotating book stand at the back, a rare sight in these parts. It was overflowing with used paperbacks, likely left behind by travelers. Spotting a copy of Arthur C. Clarke's *Childhood's End*, I snatched it up, thrilled by the unexpected find. I tossed it into Suchi's basket as she unloaded it at the counter, and then we were off.

The sun shone brightly in a cartoon blue sky filled with puffy clouds as we traveled the twisty two-lane highway that tracked the Pacific coast a few miles inland. After speeding along for about half an hour along a winding stretch bounded on either side by rainforest and verdant hills, we hit a traffic jam created by a team of road workers filling potholes, their trucks and mixers blocking the road. Noxious black fumes stained the air.

We sat immobile for more than ten minutes, the traffic building up behind us. One driver a couple of cars back laid on his horn, demanding the workers make way. What started as a lone voice soon became a chorus of horns. Her anxiety level rising, Suchi joined in. She rolled down her window and shouted at the workers in frustration, swearing like a pirate. But they just continued pouring asphalt and raking it over, oblivious to the chaos they were creating.

Having had enough, Suchi launched out of the pickup and strode up to the workers, angrily gesticulating, pointing out the long line of cars. One of the workers, a thirtyish beanpole in a jumpsuit and construction helmet, led Suchi to one side and stared at her with a blank face as she tiraded.

Taking advantage that we were alone, I asked Ahbhu: "When you and Suchi went out last night, when she made the phone call to my parents . . . did she go anywhere else other than to the phone booth?"

Ahbhu rested his chin on the seat and scoured his memory. *Suchi came here. Inside the truck, before the telephone.*

"What did Suchi do inside the truck, Ahbhu?"

Another driver exited a vehicle behind us and marched over to Suchi and the worker and joined in shouting at him like a maniac. A few other drivers flooded out of their cars and approached *en masse*, making the worker back away, his hands raised. Seeing their comrade in trouble, a couple of the other workers ran to his aid with their shovels at the ready. I feared a major fight was about to break out.

"What did she do, Ahbhu?" I repeated, keeping an eye on Suchi in case she needed our assistance.

*Ahbhu didn't see,* Ahbhu answered. *Suchi opened the door and then she closed it and went to the telephone.*

"Which door did she open?"

Ahbhu touched the passenger side door with his paw, advertently brushing against the glove compartment, and my mind ignited like a flare. Glancing over the dashboard to ensure she wasn't looking in our direction, I swiftly popped open the glove compartment and dug around inside. My fingers touched a plastic bottle under a mess of papers. Slipping it out, I peered at it. It was a half-empty bottle of Valium prescribed to Suchi.

Just then, Suchi's head jerked toward us, as if she sensed what I was doing. I flashed a smile and mimed an exasperated gesture asking how much longer it was going to take. She indicated things were under control then turned back to the worker. Feeling guilty at having invaded her privacy, I shoved the little bottle back under the papers. Moments later, the workers started clearing the road of their equipment, and the drivers dispersed back to their vehicles.

The moment Suchi climbed back into the cab, the skies parted, and we were instantly enveloped in a torrent of rain. "Oh, for the love of God!" Suchi pounded the steering wheel in frustration. Tossing up her hands in resignation, she switched on the windshield wipers and coaxed the truck forward.

As we crawled past the workers, she flipped them the bird. Then she slowly increased her speed until we were finally rattling along at around forty miles per hour. Mercifully, the rain shower ceased as abruptly as it had started. Thanking the universe for that small favor, I drew a deep breath and buried my face in my paperback, losing myself for a while in a silly story about a group of advanced aliens who visit the Earth and play babysitter to humanity.

The rest of the journey along the CA2 was a maddening combination of dangerous curves, massive potholes, herds of cows that wafted across the road, more construction, and some actual normal driving, punctuated by the occasional pit stop. Toward the middle of the afternoon, when the silence in the cab felt particularly tedious, Suchi glanced at me out of the corner of her eye and asked, "When did you first know?"

Ahbhu and I exchanged a glance, and I set down my book. "When did I first know what?" I said, certain she was asking me about the Valium, which was still weighing on my conscience.

"That you were attracted to men."

Thrown by her blunt question, I froze. Nobody had ever

asked me such a thing, not in such an unadorned way. Struggling to formulate an answer, I lowered my eyes at Ahbhu and stroked his head, tongue-tied.

"You don't have to answer if you're uncomfortable," Suchi pressed. "I just thought we might get to know each other better. But if it's too much—"

"No, it's all right." I raised my eyes at her. "I'd just never thought about it before. Not in that way."

"No?"

I shook my head. "I mean . . . I guess I was never really wired like that." I dredged deep, searching for the right words. "What I'm trying to say is I never felt attracted to *anyone*, male *or* female—not in the way you mean. I was more into reading, schoolwork, stuff at home. The only thing I lacked back then was a friend."

Closing my eyes, I cast my mind back to the cathedral, to the first time my eyes landed on that handsome acolyte in his white robe so long ago. "Then I met Gerónimo, and everything changed," I said, feeling a poignancy in the memory. "That was the very first time I felt attracted to another person."

Suchi studied me for a beat, crinkling her brow as if puzzling something out. Then she asked in a gentler tone of voice: "When was that?"

"I was sixteen," I answered, my voice barely audible. I recalled how beautiful Gerónimo had seemed to me back then, so charming and affectionate. I swallowed hard against a twinge of sadness at how things had turned out between us.

Suchi squeezed my hand, urging me on. "And since then?"

"Since then, what?" I pulled back my hand and folded my arms over my chest, feeling she was crossing a line without an invitation from me.

Startled by my reaction, a dark cloud drifted across Suchi's face. She turned away and gripped the steering wheel. "You said Gerónimo was your first. I'm asking about after Gerónimo."

"There is no *after Gerónimo*, Suchi. He's the *only* one."

"Seriously?"

"Yes, seriously."

"You're what, twenty-two, twenty-three, and you've never been with *anyone* else, ever? I'm not talking about love, obviously. I'm talking about . . . well, you know, companionship."

"I have Ahbhu." My hand dropped to Ahbhu's muzzle, and he licked my hand.

Suchi snorted. "I'm talking about sex, Isaac."

"Do I really have to spell it out? I already told you! I've. *Only*. Ever. Been. With. *Gerónimo*. That's it."

Suchi stared at me, her mouth hanging open in amazement, as if she were looking at some kind of sideshow freak— Lionel the Lion-Faced Boy or Wang the Human Unicorn. Then, covering her mouth, she suppressed a laugh, which made my blood rise.

"What about *you*, Suchi?" I lobbed a hard serve back at her. "When did *you* first know?"

If I'm honest, at that point, I didn't give a fig what she had to say. But if she was going to fish in my pond, she should be ready for me to cast a sharp hook into hers.

"I *always* knew," she struck back. "No mystery there." We'd reached a fairly straight stretch of road, and Suchi pressed down hard on the gas pedal, making the pickup rocket forward. "I even think my mother knew before I knew." She barked a bitter laugh. "She tried everything she could to *turn me normal*. Her words. Stereotypical girly shit. As if. She even tried some of her *magic* on me." She emphasized the word, taking her hands off the steering wheel and miming quotation marks in the air.

Picturing us veering into oncoming traffic or into a ditch, I dove at the steering wheel and held it steady. Not appearing to notice, Suchi lowered her hands back to the wheel and carried on with her saga.

"The more my mother tried to *make me normal*, the more

certain I became of who and what I was. I love women, period!" She quickly glanced at me. "And then I met Amparo."

The traffic ahead was slowing down. Suchi eased off the accelerator, and I let out the breath I'd been holding. After miles of driving through pure countryside, a gas station loomed in the distance, and a couple of small buildings beyond that, like a shimmering mirage, signs we were approaching a settlement.

The storm that had buffeted Suchi's face as she related her young life lifted at her mention of Amparo. The sun broke through the clouds, and she beamed an enraptured smile at the road, continuing as if on autopilot. "Not that Amparo was my first." She wagged her head at me, her smile holding steady. "There were *many* before her. And a few since. But Amparo was the one. She still is." Her voice dropped, and she swiped at her eyes. "She always will be."

"Are you the one for her?"

The smile evaporated from Suchi's face at my question.

"I mean, why are you sharing her with her husband? How can you even stand for that? Not that I'm judging; I'm just curious now that we're sharing. If you both love each other, why don't you go somewhere else together, the way you help other people do?"

Suchi's expression stiffened, and her fingers turned white on the steering wheel. Fearing I'd hurt her with my probing, I touched her arm and whispered an apology. After a moment, her grip on the wheel relaxed. She eased the pickup into the gas station as it came up and brought us to a stop alongside a pump, lowering her hands to her lap.

"I'm more than twice your age, Isaac. You think things are bad for people like us now; they were worse before, socially I mean. Especially for women. And I'm not just talking about in El Salvador. It was the same everywhere. Even in that Land of Oz you're headed to. Marriage was expected. And children. And that's what Amparo did. By the time escape was an option, she was trapped by circumstances, a daughter with serious developmental disabilities, whom I love to death, and a husband who refuses to grant her a divorce. What we have is an arrangement that works—for now at least."

A station attendant tapped on the window, and Suchi asked him to fill up the tank. Then she turned to me. "Anything else?"

"No, makes sense, I guess." I opened the door for Ahbhu, who disappeared behind the building. "I suppose I might have done the same if I'd been in your position." For a fleeting moment, the image of what *might* have been flitted across my imagination: Gerónimo and me, living our relationship under the radar. Together but separate. The very idea made my stomach churn like a cement mixer.

"It's tough stuff," Suchi said, tossing the station attendant a few bills and switching on the engine. "But it's good to talk about these things sometimes. Better than to keep it all bottled inside. So, thanks."

Ahbhu came bounding from around the corner and galloped toward us. I opened the door for him, and he jumped inside, his body radiating heat from his run in the fields behind the station.

"How much longer until we get to where we're going?" I asked, deliberately switching gears. I'd had enough of the forced rap, which seemed to have done Suchi more good than it had me. All this talk about Gerónimo had only served to bring me down. I had to get out from under him one way or another. If that meant listening to what he had to say as a first step, then so be it.

"We're less than thirty minutes away now," Suchi said, easing the truck back into the flow of traffic in the waning light of the late afternoon, our estimated five-hour trip having turned into a ten-hour ordeal. "Barring any unexpected delays, we should be arriving in Tecún Umán in time for supper."

Thoroughly exhausted and emotionally spent, I brought my legs up on the bench seat, crossed my arms, and nestled my head against the side window. "Great. Wake me up when we fricking get there."

# Chapter 24

## CIUDAD TECÚN UMÁN

As we rumbled into Ciudad Tecún Umán, the sun painted the colonial border town in warm, reddish hues, casting long shadows that throbbed along its bustling streets. The relentless journey had drained me, weariness seeping into my bones. My eyelids, burdened by fatigue, strained to absorb the town's vibrant disorder—a cacophony of color, sound, and motion pulsing through its very core—which made Ahbhu perk up, his ears twitching with curiosity. The air was thick with the roar of passing vehicles, shady market vendors loudly hawking their wares, and the hum of conversation in Spanish and indigenous languages. Perched on the edge of a river that divided Guatemala from Mexico, the town laid bare its vivid tapestry of life, a convergence of diverse faces, each, I imagined, with a different story to tell. Mine was just one of countless others.

Suchi skillfully maneuvered the pickup through the throngs of people, narrowly avoiding collisions with pedestrians, street vendors, and packs of mangy street dogs. I caught glimpses of men in wraparound sunglasses and knock-off designer jeans, lurking in the shadows cast by unmarked storefronts that spoke of mysteries behind closed doors. Ahbhu, now fully alert, lifted his head, his nose twitching to catch the scents carried by the warm breeze. Indian women in brilliant *huipiles* called out their offerings, their voices blending into a discordant chorus with the rhythmic clatter of wheels and hooves. Ahbhu's tail thumped against the floor of the pickup in rhythm with the pulse of the town.

As the sun descended, neon signs flickered to life, casting a kaleidoscope of colors on the streets. The growing darkness intensified the aroma of greasy street food that tainted the air—the sizzle of grilling meat, the scent of hand-griddled tortillas, and the heady aroma of chilies from open-air eateries made my stomach groan.

"How much longer, mommy?" I complained like a five-year-old.

"Nearly there, sweetheart," Suchi cooed, playfully matching my tone.

Turning onto a dimly illuminated, semi-deserted side street, she brought the pickup to a halt a few meters from a flickering neon sign advertising a medium-sized two-story hotel with exterior stairs and corridors. We exchanged a glance, our exhaustion mirrored in each other's eyes, hardly believing we'd finally arrived. Sensing the change in energy, Ahbhu hopped onto the seat, his tail *thwaping* with excitement. The promise of a bed and a hot meal beckoned like an oasis in the desert of our weariness.

We hopped out of the car, and I stretched my legs. Before I could say anything, Ahbhu shot out of the cab and disappeared into the shadows in pursuit of a shaggy terrier mix that had appeared from out of nowhere. "He'll be okay," I reassured Suchi, whose face registered her disapproval. "He just has to get his yayas out." Shaking her head, she shouldered her backpack and headed to the hotel, and I trailed her.

As we entered the brightly lit office, the door jangling

noisily behind us, the hotel clerk shifted his eyes at us from a TV mounted in a corner. Dressed in a white muscle shirt and bright blue jeans, the handsome thirtysomething was all business. He checked us in with an air of boredom, not bothering to look at our IDs. He was taller than a typical Guatemalan, with the broad shoulders of a swimmer or a gymnast and the biceps to match. His hazel eyes kept drifting in my direction as he transacted with Suchi, and he flashed me a friendly wink as we exited the office, keys in hand.

"Looks like *you* made an impression," Suchi said as we mounted the stairs to the second story.

"Do you think?" I asked, reddening with embarrassment.

Suchi halted and swung on me, her eyes radiating disappointment. "Give me a little credit here, please. I didn't just tumble out of the jungle!"

"Okay, yes," I admitted, smarting from the abrupt tongue lashing, "I made an impression. What of it?"

Suchi shook her head and barreled away from me down the corridor. On reaching our room, she struggled to slot her key into the keyhole. Stepping ahead of her, I tried mine. The door opened into a clean room with two double beds and a bright bathroom.

Suchi pushed past me and tossed her bag onto the bed nearest the bathroom, effectively claiming it for herself. I dropped onto the other bed and tested the mattress, which, at that moment, felt like heaven on earth.

"*Anyway*, about that desk clerk," Suchi pressed, not yet ready to let go of the subject, "he *really* wanted to eat you up like you were a piece of *pan dulce*."

"So what?"

"So, maybe you should explore that before we leave, don't you think? It's not right that Gerónimo's your only one. Not after all the crap he pulled on you. Especially, not when he's back there and you're here. Explore that side of yourself a bit more;

that's all I'm saying."

"I don't know, maybe." Her mention of *pan dulce* had made me all the hungrier. "Now, may we *please* get something to eat, and I mean proper food, not chocolate bars and banana chips."

We found a decent hole in the wall with an empty table run by a charming older woman, still attractive in her seventies, who ran the entire operation, shuttling efficiently between the tables and her kitchen. We tucked into a couple of steaming bowls of *pepián*, Guatemala's aromatic and hearty version of beef stew. We were both so hungry we asked for seconds, scarfing it up as if we hadn't eaten for a week. When we were done, Suchi placed both her hands on the table, looking like she was about to deliver unwelcome news.

"What is it?" I felt the stew curdle in my stomach in anticipation of something bad.

"I have some repairing to do," she said, "with my friends in the safehouse near here. They were expecting us tonight. So I have to go make things right with them. Also, there's a lot of paperwork I need to prearrange with them for our crossing into Mexico."

I wiped my mouth with a napkin and sat up. "You mean you're going to leave me?"

"Just for a couple of hours, maybe less. I'll be back before you know it."

I peeked through the window of the hotel office on my way back to the room. The clerk was still slouched at his desk, staring up at the TV, looking utterly bored. He straightened up on seeing me and raised his hand in a greeting, flashing a smile that wasn't easy to read. Was he flirting with me or just being friendly? It was difficult to tell. I waved back, keeping my expression neutral. Then, cautious not to send the wrong signal, I sprinted up the concrete steps to our room, two steps at a time, my heart hammering in my chest.

I was surprised to find Ahbhu lying outside the door. He stood up as I approached and greeted me with a gentle head-butt.

"How did you know which room we were in?" I asked him as I pushed open the door, the image of the desk clerk still fresh in my mind.

*Ahbhu saw*, he said, as he pattered past me. Once he'd finished sniffing around the room, he hopped onto Suchi's bed and drew up his legs, panting contentedly.

"Mine's this one." I sat on my bed and patted it.

He opened his mouth in a wide yawn and lowered his head. *Ahbhu knows.*

Of course, Ahbhu knows, I thought to myself, kicking off my shoes and feeling a twinge of jealousy at how close he had grown to Suchi, who was anything but warm with him.

"Do you actually like her?" I asked as I slipped out of my clothes and pulled the bed sheet over me.

Ahbhu blinked, and his mouth pulled into a grin. *Ahbhu likes Suchi. Suchi is good.*

"Suchi's good," I agreed. "But she's also mean sometimes. Even to you, Ahbhu!"

*Suchi is good inside. Suchi loves Ahbhu; Ahbhu loves Suchi.*

My heart sank at his words. I switched off the light and hugged the soft pillow, feeling myself drifting off. "I hope Ahbhu still loves me," I recall myself mumbling just before I dropped off.


I awoke abruptly and sat up in bed, glancing around the dark room, unsure of where I was, the image of Gerónimo softly glowing in my mind, like embers in a dying campfire. As the cobwebs cleared, I noticed Ahbhu snoring at my feet. There was an empty bed next to us, its bedspread undisturbed. Then it all came back. I reached for the digital clock. Only an hour had passed since I'd fallen asleep.

I wondered how much longer before Suchi came back. My mouth went dry at the thought she might be planning on abandoning me here. Crawling out of bed, I popped into the bathroom, where I slaked my thirst with some water from a plastic cup. Then I padded back to bed and reclined against the pillow, feeling restless and fidgety.

My thoughts drifted to the hotel clerk, at the way he'd stared at me, that wink. Was his raised hand just a greeting or an invitation? I recalled Suchi's words, encouraging me to put myself out there, that it was time for me to stop pining over the past.

I wrapped myself around the pillow and hugged it tight, trying my best to channel my thoughts elsewhere. But the more I resisted, the harder it became to unthink the image of the handsome hotel clerk with his jet-black buzz cut. Imagining him shirtless, I felt myself getting aroused—the warm flush in my face, the tingling in my core. It had been so long since I'd experienced this kind of excitement I'd forgotten how pleasurable and comforting it could be.

It was then that something clicked over in my mind: I was *so* done with depriving myself for the lost cause that was Gerónimo. Love was love, but sex was life. Jettisoning all control then, I gave full license to my imagination, my arousal transforming into a ravenous hunger, and I feasted on that hotel clerk without limits.

When I was done, I went into the bathroom to splash some water on my face, perplexed by a strange mix of emotions. I felt at once victorious and deflated and couldn't understand why. Coming back into the room, I became conscious of just how oppressively stuffy it was, as if the walls themselves were radiating a dull heat. Ahbhu was still passed out on my bed, dead to the world. In need of some fresh air, I slipped into my clothes and exited the room.

I found the hotel clerk reclined against the wall of the office, smoking a cigarette. He stood away from the wall as I descended the stairs and met my gaze. His eyes said it all. Dropping his cigarette to the ground and crushing it under foot, he opened the door to the office for me and flipped on the *No Vacancy* sign. Then, switching off the lights, he led me around the front desk to a back bedroom, where we got straight to business.

Suchi was waiting up for me when I got back to the room in the early hours. I ignored her salacious smile and fell asleep the moment my head touched the pillow. She roused me a couple of hours later, announcing it was time for breakfast. Bleary-eyed from lack of sleep, I followed her zombie-like down the stairs, with Ahbhu in tow, in direction of the restaurant she'd selected.

The hotel clerk was reclined against the wall outside the office, smoking a cigarette, exactly as I'd found him the night before. He'd changed into a crisp white guayabera, tan linen trousers, and a pair of white huaraches. His charm radiated even more intensely than it had a few hours earlier. With a playful wink exchanged between us, I signaled my readiness for another encounter anytime. A sharp whistle from Suchi interrupted the momentary distraction. Instantly snapped back to reality, I dashed forward to catch up with her.

When we returned from breakfast, I was dismayed to discover the clerk was no longer on duty. The new receptionist, a humorless young woman lacking any semblance of warmth, tersely informed me that his shift had ended. Regret washed over me as we checked out and made our way to Suchi's pickup, realizing I hadn't even asked his name.

Staring into the middle distance as we drove out of town

toward the border crossing, tight-lipped and with my arms held tightly across my chest, I battled my disappointment.

Suchi reached over and squeezed my arm. "Hey, there, Helen Keller," she tried, half serious. I looked at her without expression, her joke having fallen flat.

"Stop fixating on one person; that's been your problem all along. Think of that guy as your first notch of many. A nice one, yes, but just the first."

I shifted my sleepy eyes away from her and quipped, "He'll be a hard act to follow."

A puff of laughter escaped Suchi's lips. "In any event, it's time to look sharp." She indicated the border complex rising dead ahead with a nod. I felt my heart jolt at the sight of it as I rejoined the plot, refocusing on the reason we were here in the first place.

A procession of weary foot travelers, men, women, and children alike, two deep and stretching for blocks, shuffled along the sidewalk to our right. Their faces bore the weariness of standing under the scorching sun, exhaustion etched into their brows, shoulders drooping from the relentless heat, as they moved forward toward the border post. Suchi joined the queue of those making the journey by car, preparing for another inspection. I pounded on the seat back, signaling to Ahbhu that we were nearly there.

"That's the *Guatemalan* border post," Suchi clarified as we inched ahead. "They'll be stamping us out of the country. That's the easy part. After that we'll cross over the river that separates Guatemala from Mexico and negotiate our entry with both Mexican customs and Mexican immigration."

"Negotiate?"

"You never know with them," she explained. "Lots of petty tyrants that can frustrate one's plans just because they can. I've found it's best to go with the flow and keep one's head down when it comes to things like the vehicle search and getting our visas stamped."

Reaching into her backpack, she pulled out a sheaf of paperwork and handed me my passport. "Luckily for us, I have influential friends in high places, who helped put together everything we need paper-wise. If all goes well, we should be able to breeze right through in a couple of hours, give or take."

"They search the vehicle?" I asked, not liking the sound of that one bit. "What about Ahbhu? Maybe we should bring him into the cab. They might think you're trying to smuggle him into the country."

"We'd need a vet's certificate for that, which we don't have. And there's no time to arrange one now. But don't worry, it's usually just a cursory visual search of the bed and the interior, unless they suspect something. So just relax and play it cool, okay? This isn't my first rodeo."

Still not convinced, I shifted uncomfortably in my seat, my fingers drumming nervously against the armrest. My gaze flitted between Suchi and the border complex looming ahead, unable to shake the knot of anxiety tightening in my chest. "What about your glove compartment?" I whispered, suddenly flashing on the little bottle of Valium. "Will they search in there?"

Suchi slammed on the brakes, throwing us forward against the shoulder harnesses, forcing the car behind us to make an evasive maneuver to avoid sliding into us. Turning angrily on me, she asked, "Why would I care if they searched my glove compartment, Isaac?"

"I don't know," I stammered, conscious we were drawing unwanted attention from the pedestrians walking alongside us and the driver behind us, who was laying on his horn. "I was just saying."

"Did you look in there?" Suchi demanded, point blank, her eyes moist.

"I was just . . . I mean—"

Suchi shook her head and put the car back in gear then

pulled forward the two car lengths we'd fallen behind. "You have no right to be snooping around in my things," she intoned after an uncomfortable pause.

"I'm sorry; I was just curious. I wasn't even going to say anything about it. I mean, why would I? But when you mentioned them searching the car—"

"I have a prescription," she interrupted, "if that's what you're worried about."

"I'm nervous, that's all. All of this terrifies me. I'm not being myself."

"Then maybe *you* should consider taking one," she snapped. "It helps for exactly that sort of thing, believe me."

"I'll pass, thanks."

"I'm just saying." Suchi cast a dark glance that sent a frigid current through me. The last thing I needed at that critical moment was to make an enemy of the very person on whom I was relying.

"Again, I'm really *really* sorry, Suchi," I said, summoning the humblest expression of regret I could muster. "The last thing I wanted was to hurt or offend you in any way. It won't happen again; I swear to you." I held my hand out to her. "I hope you can forgive me. I wouldn't be able to forgive myself if I lost your friendship because of some stupid thing I did."

She stared at me as if assessing the sincerity of my apology. After a moment, she accepted my hand and squeezed it tight, transmitting in that gesture a deep well of emotion she was battling to contain. Breathing a sigh of relief at our apparent reconciliation, a lingering unease settled in my gut, whispering of unresolved tensions and secrets lurking beneath the surface. Mindful not to awaken any dormant demons, I resolved to tread carefully with Suchi from here on out, to toughen my soul, lest they consume me as well.

# Chapter 25

## ROSITA

Leaving Guatemala unfolded as seamlessly as Suchi had described. A simple exchange of *quetzals*, a perfunctory stamp in our passports, and we were on our way. Exiting the kiosk, we intertwined our fingers, silently reassuring each other as we embarked on the next phase of our journey, bound for the *Rodolfo Robles International Bridge* spanning the Rio Suchiate that marks the border with Chiapas, Mexico.

Even in that early hour, the sparkling, slow-moving river was teeming with rubber dinghies and makeshift rafts ferrying queue-jumping migrants back and forth across the waterway. As we crawled over the bridge in bumper-to-bumper traffic, I clasped Suchi's hand, grateful for all her help thus far and for her presence beside me. I couldn't begin to imagine how Ahbhu and I would have fared risking our fate on that river, the two of us against the swirling currents.

Once we were clear of the bridge, we followed the signs to the Mexican vehicle inspection station, where we were directed into a parking space by a sharp-eyed officer, his snug uniform accentuating his trim physique. Suchi disappeared into the office to handle the paperwork while I remained in the truck, surreptitiously observing the officer's movements as he went about his duties, admiring his athletic build, the confidence he exuded.

*How much longer?* Ahbhu's plaintive voice called from behind the seat.

"I don't know, Ahbhu. Maybe twenty, thirty minutes more. We still have the immigration inspection after this, which is a little farther down the road," I whispered, his whimpers tugging at my heartstrings. "Hang in there, buddy, it's nearly over."

*Ahbhu needs to go; Ahbhu is thirsty.*

My fingers tap danced on the water bottle, wondering whether there was a way to get it to Ahbhu without being too obvious. As discreetly as possible, I bent down to look under the seat but all I could see was the back of the metal panel that enclosed the hidden compartment. A loud rap on the window startled me upright, and I found myself facing the officer through the glass. Lowering the window, I was struck by a heady mix of Drakkar Noir and mild sweat radiating from the officer's freshly razored face. He did a quick look-see around the cab then focused his eyes on me.

"Did you lose something?" he asked with forced patience, resting his hand on the roof of the truck and leaning in.

Over his shoulder, I could see Suchi exiting the inspections office, shuffling a stack of papers, accompanied by another officer, the inspector I presumed, a tall, gangly man with graying hair slick with brilliantine.

Thinking quickly, I held up the water bottle, giving it a little shake. "I was looking for this, sir." Popping the cap, I took a swig and held it out to him. "Thirsty?"

Just as he opened his mouth to respond, Suchi and the inspector arrived. On seeing them, the officer stiffened to attention, deferring to his superior, and resumed directing traffic.

The inspector ordered me out of the truck, and I stood next

to Suchi watching nervously as he circled it. He passed his gloved hand around the empty bed, and studied the undercarriage, giving it a few taps here and there. In the background, the sharp-eyed officer kept looking over at us as he waved vehicles into and out of the inspection bays. I lifted my hand at him. He responded with a quick nod of his head then quickly looked away. Suchi pinched my arm as the inspector turned his attention to the interior of the cab. Her face grew tight as he ran his hand over the seat and then bent down to look underneath it.

"That's a cursory check?" I said in a low voice.

Suchi jumped forward and politely interrupted the inspection. The inspector stood, his expression a mix of expectation and impatience. Glancing around to make sure nobody was looking, Suchi closed the gap between them and produced a couple thousand Mexican pesos.

"You wouldn't happen to have some change, would you, officer?" she asked with an air of nonchalance.

The words were barely out of her mouth when the inspector snatched the cash from Suchi's hands and pocketed it. Then, signing off the paperwork with a flourish, he announced we'd passed inspection and marched back to the kiosk.

As we pulled out of the inspection bay, giddy with nervous excitement at having made it through unscathed so far, I caught a sly smile from the officer in the side mirror as he waved a discreet goodbye.

"You're really on a roll, aren't you?" Suchi remarked, glancing back at the inspection area in her rearview mirror.

"He wasn't too bad," I said, looking again in the side mirror. But we'd turned a bend in the road and lost sight of him. Now that we were headed for the immigration kiosk, the officer was old news. "By the way, Ahbhu has to do his thing."

"Now?"

"Ever since you were in the inspection office. He's thirsty, too. How are you holding up, buddy?" I asked him.

*Ahbhu is bursting*, he whimpered.

"It's bad," I said to Suchi. "Isn't there any place where we can let him out for a bit?"

"We're literally in the border zone, Isaac; there are eyes everywhere," Suchi said, "If we're seen at this point, we could get into trouble for not having papers for him."

"If we're seen, I'm sure you could buy his way in based on what I just saw back there. He's a dog, for Christ's sake. How much could it possibly cost to get someone to turn a blind eye? Look, there's a shoulder there. Pull over, please."

Grumbling a halfhearted objection, Suchi navigated onto the shoulder, waited until the VW that had been tailgating us had passed, then popped open her seat. Ahbhu rocketed out of the car and vanished into the bushes. In less than five minutes, we were back on the road, with me beaming an *I told you so* at Suchi, who ignored me, looking like she was reaching the end of her tether again.

Aside from the half hour it took to be seen by an immigration officer, we passed inspection without event, the stated purpose of our journey to visit a cousin in Puebla. The attending immigration officer, a friendly young woman with a touch of pink lipstick, stamped our passports, drawing a flirty wink from Suchi. Graciously accepting the gesture with a warm smile, she welcomed us to Mexico and waved the next person forward. It was straight-up noon.

Once we were out of sight of the immigration post, Suchi pulled to the side of the road and released Ahbhu. She called him up front, finally allowing him to sit on the seat in between us. He was beside himself with happiness, bobbing up and down, watching the passing landscape, and panting with excitement.

"We'll have lunch in Tapachula, which is literally just up the road," Suchi said as we got onto the highway, her eyes brightening with excitement. "I know a place where they make the best *estofado*."

I had no idea what estofado was, but I was hungry enough to eat anything at that point. So I flashed a thumbs-up and held tight as she pressed down on the gas and made the pickup fly.

We hit traffic on reaching the city limits of Tapachula, which turned out to be larger than I imagined. Its streets were busy with traffic and bustling with pedestrians and peddlers jostling past each other on the sidewalks. The colonial buildings lining its main drag were painted with colorful murals, and countless shops overflowed with handwoven textiles and folksy knick-knacks. The hot, humid air shimmered with the enticing aroma of sizzling meat, which made Ahbhu salivate.

Suchi found a parking spot off the charming main plaza with its whitewashed gazebo and stately cathedral gleaming bright in the intense noonday sun. Ahbhu and I followed her a short distance to a cute restaurant that, according to Suchi, boasted a large interior covered patio. On catching sight of Ahbhu, however, the light in the manager's face dimmed. He apologized stiffly that dogs weren't allowed inside. Even after I explained that Ahbhu was my service dog, he emphasized, with a pained expression, that the restaurant was not in a position to make exceptions even though he sympathized with my circumstances. Holding my hunger and frustration in check, I stepped back as a group of chattering tourists flowed past us into the main dining room. Not one to take no for an answer, Suchi waited until the last of them had cleared the reception area, then approached the manager and discreetly fanned out a few bills. He lost no time in pocketing the bribe with a curt bow and promptly escorted us inside.

The manager offered us a secluded table tucked away in a remote corner of the bustling patio. In the background, recorded marimba music competed with the lilt of lively conversation. As he departed, Suchi swiftly put in our order with him: two Chiapan estofados with extra tortillas, a couple of beers, and a beef shank for Ahbhu, subtly hinting at an extra tip if we were served *chop-chop*.

The estofado turned out to be a chicken stew that was both savory and sweet, swimming with fresh pineapple and dried fruits, carrots, and potatoes. I'd never tasted anything like it and was in heaven as I dipped into it, pairing it with freshly griddled Mexican tortillas, and cooling it off with draughts of ice-cold beer. Ahbhu contented himself with the meaty beef shank the manager had selected for him, making sure to remain well under the table out of sight of the other diners at the manager's request.

Being the slow eater that I was, I was barely halfway through my meal when Suchi pushed away her bowl and dabbed at her lips with her napkin. "I'll be right back," she announced, standing, and making a show of stretching her legs.

"Where are you going now?" I set down my fork and frowned, feeling a little guilty about my sluggish pace.

"I need to exchange some money. Plus, I want to call ahead to my friends in Tuxtla Gutierrez to find out about the state of the roads between here and there. We should ideally be leaving here no later than one thirty so we can arrive by six, before the sun goes down. Take your time. I'll be back before you know it."

And with that, before I could get a word in edgewise, she flew out of the patio, her footsteps clattering against the tiled floor, leaving me slightly stunned. I reached down and stroked Ahbhu's coat, seeking some reassurance in the contact. Ahbhu responded by rubbing his muzzle against my hand and curling against my leg.

"Do you believe her?" I asked him. I moved the bowl of stew to one side and drained the last of my beer, having lost my appetite.

*Suchi is good*, Ahbhu repeated. He turned back to the beef shank, which was long ago denuded of any meat, and gnawed on it.

As I glanced around the patio, an unexpected wave of loneliness broke over me. I reached down again for Ahbhu, only to find him peacefully snoring at my feet. With a sigh, I flagged down a passing waitress. "Could I have a bottle of water, please?" I requested. It was nearly two o'clock, and I wondered what had become of Suchi as I realized she had been gone for nearly an hour.

Just as I was about to go looking for her, she suddenly appeared in the patio, accompanied by a captivating woman with cinnamon-toned skin and a pair of Princess Leia braids framing her wedge-shaped head. She wore a thin white blouse, hip huggers, and heels, with a hand-tooled leather purse slung off her shoulder. Moving with a catlike grace, she followed Suchi, her almond-shaped eyes gleaming as she surveyed the crowded patio, a smile dancing on her red-painted lips. Each step she took drew the eyes of those nearby. As Suchi led her to our table, I couldn't help but feel a mixture of curiosity and apprehension, unsure of what to make of this intriguing newcomer.

"This is Tlaloc," Suchi said to the woman, pulling a chair out for her at the table, indicating me with a lift of her head, "my godson."

Alarm bells sounded in my brain at the subtle but significant change in my identity. I was now Suchi's godson instead of her son? I searched her face, looking for an explanation and found it in the goo-goo eyes she was making at the woman as she sat next to her.

The woman leaned across the table, her gaze lingering on me with a playful intensity. She reached out and picked at a lock that had adhered to my sweaty forehead. "I love what you've done with your hair," she purred, her lovely voice hinting at intrigue. She turned to Suchi and subtly brushed her fingertips. "Such a handsome boy." Her mischievous smile revealed a teasing gap between her two front teeth. "Just like his godmother."

Suchi's face flushed the color of a ripening plum at the unexpected compliment. "Tlaloc, this is Rosita," she stammered in an attempt to steer the conversation in a different direction.

"We met at the currency exchange office."

Sensing a new presence at the table, Ahbhu's eyes fluttered open, and he rose from the floor, cocking his head curiously at the woman. Trilling with delight, she made to pet him, but Ahbhu drew away from her, emitting a low growl.

"Steady, boy," I said, stroking him reassuringly, concerned his reaction mirrored my own initial impressions. "You two know each other, do you?" I asked Suchi.

"We've only just met," Suchi said, her eyes darting back to the woman. "Rosita was standing in line behind me, and we struck up a conversation."

"It was as if we'd known each other forever," Rosita jumped in, fluttering her eyelashes at Suchi. "A bit like destiny, don't you think?" Their fingers intertwined briefly.

Ahbhu pattered around the table and sniffed at the woman's purse. She shifted it away from him and nestled it in her lap, her smile tightening.

"You met at the currency exchange office?" I asked, trying my best to keep the skepticism out of my voice. "Where are you from exactly?" I asked the woman.

"From Tuxtla Gutierrez," she said. "The capital."

"The capital of *Chiapas*," Suchi clarified. "Where *we're* headed." She squeezed my hand in an attempt to stop me from asking questions. "We'll be giving Rosita a ride," she announced with a clear finality in her voice.

"We will?" A feeling of apprehension crept over me. "Wait . . ." I turned to Rosita. "Why is it you were in the currency exchange office if you're from around here?"

Her lips curled into a sly smile, her eyes never leaving Suchi's. "You might say I'm a kind of tour guide. People pay me in all kinds of currencies: quetzals, colones, córdobas, dólares. I accept them all. So, I'm always needing to exchange my fees into Mexican pesos. Make sense, Tlaloc?" she said, emphasizing my name with what felt like a snap of menace. I glanced at

Suchi, who hadn't caught it and was still staring at Rosita with a captivation that made me look around at the other diners in embarrassment.

"The road between here and Tuxtla Gutierrez is absolutely gorgeous!" Rosita continued, her fingers brushing against the back of my clenched fist. "Ocean views, rugged mountains, a tropical rain forest, a true feast for the senses. Like an amusement park. But it's also downright treacherous in parts. Like *all* of Chiapas, or *Chiapasland* as I like to call it. Especially at night. It's best to travel with an experienced guide. Someone like me!"

"We're lucky to have found her," Suchi said, affectionately stroking Rosita's arm.

"But I thought we *weren't* going to be driving at night," I protested, glancing at the wall clock. "Didn't you say it was a five-hour drive to our next stop?"

At that, the restaurant manager approached the table. "The kitchen will be closing in fifteen minutes," he announced, his interruption breaking the tension. "In case you wanted to order something else? Or shall I bring the check?"

"I'll have one of your extra-spicy pork tlayudas," Rosita jumped in, a spark of hunger glowing in her eyes. "With a cold cervezita, if that's all right!" She flashed her teeth at Suchi.

"It's almost two thirty," I complained.

Suchi held up her hand to silence me. "Of *course* it's all right. And it's my treat." Turning to me, she added in a low voice, "If we have to, we can bed down for the night somewhere between here and there. It's not a problem."

"In that case," I shot back, "we can sleep here, can't we?"

"Absolutely not!" Suchi's voice turned hard, angered at the challenge. "That would throw us off schedule. We need to reach Mexico City in two days, three days tops. Staying *here* would add an extra day, which we can't afford."

Pretending not to hear what we were saying, Rosita cast about the restaurant, humming along with the piped-in music, a bemused smile flickering on her lips.

One of the waitresses, a cute girl just out of her teens, arrived at the table with a bottle of beer and daintily placed it in front of her, promising to return with her dish shortly. Rosita grinned a thank you at the waitress, then snatched up the bottle and guzzled a quarter of it in one go.

Fuming, I excused myself from the table, announcing I'd be waiting outside at the pickup and sped out of the restaurant with Ahbhu. We crossed the road to the central square, where I sought shelter from the sun under the gazebo, kicking myself for petulantly abandoning the cool of the restaurant patio.

"Tour guide, my foot," I muttered.

*The new woman*, Ahbhu said, resting his head on my lap. *She has a gun in her purse.*

I sat up with a jolt as if I'd stepped barefoot on a sparking electrical wire. "What? How do you know that? And, why didn't you say something before?"

Startled by the sharpness in my voice, Ahbhu retreated, his movements weighted with a palpable sense of disappointment. *Isaac was busy*, he whimpered, his eyes reflecting a deep well of hurt.

"I'm sorry Ahbhu. But that's a *very* important detail. I need to warn Suchi."

*Suchi knows*, Ahbhu said, raising his head at me.

"She knows?" I stood up, feeling the ground shifting under me, and held onto one of the gazebo's side posts to steady myself. "Are you sure about that?"

Ahbhu nodded. *Ahbhu's sure.*

The sun was dipping to the west when Suchi and Rosita emerged from the restaurant, all giggles, unsteady on their feet. It was clear they'd both had more than a few beers.

241

"You're not going to drive like that, are you?" I asked Suchi, pulling up alongside her as she opened the passenger door for Rosita, who climbed in and scooted to the middle.

"I'm fine," she answered tersely. "Hop in."

Following her around to her side of the truck, I tugged gently at her sleeve. "You don't even know this woman, Suchi. She has a gun in her purse, for God's sake!"

Suchi pulled away from me and smoothed her sleeve, her eyes flashing dark lightning. "All women here do," she said. "For protection. Now get the fuck into the truck and be nice."

# Chapter 26

## HALFWAY TO TUXTLA

As we sped along the Pacific in the waning light, I tried to lose myself in my book while Rosita chattered on about her life. According to her, she'd been born to a middle-class family in a village outside Tuxtla Gutierrez. Her father was an automobile mechanic, her mother a baby-making machine—her words, not mine. The eldest of twelve children spaced one year apart, Rosita was forced to take charge when, at thirteen, her father was killed in some kind of accident, an explosion or a crash or something. I'd zoned out at that part of her story, which was heavy with intricate details and maddening digressions that made my brain spin. Suchi, though, seemed fascinated with every nuance, peppering Rosita with question after question.

As the principal breadwinner, lacking any skills or training but brimming with drive and imagination, Rosita supported her mother and siblings through her wiles. She bragged about all the petty swindles she'd conjured up to bring home the bacon— again, her words. An attractive and lively teenager and young woman, Rosita soon learned to carry a pistol to defend herself against grabby hands, even hinting that she'd had to use it more than once, including on some "funny uncle" who'd tried to take liberties. She drew a silent nod of approval from Suchi as we followed the darkening road away from the coast and started our ascent into the interior highlands.

"There's a rest area just ahead." Rosita pointed out a sign to our right as we whooshed past it, the headlights of Suchi's truck splashing out on the asphalt. "There are toilets and some roadside shelters there where we can stay until morning."

"How far are we from Tuxtla?" Suchi asked, squinting into the trees lining the road, appearing doubtful for the first time.

"We're about three hours away, assuming no delays," Rosita answered, patting Suchi's hand reassuringly. "Don't worry, dear, it's perfectly safe as long as I have this guy." She indicated her purse and its contents.

"I say we keep driving," I insisted, my voice tinged with unease. "I'd just as soon we take our chances on the dark road."

"That's not your decision to make!" Suchi snapped.

Over my objections, Suchi took the turnoff towards the rest area, her determination evident as we drove down the dark road, flanked by towering trees that seemed to close in on us. The only light came from the dimly illuminated complex of cinderblock buildings that loomed ahead. As we pulled into the overgrown parking lot, a sense of eerie desolation enveloped the scene, with a smattering of steamed-up cars and vans parked randomly here and there.

Exiting the truck, we stepped onto the uneven ground, the weeds brushing against our legs. Ahbhu darted into the surrounding overgrowth, disappearing into the darkness. Undeterred by the atmosphere, Rosita shouldered her purse and forged ahead confidently, beckoning for us to follow her.

Unable to contain my apprehension, I turned to Suchi, who was rushing past me to catch up with Rosita, clutching her backpack tightly. "Isn't this all a bit weird to you?" I asked.

Halting abruptly, Suchi flared her nostrils at me, looking

like a parent on the verge of losing patience with their naughty two-year-old. "Watch your tone," she growled. "I happen to *like* this woman. And I'm not going to let you ruin this bit of fun, especially after you had *yours* with that hotel guy back in Tecún Umán."

"*That's* what this is about?" I exclaimed. "I had my moment, and now you need to have yours?"

"Why not?" she retorted.

Rosita called to us from one of the buildings. "Over here, amigos!"

I looked back to Suchi, who was waiting for a response from me. "Because I don't trust her, that's why! The woman has practically admitted to being a con artist *and* she's packing a weapon in her purse."

"Oh, grow up, Isaac," Suchi spat out, her eyes flashing with irritation, before hurrying to join Rosita.

Resigned, I raised my hands in defeat and trudged across the parking lot, closing the distance between myself and the two women. Ahbhu burst out of the bushes and skidded up to us, circling and sniffing at Rosita like a vulture closing in on a piece of carrion. With a nervous glance, Rosita pointed out the men's building to our right, quickly describing its facilities while linking arms with Suchi, who didn't even deign to look in my direction. Then she led Suchi toward the women's building on our left, walking with an exaggerated sashay that felt like a deliberate taunt aimed at me. "Meet us back at the truck at the crack of dawn, boys!" Rosita called out as they stepped into the windowless hut. "Wouldn't want you to get left behind."

Once they were gone, I couldn't help but feel an unsettling sense of abandonment and an underlying fear of what the night might hold in this strange and isolated place. All was quiet out there in the open, the eerie stillness broken only by the faint rustle of leaves and the distant hum of passing cars on the highway. The tungsten lights cast a feeble glow over the asphalt, creating shadows that lingered like ghostly whispers among the cinderblock buildings. It was a desolate scene, the atmosphere heavy with a sense of foreboding.

Unable yet to retire for the night, and needing to decompress, I sought respite in a leisurely stroll along the sidewalk with Ahbhu until we stumbled upon a pair of picnic tables a stone's throw from the rest area buildings.

Stretching out on one of the benches, I gazed upward. It was a clear night, and the stars were shimmering fiercely in the vast expanse, far from the glare of city lights. I had no trouble making out the celestial band of the Milky Way rising in the east, a sight that stirred emotions long dormant within me. Tears welled in my eyes, transforming the stars into a quivering mosaic of radiant light, searing over Chiapas, a symbol of a past innocence lost. They were a poignant reminder of Time's relentless passage, its dual nature of giving and taking, like precious stones sifting through my fingers.

*Why is Isaac sad?* Ahbhu asked, contemplating me with his large liquid eyes gleaming in the reflected starlight.

I held him close and kissed his head. "Isaac's not sad, Ahbhu. Isaac's afraid."

He kissed me back and snuggled against my chest. *Ahbhu will always protect Isaac*, he promised, his voice full of emotion. *Ahbhu will die for Isaac.*

My breath caught at those words, and I sat up, feeling as if I'd been punched in the chest. "Why would you say that?"

*Ahbhu doesn't want Isaac to be afraid.*

"I understand that! But, please, Ahbhu, don't *ever* say that again! I don't know what I'd do if something were to happen to you on account of me. I wouldn't be able to live with myself."

*Ahbhu will always be with Isaac*, he said in a low voice, panting with emotion. *Even when Ahbhu goes away, Ahbhu never leaves Isaac.*

I stared at him open-mouthed, shot through to my very core

by the implication of what he was saying and too freaked out and tired to unpack it any further. What I needed was sleep.

Glancing between the ugly cinderblock hut and Suchi's truck sitting forlorn in the distance, I chastised myself for not asking her for the keys to sleep inside of it instead. Surrendering to the inevitable, I decided it was time to stop stalling and walked to the hut, dragging my feet as I went, like a condemned man being led to execution. Ahbhu met my stride, and together we entered the musky smelling hut and had a look around.

There were toilets and such in one room; next to that was a small changing room with a couple of benches. In the back I found a larger room, hazily illuminated by light from the outside lamps filtering in through a cracked skylight, containing a dozen or so empty cots. I touched one of them to assess the state of it. I was surprised to find it was dry and in good repair as if it had never been used. "Thank God for small mercies," I muttered as I lowered myself onto it, wondering about the people whose cars were parked outside.

*Ahbhu will sleep by the doorway*, Ahbhu said, crouching down, using his front paws as a pillow.

"No, Ahbhu, sleep here with me." I pulled the nearest cot closer and patted it. "Over here, buddy."

Ahbhu stood and creaked across the room like an old dog, weaving between the cots on his way over. As he settled into the cot next to me, I kept my sadness in check, hidden from him. In all our years together, I'd never contemplated a life without Ahbhu, not even after the beating he'd taken trying to rescue me from Sisler. But now he'd spoken the words, bringing the possibility of such a thing into reality. I gently stroked his side, lovingly whispering to him, until, after a few minutes, he was quietly snoring. Then I curled up and drifted off.

I awoke to the sound of furious barking echoing in the distance. Instinctively, I threw out my arm, searching for Ahbhu, only to find an empty cot beside me. Panic surged through me as I bolted outside, propelled by the urgency of the commotion. Following the sound to Suchi's pickup, I found Rosita sprawled next to it on the asphalt, screaming for help, her cries slicing through the night air, and flailing her arms against Ahbhu, who loomed over her, teeth bared, his eyes ablaze with fury. Suchi's keys dangled ominously from the truck's open door, and her backpack lay open on the ground, speaking clearly of Rosita's intention to steal the pickup and leave us behind.

Summoning every ounce of authority, I commanded Ahbhu to stand down, my gaze darting to Suchi as she emerged from the women's hut, disheveled and buttoning her shirt, her face a cauldron of bewilderment. Shadows stirred within nearby vehicles, their occupants roused out of their sleep, drawn by the turmoil unfolding, yet keeping a cautious distance.

With a surge of adrenaline, I lunged forward, wrenching Ahbhu away from Rosita's trembling form. But he continued his frenzied barking, fueled by her perceived betrayal. Rosita, her fear transforming into defiance, retreated like a cornered animal, spitting out obscenities. Then she clambered onto her heels and brandished her revolver, her hand trembling as she aimed it at Ahbhu.

"Keep that damned mutt away from me, or I'll shoot him, I swear I will," she screamed, her voice laced with desperation as she crouched toward the truck, her threat hanging heavy in the air.

"Rosita," Suchi's voice cut through the air, weighted with disappointment. "You're not going to shoot anyone."

"Who says I'm not?" Rosita retorted. "Just stay the hell back!"

As she made to enter the pickup, Ahbhu broke free from my grasp, determined to stop her. Seeing Ahbhu coming for her, Rosita pressed herself against the vehicle, double-gripping the gun, and aimed it squarely at him. Ahbhu paused mere millimeters from her, a frenzied fury emanating from every bark and growl, his mouth frothing.

"You might need these," Suchi said, extending her palm with a handful of bullets. The unexpected gesture caught us all off guard. With a dramatic flourish, she tossed them into the grass and lifted her head at Rosita with an air of challenge.

Rosita's eyes widened as she realized she'd been outsmarted. Keen to escape, she scrambled into the pickup. But before she could shut the door, Ahbhu lunged, sinking his teeth into her, and dragged her back onto the asphalt, looking for all the world as if he was about to maul her to death. Suchi and I surged forward, sprinting to Rosita's rescue, both of us desperate to prevent a tragedy.

After wresting Ahbhu away and disarming Rosita, Suchi tied her hands behind her back with some twine and sealed her mouth with masking tape. Then we spent the next few minutes deciding what to do with her.

Suchi favored tossing her into the bed of the truck and turning her over to the police at the next town. I argued for leaving her at the rest area. Either way, we realized we were probably screwed. Who knew what cockamamie story Rosita would cook up to turn the tables on us. In the end, we opted for dropping her off a couple of miles outside the next town to give ourselves a head start, then hightailing it out of Chiapas as fast as we could, even if that meant driving day and night until we reached Mexico City and dumping the pickup there.

The last image I have of Rosita was of her screaming bloody murder as we sped away just as dawn was breaking, shaking her fist at the silvering sky and vowing revenge. I'd wanted to leave her bound and gagged on the side of the road with only her legs free so she could walk to town. But Suchi thought that would only make us look worse in the eyes of the law. So, while I covered Suchi with Rosita's gun, which we'd reloaded with some spare bullets we found in her purse, Suchi untied her, ripping the masking tape from her face with a single violent tug. Then we were off.

"I hope it was worth it," I said as we sped away down the ruler-straight highway.

Suchi shot me a frustrated glance out of the corner of her eye. Nether one of us had spoken a word since we'd left the rest area, both of us too wound up to engage in conversation. But I'd been waiting for the right moment to ask the question that had been torturing me for the past hour, and I couldn't wait a minute longer.

"Well, *was* it?" I asked sharply, surprising even myself at the vehemence in my voice.

"Just shut it, Isaac."

# Chapter 27

## COYOACÁN

A couple of hours after jettisoning Rosita like excess payload on the side of the highway, we zoomed past the turnoff to Tuxtla Gutierrez, our original destination, just in case she'd managed to call ahead to report us, and we filled the tank at the very next service station we found. Suchi hadn't spoken a word other than to tersely explain our route, even after I apologized for offending her, and just kept her bloodshot eyes on the highway, a scowl marring her face, her jaw pulsating.

Careful not to attract unwanted attention from the Federal Highway Police but determined to cover the 1,000 kilometers to Mexico City as quickly as possible, Suchi tried to keep our speed steady at seventy miles per hour, which wasn't always possible considering the winding roads and diverse, mountainous Chiapan terrain. Accepting she was going to subject me to the silent treatment for the next couple of days, I settled into enjoying the ride, taking in the breathtaking vistas, reading my book, horsing around with Ahbhu, and catching up on my rest.

Driving out of the mountains, Suchi pulled into a filling station on the outskirts of Coatzacoalcos, a busy city strategically positioned along the Gulf Coast. Shattered from lack of sleep, she drove around to the back of the station to take a power nap, ordering me to wake her in thirty minutes, her first words to me in hours. Ahbhu and I took advantage of the stop to stretch our legs and jog a bit along the edge of a garbage-strewn field, and to gobble down a couple of greasy tacos from a roadside vendor.

After our brief stop, we resumed our journey, merging back onto the road and immersing ourselves in the expansive coastal plains of Veracruz. The gulf waters gleamed beautifully in the fading daylight, dappled with hues of red and orange from the setting sun, which splashed the sky with a mesmerizing swirl of colors just beyond the bustling port city. But Suchi was oblivious to it all, disregarding my admiring comments even as the lights along the roadside flickered on, signaling the onset of night, and Veracruz shimmered in the distance.

Continuing along the federal highway, we turned inland and made swift progress through the heart of the country, bypassing Puebla and Cordoba, and gunning it toward the capital. Fueling up one last time in Pachuca, just north of Mexico City, we steeled ourselves for the final stretch, battling travel fatigue as we hurtled through the darkness, the city lights on the horizon beckoning with an eerie glow.

Despite the anticipation of safely reaching our destination, with its promise of a bed to sleep in and a place to wash up, the tension inside the pickup was thick nearly a day after the Rosita debacle, suffocating even the faintest hope of conversation. Suchi, behind the wheel, was a brooding silhouette against the dim dashboard lights, her anger a tangible force in the confined space, the oppressive silence broken only by the hum of the engine and the occasional sigh that escaped her lips.

The closer we got to the city, the more the highway thrummed with activity, even at nearly midnight. Streams of exhaust-spewing vehicles jostled for space on the road amid a dissonance of honking horns and flashing lights, weaving between lanes with reckless abandon. Neon signs from towering buildings cast erratic patterns of light onto the asphalt below, creating a surreal spectacle against the backdrop of the night sky. Despite the late hour, the city pulsed with energy, its streets alive with the frenetic rhythm of urban life.

I gazed in amazement at the massive metropolis unfolding around us, feeling a breathless excitement building within me at the prospect of exploring it. Hopeful the new environment might help break the impasse, I turned to Suchi to share my thoughts. She instantly averted her eyes and leaned into the steering wheel as she took a busy turn-off, effectively shutting me out, the frenetic outside world distant and irrelevant to her, our drive through the city's labyrinthine streets mirroring the turbulent landscape of our strained relationship.

Veering south out of the central zone, we soon reached the neighborhoods bounding UNAM, the city's iconic university. As we circled around the campus, the eerie glow of the streetlights illuminated the impressive architecture, a fascinating mix of modernist and neoclassical buildings casting fleeting shadows that danced along the facades.

The complex swiftly disappeared into the darkness of the surrounding streets as we turned into a pretty neighborhood with charming cobblestone streets lined with colonial buildings, an eclectic mix of cafes and shops, green spaces, and a lovely central plaza. Even at that late hour, the place pulsed with a laid-back bohemian charm.

As we reached the end of the neighborhood's commercial district, Suchi turned onto a quiet apartment-lined street and squeezed the pickup into a tight space between a VW mini-van and a line of scooters. Then she just sat there, wordlessly collecting her thoughts. After a moment, she turned her head and stared at me, looking sad and exhausted.

"Suchi, I'm so sorry," I tried again. "I'm sorry I offended you *and* for overstepping. I should have kept my big fat mouth shut. But I can't undo it now. All I can do is apologize and let you know that I really appreciate everything you've been doing for me. You didn't have to, but you did. And for that I'll be forever grateful. It felt like a deep bond of friendship was developing between us. But now I'm afraid I've broken it forever. Have I?"

The lines on her face softened as I spoke, my eyes growing moist with pent-up emotion. Ahbhu climbed onto my lap and rubbed his head against my chest in an attempt to comfort me. Suchi lowered her eyes at him for a moment, then reached out and lightly passed her fingers through his fur, a sad smile playing on her lips. After a moment, she raised her eyes back to me.

"I *was* angry. I still am, although it's not easy to hold on to such a powerful emotion for hours, believe me. It's damned exhausting." She shook her head and stared unfocused out the window at a group of young people skipping past the pickup. "But, more than anything," she continued, "I was angry with myself, Isaac. I don't know what it is with me. I've *never* been good at picking lovers. I'm a terrible judge of character. Amparo is the only exception, and look at how that turned out. But Rosita . . . oh, my God. Rosita was the worst. She wasn't even . . ."

"It's not your fault, Suchi. The woman was a player."

"But *you* saw it!"

"I saw it because I don't trust *anyone*. That's *my* problem. And the one time I did trust someone, he screwed me over. Big time. So, yes, I was suspicious of Rosita. But I might not have made much of it if Ahbhu hadn't also been skittish around her. In the end, it was Ahbhu who stopped her from stealing the truck and leaving us at that rest stop without a *centavo* in our pockets, not me. We have him to thank. Right, boy?" I kissed Ahbhu then looked back at Suchi, hopeful we'd had a breakthrough. "Anyway, try not to be so hard on yourself. We're all messed up in one way or the other."

Suchi nodded and blinked back tears. "I guess we are, aren't we?"

"Yep. Every single one of us. The walking wounded."

I waved Suchi over to my side and we had ourselves a group hug, Suchi, Ahbhu and me, lingering there for a bit, on the verge of passing out from exhaustion. When we finally let go, having reset things for the time being, I took a breath and glanced around at the surrounding buildings.

"So, where are we and what's the plan?"

"This is Coyoacán. It's popular with university students. Nice and artsy. Frida Kahlo had a house near here. Her blue house. It's a museum now. Anyway, this is a good place for you to blend in with the rest of the young people while I sort out your visa for the next part of your trip."

"How long will that take?"

"Five days, more or less. It depends on a few variables I don't want to go into right now. In the meantime, there's a boarding house in that building there where you'll be staying. It's clean and close to the main drag. You'll have your own room with a shared bathroom down the hall, and it comes with breakfast. It's run by an older woman I know, Julia, a painter. She makes her living running the boarding house. I called ahead to make the arrangements. Julia's okay with Ahbhu staying with you." Shouldering her backpack, she made to open the door.

"What about you?" I asked, feeling I was about to get dumped again.

"Don't worry, I'll be crashing nearby with some friends and will check in on you every day. Tomorrow's Saturday. I'll call your mother first thing in the morning to let her know you're all right. Once your paperwork's ready, whenever that is, I'll bring it to you and see you off at the central bus station for the rest of your journey. In the meantime, get yourself cleaned up and make the best of your stay."

# Chapter 28

## DIEGO

Julia turned out to be an elegant older woman, nice but slightly aloof. It took a few minutes for her to answer her door, her appearance suggesting she'd been roused from sleep, as she adjusted her bathrobe and secured her hair with a delicate scarf. Despite Suchi's apologies at our late arrival, Julia greeted her warmly with a kiss on both cheeks before leading us inside. She'd transformed her luxury apartment into an eight-room boarding house, adorned with numerous of her *art naïf* paintings displayed prominently in the spacious dining room, where she explained the house rules to me—no alcohol in the rooms and no overnight guests. Suchi settled payment on my behalf for the week and slipped me a few Mexican pesos for spending money. Then she turned me over to Julia and beat a hasty retreat.

The room Julia showed me to was small but cozy, with a firm single bed, a wooden armoire, and a sink and mirror. There was just enough room for Ahbhu to sleep between the bed and the window, which opened onto a fire escape and looked out at a brick wall. I propped open the window for Ahbhu in case he needed to go out, then plopped onto the bed, still fully clothed,

256

and passed out from exhaustion.

I dreamt of rivers and blood and of being chased. I dreamt of my mother and of the volcano, of following Ahbhu through the hills, and of being trapped in a small space that got smaller and smaller until there was nothing left of me. And I dreamt of Gerónimo. His image was still lingering before me when I regained consciousness in a strange featureless room.

Daylight filtered in through an open window that admitted a cool herb-scented breeze. Sitting up, I cast about the room, trying to regain my bearings, and caught sight of myself in a mirror above a small dripping tap. Bleached blonde hair the texture of straw sticking up like a crazy mohawk, black roots growing in, framed my haggard face. Startled by my reflection, I squeezed my eyes shut as it all came flowing back.

A loud bark snapped me out of it, and I opened my eyes to find Ahbhu scampering on the fire escape, fiercely wagging his tail. On seeing me awake, he bounded onto the bed in one leap and greeted me, enthusiastically licking my face. Grabbing his body, I rolled side to side with him on the bed, laughter bubbling up as the gloom lifted.

Suddenly aware that I was starving, I tossed back the covers and climbed over the bed to the sink. "What time is it, Ahbhu?" I asked, splashing water on my face. I ran my damp fingers through my hair, determined to have it all cut off the moment I found a barbershop. It felt safe to do so now, so far from El Salvador.

*The sun is straight up*, he answered. He hopped off the bed and pawed at the door. *The Julia woman was knocking earlier, but Isaac didn't hear.*

From the sound of that, I feared I'd missed breakfast. But hungry as I was, I needed to clear something up first before I ventured out. "Ahbhu, am I safe to call Gerónimo now?"

Ahbhu contemplated me for a moment, then he settled back on his haunches. *Isaac can call Gerónimo.*

Feeling I hadn't properly formulated my question, I rephrased it: "Am I safe now, Ahbhu?"

*Isaac is* more *safe*, he said, moving back to the door and pawing at it again. *But Isaac must still be careful. Ahbhu will help.*


As I anticipated, I'd missed breakfast by two hours. Julia was kind enough, though, to brew me some coffee, which she served in the dining room with fresh fruit and pan dulce. She also placed a few pieces of chorizo in a bowl for Ahbhu. I tried to engage her in friendly chit-chat while she moved about the room. But she seemed focused on silently rearranging her paintings in preparation for an upcoming exhibition, occasionally offering a smile to acknowledge my presence.

Afterward, Ahbhu and I strolled the short distance to Coyoacán's main street, which was lively and bustling with activity, mainly with university students. Spotting an international call center slotted between a dress shop and a European style café, I popped inside, swallowing my nerves, and approached the counter.

"You can't bring your dog in here, sorry," the twentyish woman behind the counter said, turning down the radio, which was blaring The Talking Heads' "Road to Nowhere," my life story. She wriggled a black-lacquered fingernail at Ahbhu.

"He's my service dog," I explained. "I'll make sure he stays with me the whole time, I promise. I just need to make a call to El Salvador. It won't take long."

She cocked her head and crinkled her nose. "Service dog for what?"

"Epilepsy," I said confidentially, glancing around the empty shop then back at her.

"Oh," she said, drawing out the word and nodding. She snuck in a little wave at Ahbhu, who sat up and responded with a friendly bark.

I gave her the number to Gerónimo's house, and she directed Ahbhu and me to the last of a long line of phone booths, where I waited with my heart pounding in my ears. After a minute, a buzzer sounded in the booth, and I picked up the phone, my hand moist and shaking from nerves. Gerónimo's maid picked up after a couple of rings and, after a strained pause, told me to wait. Breathless with anticipation, I reached down for Ahbhu to steady myself. A moment later, I heard his voice.

"Hello," Gerónimo said softly.

I closed my eyes and let the sound of him wash over me.

"Isaac?"

"I'm here," I whispered.

"Here where?" he asked. "I've been looking for you everywhere."

Remembering why I'd called him, I sat up and steeled myself, the cobwebs of emotion clearing, and said firmly: "Never mind that. I heard you wanted to speak with me. You've been bothering my parents. That's why I'm calling."

"I . . . I wanted to tell you . . . I'm sorry for what happened." He sounded thrown by the abrupt shift in my tone. "I'm sorry I brought you there. That they pinned it on you. I never meant for any of that to happen, I promise. I've been totally devastated since then; you have no idea."

"*You've* been devastated?"

"I know, Isaac," Gerónimo said, his voice steady and deliberate. Knowing him, he'd rehearsed what he was about to say a thousand times. "I know it doesn't compare with what you and your family are going through. I just wanted you to know that I'm suffering as well."

"Well, thanks. That fixes everything."

"Which is why," Gerónimo interrupted, "I've decided to come clean with the authorities and tell them everything that happened that night. I'm going to clear your name, Isaac.

259

Come what may."

"I don't believe you. Why didn't you do it before? Why now?"

"I wanted to talk to you first, to make sure you were okay," he said. "Otherwise, what would be the point?"

"They'll probably kill you, you know," I said after a moment.

"I know," he said, his voice growing soft again. "Or maybe they won't. Either way, I have to do this. I just wanted to tell you first."

I lowered my eyes at Ahbhu who met my gaze, his own eyes full of sadness. Despite his frequent clashes with Gerónimo over the years, he knew how deeply I cared about him.

"When?" I asked.

"This afternoon, straight after we hang up."

I lowered the phone and nodded, swiping at my eyes with the back of my arm. Then I put the phone back to my ear. "I'm in Nicaragua," I said, "just outside of Managua with some people I met." Ahbhu lifted his head at the lie, and I felt suddenly ashamed.

My words were met with a long pause. Then Gerónimo spoke the last words I ever heard from him in this world.

"I love you."

And with that, he clicked off.

I cradled the receiver in my lap with Gerónimo's final words echoing in my head. Why had it all come to this? I wondered. If he really loved me, why couldn't the two of us have left together like I'd asked him? What was the point of all the suffering? I didn't get it.

Hanging up the phone, I trudged up the aisle and paid the young woman, who was tracking my movements with a worried look on her pretty face. Then Ahbhu and I stepped out into the bright sunshine where a whole other plane of existence was unfolding, happy people jostling past me, chattering about boyfriends and girlfriends, and going out, and movies and music.

Crossing the road to the central plaza, I sat on a bench and decompressed from the phone call while taking in the warmth of the day. As much as I loved Gerónimo, and as much as I feared the consequences of what he was about to do, I had to focus on the future if I was going to survive. Pining after Gerónimo had no place in that future. He'd chosen his path, and I was on mine now, for better or worse. And so, drying my face, I jumped off the bench and headed straight for the neighborhood barbershop.

The old-school parlor was busy with guys freshening up for the weekend in one of four barber chairs. The shop owner was adamant that Ahbhu had to wait outside unless I could prove he was a service dog. Ahbhu nudged my hand with his nose, assuring me he'd be fine outside, and disappeared out the door.

The owner directed me to a waiting area at the back of the shop where a space had just freed up. I sat next to a nice-looking guy engrossed in a glossy magazine. He was about my age with shoulder-length black hair held back with a pair of sunglasses pushed onto his head, dark eyes, and a pale complexion. He offered a friendly smile as I took a seat and then turned back to the magazine. Shifting in my seat to get a better look at him, my attention was drawn to his muscular arms, one adorned with a tattoo of an eagle clutching a writhing snake in its beak. Intrigued, I stole occasional glances, trying not to be too obvious, my gaze drifting down to his attire: a pair of faded 501s and a dark blue linen shirt draped casually over his solid frame. His shirt was open at the collar, revealing a delicate gold chain and crucifix nestled against a hairy chest. White slip-ons, worn without socks, completed the ensemble.

"I haven't seen you here before," the young guy said into his magazine, peering closely at a photograph before setting it face down on his lap and turning to me. "Are you new or just passing through?"

"Just passing through," I responded, masking my surprise at his directness.

"How long are you around for?"

"A couple days. Why?"

The shop owner whistled the young guy over to a barber station that had just become free.

"I'm Diego," he said, rising from his chair. "Join me for coffee next door once you're done if you have time. My treat!"

A couple of minutes later, I was called over to the barber station next to Diego's. He playfully pumped his thick eyebrows in the mirror as my barber placed a cape over me. I couldn't help smiling back at him. It was just what I needed at that moment, a friendly face. The fact that I was attracted to him made it all the better.

Diego and I maintained a lighthearted eye contact via the mirror as his barber scissor-styled his hair, while my barber passed the electric clippers over my head, removing most of my bleached locks and revealing my original color, which was just growing back in. I couldn't help but admire Diego's reflection, noting his handsome features: the aquiline nose, the high cheekbones, and the dimple in his chin. His appearance added to his allure, making it hard to look away. As my barber finished, revealing my new, short hairstyle, tinged with yellow at the tips, I found myself still captivated by Diego's striking appearance.

We were soon out the door, joined by Ahbhu, and settled at an outside table of an artsy café where everyone seemed to know Diego.

"You never told me your name," he said, once the server had taken our orders.

"I'm . . . Tlaloc," I said. The name sounded strange in my mouth, but I was careful not to reveal my real name just yet.

"Tlaloc? That's Nahuatl, isn't it?"

"Yep."

"Where are you from?"

"El Salvador."

"Ah." Diego averted his eyes a bit then looked back at me. "Sorry."

"Yeah, me too. This is Ahbhu." I patted Ahbhu's head. He panted happily. I was glad to see he felt comfortable around Diego.

The server arrived with our coffees and biscotti, and we each took measured sips, exchanging friendly smiles that suddenly felt a bit awkward.

Feeling guilty about misrepresenting myself, I decided to take a gamble with this new person who had shown me such kindness when he needn't have.

"My name's actually Isaac, not Tlaloc," I admitted. "I'm sorry for lying." I moved my coffee cup to one side, having lost my taste for it.

Diego cocked his head questioningly.

"I'm on my way to the States. It's too dangerous for me back home," I said, "You know, with our civil war and all that. I'm waiting here a few days for my onward visa. My paperwork says Tlaloc all over it. Someone picked that name for me."

Diego's face turned serious as he considered what I'd just confessed. After a moment, he slid my coffee cup back over to me, one side of his mouth pulling up into a sympathetic smile. "Not that it's any of my business," he said quietly, "but thanks for sharing that. I'm sure it wasn't easy."

Pleased he hadn't just walked out on me, I felt a little lighter, as if I'd crossed a bridge over a raging stream and was now safe on the other side. I smiled and sipped my coffee, which had grown lukewarm. "Thank you for taking it so well."

"Anyway, changing gears, why'd you chop off all your hair, Goldilocks?" he leaned forward and passed a finger over my scalp.

I shrugged. "I got tired of it, I guess. I decided to go for a new me."

"Works for me," he said, with a broad smile. "You're dead cute either way."

"The feeling's mutual," I said, feeling a warmth spread through me.

Tossing a glance over his shoulder, he scooted closer until our knees were touching. "What are you up to tonight?"

"Nothing, why?"

"What do you say we go dancing?"

"Dancing? Where?"

"There are tons of places in La Zona Rosa. I'll pick you up here at eight. We'll have dinner and then go dancing. Deal?"

I looked down at Ahbhu, who had placed his chin on my leg. "What about Ahbhu?" I asked.

Diego sat back, surprised at the question. "What about him?"

"He's my service dog. I have epilepsy."

Diego stared pensively at Ahbhu for a moment. "They won't let him in the restaurant or the clubs, that's for sure. But I suppose he can come along for the ride and wait in my car if that works. It's a two-seater."

"Thanks," I said, as we rose from the table and hugged each other goodbye. "I'm sure we can make it work."

# Chapter 29

## ZONA ROSA

Diego picked us up at eight o'clock sharp in a shiny black Mustang convertible with the top pulled down. Looking even more handsome than earlier in a pair of designer jeans and a snug black T-shirt, he wrapped me in his arms and lifted me off the ground in an exaggerated bear hug, then offered Ahbhu a doggie treat. Opening the passenger door, I was surprised to see he'd arranged a fuzzy blanket on the floorboard for Ahbhu with a small plastic food bowl brimming with kibbles. "To make sure our friend is comfortable," he said. Then flashing his perfect teeth, he squeezed my hand, and we pulled away from the café.

In the time it took for us to drive from Coyoacán to the restaurant Diego had selected, I found out he was a graduate student in psychology at UNAM on a term break, soon to start his final year. He wasn't sure what awaited him after his studies as he was getting pressure from his father to return home, to wherever he was from, to take over the family business. From the looks of his car and his jewelry, I assumed his family had money. But I didn't dare delve into details he hadn't shared. I'd learned long ago not to ask too many questions.

We hit heavy Saturday night traffic as we entered the Zona Rosa, the entertainment capital of the city. The sidewalks were heaving with people out for a good time, glowing in the glare of multicolored neon that cut through the night. Loud music blared out of scores of restaurants and nightclubs in the circus-like atmosphere as we crawled past; queues of people lined up outside each of them, chattering happily, waiting to be admitted. Diego pointed out different venues as he wound his way to our destination: his favorites, the most popular, the ones to avoid. It was all so chaotic and wonderful, I'd never seen anything like it back home, and I was filled with excitement at the prospect of diving into it with a local.

Diego had selected a nice rooftop restaurant overlooking the mayhem. He tossed his keys to the valet, plus some extra cash to look after Ahbhu, and led me by the hand up the stairs to the top of the building.

After checking in with the host, he led me to the rooftop's edge and took in my amazed expression, observing me with delight, as I absorbed the sight of the lively and frenetic atmosphere from high above. Then he slung his arm over my shoulder and led me to our table, where a bottle of champagne was waiting for us.

"Seems I've done all the talking," he said after we'd toasted the evening and placed our order. "Tell me something about yourself. Something unique and exciting!"

Keen not to put a damper on the evening with a boring recitation of my recent history, I scoured my memory banks, reaching back into my life before our country had imploded.

"I always wanted to be an astronaut," I said finally.

Diego set down his champagne glass and blinked at me. "An astronaut?"

"It's geeky, I know. But as a kid, I used to read a lot of science fiction, which led to my fascination with space and the stars. My brother bought me a telescope, as a kind of joke, I think. But I was delighted with it! Ahbhu and I used to hike to the top of the volcano we lived under to stargaze. From that, it wasn't a big leap to wanting to be an astronaut."

"You lived under a volcano?"

"Yeah, crazy, right? An active one."

"Wow! And I thought I had an interesting background."

"That's funny. I never considered my background to be interesting," I said, feeling suddenly exposed. "Anyway, what's your story?"

"I'm half Huichol and half Romani," he said, wide-eyed, waiting for a reaction.

We were interrupted by the server who deposited a plate of seafood pasta in front of each of us and poured us some white wine to accompany our meal. When he'd finally withdrawn, I looked back at Diego and confessed my ignorance about either of the terms he'd thrown at me.

"You've never heard of the Huichol people?"

I shook my head and sipped my wine to mask my embarrassment.

"What about Wixárika or hikuri? Have you ever heard either of those words?"

"Nope, never have. Should I? I'm not from around here, remember?"

"Right," he said, peering searchingly into my eyes. "So, my father, he's Huichol, which is an indigenous group from near San Luis Potosí. And my mom's Kalderash Romani, basically what some people refer to as a 'gypsy.' She's originally from Bulgaria."

My smile faltered, feeling I'd just been ambushed. "That's definitely a more interesting background than mine. How did the two of them even meet? Your parents, I mean."

Diego sat up and launched into a monologue I was sure he'd repeated countless times before. "They were both working on the same cruise ship when they were young. My mom in the kitchen, and my dad as one of the ship's gofers. They were each trying to escape their destinies, I think, especially my father who was supposed to follow in the footsteps of my grandfather as a tribal leader. Anyway, they fell in love, married, and moved back to my father's village. I came a couple of years later, the first of seven children."

"That's a lot of identities to juggle," I said, trying to square how an Indian from near San Luis Potosí could afford the luxuries Diego so obviously enjoyed. "How many is that? Huichol, Gypsy, Mexican, Bulgarian."

"And gay." Diego sat back and threw out his arms expansively as if to embrace the entire restaurant. "That's the most challenging of them all, how to fit *that* into my life, what with all the expectations on me, familial, cultural, religious. Especially as I'm the eldest son."

Taken aback by how open he was about his sexuality, I glanced around the restaurant to see if anyone had overheard him.

"Don't sweat it, dear," he said, as if reading my thoughts. "This is ground zero for the gay community in Mexico. Nobody *cares.*"

"Sorry, I'm just not used to talking so clearly about these things. Where I come from, it's more of a 'keep quiet' policy. And there isn't a vibrant scene like the one you have here." Uncertain whether I was disclosing too much or too little, and fearing I was messing things up on my first real date, I placed my wine glass down. "To be honest, I'm feeling a bit out of my depth here. I'm sorry."

Diego reached across the table and cupped my hand, which had started to tremble. "Hey, steady there. *I'm* the one who should be sorry. I sometimes forget we're in a big pink bubble here. The truth is that *most* of the world is exactly as you've described, or worse. I, of all people, should know that. Back home, where I'm from, I'm expected to hide who and what I am."

"And so?"

Diego tossed up his hands and flashed a grin. "And so I don't know. Screw the future! These days, I'm all about the present. The here and now. That's my reality. Tomorrow may never come."

I drew back my hand and stared at him, realizing he was serious. "That's ironic. Right now, I'm *all* about the future. The present is purely transitional for me. I'm moving from point A to point B if you know what I mean."

"And what about *this*, right now? You and me. How does this fit into that picture?"

"I don't know," I said, wondering the same thing. "It's not anything I was expecting. And, on that subject, why me?"

"You're the new kid in town! I wanted to show you a good time." He signaled to the server to bring the check, then looked back at me with a grin. "And because you're super cute."

"Thanks," I said, blushing at the compliment. "The truth is, this is the nicest experience I've had in a long time, maybe ever. So, thank you."

Diego raised his glass, inviting a last toast. "There you go! Never underestimate the present, my friend."

"Fine," I said, flashing a smile and raising my glass, "To the present then!"

"*And* to the future!" Diego responded, clinking his glass against mine.



We swung by the car to check on Ahbhu and found him fast asleep on the floorboard. I whispered in his ear that we'd be back soon. He opened his sleepy eyes and nodded, then nodded off again. Meanwhile, Diego counted out a few extra pesos for the valet to watch his Mustang the rest of the night and promised more on our return. Then he grabbed my hand and led me through the crowded sidewalks, never loosening his firm grip, in the direction of his favorite nightclub, the oldest gay venue in Mexico City.

As we neared the club, a symphony of thumping bass and laughter greeted us, emanating from the pulsating heart of the city's gay district. A boisterous lineup of patrons, mainly men with a sprinkle of women and a dash of tough-looking drag queens, snaked its way around the building we were headed to. Flashing lights painted the air with hues of neon while the scent of cologne and sweat mingled in the humid night air. Diego exuded an air of confidence as we maneuvered past the throng toward the front of the line. His familiarity with the bouncer, a hulking presence with bulging muscles straining against his sleek black suit, was unmistakable as they exchanged nods and grins amid the rhythmic dance music pouring out of the club. With a sweeping gesture that spoke volumes of Diego's standing in that realm, the doorman parted the sea of waiting bodies and granted us passage. As we glided past, Diego slipped a few bills into the doorman's pocket. Then, with a sense of privilege, we crossed the threshold, leaving behind the frustrated murmurs of those left in line, and entered the packed club.

As we pushed through the crowd, the vibrant atmosphere, the flashing lights, the press of bodies, and the din of loud conversation and laughter competing with the heart-thumping music overwhelmed my senses. Diego, with his magnetic presence, effortlessly commanded attention, drawing admiring glances from both the staff and the regulars. He greeted them with a warm smile and easy charm, pulling me close and introducing me as his date, making me feel welcomed and included in the tight-knit community.

We downed a couple of tequilas at the bar, and the alcohol rushed to my head, making my legs go wobbly. I leaned heavily on Diego to steady myself. In response, he leaned in and planted a wet kiss on my mouth, the taste of Cuervo Gold lingering on his lips. Just then the music softened, and he guided me to one side of the stage. "It's show time," he said in answer to my questioning looks, and we settled in to watch as the MC, a trans woman in an emerald-green evening gown and auburn wig, announced the lineup for the evening.

The drag show captivated me with its dazzling performances, and I found myself swept up in the energy of the audience, cheering and clapping along with Diego. Once it was over, we waded into the milling crowd toward the dance floor as the DJ blasted Madonna's latest. Everyone we passed greeted Diego with enthusiastic hellos and friendly hugs, his popularity only serving to heighten the excitement of the evening.

Stepping onto the dance floor, we were immediately swept up by the pulsating rhythm of the house mix. Plowing a path to the heart of the fray, we joined the celebration with abandon. Diego danced with a euphoric intensity, his hands high in the air, his eyes rolled into his head. Despite my intoxication, or maybe even heightened by it, my movements aligned seamlessly with his, our bodies grinding together in perfect symmetry. The dance floor erupted with a riot of flashing strobes and vibrant hues, flashing red, yellow, green, the spinning mirror ball above reflecting back a dizzying rainbow of light across the room.

As we surrendered to the mesmerizing mix of music and exhilaration, I lost track of all time. For what felt like an eternity, Diego and I moved as one, our bodies drenched in sweat from the fervent energy of the moment and the heat of all the bodies around us. Then, as the DJ took it down a notch, seamlessly segueing from house to pop, Diego took my hand and led me through the throng, weaving between bodies until we found refuge behind a speaker. There, amidst the pulsating bass and muffled conversations, we peeled off our shirts, our skin tingling with anticipation as we surrendered to the pull of desire, making out with a hungry passion, our mouths exploring, our slick torsos pressed against each other. Loosening my belt, he made to slide his hands under the waistband of my underpants, aiming to reach inside. Startled sober by such a bold move in public, I tugged on his wrists and extracted them from my pants, narrowing my eyes at him.

Looking confused, he wiped his mouth with the back of his hand and asked breathlessly, "What's wrong?"

"Maybe we should get a room," I said sarcastically, retrieving my shirt, which had fallen to the ground, and sliding it back on.

He reached for his T-shirt and threaded it over his head, his face turning red with embarrassment. "Sorry. I didn't—"

"I don't mind the making out," I said. "But I can't go where you were taking things. Not in a place like this. That's not who I am."

"It's my fault," he said in a low voice as we made our way back to the car. "I got carried away. I should have known better."

"We *both* got carried away." I felt bad he was beating himself up over the whole thing, especially as I'd been a willing participant up until I'd stopped it. I held his hand as we walked to let him know I wasn't holding anything against him, but it was cold and limp, so I let go.

"I'm pretty sure I'm negative, if that's what you're worried about," Diego said after a moment. "Plus, I always use protection."

"Never even crossed my mind," I said, lying to him and regretting the words the moment they left my mouth, but relieved to hear it nonetheless.

The sidewalks were a lot emptier now, shimmering in the streetlights, reflecting back the early morning dew as we strolled past the last few stragglers from the night staggering home.

The parking attendant was nowhere to be found when we reached Diego's car, which was sitting alone with the top up in a far corner of the chained-up parking lot. The sight drew an angry expletive from Diego, who stamped the ground in frustration. Ahbhu trotted across the asphalt to us, and I ran to meet him. He said he'd tried to stop the attendant from leaving, but the attendant seemed in a hurry for something. The attendant had left a note inside the car for Diego and the keys behind the front tire. Diego stared at me like I was crazy when I relayed the information. Then he looked at Ahbhu, tilting his head slightly in confusion.

"Just check," I said, nuzzling Ahbhu and kissing him.

Diego jogged to his car and retrieved his keys from exactly where Ahbhu had indicated. Opening the car door, he emerged a moment later with a piece of paper. It was an apology from the attendant, who'd been called home for a family emergency. Diego sighed in relief, his eyes moist from his receding anger. According to the note, the parking lot key was with the caretaker, whom we found by knocking on the back door of the restaurant. In less than ten minutes, we were on the road back to Coyoacán.

"Ahbhu talks?" Diego asked after a few minutes of silent driving.

I glanced at him for a beat, then reached down and kneaded Ahbhu's fur. "Sometimes."

Diego's gaze drifted briefly from the road to Ahbhu then back again.

"Crazy, right?" I said.

"Not necessarily," he said, his voice catching strangely in his throat. "Remember I told you my father's Huichol?"

I nodded, not seeing the connection.

"We're known worldwide for our vibrant yarn paintings depicting our beliefs and our cosmology," he explained with a hint of pride. "We call them *nierika*; outsiders call them *tablas*. They bring in a lot of money to our village. Besides nierika, we're also known for our traditional spiritual practices centered around *hikuri*, a sacred plant we use in our religious ceremonies and rituals for healing, divination, and spiritual connection."

"You mean like a kind of drug?"

"Some people use it that way, outsiders mainly who buy it on the black market. But when used properly during a ceremony guided by a healer, like my father, hikuri is a tool for spiritual insight, self-discovery, and expanding one's consciousness. Participants in a ceremony are able to explore the boundaries of perception, the interconnectedness of all things, and knowledge beyond ordinary reality."

"Right, but how does that have anything to do with Ahbhu?"

"I'm getting to that," Diego said, slowing down as we rounded a traffic circle and entered the university zone. He was staring straight ahead, focused on some vague point in the middle distance.

"One of our most fundamental beliefs is in the concept of *nonordinary reality*, the idea that all living beings, *including animals*, have their own forms of consciousness and knowledge. By accessing altered states of consciousness, or heightened awareness, with the help of hikuri, some of us are able to communicate with animals on a deep level and learn from their wisdom and insights. Maybe that part of *your* consciousness is naturally more developed than most, which might explain why you're able to communicate with Ahbhu."

"Interesting theory. But maybe *Ahbhu's* the one with the special ability."

"Maybe. But that doesn't take away from the fact that it's a two-way communication between yourselves, from what I understand."

Ahbhu was doing his best to follow our discussion, his head bobbing back and forth between us as if watching a ping-pong match, probably not understanding a word we were saying.

"Did you hear that, Ahbhu! You're my special boy," I whispered, scratching his head. Ahbhu responded by climbing into my lap and letting out a happy groan.

Diego chuckled at our interaction as he pulled up in front of Julia's and switched off the car. We sat quietly for a bit, watching the sky brightening with the advancing dawn; the only sound in the car was our quiet breathing, both of us delaying bringing our date to an end. Then, catching sight of Julia raising the blinds in her front room, I felt it was time to break the impasse. I turned to Diego, ready to take my leave. But before I could get a word out, he took hold of my hands and held my gaze.

"Let's give it another try," he said. "Tonight, if you're not busy. No clubs. Just a quiet dinner someplace local and some quality time after."

"I'd love that," I said, relieved not to be ending things on a sour note and looking forward to spending my final hours with him before embarking alone on the final leg of my journey. Agreeing to meet at Julia's at seven that evening, we kissed each other goodbye, and I watched from the sidewalk as he disappeared around the corner at the end of the street.

# Chapter 30

## JULIA INTERVENES

"Was that the del Castillo boy?" Julia asked the moment Ahbhu and I stepped into her apartment. Draped in a multicolored apron, she was busily setting the table for breakfast. Not hearing a response from me, she stopped what she was doing and turned to me, holding a plate in her hand.

"I don't know," I said, caught out by the question. "I only know him as Diego."

"Yes, that's right. Diego del Castillo. He rents a room at my friend Isabel's house. How do you know him?"

"I met him yesterday afternoon at the barbershop. Why?"

"Just curious," she said, inspecting the table and adjusting the cutlery. "He's something of a celebrity around here, that one, quite the man about town from what I understand—not to mention his uncle is Chamba del Castillo, the internationally renowned artist famous for his yarn paintings."

"You mean *tablas*?"

Julia halted her work. "So, you *do* know."

"Diego told me about the yarn paintings, not about his uncle."

276

"I see," she said softly. "Chamba del Castillo produces such detailed and culturally rich work. And it's not just his yarn paintings. Your friend's uncle is equally renowned for his murals; one is even displayed in the Louvre in Paris. The man's a legend."

Beckoning me into the kitchen, she poured me some coffee in the midst of her preparations. "Are you and Diego dating?"

"He invited me out last night. Dinner and dancing. I'm not sure that qualifies as dating." I stretched my arms and suppressed a yawn, eager to catch up on my sleep. "Anyway, we're seeing each other again tonight," I said as I rose from the table and deposited my coffee cup in the sink.

"Two nights in a row!" Julia exclaimed. "That's impressive."

"We're meant to have dinner locally," I said. "I'm not sure where yet."

"Why not here?" Julia said, wiping her hands on a dish towel. "I'm happy to prepare the two of you a nice, romantic dinner, complete with wine, candles, and music to match the mood. And if things go well," she added with a wink, "I may even turn a blind eye to my rule about overnight guests."

Her offer caught me off guard, coming as it did from out of the blue. "Thanks, Julia, that's … very generous. I'd have to check with him first, of course. He may already have made other plans. Plus, I'm not sure I could afford it."

"Surprise him!" Julia said. "And don't worry about the money. As long as I'm able to have a quick chat with the boy about his uncle, that will be compensation enough."

I knew there had to be a catch—a gourmet dinner in exchange for the chance to chat with Diego. It wasn't such a bad deal, though, even if Julia's motives weren't entirely altruistic. I flashed a noncommittal smile and told her I'd let her know one way or the other, then headed to my room, weaving past the first few boarders entering the dining room.

When I woke up at 2 p.m. after a six-hour nap, Julia had already made all the arrangements for the evening. She'd called Diego's landlady, suggesting that he shouldn't make dinner plans elsewhere. I listened in wide-eyed disbelief, suppressing my displeasure at the subterfuge she'd orchestrated, as she excitedly served me lunch ("on the house") and detailed the elaborate menu she'd planned for the evening.

Suchi arrived just as Julia was describing the Oaxacan pavlovas she'd commissioned from Cayoacán's best baker as one of our desserts; the other was a surprise. Momentarily distracted by Suchi's warm embrace, Julia quickly refocused and continued outlining her plans while Suchi observed us with bemusement.

"So, what's this all about?" Suchi asked once Julia had finished.

"The young man has a date tonight with someone very special!"

Suchi tossed a glance at me. "You work fast," she said, lightly scoffing. "What does that have to do with you?" she asked Julia before I could rise to the jibe.

"Your young man's beau is the nephew of a world-famous indigenous artist, one of my favorites, in fact. He's very kindly agreed to introduce me. Of course, such a kind gesture deserves reciprocation. Hence, I've offered to host a nice, intimate evening for them."

"Well, that's *awfully* nice of you, Julia," Suchi replied, with a barely perceptible hint of irony. Turning to me, she added, "Isn't that awfully nice of Julia, Tlaloc?"

"It's amazing," I replied. "Thank you, Julia." Getting up from the table, I hugged her, resigning myself to going with the flow while silently hoping for a better evening with Diego.

"Oh, one more thing, young man," Julia called out as Suchi

and I withdrew to the drawing room. "I've taken the liberty of selecting some items of clothing for you given your limited wardrobe. You should look extra nice tonight. You'll find it all in your armoire."

Trading a quick look with Suchi, I thanked Julia again. Then we closed the door to the living room and dropped onto the sofa.

"I didn't have anything to do with that," I blurted out to head off a scolding. "She engineered the whole thing."

Suchi waved her hand dismissively. "Never mind that; that's just Julia. And don't even get me started on that goddamned haircut. The important thing is that your papers came through faster than we expected. We'd like you to leave tomorrow."

"Tomorrow?"

"Yes, tomorrow. Our contact in Tijuana will be expecting you to check in with him no later than a week from now. That gives you a full seven days to make the trip, which is plenty of time, factoring in any delays. The quickest way there is by long-distance bus, seventy-two hours tops with transfers and layovers. I'll write it all out for you."

Unprepared for the news, I stared out the window as she spoke, my mind all a jumble, trying to formulate my thoughts. Ahbhu was racing up and down the sidewalk like a sprinter training for a track meet. Overhead, the sky was turning dark with an approaching storm.

"Also," she continued, "I've been in contact with your parents. They're wiring some money for you this afternoon. I'll have it ready for you when we meet in the morning. Be ready at seven."

"It's too soon," I said, looking back at her. "You said I'd be here a week or so."

"Yes, tops. But your visa came through sooner than that. That's a good thing."

"But . . ."

"But what? You can't stay here, Isaac. You're a Central American without papers in Mexico, where we're not particularly welcome in the first place; *plus* you don't know anyone here. Also, your job prospects are nil. Finally, and most importantly, unlike here, in America there's a whole legal regime and a raft of organizations that help gay and lesbian migrants apply for asylum. No, Isaac, tomorrow is the day." She touched my leg in an uncharacteristic show of sympathy, her face softening slightly. "My advice is that you enjoy tonight . . . notwithstanding my artist friend." She nodded at the closed door and added in a lowered voice. "She means well, our Julia."

Diego arrived promptly at seven amid a deluge of rain, dressed all in white, clutching a bouquet of dripping roses, and beaming a winning smile. I'd beaten Julia to the door at the sound of the buzzer and greeted him warmly, our lips lingering in a kiss. Then I ushered him into the dining room, which Julia had transformed into a haven of opulence. The space resembled a high-end restaurant, the dining table adorned with a crisp, white tablecloth that contrasted elegantly with the dark wood. Flickering candles in an ornate candelabra cast a soft, romantic glow while a piece by Chopin played in the background on an old turntable.

I introduced Diego to Julia, making sure to add that besides being our host, she was also a talented painter. Mildly abashed, Julia graciously accepted the bouquet from Diego and promptly returned with a crystal centerpiece crafted from the roses he had brought. Despite the rain outside, the room exuded an air of sophistication and charm.

"I'm speechless," Diego said once Julia was out of earshot. "When Isabel said you had a surprise, I never imagined anything like this." He glanced around the room in fascination then looked back at me. "To what do I deserve such an honor?"

Julia returned to the room bearing a bottle of champagne

and popped the cork, crying out with delight as it shot across the room and smacked into a lampshade, knocking it cockeyed. "I never liked that one much anyway," she joked as she filled our fluted glasses and withdrew again.

"This was Julia's idea," I confessed, slightly embarrassed. "She saw you dropping me off this morning and then offered to do this."

"Why?"

"Something to do with your uncle, she said. About him being a famous artist. She wanted to meet you. *Sorry.* I wanted tonight to be special like we planned. But she highjacked it before I knew it, and I didn't have the heart to turn her down."

"Nothing to be sorry about. I get it. Anyway, let's make the best of it, shall we?" He raised his glass. "To a special night!"

"To a special night," I echoed as we clinked glasses and surrendered to the full Julia experience.

To my relief, Julia mostly left us alone, coming into the room only when it was time to serve the next course of our French-inspired dinner, designed around her main course of chili-spiced *duck a l'orange*.

Over the course of our meal, I learned more about Diego's intriguing background. He told me about how his mother had been initially disowned by her influential family for eloping with an outsider. But when Diego was born, she reconciled with her parents on the condition that she send Diego to Bulgaria when he turned six. In the ten years he spent there, he grew very close to his wealthy grandfather. And despite his moving back to Mexico when he turned sixteen, much to his grandfather's disappointment, Diego inherited a substantial sum of money on his grandfather's passing.

"How did that go over with your parents and siblings?" I asked.

Diego shrugged. "I made sure they all benefited. We're close, so it wouldn't have been a problem anyway. But, still, we're fine."

In the lull that followed, my fork hovered over the last piece of duck as I debated whether now was a good time to break the news about my departure.

"Not hungry?" he asked, sopping up the last of the orange sauce with a piece of tortilla.

"I'm just taking a break. It's a lot of food."

He nodded and wiped his mouth. "Anyway, I have something to tell you."

"I have something to tell you first."

He slid his plate to one side and folded his hands on the table as if in anticipation of something serious.

"My visa came through earlier than I expected. I'm leaving tomorrow morning."

Diego pulled back his hands and sat up.

"My friend Suchi, the woman arranging it all, she's dropping me off downtown to catch a bus to the border."

"That's a hell of a long way."

"Seventy-two hours she said."

"At least! What *I* was going to tell you was that I'm supposed to leave for home tomorrow. Why don't you ride with me? I'd love to show you where I'm from, introduce you to my parents. My father's super curious to meet you and Ahbhu, so this is actually fortuitous."

"You told your father about me and Ahbhu?"

"He and I spoke earlier today. I told him about, well, you know . . ." he glanced in the direction of the kitchen and lowered his voice. "Needless to say, he's intrigued."

Feeling excited at the prospect of spending more time with Diego, but worried the detour might upset Suchi, I explained I was supposed to arrive at the border in no more than a week. Diego reassured me I would make my schedule even if he had to drive me there himself.

"*Et voilà!*" Julia exclaimed, appearing in the room bearing a flaming plate, which she placed in the center of the table. "My version of cherries jubilee for your first dessert!"

As she cleared our dinner plates and replaced them with dessert bowls, she proudly explained the dish, candied cherries flambeed with mezcal, which she spooned over vanilla ice cream with dark chocolate sprinkles once the alcohol burned off.

"Why don't you join us, Julia, please," Diego said, offering her a warm smile and nodding at an empty chair. "I want to hear more about your lovely paintings."

Julia's face lit up at the invitation, and she hurried to retrieve another bowl from the sideboard. Diego winked playfully at me, then graciously proceeded to quiz Julia about her artwork over the next half hour, promising at the end to introduce her to his uncle the next time he exhibited in Mexico City.

After dinner, Diego and I retired to my room, where, after a brief impassioned fumble, we fell asleep in each other's arms.


When Suchi arrived the next morning, she eyed Diego suspiciously as I explained that I'd be riding with him part of the way. Despite Suchi's initial hostility, Diego calmly outlined our route, including the point at which I'd rejoin the itinerary she had prepared. Ahbhu, showing his approval, eagerly scrambled onto Diego's lap, accepting a doggie treat from his pocket.

Seeing herself outvoted, Suchi raised her hands in mock surrender and pulled me into a warm, lingering hug. She urged me to be careful, casting a backward glance at Diego, then handed me an envelope stuffed with cash and made me promise to call her at her home in San Salvador the moment I arrived safely in Tijuana.

# Chapter 31

## THE CLAIMING OF AHBHU

Diego and I arrived at his village, exhausted, after a full day of driving punctuated by brief stops along the way where he pointed out some stunning colonial towns as well as a couple of archaeological sites. As we turned off the main highway, brilliant moonlight bathed the landscape, casting long shadows across the rugged terrain. The air was crisp, carrying the faint scent of earth and distant smoke. The steady hum of crickets filled the night, pierced through by the occasional screech of a night bird, as we drove through the dark lanes of his extensive village, made up of scores of one-story adobe houses and thatched buildings.

Diego had fallen quiet as we progressed over the bumpy dirt roads to the far end of the settlement where his family lived. Their home was somewhat removed from the rest of the villagers, in a sprawling rancho that reflected their prosperity. Ahead, the rancho's iron gates loomed in the moonlight, their imposing presence softened by the gentle swaying of the surrounding trees. Diego exited the car and pushed them open, the gates creaking slightly on their hinges. Then we drove down a long drive, flanked by tall pines and blossoming jacarandas.

Arriving at the family compound, we parked to one side of the rambling main house amid a collection of vehicles, both old and new. Diego's parents, Don Federico and Doña Lenka, were waiting for us on the porch. Don Federico, a towering figure in a white tunic, exuded a quiet strength as he pulled Diego into an emotional hug. His demeanor was stoic yet affectionate, his deep voice carrying a hint of gravel as he welcomed his son home. Doña Lenka radiated warmth and hospitality, her gentle smile lighting up her features as she waited her turn to embrace Diego. Despite her slim frame and friendly smile, she embodied a quiet strength and resilience.

Diego introduced me as a dear friend and fellow traveler. Doña Lenka's eyes sparkled with maternal pride and, in heavily accented Spanish, she warmly invited me into their home with a graceful sweep of her hand. Don Federico, by contrast, stood back slightly, studying me with his intense dark eyes. His gaze was penetrating yet not unfriendly, and I sensed a depth of wisdom in his silent scrutiny. Looking past me, he spotted Ahbhu, who had paused halfway between Diego's car and the house, standing at full attention with his ear perked up and alert.

"This is *la criatura* you spoke about, hijo," he affirmed to Diego, not taking his eyes off of Ahbhu.

"His name's Ahbhu," I said, finding it strange his being referred to as a *criatura*, a creature.

"Yes, Papá," Diego said, glancing sidelong at me. "This is the one."

"Ahbhu, come here," Don Federico ordered, squatting on the stoop and holding out his hand.

Without a moment's hesitation, Ahbhu moved to Don Federico, who wrapped him in his arms and pressed his face against Ahbhu's head. I started at the gesture and made to intervene, but Diego held me back, signaling to allow his father space as Don Federico whispered something into Ahbhu's ear. After a moment, he released him and stood. Ahbhu stared at him, mesmerized, and wagged his head side to side. It was obvious something had passed between them, something I wasn't privy to. Feeling a pang of jealousy, I waved Ahbhu over. Don Federico, reading my emotions, draped his arm over my shoulder and led me into the house with Ahbhu following closely at his heels.

Despite the late hour, the house was alive with activity as several of Diego's siblings popped in and out of the living room where Don Federico received us, while Doña Lenka prepared dinner for Diego and me. They showered him with hugs and kisses, their admiration evident on their radiant faces, and were equally welcoming of me. In the meantime, Ahbhu had crawled into Don Federico's lap the instant he sat in his throne-like chair at the end of the room. I shot Ahbhu a questioning look. He responded by turning his head into Don Federico's barrel chest, who stroked his fur and whispered to him in a language I assumed was Huichol.

"Diego tells me you will be with us for a day or two," Don Federico said, looking back and forth between the two of us sitting next to each other on a leather love seat.

"No more than that, Señor. I'm expected in Tijuana in six days."

"Yes, I've been told," he said plainly.

I glanced questioningly at Diego, who nodded in affirmation, gesturing at Ahbhu as the source of the information.

Astonished by the revelation, I raised my eyes at Don Federico. "You're able to communicate with Ahbhu?"

"Only on a very basic level," he admitted, smiling at Ahbhu, who gazed up at him.

"How?" I asked.

"The question is more how *you* are able to communicate with him."

"I have no idea."

Don Federico nodded, keeping his eyes on me. "Diego has

explained to you about our ceremonies." Don Federico never asked questions. He only made statements.

"Yes, he explained. Why?"

"You're curious; you want to see. Correct me if that's not the case."

"Yes, I'm curious." I looked at Diego who directed my attention back to his father with an upward tilt of his head. "Is that even an option?"

"It's an option," Don Federico answered. "More than seeing, you will participate, and I will guide you. And, if you grant me permission, we will *both* commune with Ahbhu on a deeper level—to better understand how you and he are able to speak to each other without the aid of hikuri."

I glanced at Ahbhu who, together with Don Federico, was watching me from across the room, waiting for a response.

"Is it dangerous?" I asked. "For Ahbhu, I mean."

"Ahbhu needs only to be present. The ceremony will pose no danger for him whatsoever."

"My father has been a guide for over thirty years," Diego reassured, "He knows what he's doing. You'll both be safe."

"Okay then. I agree," I said with a modicum of caution.

"Good." Don Federico rose from his chair and turned Ahbhu over to me. "Tomorrow in the early morning, we will travel to Wirikuta, our sacred desert, three hours from here. We will commence our journey from there."

As if on cue, Doña Lenka appeared in the doorway, and waved us to the dinner table.

"Of course, tonight you will eat," Don Federico added, "and then you will rest. You will need all your energies for tomorrow."

And with that, he entrusted us to his wife, who had us in stitches for the rest of the evening with hair-raising stories about her former life in Bulgaria.

After dinner, Diego and I took a stroll outside before retiring to bed. I missed Ahbhu, who, having turned quiet and contemplative, had stayed behind. But I decided to keep it to myself, considering how comfortable he felt around Don Federico.

Once Diego and I were out of view of the main house, he took my hand and led me into a small hut behind a secluded stand of trees where he drew me into his arms. I could feel him getting hard as he kissed my neck and nipped at my ear, his breath shallowing.

"Are you sure it's okay to do this here?" I whispered, trying to buy time as he was a lot further ahead of me. "What if somebody sees us?"

"Nobody comes here, not at this time," he whispered back breathlessly. "Plus, my parents are going to put us in separate rooms tonight. So this is our one and only chance."

"Separate rooms?"

"Don't ask so many questions," he said with a twisted smile. "Not now. Unless you don't want to." He leaned in for a deep kiss, and I opened my mouth to receive it.

As we mauled each other hungrily, I was overtaken with an intense desire for Diego unmatched by anything I'd ever felt with Gerónimo. Stripping off his shirt, I explored his chest and arms with my mouth, urged on by the taste of him, the smell of him; then I yanked down his jeans. Diego moaned softly as I took him into my mouth, bringing him close to climax a few times. He returned the favor before leading me to a hard cot in a corner where he pressed a condom into my hand and surrendered his body to me.

Once we'd exhausted ourselves, we sat on the edge of the cot, leaning heavily against each other, quietly catching our breath, our bodies gleaming with sweat. Then, reluctantly, we got into our clothes and trudged back toward the house.

As it came into view, Diego let go of my hand and walked the rest of the way, a little ahead of me. Doña Lenka received us with a tight smile as we passed through the doorway. Diego and I separated, and Doña Lenka ushered me to the guest room on the second floor. I was happy to find Ahbhu there, snoring peacefully at the foot of the bed.

Don Federico roused me at four in the morning, impressing on me the importance of reaching Wirikuta in time for the sunrise. Despite having managed only five hours of rest, I felt refreshed and eager for the forthcoming experience. With a gentle call, Don Federico beckoned Ahbhu, who sprang to life at the sound of his voice, offering me a brief yet affectionate lick. As they vanished through the doorway together, a renewed sense of jealousy stirred within me at Ahbhu's growing bond with Don Federico.

The bracing shock of freezing water on my face served to fully awaken my senses as I hastily prepared myself in the guest bathroom. Then I dashed downstairs where I found them all gathered around the kitchen table: Diego, Doña Lenka, Don Federico, and Diego's youngest brother Francisco, all clad in pristine white tunics adorned with elaborate embroidery, draped ponchos, and handcrafted necklaces. The sight surprised me and I suddenly felt self-conscious in my blue jeans and T-shirt.

After a hurried breakfast of beans, tortillas, and hot coffee, we congregated in a sleek modern pickup truck driven by Francisco. Don Federico rode shotgun with Doña Lenka in the middle and Ahbhu at his feet. Diego and I wrapped up in blankets and nestled in the bed of the truck as we drove out of the gates under a star-splashed sky. Just before leaving, Don Federico had pulled me aside and instructed me to do my best to turn inward and examine myself during our three-hour journey to Wirikuta, assuring me that such spiritual work would serve to prepare me for the ceremony.

"I love this ride," Diego whispered as we sped along the road, his warm fingers intertwined with mine under the blanket. "I've been taking it as long as I remember. I missed it when I was in Bulgaria. It's part of the reason I came back."

"What's it like? The hikuri?" I asked, fixating on the aspect of the ceremony I was most curious about.

"You'll see with your heart," he answered cryptically. "But it's best not to focus on that, Isaac. More than anything, this is a spiritual journey. Hikuri is there to help us connect with our inner selves and the spiritual realm, but only when we're guided by a *marakame*, a healer like my father."

My chest tightened at his mention of the spiritual realm. Never having been much for that aspect of religion, the idea there might actually be something out there and that I might be connecting with it both fascinated and terrified me. I squeezed his hand tightly and he squeezed back. Then he unlaced his fingers from mine and rubbed them against his tunic.

"This is a pilgrimage," he uttered. He narrowed his eyes until they were just slits, staring intently into the receding distance as the truck ascended the winding road into a landscape that was becoming ever more barren of vegetation. "It's time for us to concentrate."

# Chapter 32

## WIRIKUTA

When we finally arrived at Wirikuta, the sky was beginning to lighten, which created a sense of urgency among Diego's family, who were keen to make it to the summit in time to see the rising of the sun. Don Federico distributed straw hats decorated with feathers and colorful bangles to Diego and his brother and donned one himself. Diego's mother handed me a baseball hat, "for the sun," she said with a playful wink.

Francisco led the way along a rocky path up a steep hill, while playing a mournful tune on a stringed instrument resembling a rustic violin. Diego's mother followed behind, tapping out a rhythm on a small drum. Don Federico brought up the rear, chanting a song in the Huichol language that grew stronger as we promenaded to the summit of the hill, the stars blinking off above us.

Diego held my arm as we walked, making sure I didn't stumble, while chanting in unison with his father. Ahbhu ran past us and fell in alongside Don Federico and matched his stride. The sight was like an ice pick to my heart. I felt sure Don Federico had cast some kind of spell on Ahbhu, perhaps intending to keep him. Perhaps he'd even lured me there via Diego with the intention of taking Ahbhu from me once he'd learned of Ahbhu's ability to speak. One thing was certain, Ahbhu hadn't directed a single word to me since we'd arrived at Don Federico's. As if registering my thoughts, Don Federico looked back at me and spoke a few words in Huichol, slow and deliberate, words that made Diego lose his footing, narrowly avoiding falling onto one knee. Then he turned back and carried on with his chanting. Diego cast a questioning glance at me as I helped steady him.

"Something's wrong with Ahbhu," I said out of the corner of my mouth. "He's not the same since we arrived at your place. He won't talk to me; he's acting all zombie-like, except when he's with your father. I'm worried."

"Nothing's wrong with Ahbhu, Isaac. He's a special dog with a special soul, and my father's a special man who has a way with special animals. Please, try not to worry. It won't be good for you, for the hikuri."

We reached the summit a few minutes later, a barren platform at the top of the world it seemed. Don Federico and his family gathered around a ceremonial stone circle to make offerings of incense and food. A few meters away stood a small hut Diego explained was a sacred shrine. Drifting to the edge of the summit, I gazed out at the magnificent sight of the desert unfolding below and around us, a hypnotic expanse of hills and valleys, scrub and sand, that seemed to go on forever, growing ever sharper in the swirl of colors of the advancing dawn. A sharp whistle brought me back to myself. Wiping my face, I jogged over to the ceremonial circle where they were all waiting for me.

"This is Wirikuta, our sacred place, located on the ancestral lands of our people," Don Federico explained, half speaking, half chanting, in Spanish for my benefit. Diego and the others continued their quiet singing. "Wirikuta is the birthplace of the sun," Don Federico declared. He punctuated the statement by throwing out his open palm at the hills in the exact moment the sun burst blazing over the horizon and set the desert alight. Ahbhu shot to the edge of the summit and bayed at the circle of fire as it ascended into the sky. Awestruck, my knees buckled and Diego rushed to me and held my arm to keep me from keeling over.

Don Federico turned back to me with a broad smile, his face glowing in the reflected light, elated we'd made it in time for me to witness, as he put it, the birth of a new day.

"We Wixárika have kept our rituals and traditions alive for thousands of years, long before the Spanish reached our shores," he said proudly. "Generation after generation we've honored our relationship with the earth and the original elements of life: fire, water, earth and air. Wirikuta is the place from which we originated. Over the centuries, though, our people have scattered, like chaff in the wind, to towns and villages around Mexico. Even so, Wirikuta has remained a place of pilgrimage for our people. We journey here during sacred festivals, some of us on foot, from wherever we happen to be. Most importantly, Wirikuta is also the home of hikuri, the sacred plant we ritually ingest to receive the gift of seeing. We are here today for a *private ceremony*. Are you ready to begin, young man?"

I glanced at Ahbhu, who was still at the edge of the hill, mesmerized by the sun. "I'm not sure, Señor."

Don Federico beckoned to Ahbhu with a whistle; he was with us within seconds. Don Federico then indicated the ground next to me, and Ahbhu sat down, gazing up at him.

"And now?" Don Federico asked.

I raised my eyes at Don Federico and met his penetrating gaze. "What's happening to Ahbhu, Don Federico? Ever since we arrived, it's like he doesn't recognize me, his owner, the person who rescued and raised him and has loved him since he was a pup. It's almost as if he's become *your* dog now." I looked at Ahbhu, hoping for a reaction, but he continued to stare at Don Federico.

"You speak in terms of ownership," Don Federico answered softly. "We don't own the creatures we encounter or any other part of nature for that matter."

"Ahbhu is *my* dog, not yours," I asserted. "When I leave here, he's coming with me."

"You're angry Ahbhu feels an affinity for someone other than yourself."

"That's not it. He's felt an affinity for certain other people before. But he's always recognized me as . . . as his friend. This time it's different. What did you do to him?"

"I haven't done anything to him. But, make no mistake, Ahbhu is aware in a way other creatures like him aren't. He and you have been communing on a plane of consciousness that is slightly removed from the one in which we move. This says something about you as well. I'm *also* able to access that plane. Ahbhu's reaction is simply one of fascination that another human is able to connect with him."

"Cashtōka was able to communicate with him," I said. "And he didn't get like this with her."

Ahbhu lifted his head at my mention of Cashtōka and let out a whimper.

Don Federico lost concentration at this new information. "Who is Cashtōka?" It was the one and only time I ever heard him ask a question.

"Cashtōka is a Mayan woman who helped us back home. She gave Ahbhu and me food and shelter when we found ourselves in difficulty. She was able to speak with him. The two of them even bonded. But he *never* withdrew from me the way he has now."

"This woman, Cashtōka, was a shamana," Don Federico said.

"No, her mother was."

Don Federico looked away from me for a moment; then he

looked back at me with a humorless smile. "Don't worry, young man. Your relationship with Ahbhu is not in any danger."

Ahbhu glanced up and met my gaze, a flicker of recognition returning to his eyes. He lovingly nuzzled his head against my leg. As I rubbed the sweet spot behind his ear, I felt a wave of relief spread over me, like an icicle melting in the sun, its once sharp edges softening into a gentle trickle of warmth.

"I'm so sorry, Don Federico." I cast an embarrassed glance at Diego and his family. "Ahbhu's all I have left at this point. I just—"

Don Federico squeezed my shoulder. "There's no need for apologies, young man. It's time to let go of all your fears, time to gain spiritual insight, to get to know yourself on a deeper level and expand your consciousness—if you're ready."

Squatting next to Ahbhu, I kissed him and stood. Focusing on Don Federico, I signaled I was ready.

Don Federico lit incense and passed the smoking censor over my body while he chanted prayers and Diego, his brother, and his mother played instruments in the background. Then he waved feathers and branches over me and asked me to silently confess to the gods, whichever ones I believed in, or to the universe, so as to journey with a clear conscience. He repeated this to each member of his family, each of whom repeated the prayers.

Once we were done with our confessions, Don Federico lit what he called a sacred fire and invited us to express gratitude, ask for blessings, or seek his guidance, each of us in turn out of earshot of the others. When it came my turn, I asked him what he foresaw for me in my journey ahead. Holding me in his firm and steady gaze, Don Federico confessed he couldn't see into the future, but he promised to seek an answer from the hikuri.

We followed Don Federico into the sacred hut, which was

filled with feathers and intricate yarn work, half-melted candles, and a rainbow of offerings of every kind, from simple knick-knacks to animal skulls to snow globes. We sat in a semicircle inside the cozy space. I was pressed up against Diego with Ahbhu between my legs; next to Diego was his mother and next to her his brother. Then Don Federico distributed the hikuri buttons to each of us. I brought mine to my nose and sniffed at it. It smelled earthy and slightly fruity. Diego leaned over and offered to peel it for me, and I handed it to him. Digging his thumbnail into the green skin of the button, he peeled it back and revealed the pale yellow flesh inside. Then he squeezed off a piece, about the size of a grape, and handed it to me.

Don Federico led us in a prayer of thanksgiving, both in Huichol and in Spanish, asking the hikuri for guidance and blessing, and a deeper spiritual connection. Then, placing the hikuri in his mouth, he indicated for us to do the same.

The moment I bit into the hikuri, I recoiled at its bitter taste. I found it overpowering and challenging to tolerate as I chewed its slimy fibrous flesh and its juices joined with my saliva. I recall accidentally dropping a small piece and reaching around on the ground for it when I was suddenly slammed with an intense feeling of nausea and a pain in my gut. I doubled over on the verge of vomiting. Diego rubbed my back, reassuring me the discomfort would soon pass. Don Federico echoed this and urged me to relax and embrace the experience.

I closed my eyes and held still and soon found the aching in my gut gradually replaced by a tingling warmth that spread throughout my body. Once the pain had subsided, I slowly unfolded, buoyed by an odd lightness in my body, and opened my eyes.

The room was awash in bright colors, at once fluid and razor sharp. Diego and the others glowed as if enveloped in bright halos of radiant light, their voices mingling in a harmonious chorus of words I didn't understand. I reached for Diego and he beamed back an outflow of love from eyes as wide as the hikuri buttons themselves. We touched hands, palm against palm, and I felt them sizzle against each other as every nerve ending of my body came alive. The contact ignited a mixture of empathy and euphoria that flowed into and through me and expanded outward into the sacred space of the hut, and into the universe beyond.

With Don Federico's voice resonating in my mind, guiding me as my spirit ascended, I journeyed out of Wirikuta. Through a kaleidoscope of cosmic vistas, I sped through both space and time, weaving a path through Orion and the Pleiades, until I descended over my war-torn homeland. Beneath me, the land seethed with the fury of erupting volcanoes, casting a fiery glow astride the landscape.

Spotting El Boquerón, belching fire in the distance, I dipped toward it and beheld the wreckage of my family home, perched precariously on its smoldering flank. In a surreal blur, I witnessed my beloved mamá, stumbling alone amid the debris, her anguished cries piercing the sulfurous air, calling out my name. With a heart as heavy as osmium, I longed to reassure her, to let her know I was safe, but her image swiftly faded, a shimmering mirage in a searing desert.

In her place emerged the haunting image of Gerónimo, frightened and imprisoned in a dank cell, his form battered and broken. With a jarring clang, soldiers burst into the cell and seized him, dragging us *both* through echoing corridors to a gravel-strewn yard. Bound to a post, I faced a grim line of rifles, their menacing gaze fixed on me.

*Don't do this, young man*, pleaded Don Federico, his voice full of compassion. *You cannot exchange one person's destiny for another's. Come back.*

Yet, despite his urging, I couldn't abandon Gerónimo, my heart torn by my love for him. As the countdown to execution echoed in my ears, I clung to hope amid his impending annihilation, unwilling to let go of the bond that connected us.

"Ten, nine, eight," the commander's voice thundered.

*Come back, young man!* echoed Don Federico.

"Seven, six," the world narrowed to a single, harrowing moment of reckoning.

I squeezed my eyes shut, preparing for the inevitable, the smell of rotten eggs filling my nostrils, the taste of metal on my tongue.

*Isaac, come back!* I heard Diego shout, his voice merging with Don Federico's in a chorus of desperation.

"Two!"

A silent plea for redemption echoed inside me, igniting a last flicker of determination, as I bargained with the Universe for Gerónimo's life.

"One!" With a deafening roar, the scene around me refracted into an incomprehensible spectrum of colors before everything dissolved into blackness.

I gradually emerged out of the trance as if rising from the depths of a deep lake to the sun-dappled surface. Refreshed but exhausted, I felt a pulsing ache in all my limbs, surrounded by a confusion of voices. The only word I recognized was my name repeated over and over again, the air around me pungent with smoke. As my eyes fluttered open, I found myself staring up at Diego's concerned face. Beyond him stood his parents, Don Federico and Doña Lenka, grasping onto each other and babbling words I didn't understand. We were still inside the hut, engulfed in a swirl of fumes. Diego passed his hand over my forehead, peering into my face. Seeing I'd regained consciousness, he smothered a cry and turned to his parents announcing that I was back.

"What happened?" I croaked. My throat felt parched.

"Isaac, thank God!" Diego said, his voice hoarse with

emotion. He handed me a cup of water and waited until I'd drained it while in the background his parents tearfully embraced each other, clearly relieved. "You had a seizure. We weren't sure what was happening at first. But then I remembered you said you had epilepsy."

Feeling suddenly gripped by a sense of desperation, I looked around for Ahbhu. "Where's Ahbhu?" I asked. "He was supposed to help me."

Diego sat up and looked around. Don Federico let go of his wife, his face filling with anxiety, no longer looking like a man in control. He cast about the hut, calling out Ahbhu's name. Then we all took up the chorus. Francisco disappeared outside. He was back within minutes, breathless and frightened.

"I found him. He's in the circle of stones. Something's wrong." He wagged his finger at the door.

Diego helped me up and we all exited the sacred hut into the late afternoon and rushed to the stone circle, where we found Ahbhu collapsed, his eyes half open and glazed over, his mouth bubbling foam.

"Ahbhu!" I screamed, drawing him into my arms, wiping his mouth and kissing him as he groaned. I swung on Don Federico, who crouched next to me and tenderly examined him. "What's wrong with him?" I cried.

"These are signs of intoxication," he said, looking around at his family. "All of you ate your hikuri."

Diego, Doña Lenka, and Francisco were huddled together watching on, their faces full of fear. They nodded to Don Federico that they had.

Then he turned to me, waiting for my response.

I recalled the small piece of the hikuri that had skittered out of my hand when I bit into it. The sudden realization of what had happened slammed me. Ahbhu had eaten my morsel. I leveled frightened eyes at Don Federico, who was staring at me.

"No, Don Federico, not all of it!" I whimpered. "I accidentally dropped a little piece. I tried to find it, but—"

"Search the shrine!" Don Federico said to his son Francisco. "Scour every inch of it!"

"What if Ahbhu ate hikuri?" I asked, my voice trembling.

"Hikuri is toxic to animals," Don Federico answered. "If Ahbhu ate hikuri, he would have experienced some of the same effects that you did, but without the benefit of a guide. After that, he would have either passed from this world or become very ill, depending on the amount he ingested."

Francisco emerged from the hut and signaled that he hadn't found anything. Don Federico turned back to me, his eyes full of sadness. He held out his arms for Ahbhu, and I transferred him into them. He whispered to Ahbhu, who responded by shifting his head and baring his teeth in a weak attempt at a smile. Lowering his head to Ahbhu, Don Federico kissed him and handed him back to me.

"We must get Ahbhu to a veterinarian urgently. I know of one in San Luis Potosí. Come, we must hurry."

"Will he die?" I asked Don Federico as I rushed with Ahbhu in my arms on our way back to the truck, with Diego supporting my steps.

"We all die," Don Federico answered with a tinge of anger in his voice. "But if Ahbhu is seen by the veterinarian, he will not die today."

We sped to San Luis Potosí along the deserted highway. Don Federico administered fluids to Ahbhu in the cab, which he said was essential to ensuring his survival, while I rode with Diego in the back, clutching onto him and holding back the surge of sadness and guilt threatening to undo me. Diego did his best to comfort me, reassuring me it wasn't my fault, his eyes full of tears. "*I'm* the one that should have been monitoring your taking of hikuri . . . *I'm* the one that brought you and Ahbhu here! This is *totally* my fault, not yours."

We reached San Luis Potosí at sunset, driving straight to the vet's house through the darkened streets. Don Federico leaped out of the truck, cradling Ahbhu in his arms, and urgently knocked on the door. After what seemed like an eternity, the vet—a weathered man in his forties with a splash of white hair—answered the door, clearly displeased at having his dinner interrupted. After a quick exchange of words and money, the vet ushered us into the back room that served as his clinic.

He wasted no time in getting to work, listening intently to Don Federico's explanation while assessing Ahbhu's condition. The vet's practiced hands moved deftly as he conducted a thorough examination, starting with listening to Ahbhu's heart and lungs, checking for any irregularities. Ahbhu, visibly uncomfortable, let out a soft whimper as the vet gently pressed on his abdomen, checking for any signs of pain.

Satisfied with his initial assessment, the vet prepared a syringe, carefully measuring out a dose of some medication before administering it to Ahbhu with a practiced hand. To my relief, he assured me that Ahbhu would probably be all right, but that he wanted to keep him overnight for observation just in case. Still fearful of the outcome, I tenderly hugged Ahbhu, who seemed more alert than when we'd first arrived, and promised him I'd be back the next day to pick him up. He licked my hand and uttered his first words to me since we'd arrived at Don Federico's.

*Ahbhu is sorry.*

# Chapter 33

## EL GARROBO

"I need to call my mother," I said to Diego once we reached his house, explaining to him what I'd seen in the vision.

Overhearing our conversation, Don Federico intervened: "What one sees in visions is rarely literal, young man. Sometimes it's purely symbolic. Perhaps, in this case, your subconscious was trying to reveal something critical to you—the breakdown of your home, your mother in distress—it's possible you feel responsible for the chaos."

"But that's just the thing, Don Federico. I *am* responsible for the chaos! Disaster follows me wherever I go. I've never been able to catch a break in this life. People are suffering because of me—not to mention Ahbhu! That's what your blessed hikuri showed me."

"If *that's* what it showed you," Don Federico countered seamlessly, "it was because it wants you to break free of that cycle, whether real or imagined. *That's* the spiritual work you're destined for."

"Thank you for that," I said, feeling taken down a notch. "Still, I'd like to call my mother, to make sure everything is all right."

"Of course!" Diego said. He escorted me to a paneled study off the living room and indicated an old-fashioned dial phone on the desk. Then he made to exit the room to give me privacy.

"Please stay, Diego," I said, needing some moral support. He pulled a chair next to me as I picked up the receiver and dialed.

The phone rang a few times, but there was no answer. I hung up and retried the number. Again, no answer. Feeling a cold sweat break out on my forehead, I dialed my brother Neto. His phone rang a few times before diverting to his answering machine. I hung up without leaving a message and tossed a worried glance at Diego, considering whether I should call Gerónimo's parents.

"Maybe you should try your friend Suchi. She might know something."

I nodded tentatively, unsure whether Suchi would be back in San Salvador so soon. Digging her number out of my pocket, I dialed it. A woman answered on the second ring.

"Amparo?" I asked. My question was met with a long silence. "I'm Isaac," I tried. "Do you know who I am?"

"Yes, I know," she said in a hushed voice.

"I'm so sorry to disturb you. Is Suchi there?"

"I'm expecting her tomorrow," she said after another long pause. "Have you arrived?"

"Not yet. There's been a delay. But soon. I just need to speak with Suchi urgently. When do you expect her?"

"Tomorrow evening," she said, then quickly hung up.

I returned the phone to the cradle and frowned at Diego. He took my hand and, with a swift glance at the door, kissed it.

"This is so messed up." I lowered my head in frustration. "They're expecting me in Tijuana. But now with Ahbhu, I don't know if he'll be okay to travel."

"You can stay here for as long as you need, until Ahbhu is fully recovered or even longer. Or you can come back to Mexico City with me."

"I can't do that, Diego. I have a plan. People are waiting

for me: the guy in Tijuana, my mother's cousin in Los Angeles. That's where my future lies, not here. But thank you. I'm super happy I met you. I've appreciated all your hospitality and the special times we've spent together."

"Fine, but at least let me take you to Tijuana."

"Either way, it's still a long journey."

"I meant by plane."

"Plane?"

"I have a good friend with a private jet in San Luis Potosí. I'll call him right now and see if he can fly us to Tijuana, either tomorrow or the next day, once Ahbhu is ready to travel. It's a two-hour flight, maximum."

"But what about immigration control?"

"We're talking about San Luis Potosí, Isaac, not Mexico City. Just leave that part to me."

The vet discharged Ahbhu the next morning with a strongly worded caution that he should be allowed to rest for at least a week. The hikuri had so depleted his energies, he said, that unless afforded proper time to recover, Ahbhu might relapse into a coma or worse. He looked skeptical when Diego asked whether Ahbhu was well enough to fly. Diego clarified it would be in a private jet and that he'd arrange to transport Ahbhu to the airport without the need for him to walk.

"As I stated," the vet said, exchanging a concerned look with Don Federico, "I'd prefer that the poor animal rest *before* traveling. But, if it's a matter of urgency, as long as he can rest properly on the other side, I won't oppose it."

I gathered Ahbhu's trembling body into my arms and stared into his eyes. He smiled weakly, gently panting, and nodded, letting me know he was feeling better.

Don Federico laid his hand on my shoulder. "Let Ahbhu

rest here, Isaac. Call ahead to your people and explain what happened. Surely they'll understand."

"Thank you, but I can't, Don Federico. I'll make sure he rests when we get to Tijuana, I promise. But I can't delay any longer." I kissed Ahbhu and he licked my nose in response.

"I'll stay with them, Papá," Diego promised. "I won't leave until I see they're properly settled somewhere Ahbhu can recover."

The vet scribbled out the name of a colleague in Tijuana and offered to call ahead to book a follow-up examination, which we all agreed was a good idea. Then we were off to the airport where I bade Don Federico and Doña Lenka goodbye while Diego greased the palms of a couple of airport officials and an immigration agent.

We soon boarded Diego's friend's jet with Ahbhu at my feet resting in a soft-sided carrier. After a smooth, mercifully uneventful flight, we were back on the ground in an airport limousine, riding through the gritty streets of Tijuana in search of the safehouse.

The limousine made slow progress down Avenida Revolución, the city's main commercial drag, whose frenetic, bustling sidewalks contrasted sharply with the dense, sluggish traffic. Exhaust-belching cars, busses, and trucks drifted languidly in and out of unmarked lanes, the drivers sounding their horns with each erratic maneuver they attempted.

After nearly an hour of battling through the automotive fray, our driver turned out of the river of vehicles and drove along the border wall, through trash-strewn streets, trying his best to avoid the potholes and stray dogs that darted out without warning. After several fits and starts trying to locate the address Suchi had given us, the driver made a left onto a dirty, nondescript lane and crawled forward to where it ended against a crumbling brick wall. "That's it, I think." He pointed at a blue door set in a wall to our left, the only door in the lane.

Diego and I exchanged doubtful glances as we stared at the door. Ahbhu perked up his head and sniffed the air, emitting a low growl.

"Are you sure?" Diego asked.

The driver held his hand out at the door and answered dryly, "There's only one way to know that, isn't there?"

We rapped on the door a few times before it swung open to reveal a swarthy, middle-aged man with dark, darting eyes. His ink-black hair was cut military style, and his face bore deep lines, framed by a close-cropped beard. "Who are you?" he asked, looking past us at the van, then back at us, his suspicion palpable.

"Suchipila Ramirez gave me this address," I said, grasping Suchi's scribbled note of introduction.

He snapped his fingers for the note, read through it, then handed it back at me. "We've been waiting for you. Who's this?" He raised his head at Diego, who bristled at being referred to in the third person.

"He's my friend."

"There's nothing in there about a friend," the man said, gesturing at Suchi's note. "Just about a dog."

Diego dug a small wad of cash from his pocket. "I'm here to inspect the place before I leave him with you." The man's eyes gleamed as Diego counted out a few large bills. "Is this enough?"

Identifying himself as El Garrobo, he pocketed the cash in his weathered jacket before leading us on a tour of the facility. The converted warehouse boasted a grassy yard in the rear as well as amenities such as separate dormitories for men and women, each equipped with a pair of bunk beds, a couple of clean bathrooms, and a sparsely furnished lounge overlooking the yard. El Garrobo told us he lived on premises.

"Where is everyone?" I asked, unsure of how comfortable I'd be alone with El Garrobo, who exuded a slight air of menace.

"You're the only one for the moment. I'll be taking you and your dog across early tomorrow morning before the sun comes up."

"About that," Diego cut in, "his dog isn't well. He'll need to rest for about a week beforehand."

"That's impossible," El Garrobo snapped. "I have a group of people coming next week, four in total. I can't attend to them as well as this guy and his dog at the same time, not to mention there's the issue of cost. I wasn't paid to house them for more than a couple of nights. No, it's tonight or not at all."

"Don't worry about the cost; I'll cover your fee. But it's imperative that the dog is allowed to rest until he's ready to make the crossing. Understood?"

"All right. But it won't be cheap," El Garrobo said.

"As I said," Diego responded, "I'll cover it. I'll pay you an advance now, and the rest once they're safely on the other side."

El Garrobo locked eyes with Diego, sizing him up; then he let out a sarcastic chuckle. "Sure, why not?"

"That's a wise decision," Diego replied. Without removing his eyes from El Garrobo, he instructed me, "Bring in Ahbhu while I settle things here."

When I returned a couple of minutes later with Ahbhu limping along behind me, Diego had concluded his negotiations with El Garrobo. Although we'd only requested a week, El Garrobo had demanded payment for two full weeks of room and board for both Ahbhu and me, which Diego was prepared to pay. Diego and I then withdrew to the men's dormitory and set up a place on one of the beds for Ahbhu to sleep.

"Thank you for everything, Diego," I said, hugging him tightly. "I don't know how or when I'll ever be able to repay you for all of this."

"There's no need for that." Diego's eyes reflected a kindness I'd never seen before in anyone I'd ever met. "Just *promise* me you'll contact me if you need anything at all while you're here. Absolutely anything."

"Yes, I promise."

"I'll *always* be there for you, remember that!"

"Thank you, Diego."

"And don't forget to call me once you and Ahbhu have made it across."

Then he tried handing me an envelope fat with cash, which I categorically refused on the grounds I didn't want to take advantage of his generosity. When he reminded me I still needed to make a visit or two to the vet for Ahbhu, which might prove expensive, I reluctantly accepted a portion of the money. And with that, Diego walked out of my life, and I was left staring at four blank walls in the deathly stillness of the safehouse. Crawling into bed with Ahbhu, I cradled his warm body, muffling my tears against his bristly fur.

# PART IV

*Tijuana, Mexico: February 7–14, 1986*

# Chapter 34

## FULL CIRCLE

"Get up, you!" El Garrobo's voice pierced through the dark haze of my grief as I held Ahbhu's trembling body. "It's time to get moving. The others are waiting!"

A week had passed since Diego left me at the safehouse. During that time, Ahbhu had grown weaker, showing no interest in food and barely able to swallow the water I poured down his throat. Our visit to the vet had been met with grim-faced declarations and advice to keep him well hydrated. But Ahbhu had yet to turn the corner. His emotional disappearance on the eve of our scheduled crossing had pushed El Garrobo over the edge.

"I'm sorry, señor," I said, forcing back tears. "There's no way we can make it tonight, not like this. Look at him; he can barely move."

"Then carry the damned thing!" he yelled, his face flushed with anger. A few of the others peeked through the doorway, drawn by the commotion.

Fed up with El Garrobo's abuse, I leapt off the bed and faced off with him. "Ahbhu is not a thing!" I shouted. "And if you can't find even an ounce of compassion in that black heart of yours for him or for me, then you can go screw yourself, you goddamned money-grubbing bully!"

"Hey!" he said, holding me back, "There's no need for name calling. Just calm down."

"All I ask is that you let us stay until morning, until I can make other arrangements; then we'll be out of your hair for good. Can you do that?"

"There's no need for you to leave. You're paid up for two weeks. But a delayed crossing will cost you extra. Let your rich friend know it'll be a thousand dollars more."

"In your dreams! He already promised you more money once we're safely on the other side. If you want to see any of that, stop trying to squeeze me for more."

El Garrobo spat on the floor and glared at me before finally relenting. "All right, mocoso, you win this one. Just make sure the dog's ready to cross a week from today."

I was relieved Ahbhu was still with me the next morning. His tongue lolled out of his mouth as he opened his eyes and focused on me. With a glimmer of recognition, he smiled weakly and licked my hand. Outside the door, El Garrobo was banging around, and I shuddered at the memory of our argument, desperate to avoid another confrontation with him in front of Ahbhu.

I offered Ahbhu some water and a few kibbles. He sat up and tried his best. But all he could get down was a small morsel, which was more food than he'd had in a week. I rewarded his effort with an encouraging hug. Maybe this was Ahbhu's corner.

As we rode to the vet in a taxi, crawling through the morning traffic, Ahbhu lifted his head and watched the passing city, gently panting. His interest fanned a spark of hope in me. I rolled down the window for him as the cab wended its way into the city's *Zona Rio* and down the *Bulevar de Los Héroes* with its massive traffic circles. Ahbhu leaned his head outside, relishing the breeze generated by the taxi's forward movement.

Arriving at the strip mall where the vet's office was located, Ahbhu declined to be carried, insisting he walk on his own steam. I resisted, feeling hurt by his refusal, but instead chose to see it as another good sign.

The vet, a kindly gentleman who had taken a liking to Ahbhu during our prior visit, examined him while I watched on, chewing what was left of my fingernails. When he finished, the sorrowful expression on his face extinguished any hope that had been building inside me.

"This boy is not getting better," he said sadly. The statement was a stab to my heart.

"But he's shown improvement today," I said, holding onto the examination table for support.

"It happens sometimes, that brief spurt of energy. But his vital signs say it all. Your Ahbhu is dying."

Ahbhu glanced up at me at those words. Choking back my sadness, I took his head in my hands the way I'd done ever since he was a pup, gazing deep into his eyes, beaming love into him.

"How long?" I asked quietly.

"It's impossible to say. It could be days; it could be—"

"Weeks?"

"No, young man." The vet placed his hand on my shoulder. "Not weeks. Perhaps hours."

"Is there any possibility he could recover, doctor? Any at all?"

"Anything's possible, of course." The vet absently stroked Ahbhu's fur. "But I don't think it's probable. Not in this case. If I thought otherwise, we'd be having a different conversation. My advice is that we end the poor animal's suffering today rather than prolong the inevitable. That way you can say goodbye to him properly. On your terms."

I closed my eyes and took in the doctor's dreaded words. Such a thing had never crossed my mind, not in a trillion lifetimes. "May I have a moment, please?" I whispered. "Alone with Ahbhu?"

Gently caressing Ahbhu one last time, the vet nodded and slipped out of the room, leaving the two of us alone. As I searched for something to say, Ahbhu nudged my hand with his wet nose.

*Let Ahbhu go, Isaac,* he pleaded. *It's time for goodbye.*

"It's too soon, Ahbhu," I cried. "We were supposed to have another eight years together! How can I possibly agree to that?"

*It's time,* he repeated, his voice growing fainter, his eyes fluttering. A strange groan emanated from inside of him that made the bottom drop out of my stomach. A moment later he refocused on me, his eyes burning bright with a final burst of energy, and spoke as I sobbed into my hands: *Go to America. Remember Ahbhu. Kiss Suchi and Diego. Make Ahbhu happy . . . it's time for goodbye.* Then he lowered his head onto his paws and closed his eyes.

A few minutes later, I called the vet back into the room. He checked Ahbhu's vitals one last time then turned to me, looking slightly confused. "But . . . he's gone."

I nodded numbly, having realized the same thing within moments of Ahbhu's final words. Ahbhu had left on his own terms. He'd saved me from making the impossible decision that had to be made. He'd said goodbye. Now it was up to me to find any good in that goodbye. I feared for myself if I couldn't.

The vet refused payment for his services, accepting only a fee for the disposal of Ahbhu's body. Afteward he poured me a shot of mezcal, and we somberly toasted Ahbhu's memory. Although I wasn't a drinker, I downed three more shots with the vet's blessing and stumbled out of the clinic into the harsh sunlight, bleary-eyed, aimlessly wandering in the general direction of the main boulevard.

Spotting a bar the next block over, I headed toward it and took up residence in a dark booth. I sobbed into a beer mug while Mexican rancheras played on a jukebox and a few people bobbed to the music on a small dance floor at the back.

Ahbhu's last words played a tortuous loop in my head. Kiss Suchi; kiss Diego, he'd said. I'd been trying to manage on my own since I arrived, resisting the urge to call for help, stubbornly determined not to bother anyone until Ahbhu and I were safely on the other side. But now that he was gone, I knew I was going to have to reach out for guidance. It was either that, or, with my luck, I was destined to end up in a ditch somewhere. For now, though, it was time to anesthetize myself into oblivion until I was ready to wake up from this nightmare.

When I was nearing the end of my second beer, I caught the attention of a tall guy in his thirties or thereabouts, in a cowboy hat, black jeans, and boots. He slid into the booth next to me and, flashing his teeth, placed a brimming mug on the table to replace my empty one. His hand on my thigh under the table left no doubts as to his intentions.

We exchanged a few words I can't recall and, after a few more sips of beer, I followed him into the restroom and into a stall where he dropped to his knees and serviced me, no strings attached. Once he was done, he thanked me with a curt nod and left me alone. I'd felt a moment of consolation in the midst of the release. But now that it was over, I felt worse than ever and lowered myself to the floor of the stall and wept for Ahbhu.

By the time I exited the restroom, the bar had filled up with the afternoon crowd. It felt suddenly claustrophobic. The cowboy was chatting up another guy by the entrance. As I passed him on my way out of the bar, he averted his eyes and pretended not to know me when I said goodbye.

I trudged back to the safehouse, my only remaining tether to reality in that horror show of a city, the weight of grief dragging at my every step. The fading sunlight cast eerie shadows across the deserted alley, amplifying my sense of isolation. The distant rumble of traffic and faint echoes of laughter served as haunting reminders of the world outside, a world I no longer felt a part of.

Desperate for refuge, I rapped hard on the safehouse door. After a few minutes, El Garrobo begrudgingly opened the door, scolding me for the disturbance. Ignoring him, I brushed past him and retreated to the solitude of the men's dorm where I collapsed onto my bunk, seeking solace in the darkness. An instant later, El Garrobo was at my side.

"You're alone?" he asked.

"Obviously I'm alone!" I answered back.

"Where's the dog?"

Curling up tightly, I bit my lip against the urge to scream and squeezed my eyes shut.

"Oh . . . sorry," he said. "Anyway, your friend Suchipila has been calling for you all day."

"What does she want?"

"The hell if I know. But she said she needs to speak with you ASAP. She sounded pretty cut up if you ask me."

Sitting up on the bed, I wiped my face and looked at El Garrobo, who loomed over me like an ogre. "Can I at least use your phone? You can put it on my tab."

"Go ahead, use it." He waved a hand toward the lounge. "We can settle up later."

Suchi answered on the first ring. Before she could get in a word, I burst out crying at the sound of her voice, tearfully recounting what had happened to Ahbhu. When I finished, the phone fell quiet, as if I'd lost the connection. "Suchi?" I asked, my voice shaking. I glanced over my shoulder and saw El Garrobo hovering in the background, listening in on my conversation. "Are you still there?" I asked.

"I'm here, Isaac," she said, quietly. "I have some news. It's about your father."

"My father?" I sat up with my heart in my mouth. "What's wrong with my father? I've been calling them since I was at Diego's, but I haven't been able to get through."

"Oh, Isaac . . ."

"Just tell me, Suchi."

"A bomb exploded downtown at a community center last week. Your father was in the next building. Your brother, too."

"Were they injured?" I asked, fearing the worst.

"They were killed, Isaac. Both of them. Your mother told me. The poor woman's been in pieces. She's staying at your uncle's in Santa Ana for the time being; they're taking care of her. I'm so sorry."

I put the phone down and gritted my teeth, pounding down my panic, unsure I could withstand another blow but conscious I had to press through it regardless, as long as my mother was still alive. Taking a long, measured breath, I put the phone back to my ear.

"I'm going back, Suchi."

"Isaac, no. It's still too dangerous."

"There's nothing here for me, Suchi! My mother needs me, now more than ever. I can't just ignore that and carry on with my own plans. I absolutely *have* to go back."

"What if your mother were to join you?" Suchi countered. "The two of you could cross together."

"What? Are you—"

"Hear me out! It makes total sense. You're alone and she's alone. You could both start over again in America, together."

"And how in God's name would she even get here?"

"I'll bring her, of course," Suchi said matter-of-factly.

"All the flipping way to Tijuana? That makes *no sense.* My mother is in no condition for that kind of a journey. Not at her age, and not while she's in mourning."

Suchi fell quiet at that. In the silence that followed, I reflected on her words, trying my best to be dispassionate despite the emotional turmoil I was experiencing. The logic of what she was suggesting was sound in principle, just not in the execution. My mother was in no condition to undergo a fraught and grueling two-week land journey. On top of that, I had no idea what she herself would have to say, considering the devastating loss we'd just suffered.

"Leave this with me, Suchi," I said finally, consciously restraining my skepticism. After all, she was doing all of this out of the goodness of her heart, not out of any real obligation. I owed her and her mother so much. She deserved my consideration regardless of how far-fetched her idea appeared. "I'll talk to my mother and see what she has to say. If she's up for the journey, I'll let you know. I'll let you know *either* way. And thank you for everything."

After making it past the gatekeepers—a cousin, my aunt, and finally my uncle—none of whom could believe they were actually hearing my voice this side of the grave—I was put through to my mother. Still in a state of shock at the sudden loss of both her partner in life and her firstborn son, she was at a complete loss as to how to react to my telephone call. Bereft and elated at the same time, but ever the stern pragmatist, she held her emotions in check as I tearfully commiserated with her, explaining that I'd only just heard the news. I was saddened to learn the funerals were to take place the very next day.

"I'll come back as soon as I can," I promised. "I have a friend who might be able to help me get there even as soon as tomorrow."

"Mijo," she said, firmly, "don't come back. This is no place for you."

"But Mamá—"

"I don't want to lose my last son to this madness!" she interrupted, her voice edged with anger and frustration. "You carry on, you hear me? Make a new life in America, you and Ahbhu. Perhaps one day I'll be able to join you. For now I'm fine here with Paco and Elsie." She said the last part loudly, as if for the benefit of my uncle and aunt, whom I pictured in the same room with her.

"Ahbhu's gone, Mamá," I said, faltering at the mention of his name. "He . . . he got sick and . . . I've only just gotten back from the vet's where he passed."

"Oh, mijo, I'm so sorry." The dam holding back her grief burst at the unexpected news. She broke down and wept, and I joined her, embarrassed to be losing it within earshot of El Garrobo. I shot him an angry look over my shoulder and waved him away, and he disappeared into the shadows.

Once we had recovered our voices, I ventured, "Suchi thinks you should join me *now*, now that we're both alone. She thinks we should cross over together. I told her that was a crazy idea."

A knock at the safehouse door distracted me. El Garrobo sped down the hall and, after the exchange of a few words, he admitted a couple of guys around my age, both of them road worn and bearing backpacks, new clients I assumed. I turned back to the phone.

"Mamá?"

"How would I get there?" she whispered, signaling by her change in tone that she was not keen on being overheard, not on this subject.

"You mean you'd consider it?" I said, feeling suddenly short of breath.

"Yes," she said after a moment, the firmness returning to her voice. "I'd consider it."

"It's a long trip, Mamá. Suchi offered to bring you. But it's much too hard and risky. I'll see if there's another option. In the meantime, just focus on Papá and Neto. It kills me I can't be there in person. But believe me Mamá, I'm with you in spirit, right there by your side. I love you Mamá."

"Just a couple more calls, I promise," I said to El Garrobo as he showed the new guests around. He waved me off dismissively, not seeming to care either way. So I quickly dialed Diego's number. Doña Lenka answered and put me through to Don Federico. Though pleased to hear from me, he sensed I was troubled and invited me to share with him. After a moment of hesitation, unsure of how he would take the news about Ahbhu, I brought Don Federico up to date with everything that had happened since I'd last seen him. As I feared, he let out an animal cry on hearing of Ahbhu's passing. But he soon recovered, offering his profoundest condolences. He promised to honor Ahbhu's memory with a ceremony involving special offerings and prayers, as well as by commissioning a yarn painting to hang in the shrine at Wirikuta. As Don Federico spoke of his plans for Ahbhu, a comforting warmth spread through me, calming the maelstrom of emotions that had been surging through me for the past few weeks.

Although Diego had already left for Mexico City, Don Federico assured me he could get hold of him quickly and asked me to remain by the telephone. Less than ten minutes later, I was speaking to Diego. Without a moment of hesitation, he offered to fly my mother up to Tijuana in his friend's jet after the funeral if she was up for it. Within a matter of thirty minutes—between Diego, Suchi, my mother, myself, and El Garrobo—arrangements were put in place for my mother to arrive in Tijuana in three days' time.

# Chapter 35

## EMBRACING EXCESS

Not knowing what to do with myself for the next three days, and desperate to escape the overwhelming weight of grief that threatened to suffocate me, I fell in with Adán and Mario, the Honduran guys who had shown up at the safehouse and were now my bunkmates. It turned out they were a couple, together since childhood, both heralding from the same poor Tegucigalpa neighborhood. Threatened by their families to keep their relationship secret, they'd connected with the same network Suchi was part of and, with money they'd saved over the years, made their escape. I couldn't but envy their willingness to choose each other over their families and make a new life together despite the risks and uncertainty.

Adán turned out to be the more gregarious of the two, short and built like a rugby player. He spoke enthusiastically of their plans to settle in San Francisco. They were ready, he said, to dive headfirst into the gay scene there, the clubs, bars, and underground parties. It was clear from the way he was speaking that they weren't particularly monogamous, which I found strangely intriguing. Mario, the cuter of the two, lithe and graceful as a cat, observed Adán as he spoke, quietly sharing his excitement, and glancing at me every so often, gauging my reaction. We ended up making plans to go out that night to explore what Tijuana had to offer based on an itinerary Adán had pieced together long before arriving in town.

Our first stop that night was a glittering bar with a youngish crowd in the *Zona Centro*. The place was in full swing by the time we arrived, packed tight with both locals and tourists sipping on colorful cocktails and singing along to Mexican pop songs. Adán offered his hand as we weaved our way to the bar with Mario following close behind. Once there, Mario and I downed tequila shots and a couple of Coronas while Adán made out with a beefy black guy with a military haircut standing next to him at the bar.

"You're not jealous?" I asked Mario, who watched on amused as his boyfriend mauled the other guy.

He shook his head and grinned. "Adán fishes for the two of us," he said with a wink.

"Guys, this is Jacques." Adán introduced his conquest in passable English, a marine from Camp Pendleton just over the border. His striking green eyes sparkled in the dim light of the bar as he took us in. Adán wrapped his arm suggestively around Jacques' waist. "That's my boyfriend Mario," he said, kissing Mario on the mouth. "And this is Isaac, our new friend."

"Hey!" Jacques said, suggestively pumping his eyebrows.

"What do you say we quit this place and go dancing?" Adán said.

"I'm game," Jacques answered. Mario and I looked at each other and quickly downed what was left of our beers. Then we were out the door and on our way to Excess, a massive dance club in the Zona Rio, where the house music pounded, the alcohol flowed, and bodies writhed on a darkened dance floor shot through with high-energy lasers and strobes.

The four of us lost ourselves in the fray, stripping off our shirts and flailing in time to the music, embracing the madness, releasing our stress. Echoing back the soundtrack, the crowd took up a chant, fists in the air, an orgy of defiance and celebration.

In the midst of it all, I dropped to my knees and let out a howl that cut through the air, drawing attention from those around us. Diving to my rescue, Jacques pulled me up and joined in, and soon the whole crowd echoed our cry.

The music intensified as we lost ourselves in the moment. Jacques grinned, tears of release in his eyes, and he planted a kiss on my mouth. "Thanks, man," he shouted. "I really needed that!"

"Likewise!" I shouted back as Adán and Mario pulled us into a sweaty group hug.

Wasting no time, we were soon out of the club and checked into the nearest motel where we left all rules and inhibitions at the door and consumed each other in every way possible. The frenzied sex lasted for hours, pausing and repeating until check-out time. Then, smiling ear to ear, Jacques beat a hasty retreat back to Camp Pendleton, and Adán and Mario and I hopped a cab back to the safehouse where we collapsed on our bunks until the late afternoon.


"Tonight we're visiting a sauna," Adán announced over dinner, exchanging a playful look with Mario. El Garrobo, who was distributing tortillas among us, arched an eyebrow and grumbled something to himself. "That dude needs to get laid," Adán said once he'd left the room.

"I'll pass on that, thanks," Mario said, with a touch of humor. Still, I got the feeling that even El Garrobo wasn't off limits as far as Adán was concerned if push came to shove.

"Wanna come along?" Adán asked me.

"I'm worn out from last night," I said, "fun as it was."

"Come on, man! We'll have even *more* fun than last night.

I've heard the place is packed full of hot guys ready for action. We can cut out all the preliminaries—the drinking, the dancing and romancing—and get straight to it, with as many men as we can fit in, one-on-one, two, three, anything goes. You liked that Jacques guy, right? Well, there are plenty of Jacques' there! If it's a dud night, we can always come back here and have our own party."

My appetite for sex had been awakened the night before and was gnawing at me, growing ever more acute with Adán's compelling description of the sauna. And, as exhausted as I was, the thought of another night of excess far outweighed the prospect of spending an evening alone with El Garrobo the ogre, or on my own in some sad bar, crying into a beer, pining for Ahbhu. No, I needed once and for all to exorcise my grief. And the intense pleasure I'd found in sexual abandon was exactly what I needed.

Forcing a grin, I agreed to join them for one last night. After that, my mother would be arriving, and I needed to be ready to play the good son. For now, though, I was ready for anything.

Just as Adán predicted, the sauna was humming with men of all ages, mainly Mexican with a smattering of Americans, hungrily cruising up and down the corridors in nothing but towels, condoms at the ready. I'd heard about such places from friends of Gerónimo, veritable sexual playgrounds equipped with cubicles of various sizes for hooking up, steam rooms, jacuzzis, and showers, where people lost no time, in full sight of anyone in the vicinity.

Adán, Mario and I changed out of our clothes, with the plan of splitting up and meeting again in a couple of hours in the lounge to check in on each other. As I made to move out of the locker room, Adán grabbed my wrist and pressed something into my palm. Glancing into my hand, I found a postage stamp with an image of Mickey Mouse in a sorcerer's robe printed on it.

"It's a hit of acid," Adán explained in answer to my questioning look.

I hesitated, my mind unexpectedly swirling again with painful memories of recent tragedies. "I don't do drugs," I said, my voice barely a whisper, my hand trembling as I offered the tab back to him.

Adán pushed it back at me. "Try it this once," he urged. "It might help whatever's got you down. Not to mention it makes the sex all the more intense. If you don't like it, you don't have to do it again." He dangled another tab in front of my nose, then popped it in his mouth. "Your turn."

I looked at Mario, who offered a supportive nod before popping one as well and wandering off.

With a heavy sigh, I shrugged and placed the stamp on my tongue.

"That's a good boy," Adán said with a victorious smile. "And you're welcome!" Then he disappeared in pursuit of a hairy-chested Mexican guy with a thick moustache, who had poked his head into the locker room.

As the tab dissolved on my tongue, it left behind a bitter, coppery taste accompanied by a queasiness that didn't sit well with my emotional state. Keen to clear my mouth of the unpleasant taste, I wended my way to the bar past a procession of men and ordered a bottle of mineral water. Then I sat on a bench seat in the corner to watch the comings and goings, hoping the funk I'd fallen into would pass once the acid kicked in.

I found myself reflecting on the last time I'd seen Ahbhu on the vet's table. I couldn't get over how brightly his eyes had burned in his final moments before growing so cold and pale. We'd spent nearly a decade together, but now that he was gone, it was as if he'd vanished from my life after a brief spell, like a dream whose images disperse and drift away, receding into the hazy morning light on waking. His last words haunted my mind: "It's time for *good*-bye." *How could I possibly find any good in that?* I thought.

An endless stream of men paraded past as I ruminated in my corner, their fleeting glances barely registering as I nursed my drink. Among them, one stood out—a handsome, well-built Latino with a sharp haircut, a thin moustache, and piercing dark eyes, exuding confidence as he approached. His presence was magnetic, drawing my attention despite my disinterest in conversation.

He slid onto the bench beside me, a smirk on his lips as he tapped my bottle with his. "Is that all you're having?" he asked with a hint of flirtation.

Cutting to the chase, I reached up and kissed him on the mouth. Surprised at my directness, he drew back and blinked at me. Setting aside his bottle, he dove in for more. Within moments we'd dipped into an empty cubicle and swiftly lost our towels. Then he dropped to his knees and serviced me. After a couple of minutes, he rose to his feet, placed his hands on my shoulders and pushed me onto the ground, pressing my face into his groin. Shocked by the aggressive reversal, I pulled away from him, stumbling backward against the cubicle. He cocked his head at me, looking thoroughly confused.

"Sorry . . . sorry," I muttered, standing and searching for my towel, "maybe later."

"Maybe later what?" he snapped, snatching his towel from off the floor and tying it around his waist. He raised his head at me as if demanding a response.

I folded my arms defensively, still naked and feeling vulnerable in his presence. "Nothing . . . I'm just not feeling myself tonight. I'm sorry," I said, hoping to convey my change of heart without causing offense.

His reaction was unexpected, a subtle bristling of his demeanor, a flicker of irritation. "You're not into me, I get it," he retorted, pulling open the door and casting a disdainful glance in my direction. "All you had to do was say so."

Confusion mingled with a growing sense of unease as his words hung in the air. Suddenly, the cubicle seemed to shift and warp around me, the edges blurring into a mirage-like shimmer of color. Disoriented and overwhelmed, I sat down on the bed, searching for clarity in the shifting surroundings. As I looked up at him, he had already begun to retreat out of the cubicle, his figure outlined in an ethereal glow.

Feeling like I was on the brink of losing my mind, I locked the door behind him as I grappled with the unexpected effects of the acid. Draping myself in the bedsheet, I settled onto the floor, wrapping my arms around my knees, trying to steady myself against the effects of the drugs.

A swirling vortex of darkness enveloped me, filled with fragmented images of my past: my mother, Arturo, the bloodshed of the massacre. They whirled around me relentlessly. Amid the chaos, a pinpoint of light materialized at the center of the cyclone, unwavering in the midst of the turmoil. It grew larger, drawing nearer, until it resolved into the image of Don Federico's disembodied head. His eyes, brimming with warmth and wisdom, held me transfixed, anchoring me in the storm.

Grateful for his calming presence, I reached out, yearning for his touch. But just as my fingers brushed the air, Don Federico's head ascended like a helium balloon, his gaze unwavering. Hovering above me for a moment, his face transfigured into the radiant visage of Ahbhu. His presence exuded compassion and understanding as he regarded me.

*Isaac*, Ahbhu said, his voice a gentle murmur, *do you truly believe that all this anguish does justice to our bond?*

I blinked, finding the surreal sight of my beloved friend both comforting and disorienting. "Ahbhu?" I whispered, a blend of awe and longing flooding my senses.

*Enough with the tears and sorrowful displays, Isaac,* Ahbhu continued, his voice like a soothing balm. *Instead, honor our bond by living a life filled with kindness and compassion. That's how you can pay tribute to our love. That's Isaac's good in goodbye.*

I wiped away my tears, the haze of intoxication slowly dissipating in the presence of Ahbhu's ethereal wisdom. "I miss you terribly, Ahbhu," I confessed, my voice shaking with emotion.

Ahbhu drew nearer, offering a tender nuzzle, a poignant reminder of our cherished moments together. *Ahbhu misses Isaac just as much. But remember, Ahbhu will always live in your heart.*

With those words, the vision of Ahbhu faded, leaving me alone in the cubicle, my mind gradually clearing. I wondered how long I had been lost in that surreal encounter. Emerging from the cubicle, I found the corridor nearly deserted. The sauna had emptied, save for a few stragglers stumbling in search of their final conquests. It was four in the morning, and Adán and Mario were nowhere to be found.

Changing back into my clothes, I exited the sauna and flagged down a passing cab. By four thirty, I was back at the safehouse, having roused El Garrobo from a boozy stupor. Surprising him with an apologetic peck on his stubbly cheek, I headed straight to the dorm room and collapsed on my bunk fully clothed.

# Chapter 36

## BREAKING THROUGH

I received a call from Diego later that afternoon. All the arrangements were in place to fly my mother up the following day. Suchi would pick her up in the morning and drive her to the airport where Diego would take over. He would accompany her on the flight, making sure everything flowed smoothly. Once in Tijuana, he'd bring her to the safehouse. They'd already brought El Garrobo up to speed and agreed on terms with him, including the date for our crossing, in the early morning of February 14, 1986.

I called my mother to ensure she was on the same page with us and was surprised to hear she was looking forward to the journey, despite the fact she'd just laid to rest her partner of forty years and her eldest son. She was ready to quit the country of her grief and remake her life with me, far from the unrelenting menace and bitter memories that surrounded her.

I spent what was left of the day engrossed in a book, deliberately slowing myself down in preparation for my mother's arrival. Adán and Mario had arrived back from their night out when I was getting up, chagrined that they'd lost track of me at the sauna. Politely declining their invitation for another night of prowling, I explained my need to be clearheaded from here on out.

The next morning, Suchi called to confirm she'd dropped off my mother at the airport. I was beside myself for the next few hours, pacing the safehouse, nervously wringing my hands. At his wits' end with me, El Garrobo ordered me into the backyard and shut me out of the house. I spent the rest of the morning in fitful meditation under the hot sun in a lounge chair, anxiously awaiting my mother's arrival.

El Garrobo called me back into the house at noon. Diego was calling from the airport to report they'd arrived safely and would be at the safehouse shortly. Thirty minutes later, I was wrapped in my mother's embrace, her thin arms enveloping me tightly as we wept on each other.

A chilling breeze swept through the desolate landscape in the early hours, carrying the faint scent of distant sea salt. I found myself huddled against a cold chain-link fence under the cover of darkness alongside my mother and Adán and Mario, two thousand meters from Tijuana's San Ysidro crossing. Every sixty seconds, a blinding flash of light from an American beacon split the night, briefly illuminating the nervous faces around me.

El Garrobo's hushed instructions were barely audible over the whistle of wind through the fence. When he considered it optimum, he guided Adán and Mario through a small opening, their footsteps barely making a sound on the soft earth. They disappeared into the darkness on the other side, phantoms vanishing into the night.

El Garrobo then approached my mother and me, his shoes crunching on the gravel. The ground beneath us was uneven, and I could feel the cold, hard surface digging into my worn-out trainers.

"When I give the signal, go through the opening and run to your left, staying as low to the ground as possible. You should find the car waiting for you five hundred meters down the access road. Understand?" El Garrobo whispered, his breath condensing in the chilly air.

"Yes, sure." My voice trembled, and I shivered involuntarily, my fingers tingling with nerves. I glanced at my mother, who tightly gripped my arm, her fingernails digging into my skin. The sharp sensation sent a jolt through me, reminding me of the danger we faced. "Are you all right, Mamá?"

She stared into my eyes before turning to El Garrobo. "What do we do if they catch us?"

"Don't worry, Señora; they won't. Just follow my lead, and one of my team will meet up with both of you in San Diego tomorrow if all goes well. *De acuerdo?*" El Garrobo reassured her with a gentle touch of his hand, a flash of light momentarily enhancing his earnest expression.

My mother looked back at me, concern furrowing her brow, the distant whirring of desert cicadas adding an eerie soundtrack to our predicament. "We don't have to cross tonight, mijo. Not if you're not ready." Her comment drew a sharp look from El Garrobo.

"Don't worry about me, Mamá. Are *you* ready?" I asked, trying to sound confident despite the doubt eating away at me.

El Garrobo looked around, wringing his hands, his face glistening with sweat in the dim light, his eyes appearing red and tired in the darkness. "Come on, come on, make up your minds already," he muttered under his breath.

I held my mother even tighter, feeling the rapid thump of her heartbeat against my chest. The chilly night air intensified the heightened sense of urgency coursing through my veins. "Okay," I said to El Garrobo, trying to ignore the biting cold seeping through my thin clothes, "let's do this."

El Garrobo let out a long breath that dissipated into the

crisp night air. Then, he guided us toward the breach in the fence, holding it open with one hand, the metallic clinks resonating in the stillness. Placing his other hand on my back, he waited for the next flash of light. The suspense hung heavy in the air, our heartbeats pounding in unison, a relentless rhythm matching the intensity of the moment.

When it came, the blinding light nearly overwhelmed my senses, momentarily disorienting me. "Now! Go! Head to the left," El Garrobo whispered urgently, his voice almost drowned out by the sudden rush of adrenaline in my ears.

Hand-in-hand, my mother and I slipped through the opening and hurriedly made our way to the left, moving as fast as we could. The gravel shifted as we sped across it, making each step a precarious gamble in the darkness. We searched for the access road where El Garrobo said the car would be waiting, relying on our senses to navigate through the obscurity.

The next flash of light startled my mother, and the sudden brightness caused her to stumble on some loose rubble and fall to the ground. I dove towards her, just as she cried out in pain.

"Mamá!"

"It's my ankle, mijo," she whimpered, the distress evident in her voice. I could feel her trembling against me as I pulled her closer.

With the next flash of light, I noticed her foot was twisted unnaturally to the left. The sight made my stomach churn. Panic surged through me as I scanned the surroundings for help, the darkness seeming to swallow us whole.

Gathering my mother into my arms, I held her close to my chest, trying to decide whether to go back or continue forward.

"Ay!" she cried out, immediately covering her mouth, the sound echoing in the night.

"It's okay, Mamá," I reassured her, my voice shaky, my body bathed in sweat. "Please, don't worry. We're almost there." I felt on the verge of collapsing from exhaustion and fear, but I knew

I had to keep moving forward. There was no turning back now.

Standing with my mother in my arms, she felt like a shaking bundle of sticks, like kindling for a campfire. I squinted in the direction of the access road, blinking against another blinding flash of light. Determined, I did my best to carry her the rest of the way, my vision impaired by the beacon's brightness.

Suddenly, a voice emerged from the shadows, piercing the darkness. "United States Border Patrol! Stop!"

I froze, my eyes struggling to adjust to the light shining directly in my face. Another light appeared from the corner of my vision, illuminating the figure standing before me, a US border agent in a fatigue-green uniform, holding a flashlight in one hand and a drawn gun in the other. Now that he had backup, he holstered his flashlight and approached me.

"Put down the lady and raise your hands!" the agent growled in Spanish.

"She's injured," I pleaded, holding my trembling mother close to my chest.

"I won't ask again," the agent warned.

As gently as I could, I carefully placed my terrified mother in the dirt. I kissed her on the cheek before standing up to face the agent and froze as I recognized the guy I'd rebuffed at the sauna two nights before. Forcefully pushing me onto my knees, he stepped around to handcuff me behind my back. "Welcome to paradise," he grunted into my ear.

"We're seeking asylum!"

"Shut the fuck up," the agent snapped as he secured the cuffs and hauled me to my feet. "You can save your sob story for the station."

The second border agent, a stocky Asian man, tried to help my mother up by the arm, but she cried out in pain.

"Hey!" I screamed. "I told you she's injured."

The second agent straightened up. "We should call for backup," he said to his partner.

"Nah, the four-by's not far. I'll wait here with them while you go get it."

"Are you sure? What if there are others?"

Our agent chuckled and patted his revolver. "Don't worry about me, Tran. You'll be back in no time. Radio it in if you want, just to let them know."

I watched the darkness swallow up Agent Tran as he hiked across the dirt into the distance. Then I looked up at our agent, who was busy propping his flashlight on a nearby boulder for illumination.

"Are you okay, Mamá?" I whispered.

My mother flashed tear-filled eyes at me. "I'm sorry, mijo," she answered. "This is my fault."

"It's nobody's fault, Mamá," I said in a low voice as the border agent walked back towards us. His uniform looked to be a size too small as he seemed literally stuffed into it.

When he reached me, he yanked me up by one arm. It was then I noticed his nametag, *O. Vasquez*, and made a mental note of it.

"Small world, isn't it?" he said in English, stopping a moment to glance at me with a hint of threat in his eye. My heart dropped as I realized I was probably in for it. Then he pulled out a notepad and flipped it open, switching back to Spanish. "What's your name?" he asked.

"My name's Isaac Perez. I'm from El Salvador."

Vasquez scribbled into his pad and lifted his head at my mother. "How about her? What's her name?"

"Miriam Perez, my mother. She's also from El Salvador."

Vasquez made a few more scribbles. "You wouldn't happen to have any ID on you, would you?"

"We both do."

Vasquez gave me a thumbs-up and returned to his pad, his pen poised over it. "Why did you leave your home or country of last residence?"

"I was afraid. People were looking to kill me, like they killed my brothers and my father."

"What kind of people?"

"Soldiers."

"Why would soldiers want to kill you?"

"They didn't like our politics, I guess."

"Politics, right." Vasquez scribbled a bit more in his pad. In the distance, the rumble of a car approaching caused him to stop for a moment; then he turned back to his pad. "Do you have any fear or concern about being returned to your home country or being removed from the United States?"

"Yes, of course. If they knew I was back, they'd hunt me down and kill me. I have no doubt about that."

"What about her?" Vasquez lifted his head again at my mother.

"Yes, her too. Our whole family was targeted," I answered, following El Garrobo's instructions. "She and I are the only ones left."

We were interrupted by the headlights of the four-by-four as it rounded a boulder and came around to where we were standing. Tran climbed out and approached us.

"See," Vasquez said to Tran, "that wasn't so bad, was it?"

"I radioed ahead to the station. They're expecting us. The medic's still there."

"Perfect," Vasquez said. "I was just having a nice chat with this one." He indicated me with his pen. "Why don't you go on ahead with the mother? We'll catch up with you in a bit. I'll just finish up with him and head back in the squad car."

"No, wait," I said, as Tran gathered my mother in his arms and carried her to the four-by-four. "I'm going with her."

"You'll join her shortly," Vasquez countered. "See you at the station," he said to Tran, who jumped into the four-by-four and sped away.

Angry, I reluctantly allowed Vasquez to lead me by the arm

along the border fence in the direction of San Ysidro, neither of us saying a word. My mind churned with worry for my poor mother and about what was coming next.

After around twenty minutes, we reached the port of entry, where we climbed into a squad car, with me seated in the back seat behind a grate and Vasquez in the front. The car roared to life, and Vasquez set off up the highway.

"Where are we going?" I asked.

"For a little ride."

"Why?"

Vasquez remained silent and continued to drive until we reached a turn-off a few miles north of the border. Then he headed inland into the scrub hills, over an unpaved service road, and parked the car within an outcrop of rocks. He turned off the engine, exited the front of the car, and sat in the back with me.

"Now, then, Perez," he said with a tight grin, "welcome to the land of opportunity."

I raised an eyebrow. "I could have sworn you said 'welcome to paradise' back there. Which one is it?"

Vasquez studied me for a moment, his expression serious. "It's the land of opportunity, smart ass. This just happens to be your lucky day."

I averted my gaze. "What do you mean?"

Vasquez leaned in closer, his voice low and deliberate. "We have unfinished business. Now's your chance to make it up to me."

I shook my head, hardly believing where this was heading. "I have no idea what you're talking about."

Vasquez locked eyes with me. "You know *exactly* what I'm talking about."

I met Vasquez's gaze. "Take me to my mother! She's injured and doesn't speak English."

Vasquez raised his hands in a calming gesture. "Hang on,

guy. We need to clear something up first, and then you can see your mother."

Confusion washed over my face. "What do we need to clear up? We had our moment, it didn't work out, end of story. I'm not going to say anything about the sauna if that's what you're worried about."

Vasquez grinned, inching closer until our knees touched. Feeling uneasy, I shifted away and positioned my handcuffed hands near the door handle.

"I'm not the one that should be worried," Vasquez said, his voice low and threatening. "Remember, I said, 'Welcome to the land of opportunity'?" He dropped his hand into his lap. "Well, this is your opportunity to redeem yourself. After that, you're home free."

I gasped, my eyes widening as I watched Vasquez unbuckle his belt. "What do you think you're doing?"

Vasquez unbuttoned his pants, revealing a pair of black briefs. "It's more a question of what *you're* going to do."

He pulled his shirt up slightly to expose his hairy navel and tugged at the elastic band of his briefs. "A little favor from you earns a big one from me. Simple as that. All you have to do is finish what you started."

My voice trembled with disbelief. "You can't be serious."

Vasquez's expression hardened. "Deadly serious. Don't worry, it'll be over before you know it." He winked at me and lowered his trousers, exposing himself. "Now get to it."

I glared at Vasquez, my mind racing for a way out of this horrifying situation. I glanced outside the squad car, assessing our surroundings. We were parked at the end of a secluded service road, far from any main routes. Even if I managed to escape the car, I knew I wouldn't stand a chance against his superior size and speed. And then there was my mother, waiting for me, unaware of the danger I was in. I realized I was running out of options.

As I processed the gravity of the situation, a wave of nausea washed over me, causing me to double over. I let out a loud groan, startling Vasquez. The tremor intensified, spreading from my stomach to my chest, leaving me gasping for breath. My body trembled uncontrollably, the intense surge of emotions coursing through me like a flow of lava. In an instant, the eruption reached my heart, fueling a surge of rage that propelled me towards Vasquez.

"Are you fucking kidding me?" I screamed. "I survived a civil war, earthquakes . . . the murder of my father and brothers, a four-thousand-mile journey from hell . . . the loss of my best friend in the world . . . only to face this? What the fuck???" Tears streamed down my face as I pounded my head against the side window of the squad car, my cries echoing in the confined space.

"Hey! Calm down, Perez!" Vasquez tried to restrain me, but I shook him off, my desperation intensifying as I continued to assault the window.

"Ahbhu! Ahbhu!" I cried, my voice filled with anguish. I swung on Vasquez, baring my teeth. "Grrrr! Grrrr!!!! Ahbhu! Ahbhuuuuuu!"

Vasquez scrambled away and reached for his service revolver. "Are you out of your mind? Stop that!"

His eyes flashed panic as I arched my back and emitted a long, spine-chilling howl. Then, with a surge of strength, I yanked the door handle and tumbled out of the car, landing on the dirt.

"Ahhhhhhhhbhu! Ahhhhhhhhbhu!!!!!!!" My cries filled the air, my desperation reverberating through the desolate surroundings.

Vasquez hurriedly circled the car, pointing his gun at me. "Stop that, I said! Now!"

My voice dripped with defiance as I hauled myself to my feet, my gaze locked with Vasquez's. "What? You're going to shoot me?" I taunted. "Go ahead and shoot, you coward! Welcome to the land of opportunity, right? Well, here's your chance! Shoot an unarmed immigrant who never harmed anyone in his goddamn life. Give it your best shot, pendejo!"

I staggered towards him, my eyes wide and nostrils flaring. I could feel the weight of every hardship I'd endured—the civil war, the murder of my brother, the treacherous journey, the loss of my Ahbhu. Each step brought me closer to him, my fear burning away in the face of my anger and determination. "Take your shot!" I dared him. "And look me in the eye when you do it!"

Vasquez stood there, mouth agape, the barrel of his revolver pressed against my chest. I could see the hesitation in his eyes, the conflict warring within him.

"What are you waiting for, buddy?" I growled, now utterly fearless. I had faced death before, and I was ready to stare it down again, come what may. "Do it. Fire!"

Vasquez's mouth hung open, his eyes darting between me and the gun. For a moment, I thought he might actually pull the trigger. But then, to my surprise, he closed his eyes and lowered the weapon, leaving a faint red line on my chest.

I dropped back a few steps, my heart racing as I squatted in the dirt, trying to steady my trembling limbs. The cool breeze did little to calm the storm raging inside me. Vasquez staggered back to the squad car, leaning heavily against it for support.

For a moment, neither of us spoke, the weight of the aborted confrontation hanging heavy in the air.

"Can we go now, please?" I rasped finally, my voice hoarse with exhaustion. "I really want to see my mother. Your partner must be wondering what happened to you."

Vasquez nodded silently, gesturing towards the car with his gun. I approached cautiously, my eyes never leaving him. "Can you uncuff me, please?" I asked, trying to keep the bitterness out of my voice, keen not to reescalate.

After a beat, Vasquez pulled out a set of keys and uncuffed my wrists without a word. I massaged the circulation back into my wrists as I slid into the back seat, strapping myself in. Despite my fury at his attempted assault, I kept my thoughts to myself; he still held all the power.

As Vasquez started the car, I gazed out at the darkened landscape, trying to make sense of everything that had just happened, feeling increasingly desperate about my mother. After a few moments, Vasquez spoke, his voice barely above a whisper. "What the fuck was that back there?"

"I should ask the same thing," I said, careful not to sound confrontational.

"Yeah, but . . . that was fucking scary. I never expected—"

"I don't know what to say, officer. I've been through a hell of a lot. I guess I reached my limit. I guess I should be grateful you backed down." I held his gaze in the rearview mirror then looked aside, aching to be reunited with my mother.

"I'm *sorry* about what happened back there," he said after a beat, sounding a note of genuine regret. "I'm not like that, really. I don't know what got into me."

I raised my eyes to him, surprise and disbelief written across my face. Was the jerk actually apologizing? "Forget it," I murmured, my anger slowly dissipating, replaced by a weary desire to move past the confrontation. "We all have our demons."

Vasquez nodded, his expression pained. "I wasn't thinking straight," he added. "I haven't been for a long time."

I studied him for a moment, sensing a touch of anguish in his voice, an unexpected vulnerability I found uncomfortable.

"Like I said, officer—"

"Just hear me out, Perez, please," he pleaded, his voice tinged with desperation.

I hesitated, unsure how to react. Considering it was best to keep things civil, though, I raised my shoulders and nodded.

"I was just coming to terms with my sexuality a couple of years ago," he said in a low voice, reducing speed. "I came this close to coming out to my conservative parents. Then AIDS happened and spooked me back into the closet. Before I knew it, I was married with kids."

"You're married?" I said, thrown by the revelation.

"With two little girls."

I blinked at him, feeling suddenly confused. "So how does that work exactly if you don't mind my asking? You're married and still sleeping around with guys, going to gay saunas . . .? What happened to your being spooked?"

"That wasn't my intention. I was *completely* loyal to my wife for the first couple of years. But then . . . I couldn't deny I was still attracted to men. Hard as I tried, I couldn't shake that. Eventually, I slipped up. Now it's a regular thing. It's a torture, this double life. The guilt is killing me."

"But . . ." I flashed on Gerónimo, on his willingness to live the same lie for the sake of society, on Suchi and her arrangement with Amparo. Things like this weren't meant to happen in America where love was love. Or maybe I'd gotten it all wrong. I looked away from him again, questioning for a moment whether I'd made a mistake coming here.

"But what?"

"Why are you telling me all of this?" I asked, catching his gaze in the mirror again and refocusing.

"I thought I owed you an explanation. I'm fucked up in the head. I wouldn't blame you if you reported me."

"Is *that* what you want?" I asked, incredulous that he would suggest such a thing and touched with a modicum of sympathy for his situation.

"Maybe that's what I need."

"Maybe what you *need* is to stop living a double life, not to mention you probably need some serious therapy. That's what I think at least, for what it's worth."

Vasquez nodded. "Thanks, man. You're probably right. Thanks for hearing me out. And, again, I'm sorry."

"No worries," I said, grateful to be finally moving on and

setting my mind on what was waiting for me. What was past was past. It was time to reorient myself to the future, whatever it held for me. "Are we nearly there?" I asked, straining my neck to look down the highway.

"Almost. Where are you headed once you're released?"

I crossed my arms and locked eyes with him again through his rearview mirror. "I have no idea. Why?"

He glanced at me over his shoulder. "Maybe I can look you up and make it up to you somehow? I'm Oscar by the way." Vasquez's voice held a hint of hope.

Groaning inwardly, I fought hard against the instinct to lash out at him, especially after everything he'd just shared with me. "Listen . . . Oscar," I said as gently as possible. "I appreciate the explanation and your candor, really I do. And I'm sorry you're where you're at in your life. But right now, I don't have the mind for *anything* except making sure my mother is all right—that's first and foremost—and for getting in our applications for asylum. After that, who knows. So, *please*, for the love of God, just get me to my mother, and I'll forget anything ever happened back there, I promise."

# Chapter 37

## EMERALD CITY

Still reeling from my encounter with Vasquez, I spent the next couple of hours decompressing in the corner of a holding cell, waiting for the duty agent responsible for asylum claims to arrive. By the time she did, Vasquez was long gone. The fact I was the first called out of the cell made me wonder whether he'd had anything to do with that. I never found out.

I was finally reunited with my mother at the duty agent's desk, where we made our respective applications. I was relieved to see she'd been patched up and was a lot calmer than I'd expected. The duty agent, a long-legged blonde woman with a poker face who spoke basic Spanish, allowed us a quick hug before diving into our stories with business-like efficiency.

As coached by Suchi and Diego, I steered clear of any mention of the murdered soldier or my participation in the ceremony at Wirikuta, as neither of these was likely to serve me well. I focused instead on the targeting of Arturo, the deaths of my father and only remaining brother, and my fear of returning to El Salvador.

In the time it took for the agent to take down our stories

and prepare the applications, bond was posted by my mother's cousin Elías, whom Agent Tran had allowed her to call when they'd first arrived at the station. By the time we were done, Elías had arrived at the facility with his wife and their two young children to pick us up.

As we emerged from the facility into the bright sunlight of a glorious day and the fresh scent of the ocean in the air, my knees nearly gave way from the sense of freedom that flooded over me. Taking a moment to process it all, I absorbed my surroundings, the busy parking lot, the shiny new cars and four-by-fours whizzing past on the freeway, and beyond, the fields of strawberries. It all seemed so normal compared with what I'd just gone through.

Casting a quick glance back at the facility, I noticed it was built against a backdrop of hills, lush from recent winter rains. Among them, a cone-shaped peak stood near the facility, its switchback trail winding up to the summit, triggering a flood of memories: El Boquerón, the symbol of my conquered childhood fears, my hikes with Ahbhu, the sanctuary it had provided in my later years.

"What's wrong, hijo?" my mother asked, gently pulling on my arm. "Elías is waiting." She raised her head at her cousin and his family, who had stopped on the sidewalk ahead, expectantly looking back at us.

"There's something I have to do, Mamá. I'll be right back, I promise." I planted a kiss on her cheek as I turned her over to her cousin. Then I sped off toward the hill.

Attacking the well-worn trail, I hoofed it to the top in about a half hour. Pouring sweat by the time I reached the summit, I paused for a moment to catch my breath. Then I turned around.

My breath caught at the sight of the Pacific, calm and massive, breaking along the shoreline, its waters reflecting the brilliance of the noonday sun. Tracing the coastline, I saw San Diego rising in the distance with its handful of skyscrapers, their glass facades glimmering in the sunlight. The cityscape was crisp and clear against the backdrop of a clear azure sky, while the golden beaches and rugged cliffs accentuated the natural beauty of the coast. Despite the distance, I could feel the vibrant energy of the city pulsating from afar. Memories of Ahbhu filled my mind, his unwavering loyalty and boundless love guiding me through the darkest days. Though physically absent, I could feel him right there next to me on that hill, ready to take on our next challenge, our next adventure.

With a silent vow to make Ahbhu proud, I extended my arms towards the city, in a gesture of blessing, an embrace, an act of defiance. I had no idea what awaited me in that shiny new land. Whether good or bad, there was no going back now. Either way, I was ready to take on whatever the future threw at me.

The distant honk of a car horn roused me out of my reverie. Looking down from the hill, I spotted Elías waving frantically from the parking lot below. Flashing him a thumbs-up, I stole a final glance at the city and descended the hill.

# El Salvador Timeline

## Pre-Columbian Era (before 1524)

- 2000 BCE–250 CE: The Mayan civilization thrives in present-day El Salvador, leaving behind archaeological sites such as Joya de Cerén.

- 535: The Ilopango volcano, located near present-day San Salvador, erupts, causing widespread devastation and impacting the local population.

- 900: The Pipil people, an indigenous group, migrate to the region from present-day Mexico and establish settlements.

## Spanish Colonization (1524–1821)

- 1524: Spanish conquistador Pedro de Alvarado arrives in El Salvador, encountering the country's volcanic landscape, and begins the process of colonization.

- 1658: The eruption of the San Salvador volcano (nicknamed "El Boquerón") causes significant damage to nearby communities and affects the local economy.

- 1821: El Salvador gains independence from Spain but remains economically dominated by European plantation elites. Despite this dominance, indigenous peasants continue to farm their communal lands. The country joins the newly formed Federal Republic of Central America.

## Early Independence and Political Instability (1821–1932)

- 1839: El Salvador secedes from the Federal Republic of Central America and becomes an independent republic.

- 1854: The Santa Ana volcano erupts, destroying everything in its path and taking life in the surrounding areas.

- 1880–1890: The government confiscates communal lands from indigenous peasants on behalf of plantation elites, forcing many peasants to become laborers in the growing coffee industry.

- 1917: El Boquerón erupts again, causing a powerful earthquake that leads to widespread destruction and loss of life.

- 1930s: The Great Depression exacerbates economic difficulties for peasants, who, having previously lost their lands, now lose their jobs.

## The Coffee Republic (1932–1979)

- 1930s–1970s: El Salvador becomes known as the "Coffee Republic" due to its increasing reliance on coffee exports for economic growth.

- 1932: Indigenous communities mount an insurrection against the military government, which responds by killing between 10,000 and 30,000 people in a massacre known as La Matanza. Power becomes even more concentrated in the hands of wealthy elites and the government. Indigenous people are systematically forced to assimilate or go into hiding.

- 1969: El Salvador and Honduras fight a war over a disputed border, leading to the expulsion of nearly 300,000 Salvadorans from Honduras.

- 1970s: Increasing social and political tensions lead to protests and leftist guerrilla groups' rise. Government repression further polarizes society.

- 1977: Bishop Óscar Arnulfo Romero is named archbishop and becomes a vocal critic of the military junta in power and the unequal distribution of wealth. His outspoken defense of the poor brings repeated threats to his life.

## Civil War (1980–1992)

- March 24, 1980: Archbishop Romero is assassinated, triggering a full-scale civil war.

- 1980–1992: El Salvador undergoes a brutal civil war fought between the right-wing government, supported by the US, and left-wing rebels, backed by Cuba and the USSR. Approximately 750,000 people are killed, one million are displaced internally, and another one million flee the country, seeking refuge primarily in the United States and in neighboring Central American countries.

- 1990–present: The US grants Temporary Protected Status (TPS) to Salvadorans fleeing violence.

- 1992: The Chapultepec Peace Accords are signed, officially ending the Salvadoran Civil War and initiating comprehensive reforms to promote reconciliation, demilitarization, and democratization.

## Post-War Era (1992–2009)

- 1990s–2000s: Deportations of Salvadoran gang members from the US lead to a rise in gang violence in El Salvador.

- January 1, 2001: El Salvador adopts the US dollar as its official currency to stabilize its economy.

- January 13, 2001: Two deadly earthquakes strike El Salvador, causing widespread devastation and further destabilizing the economy, leading to an increase in TPS grants for Salvadoran migrants to the US.

## Contemporary Era (2010-present)

- 2014: Salvador Sánchez Cerén becomes the first former guerrilla commander to be elected president.

- 2019: Nayib Bukele is elected president, prioritizing the gang problem and restoring civil order with a controversial iron fist policy.

- 2021: President Bukele introduces a bill to allow El Salvador to become the first country to adopt Bitcoin as legal tender, claiming it would generate jobs and promote financial inclusion. The Legislative Assembly passes the bill.

- 2023: Former President Mauricio Funes (2009-2014) is sentenced to twenty years in prison in absentia because of negotiations related to gang truces he made while in office as well as for tax evasion and corruption.

- 2023: Statista and other sources name El Salvador the safest country in Latin America and the Caribbean, with just 2.4 homicides per 100,000 inhabitants.

- 2024: Nayib Bukele is reelected president, winning over 85 percent of the vote, for an unprecedented second term.

# Sources and Further Reading

White, Christopher M., *The History of El Salvador (The Greenwood Histories of the Modern Nations)*

Floras-Lopez, Isabella and Hansen, Einar Felix, *The History of El Salvador: From Maya to Modernity* (2023)

Menjívar, Cecilia and Gómez Cervantes, Andrea. "El Salvador: Civil War, Natural Disasters, and Gang Violence Drive Migration." Migration Policy Institute (August 29, 2018)

Martínez de Quintanilla, A. B. "AIDS in El Salvador." National Library of Medicine (1992)

Roy, Diana and Klobucista, Claire. "What is Temporary Protected Status?" Council on Foreign Relations (September 21, 2023)

"Temporary Protected Status for El Salvador." Catholic Legal Immigration Network (2018)

Swiston, Andrew. "Official Dollarization as a Monetary Regime: Its Effects on El Salvador." IMF Working Paper (June 2011)

Quesada, Juan Diego. "Bukele, the Iron Fist Leader Without Rival in El Salvador's Elections." El País International (January 28, 2024)

"Statista Ranks El Salvador as Safest in the Region." El Salvador News (March 19, 2024)

Ward, Susie Violet. "El Salvador Embraces Future with Bitcoin as Bukele Secures Historic Victory." Forbes (February 5, 2024)

# About the Author

Orlando Ortega-Medina was born in Los Angeles. He studied English Literature at UCLA and has a Juris Doctor from Southwestern University School of Law. At university, he won the National Society of Arts and Letters Award for Short Stories.

Ortega-Medina's short story collection *Jerusalem Ablaze* was shortlisted for the Polari First Book Prize (2017). In 2018, he was named the Marilyn Hassid Emerging Author for the Houston Jewish Book & Arts Festival. Ortega-Medina went on to release a series of gripping novels, including *The Death of Baseball* (2019), *The Savior of 6th Street* (2020), and *The Fitful Sleep of Immigrants* (2023). Ortega-Medina lives in London, where he directs the US immigration law firm of Ortega-Medina & Associates.